AN AIRLESS STORM

COCHRANE'S COMPANY, BOOK TWO

PETER GRANT

SEDGEFIELD PRESS

This book is dedicated
to my friend and fellow author
SARAH HOYT,
who encouraged me to get started
on my own writing career,
and supported my fledgling efforts
with enthusiasm. Thanks, Sarah!

CONTENTS

CRIME AND PUNISHMENT

KEDA

The prisoner was trembling as the jailers unlocked his cell door, cuffed his hands behind his back, and led him out into the corridor. The escort commander, a stone-faced major, inspected him from head to foot, and grimaced in distaste. The fear-stench added a sour, bitter overtone to the already rank odor of the man's grimy clothes and unwashed body. *Then again, why bother letting inmates here wash?* he thought to himself. *None of those in this corridor will stink much longer.*

He led the prisoner and his guards down the passage to a heavy double door. It opened onto an enclosed courtyard, its green grass contrasting with the dark, damp stone of the crenellated walls around it. Several observers looked down in silence from atop them, dressed warmly against the damp chill. They watched as the major signed a form, accepting custody of the prisoner. The guards went back inside, and the doors closed behind them.

The waiting escort snapped to attention at the command of

their sergeant. He marched them behind the officer as he escorted the stumbling, shivering prisoner down the graveled path, then turned ninety degrees toward the rear wall. He led the prisoner toward a thick head-high wooden stake planted firmly in the ground, two meters before the wall. Behind it, a thick pile of sandbags had been erected against the stone. A few pock-marks in the wall at its edges showed where it had sometimes failed to provide an adequate backstop against poor marks-manship.

The sergeant halted the escort, formed them into a single line and dressed the rank, while a corporal went forward to assist the officer. The two of them briskly, impersonally turned the man to face the line of soldiers. The corporal went down on one knee and tied his feet together, then tethered them to the base of the stake. The officer waited until the prisoner's feet had been secured, then took from his inside jacket pocket a formal decree. He unfolded it and read it aloud.

"For the crime of selling advanced military weapons to unknown enemies of the state, in dereliction of his duty and responsibilities, and to the grave detriment of the security of Keda and its star system, Lieutenant-Commander Wira bin Osman is hereby sentenced to death by firing squad. The sentence is to be carried out within one week from this date."

He folded the document and returned it to his pocket. "Do you have any last words, prisoner?"

"I – you can't do this! I have the right to appeal the sentence of a military court-martial to the Supreme Court of Keda! My – my lawyer is –"

"Your lawyer has already filed your appeal, prisoner. By edict of the President of the Supreme Court, it has been rejected without a hearing. The sentence of your court-martial stands."

"B-but... I..." Tears came to the prisoner's eyes, and his knees wobbled, as if he were about to fall.

"Control yourself, damn you!" Revulsion curled the major's lip.

"Your execution will be televised. At least try to die like a man, even if you could not live like one!"

"I..." The condemned man seemed to find a last reserve of courage. He drew himself up. "Major, I... I am being murdered to cover up the crimes of my superior officers. *They* sold those weapons, not I." His voice was hopeless. "Who will bring *them* to justice?"

The officer did not answer. He nodded to his corporal, who produced a length of black cloth and briskly, impersonally, tied it over the prisoner's eyes; then he pulled a small white card from his pocket, and pinned it to the convict's shirt over his heart. Snapping to attention, the two soldiers turned their backs on the doomed man and marched back to the firing squad. The major took up his position at one side, while the corporal retrieved his rifle and joined the line.

The sergeant bellowed, "Ready!" The eight-man squad snapped to attention.

"Load!" There was a rattle of metal on metal as beads were chambered.

"Aim!" The firing party took a half-step back with their right legs and lined their weapons at the prisoner. The trembling man against the post tried to stand straighter, as if that would somehow control his shivering. It did not.

"*Fire!*"

The shots crashed out as one. The electromagnetic mechanism of the rifles in the soldiers' hands accelerated their projectiles to hypersonic velocity as they left the muzzles. The impact of the rounds raised puffs of dust from the card and the prisoner's grimy white shirt beneath it, before both were stained with red as blood gushed out. The man slammed back against the post, crying out once, short and sharp; then he toppled slowly, stiffly, to his left. The card came loose as he fell, fluttering downward through the air. He bounced once on the grass, rolled halfway onto his back, and lay still.

The major marched briskly forward from his position at the
side of the firing squad, unbuckling the flap of his holster and
drawing his pulser. He stood over the prone figure, aimed down
at the black band around its eyes, and fired once – then skipped
back with an exclamation of disgust as a few drops of blood splattered on his gleaming, immaculately polished boots. The
sergeant bellowed a command that sent the corporal scurrying
forward, pulling out his handkerchief to wipe the footwear clean.

The firing squad formed up in two ranks, and the sergeant
marched them down the path toward the portal. The major
returned his pulser to its holster, then followed his men, walking
briskly. Others, menials, would clean up the mess. He had more
important duties to attend to.

Of course you died to protect your superiors, he thought disdainfully as he closed the door behind him and turned down the
corridor toward his office. *What else did you expect? You didn't seriously think they were going to take the blame, did you? In your shoes,
I'd have been sorrier for my wife and children than I was for myself.
Their punishment is only just beginning.*

A FEW WEEKS LATER, a man sitting at a desk aboard a freighter
orbiting a distant planet watched a vid recording of the
Commander's execution. His face was impassive as the officer
collapsed, and the major delivered the *coup de grace.*

The announcer's voice rose in impassioned approval as the
vid cut to a family home in a suburban setting. A young-looking
woman was dragged out of the front door, screaming hysterically,
looking back in anguish at two uniformed policemen who were
carrying a young boy and girl out after her. They were probably
not more than two or three years old, clearly twins. They were
crying, struggling, reaching out for their mother. The officer
dragging her paid no attention to her pleas. He threw her bodily

into the back of a van, and slammed the door in her face. The two children were deposited, less roughly, in the back seat of an unmarked car, where an iron-faced female officer accepted custody of them. The vehicles drove off in different directions.

"So?" he said expressionlessly as he cut off the playback, looking at the man standing before his desk. "That was only to be expected. Why did you bring it to my attention?"

"I... I thought it might interest you, sir."

"It doesn't. She'll end up in a brothel somewhere – she's still young enough and attractive enough that they can make some money out of her. The children will probably end up there too, once they're older, if they grow up pretty enough. If they don't, it'll be the mines for them, to be worked to death as slave labor. That's the way of things on Keda."

"Ah... I thought..."

"You thought we should do something for them, since our actions led to the death of their husband and father? Rescue them, perhaps?"

"Er... yes, sir."

"You are too sentimental, Flamur." The man's voice was frosty with disapproval. "They are nothing, and less than nothing. That, and worse, happens to little people all over the settled galaxy, every single day. If we cared about all of them, we would have no time or resources to devote to our cause. I will make allowances for your error this time, because you are still young enough to be needlessly sentimental; but see to it that you learn to ignore such inconsequential nonsense. If you do not, you will be useless to us."

"I hear and obey, sir!"

"Very well. Return to your quarters. I will have another mission for you soon."

"Yes, sir."

The man behind the desk watched him go, then brought up his terminal display once more and began scanning figures. As he did so, he thought with satisfaction of the sixteen missile pods secured in two of the freighter's holds. Five years ago, Keda had bought a division of four frigates, each carrying four missile pods. Every pod contained sixteen main battery and sixteen defensive missiles. It had also bought a set of reload pods for all four ships. Those reloads had changed hands a few weeks before, after transfer of what he still thought was an exorbitant sum in gold to a senior officer. It had been paid into an off-planet account, where it would ensure his comfortable retirement as soon as he could gather his family and flee Keda, never to return. He might already have done so, for all the man knew – or he might have failed, to be executed in his turn, and his family suffer as well. That was of no consequence.

The only thing that mattered was that he was fulfilling the charge laid upon him personally by the leader of the Brotherhood. "Get us modern missiles, and fire control systems to direct them, Ylli," Agim had urged. "I do not care if you have to pay high prices. Our peril grows, and our need is great. We can buy ships and convert them, but cannot buy up-to-date weapons for them – at least, not through legal channels, although we are working to change that. Until then, you are the best man I have for this job. Do not fail us!"

The latest acquisition meant he had acquired a total of forty-two missile pods from four different planets, containing many times that number of missiles. Fire control systems were more difficult, but he had his deputy tracking down special software, developed by a mining planet that could not afford to buy the military systems it needed. Their program ran on readily available asteroid survey systems, converting them and their long-range sensor panels into a better-than-passing semblance of a fire control system. His second-in-command was due to report back soon.

Meanwhile, Ylli had one more planet on his list of possibilities. Even if it did not pan out, provided his deputy had succeeded, they could all go back to Patos in triumph, to receive Agim's grateful thanks and the reward that would surely accompany them.

NEW SKYROS

The executive scrolled through the electronic document, and nodded in satisfaction. "Kreshnik Security's articles of incorporation, and its company registration, all appear to be in order, Mr. Cela. All we need is an end user certificate from the planet, then we can accept your order. What warships do you require?"

"As you know, a civilian company can't operate armed vessels carrying more than two missile pods. However, our first client, Tarakan, wants more powerful ships. That means they'll have to buy them in their own name. Kreshnik will provide the initial crews, and help them train their own spacers to take over from us. Another thing: there must be no announcements, no publicity, no press releases, even upon delivery. Tarakan wants everything kept entirely confidential."

"I understand. We've made similar arrangements in the past."

"Good. I'll have Tarakan's end user certificate for you within a few weeks. Meanwhile, may I look over some of the ships you have under construction, to familiarize myself with them?"

"I think we can accommodate you. We have two destroyers currently on our ways, as well as a courier ship and a freighter."

"Good. Destroyers are what our client will probably order, perhaps a full squadron of eight of them, plus a depot ship. They will be most interested to hear my views on your design."

The businessman's eyes didn't flicker at the thought of Tarakan buying a three-and-a-half-trillion-drachma squadron of destroyers. By rights, so minor a planet should not be able to afford even one of the warships. *Good,* Cela thought as he watched the man. *If you're not turning a hair at that, it means you'll ask as much for your ships as you think we can afford – probably at least twenty-five percent above your list price – and see if we'll pay it. If we do – and we will – then you'll know we're up to no good... but you'll take our money anyway, because at least on paper, everything will be legal. That's all people like you worry about.*

"How long will it take to build the ships?" he asked.

"We'll have to finalize what your client wants – weapons, systems, accommodation, and so on. We tailor our basic design according to customer requirements. That will take some time – how long is up to your client. After that, we'll order long-lead-time items while we begin programming our robotic constructors. I think we can start building the first two ships about eighteen months from now, and complete two ships every eight to nine months, thanks to our ultra-modern methods."

"That may be too slow for our client's needs. Is it possible to build them faster?"

The executive looked surprised. "Well, yes, it is, but that would cost more – quite a lot more. You see, we have other orders. We try to keep our ways filled, for greater efficiency. We would have to slot your orders in among our existing commitments. If you wish, we might be able to persuade some customers to delay their orders, and give you their slots in our schedule. However, you would have to pay them to do so, and they'll charge what the traffic will bear. It won't be cheap, and it may not be feasible if they won't agree.

"Alternatively, we can open another building way, dedicated to your order, and hire engineers and technicians to staff it. With that, and given speedy approval of your plans, we can begin construction in six months, and deliver two ships every eight months after that. The depot ship would be slotted into our regular production schedule, to be ready with the second or third pair of destroyers. However, given our additional staffing costs, plus the expense of starting up and shutting down a building way specially for you, the price of your warships will be at least fifty percent over list."

Cela fumed internally. *Greedy bastard! You're already pretty sure what's going on, and you're testing the water to see how deep you can gouge us!* However, he did not let his thoughts show on his face.

"I'll have to discuss that with our client. It'll be their decision, you understand."

"I do. Ah... in what currency will they be paying?"

"I don't know, but it's probable they'll pay in gold. They have abundant mineral resources."

The businessman could not keep the greed out of his eyes. Gold would make it much easier to siphon off part of the payment for himself and his fellow directors. The shipyard could also declare a much lower income for tax purposes, because gold could not be tracked like a normal bank transfer. "Provided their gold passes assay, that will be very satisfactory."

I'm sure it will, Cela thought sourly as he came to his feet. "Very well, Mr. Metaxas. Let's go and look at ships."

He wondered, as he walked down the corridor with his host, how much the Brotherhood would have to pay to a couple of Ministers of State on Tarakan to get the end user certificate, and have them verify it if questions were asked. It was the last piece in the plan they had crafted to evade interplanetary legal restrictions, and get their hands on major modern warships. Whatever it cost would be money well spent, if it meant the defeat of their enemies.

PATOS

Agim worked late into the night, reading electronic documents on his terminal display and ruffling through old-fashioned paperwork – still the preferred method of communication when interception might spell disaster. Paper could be burned. Electronic data could not.

At last, with midnight fast approaching, he leaned back in his chair, stretching and yawning. He rose, went to the balcony door, and stepped out into the fresh night air, looking out over the city.

So... he thought. *Pali has bought four fast freighters. Two are already at our base, the others are on their way. Ylli has found us missiles, and fire control systems for them. We don't have a shipyard there, but our repair ship can install everything. It's already prepared the first two to install their missiles. We can have them all operational within a year to eighteen months, if everything goes well. Meanwhile, Cela is arranging our new warships. By the time our first two armed merchant cruisers are ready, the first pair of destroyers should be on the building ways. In three to four years, we shall have a fleet to be reckoned with, rivaling those of all except larger planets.*

He suppressed an upwelling of anger and frustration as he thought of the Patriarch. It was so *unfair!* He had set them on fire with his vision of the Fatherland, and they had followed him... and then he had vanished, his vision yet unfulfilled, while trying to punish their enemy for interfering. They would have justice for him, as soon as the armed merchant cruisers were ready, and doubly so when the destroyer squadron was operational.

Eufala, or Hawkwood, or whatever you are calling yourselves now – we are coming! We shall avenge our Patriarch in your blood!

2

EXPANSION

CONSTANTA

Dr. Elizabeth Masters looked radiant in her white dress as she emerged from the registry office. Beside her, Captain Dave Cousins, wearing the full, formal uniform of his rank, tried to look suitably dignified, but his efforts were marred by the proud grin that insisted on flitting across his features, every time he forgot about controlling them.

Cochrane shook Elizabeth's hand, then the groom's. "Congratulations to both of you. Why you waited three years to tie the knot, I have no idea. The rest of us knew this was coming within a couple of weeks of the two of you signing on."

"Thank you, Commodore," Dave replied, smiling. "The waiting wasn't our idea. It's just that you had us jumping around so much, we never had time to figure out where we want to live, or house-hunt, or any of the other things that go into a marriage. It's only in the past six months that we've managed to get that right."

Elizabeth nodded. "Thanks for giving us enough time off to do that, sir."

"It was a pleasure. I'm looking forward to you setting up our base hospital facilities when you get back."

"So am I, sir – but today's not about medicine." Her eyes twinkled. "When will we hear wedding bells for you and Captain Lu?"

Beside him, Hui shook her head. "Give us time. We've got a lot to sort out before we can make plans like that."

Cochrane said firmly, "Forget about us. You two go off and enjoy yourselves on honeymoon!"

As soon as they got back to the Headquarters building, Cochrane sent for Commander Frank Haldane. The Commander had joined the company the previous year, after falling foul of the same offshoot of the Albanian Mafia that had seemingly declared war on Hawkwood.

Like him, Haldane was still wearing the first-class uniform that he'd put on for the wedding. He grinned as he entered Cochrane's office suite. "Looks like we're both dressed up for a formal Mess dinner, sir."

His boss laughed. "It's been several years since I attended one of those. We didn't carry over that military custom when we formed a private space security company. Still, they had their moments – particularly after the meal, when senior officers and their guests had left, and the rest of us could get down to the serious business of having fun."

Haldane's eyes sparkled. "I could tell you a few stories too, sir, but I suppose that's not why you sent for me."

"No, it isn't. Help yourself to a drink, if you like. I shall. The sun's got to be over the yardarm somewhere in the galaxy by now!"

They each poured themselves glasses of their favorite tipple, then sat down in the corner armchairs. Cochrane began, "I've been giving a lot of thought to what happened last year in Mycenae, when the Brotherhood attacked us. We were very lucky indeed to survive that."

"Yes, sir. If you hadn't installed that surveillance satellite constellation, you wouldn't have spotted them until they were right on top of you; and if you hadn't had one modern warship in service by then, allowing you to ambush them, you would have been massacred."

"You're right. A lot of the breaks went our way, but they could easily enough have gone in the enemy's favor. We're ramping up our fleet as fast as we can, given limitations of time, money and construction, but I'm sure the Brotherhood's doing the same thing. They're in this too deep now to back out, particularly after we destroyed two of their warships. They're bound to hit back at us. It's a matter of pride, and the Albanian Mafia's never been short of that. Besides, if they don't hit back, they'll appear weak, and that'll encourage their other enemies. They can't afford that.

"I've started a complete reassessment of where we are, in terms of facing that threat as well as catering for future expansion. Two more planets have already approached us about providing security for their systems. I hope they'll be the first of many. I'm going to concentrate on heavier firepower, something that can handle a major attack if it comes. I want you to look at our overall fleet size and composition apart from that. How many ships are we likely to need to patrol a typical star system? What types of ships, and what numbers of each? What about sustaining the effort, allowing for resupply, routine maintenance, crew changes, and so on? I'd like you to put your mind to those issues, and come up with a proposed fleet size and composition for Hawkwood Security."

"Can do, sir. What's the deadline?"

"Let's get together with Dave Cousins when he returns from honeymoon. As my second-in-command, he'll need to be part of our planning. I'll also bring Hui into it. As a Captain in Qianjin's Fleet, she can bring her professional experience to bear on the problem. If the four of us agree, I think we can accept that the plan will work. Can you be ready in, say, two weeks?"

"I can, sir."

"Good. Let's pencil that in on the calendar, and then get started. There's a lot to do."

THE FOLLOWING DAY, Cochrane called in Caitlin Ross, his intelligence specialist. She'd served as a Lieutenant-Commander in the New Orkney Cluster, and done sterling work in that field. He'd tapped her to do the same thing for Hawkwood Corporation.

"I asked you to find out everything you could about the Albanians," he began. "How much progress have you made?"

She frowned. "Enough to tell me I won't make enough progress here, sir. There just isn't that much information about Albanian Mafia activities on planets like Constanta, where they've never operated. I'm going to have to find good sources, then go to them to learn what you need."

"I figured as much. Do you have any in mind?"

"I thought of the Interplanetary Police Union on Neue Helvetica, but they're specifically a law enforcement information clearing house. They won't share their files with non-approved outsiders, and besides, they probably won't have much about the Albanians from the inside. I need to find a source that's already butted heads with the Albanians, and can tell us what it was like on the receiving end. We can compare that with our own limited contact with them, and see what else might come up. Also, they might know more sources to approach. I think it's going to be a long-term project, sir, and a big one."

"I'm afraid you're probably right. I have one source to suggest as your starting point. Hui is an Intelligence officer with the Qianjin Fleet. She can introduce you to their people, who almost certainly know a lot more about the Albanians than we do." He forbore to mention that since the Dragon Tong, one of the most feared criminal organizations in the settled galaxy, was headquartered on Qianjin, its Fleet database would surely incorporate everything the Tong could contribute to the planet's security. It was likely to know as much, if not more, about organized crime as any police or security organization.

"I'll ask her to write you a letter of introduction," he continued. "I'll also talk to a couple of my contacts, who have knowledge of Qianjin's... shall we say, less official resources. I think you may be able to learn enough there to figure out where to go next, and what to do there."

Caitlin smiled eagerly. "Thank you, sir. There's just one problem. I'll have to be away for a long time, certainly months, perhaps as much as a year or more. I'll be able to report back from time to time, but I'll be gone so long I don't think I'll be able to handle your other intelligence needs."

"I agree. You'll have to delegate that job to two or three of your subordinates. Pick ones you trust. I'll make a courier ship available to you. I'll also fund you generously, using interplanetary bearer bank drafts, cash in hard currencies, and gold. You don't know what your expenses will be or who you might have to bribe."

"Thank you, sir." Her eyes twinkled. "If I get the chance to go shopping..."

He laughed. "I'll trust you not to spend it all on fripperies!"

CAITLIN HAD BEEN GONE for almost a week by the time Dave Cousins returned from honeymoon. As soon as he was back at work, Cochrane summoned him to join Hui, Frank and himself in his spacious corner office. It was labeled, not with his military-style rank, but as Managing Director of Hawkwood Corporation, the space security company he'd founded – at first under another name – three years before.

He began, "A year ago, Frank and I began planning the doctrine and tactics we'll use with our frigates. More recently, I asked him to look into our fleet mix, in the light of both last year's attack and the possible expansion of our operations. He'll address that with us, after which I'm going to talk about adding some heavier firepower. Over to you, Frank."

"Thank you, sir." Commander Haldane looked around as he spoke. "I've looked at Hawkwood's situation three different ways. The first is what we've learned about security operations at Mycenae. The second is possible future customers. We're talking to two right now. The third is our fight with the Albanians, which we didn't ask for, but which is going to be a headache for the foreseeable future.

"At Mycenae, we saw that our old patrol craft simply couldn't cut it against even outdated opponents. We were damned lucky to lose only one to those destroyers' missiles. We learned that we need modern, up-to-date sensors and weapons to face any serious threat. There are no short-cuts.

"Both of the planets talking to us at present are facing multiple problems. They're dealing with smugglers, occasional piracy of ships heading to and from orbit, and illegal asteroid mining. Their problems might have been addressed more simply and cheaply a few years ago, but they let things get out of hand. Now, they need high-end solutions. We can offer that, but only if they're willing to pay high-end prices. A lot of planets can't afford them – but low-cost solutions won't actually *be* solutions. They'll be panaceas, like bandaging a wound without treating the infection inside it. We have to offer enough ships, with enough power and performance, to deal with all those problems.

"Finally, there's the Albanians. We think they have at least a couple more destroyers, bought as scrap from Anshun a decade ago and refurbished. They may have smaller armed ships, too.

They're sure to try to replace the ships they lost at the Battle of Mycenae last year, and probably add more, either by converting fast freighters into armed merchant cruisers – which is their easiest short-term option – or getting their hands on actual modern warships. Whatever they do, they'll pose an increasing threat. The Commodore will address that in a moment.

"Putting all those factors together helps to define the size of the fleet we'll need. The absolute, rock-bottom minimum to patrol any star system at a basic level, and deal with low-level threats, is four corvettes. There'll also have to be a depot ship, to provide base facilities. One corvette at a time will be at the depot ship for crew rest, routine maintenance, and resupply. The other three will be patrolling the system. They've got the speed and endurance to cover the distances involved, and the firepower to take care of the average pirate or smuggler. However, four of them won't be enough to cover the whole system, all the time. We'll have to help them by using a system surveillance satellite constellation. That can pinpoint traffic anywhere within three to four light-hours of its position, allowing us to send our ships to intercept it if necessary. It's expensive, but it'll be essential. Without it, we'd need two to four more corvettes, which would be even more expensive.

"The detachment will need support ships. Rapid communication is a must, to call for reinforcements if things get bad, or send for urgently needed spare parts, or whatever. That means a high-speed courier vessel always on standby, in case of an emergency. Another will carry routine communications to and from Headquarters. In other words, we'll need two communications ships, alternating those tasks every month. We also need a fast freighter to resupply the detachment every month, assuming we can't buy all the supplies we need locally, and shuttle relief crews, spares and other necessities to and fro.

"We've just defined our minimum level of commitment: four corvettes, one depot ship, one fast freighter, two high-speed courier ships, and a system surveillance satellite constellation. Eight vessels, with five to six hundred officers and spacers. That's our smallest practical deployment. Given their capital and operating expenses, we'll need a fee of at least a billion Neue Helvetica francs per month to cover their costs, plus give us a reasonable after-tax return on our investment."

Hui winced. "That's a huge expense for anything but a wealthy planet – and wealthy planets will have their own System Patrol Services, well-equipped enough that they won't need Hawkwood."

"You're right, ma'am. That's where asteroids come in. A couple of years ago, Captain Cousins suggested we could accept a minimal monthly fee, plus the right to prospect for an agreed number of asteroids in that system. We can use the prospector bots we confiscated from the Albanians and the Callanish consortium in Mycenae, and buy more if we need them. If we find a few dozen high-grade asteroids, rich in precious metals or rare earth minerals, we'll get more money than if we charged a full fee, and the client wouldn't have to pay much in cash at all."

Cochrane nodded. "We'll have to have an ironclad contract, specifying how many asteroids we can harvest, of what minimum value, and get agreement from anyone who already has exclusive rights to exploit the asteroid belt. If we can get all those elements in place, I think we'll do well. Both prospective clients are discussing them with us right now."

"How much do you think you might get for your asteroids?" Hui asked.

Frank grinned. "We've just collected the harvest from a deserted star system that nobody wants, because survey ships said it didn't have enough resources to be worth colonizing or exploiting. We turned our bots loose in its asteroid belt about fifteen months ago. I took HCS *Orca* to collect them last month, along with twenty-seven asteroids they'd beaconed for recovery. Even though they aren't as good as many of the asteroids we got from Mycenae, the refinery ship at Barjah reckons we'll get five to six billion Neue Helvetica francs as our half-share after processing."

"*Six billion?* From a system the surveyors said wasn't worth exploiting?"

"Yes, ma'am. We think there are probably more like that; and in a system with richer resources, like most of those with settled planets, we expect to do a lot better. That makes our fee requirement much more achievable."

"It does! You'll need working capital reserves, to tide you over until the asteroids can be refined; but given the proceeds from those you've already harvested, that shouldn't be a problem."

"That's the way I see it," Cochrane agreed. "What's more, our share is only half the asteroids' value. The refinery ship gets the other half. If, in due course, we buy our own refinery ship, we can keep all the proceeds. I don't want to do that now, though. At present, we need to focus all our efforts on expanding our security operations and dealing with whatever the Albanians have up their sleeves. A refinery ship can be tabled for future consideration. Carry on, Frank."

"Yes, sir. Moving on from that basic level, if a system has a lot of serious problems and needs more than minimal patrolling, we'll need to send more ships. Mycenae, for example, because it's a very large binary star system, needs at least six corvettes to cover it even sparsely, plus the four old patrol craft operated there by the New Orkney Enterprise. If they weren't there, we'd need eight corvettes. What's more, corvettes are fine for patrolling and dealing with minor opponents like pirates and smugglers, but they're outclassed against more heavily armed enemies like those we faced last year." His audience nodded grimly.

"To deal with opponents like that, we'll need our forthcoming super-frigates, with their big cruiser-size missiles. However, their capital and operating costs are more than twice as high as a corvette's. For big systems with serious security issues, we might need six to eight corvettes, two frigates, and two depot ships, plus two communications vessels, a freighter, and the surveillance satellite constellation. All that gets very expensive, very fast. We'll need to charge well over two billion francs per month for a deployment like that – or they'll have to give us a lot more asteroids."

Cousins winced. "They sure will! What's more, if we assign that many ships to one system, we'll be short of ships to send to others."

"At our present and planned fleet size, yes, sir, we will. That's why I suggest you order a lot more corvettes. They're Hawkwood's maids-of-all-work, and our most economical solution. Our current plans include nine of them, the last two of which are currently building."

"We've ordered one more, although our total will remain nine," Cochrane informed him. "If you recall, our first corvette, *Amanita,* was Kang Industries' prototype, which we bought used. All those built for us were lengthened, to provide bigger crew quarters, a brig, more damage control storage, and a larger sick bay. We also gave them full-size destroyer antenna arrays, to upgrade the performance of their fire control systems. They meet our needs better, so I've arranged to sell *Amanita* back to Kang, and buy a larger model to replace her."

"I get it, sir. In that case, I suggest you order at least seven more right away. That'll give you a fleet of sixteen corvettes in all; three divisions of four operational vessels, plus one of ships undergoing maintenance or training new crews. Any two divisions are likely to be busy in client systems. If a customer needs more, they can be drawn from the third division; or, if all three divisions are busy, frigates can fill in for them in the short term. You have nine super-frigates on order, right, sir?"

"Yes. I'm figuring on two divisions of three operational ships, plus a third division of three frigates under heavier or long-term maintenance, or protecting headquarters."

"Uh-huh. Sir, I'd like to propose that you consider two-ship divisions instead. One or two divisions can be allocated to an emergency response force. They'll be at our main base, ready to reinforce any of our client systems in an emergency, or respond to anything the Albanians might try, including defending our headquarters. You'll want two more divisions to operate in support of our corvettes in larger systems with more serious security problems. A fifth division will be for frigates undergoing maintenance. I therefore suggest you may need ten to twelve frigates in all."

Cochrane frowned. "Trouble is, those are expensive ships. We can buy two and a half corvettes for the price of one frigate."

"Yes, sir, but two and a half corvettes can't do all that a frigate can – and they're not the only expense. You need to figure on one depot ship for each corvette division, plus at least two for your frigates. You have four depot ships on order, so you should plan for two more, plus at least one spare to allow for routine maintenance. Finally, there are support ships. If we're operating at, say, three planets, that's two courier ships for each deployment, plus at least two for Headquarters use, and a couple undergoing maintenance or crew rest. You also need a fast freighter to resupply each deployment every month, and one to support your emergency response division in the field. We're talking about ten to twelve courier ships, and at least six fast freighters. You'll probably also need another repair ship in due course, because there'll be too much work, spread over too great an area, for one to handle."

There was a long silence. Cousins broke it by saying, slowly and carefully, "We've already committed twenty-two billion Neue Helvetica francs to pay for nine corvettes, nine frigates, four depot ships, four courier vessels, and our present freighters. Now you're telling us we need to budget at least *another* twelve to fifteen billion, for even more ships?"

Frank shrugged. "Sir, you heard my analysis of the likely demands on our fleet. If it's accurate, that's how many ships we're

going to need. We paid for our present orders by recovering illegally beaconed asteroids from the Mycenae system. I just
collected another six billion francs' worth of asteroids from a
deserted system. It's not like there are no more where those came
from. I think we can fund this."

"Yes, but there's also the cargo shuttles, cutters and gigs that
each ship will need, plus more spacers to crew them, plus more
support facilities, plus... dammit, we'll have more ships and
personnel than the Fleet of a major planet, if this goes on! We
may even have to set up our own shipyard to maintain them all!"

"Yes, sir; but we'll be securing three or four planets or star
systems with them. That's the reality of Hawkwood's business."

Cochrane scratched his chin thoughtfully. "I must say, I agree
with Frank's analysis so far. However, what I propose may change
the number of frigates we need. I'll lay long odds the Albanians
are buying more armed ships right now, by hook or by crook,
legally or illegally. In their shoes, I'd do everything I could to get
more and better warships, to fight anything of inferior size or
power – like our corvettes, for example, which by now they must
know we have. I'm not sure if they've learned about our forthcoming frigates yet, but they soon will. They'll be buying ships to
counter such vessels, so we need to increase our firepower to
match them.

"We already know they have destroyers, even if they're old
and out-of-date. They'll probably modernize those they have left,
and may try to get more. I want firepower enough that even those
ships won't be enough to face us. A destroyer typically carries one
hundred to a hundred and twenty main battery missiles, and the
same number of defensive missiles. A cruiser usually doubles
that – two hundred to two hundred and fifty of each."

Hui interjected, "But cruisers cost a fortune! With all their
systems and weapons, they run three to four billion francs apiece,
and they need big crews, too. Qianjin's Fleet couldn't afford to
replace our four old cruisers. Instead, we chose to refurbish and

modernize them, and even that cost as much per vessel as a new destroyer. Surely Hawkwood can't afford ships like that?"

Cochrane shook his head. "No, we can't; but even so, I want to get as close as possible to cruiser-level firepower. I thought first about armed merchant cruisers. However, there's the problem that, according to United Planets regulations, as a private company, we're not allowed to operate armed ships with more than two missile pods. Whatever we do has to take that restriction into account, otherwise our ships risk arrest whenever they call at a planet with a conscientious System Patrol Service.

"Frank mentioned that we'll need more freighters. They might also offer a solution to our heavy hitter problem. There are several commercial fast freighter designs, of three-quarters to one million tons capacity, that can achieve speeds of up to one-quarter Cee, fully loaded. They aren't built to military standards of toughness, of course, but they also cost much less than a military-grade transport. A new fast freighter of that size sells for a hundred and eighty to two hundred million francs. That's less than half the price of a corvette – although, of course, they aren't stuffed with military-grade systems and weapons, like a warship. The thing is, they can do a lot more than just carry freight. Some of their cargo holds can be used to convert them into arsenal ships."

Frank looked puzzled. "I'm not familiar with the term, sir."

"That's because no major Fleet has used them for a long time, due to their limitations. The idea arose early in the Space Age, back on Old Home Earth, for use in wet-water fleets. Briefly, an arsenal ship carries a lot of weapons, but has no systems to control them herself. They're fired at the command and under the control of warships accompanying her. Basically, she's a missile truck."

Frank's eyes lit up. "Oh! I get it. Yes, that would limit her. If you don't have warships with her to guide all her missiles, she's dead weight. I suppose she can't even defend herself."

"True. However, we'll have enough ships to protect her, using her own defensive missiles as well as theirs. There's no reason we can't equip some fast freighters to serve as arsenal ships when needed, or even dedicate some to that role. We can build the necessary reinforcement into their hulls. When needed, we'll simply load missile pods. What's more, we won't have to observe United Planets restrictions by loading only two pods, because the arsenal ship can't fire or control its own missiles. It merely transports them, so it's not classified as an armed ship. We could load a lot more than just two missile pods."

"Oh, yes!" Hui said, her excitement obvious. "Why not six, or eight, or ten? The fire control systems on your frigates and corvettes can control up to a hundred and twenty main battery missiles, and the same number of defensive missiles. Put two of those freighters, each with eight of your super-frigate-size missile pods apiece, in formation with four of your corvettes, and the warships can control and direct everything the freighters can launch. That's like having two cruisers."

By now everyone was smiling, leaning forward eagerly. Frank added, "And the warships will still have their own missiles in reserve, for a second salvo if necessary. It'll be like a double whammy!"

"We can also make the freighters less visible," Cochrane went on. "If we apply to their hulls the same stealth coatings we use on our warships, their radar cross-section will be reduced – even more so if we remove radar-reflecting protrusions, or put fairings over them. If they use minimum gravitic drive power, or shut down their drive and rely on reaction thrusters, they might be able to sneak up to within a million kilometers of an enemy base or formation, then fire at point-blank range. That many missiles, that close... they'd never be able to stop them all. It'd be a slaughterhouse!"

"Think of them on defense, too, sir," Frank said. "Instead of needing to keep three or four expensive frigates at headquarters for defense, you could have one arsenal ship, plus two corvettes to control her missiles. I'd hate to be aboard an enemy ship poking its head into *that* hornet's nest!"

"How could we buy so many missile pods without arousing suspicion?" Cousins asked. "We need to keep the arsenal ships under our hat until we need them, so an enemy doesn't know what's waiting for them."

"We'll be buying the same missile pods for our frigates," Cochrane pointed out. "We can simply order a lot of reloads. We can use the excuse that we'll base them in all the systems where we operate, even if frigates aren't deployed there. In case they are, they'll find reloads waiting for them. It's threadbare, I know, but I think Kang Industries will wink at it. They'll be making a lot of money selling us the pods, after all. We might buy more freighters from them, too, to sweeten the pot and make them more cooperative."

Frank grinned. "You've still got all those old missiles taken off the New Westray patrol craft, haven't you, sir?"

Cochrane looked surprised. "I didn't know we still had them. They were all unserviceable, of course. I thought Sue had gotten rid of them."

"Last I heard, sir, they were in a hold aboard *Humpback,* our warehouse freighter, waiting for disposal. I was told there were well over two hundred main battery missiles, and at least as many defensive units. What if you transfer them all to a separate ship – an old, cheap one – then arrange for an 'Albanian attack' that steals or destroys it? You can swear with a straight face, even under truth-tester examination, that Hawkwood really has lost that many missiles, and you need to replace them. What more logical reason to order a lot of missile pods from Kang?"

By now they were all laughing. Frank continued, "You could even order twice as many, because you want to keep reserve supplies in two different places. That should be good for at least twenty new pods, maybe as many as thirty – enough for a full load-out of three or four arsenal ships."

"I'll think about that, and see if we can make it work. Over and above the missiles, we'll need an auxiliary reactor for each ship, to provide startup power to the missiles' reactors and run the pods' mass drivers, which will launch the missiles on command. The warships accompanying the arsenal ship can program them via datalink before launch, and guide them once they're fired. If worse comes to worst, after firing, we can dump the used missile pods and wiring harness into the nearest star, then bring the freighter back with empty holds, as if nothing had happened. Any investigation will have to prove what we did. They'll find that very hard."

He looked at Frank. "You said we'd need four or five fast freighters. If we order ten of them, and modify, say, four to six in this way, we'd have some as dedicated fast freighters, plus the two smaller ones we already have. Some of the arsenal ships can also be used as freighters until they're needed, when we'd load their missile pods; or we might keep them loaded, standing by to defend our headquarters or a major base like Mycenae, along with a few corvettes to control their missiles. How does that sound?"

"Like a winner, sir," Frank said, grinning. "What about frigates? Will you still need them?"

"Oh, yes! We still need warships more powerful than corvettes, to help the smaller ships in more dangerous systems. Arsenal ships can't patrol independently, but frigates can. On the other hand, we might be able to make do with fewer frigates. We'll have to try out this combination of vessels on operations, and see what fleet mix will work best for us."

"There's another aspect," Hui pointed out. "If you need to send out a squadron for an extended mission – for example, looking for the Albanians' base – the arsenal ships will have plenty of space available in the holds not used for missile pods.

They could carry enough stores to supply the whole squadron for months, without having to call at a planet or be resupplied from our base. Give it an arsenal ship, plus four corvettes to search through star systems, and maybe a frigate or corvette to stay with the arsenal ship, plus a couple of fast courier vessels to keep in touch, and the squadron would have tremendous operational flexibility."

Cochrane nodded. "Very well. I think we can all see the possibilities here. Dave, I want you and Frank to put your heads together over the next month. Start working out how we can fit arsenal ships into our operations. I must visit Kang Industries soon, to discuss our forthcoming frigates, so I'll inquire about more corvettes, depot ships, courier vessels and fast freighters while I'm there. Frank, in two months you'll assume command of our frigate prototype, HCS *Bobcat*. You'll spend three months working her up, wringing her out, and seeing what needs improvement. Expedite that, if possible. Let's get a list of what needs to be improved, so Kang can incorporate it on their production line, and *Bobcat* can be modified accordingly. Once we have a better idea of her capabilities and potential, we'll decide whether to increase or decrease our frigate order."

"Yes, sir." Frank hesitated. "Ah... something just occurred to me, sir. You realize that, if we order what we've discussed this morning, we're going to have more warships than most planets, rivaling even a decent-size military fleet? What's going to be the reaction of Constanta or Rousay when they learn that? We have licenses from both planets to operate armed spaceships, but I can't think of a single politician who won't be worried by our size. With a fleet that big, we could crush both of their System Patrol Services and take over both planets' orbitals, anytime we wanted to. They probably won't be very happy about that, sir. In their shoes, I wouldn't be, either."

Cochrane frowned. "Dammit, you're right! We're going to have to look at basing our fleet more evenly across both planets, to spread our ships around and look less threatening. Even that may not be enough."

Hui suggested, "Why not talk to Barjah? You've been taking your asteroids to the Dragon Tong there for several years, to be refined. They could talk to the people they know in the government. I'm sure you could get a license for Hawkwood there, too. If you split your fleet across three planets, plus the Mycenae system, you should be able to stop people realizing how big it's grown. With all the courier ships you're ordering, you could maintain adequate control. For a big operation, you could have the ships rendezvous at a deserted star system, to brief them all together."

Cochrane's frown cleared. "That's brilliant! It might even stop the Albanians figuring out how big we're getting. That may lead them to go on underestimating us, just as they did in Mycenae last year. Yes, Barjah will do nicely. I'll go there as soon as I've seen Kang Industries, and talk to Mr. Huang and Mr. Hsu." He smiled at her. "Care to come along?"

"Try to stop me! I'm your liaison officer, remember?"

The other two laughed. Frank said, "I'm not going to say a word about liaisons. No. Really, I'm not. I –"

He ducked, grinning, as Hui and Cochrane both took mock swipes at him.

3

UPGRADE

PATOS

The stone-faced security team tramped down every corridor and through every partitioned room, eyes flickering up and down and from side to side, hands lifting, fingers probing, missing nothing. They paid particular attention to a corner office, ornately carpeted and paneled in wood, and an equally plush boardroom in the adjacent corner.

The team leader turned to the building owner, who had hovered attentively by his side to answer questions during the inspection. "What about the windows?"

"As you specified, Mr. Tanush, we replaced the standard double-glazed windows with nitrogen-purged triple-pane units. Your people watched as we put them in."

Tanush glanced at one of his subordinates, his eyebrows rising, and nodded in satisfaction as the man agreed. "They were as we specified, sir."

"Have you tested them?"

"Yes, sir. We used a laser from various distances to try to

detect vibrations from voices inside, and record them. We could not."

"Very well." He looked back to the owner. "Thank you for making all the changes we requested. I shall inform Mr. Nushi that you have fulfilled our requirements to the letter. He will pay you the balance of our deposit, plus the first quarter's lease in advance, as agreed. We shall move in next week."

"Thank you, Mr. Tanush. I'll have our workers ready to help."

"That will not be necessary. We shall provide our own people."

"As you wish. I hope you will enjoy your tenancy."

After the team had left, the owner walked back to the board-room. Idly, he looked out through a pane of sparkling-clean glass, then glanced down at the bottom of the window. Nothing out of the ordinary was visible to the naked eye. Smiling, he nodded to himself, then turned and left the building, locking it behind him.

TWO WEEKS LATER, elaborate precautions preceded the first board meeting in the new premises of Kreshnik Security Services. The security team swept the entire building for listening devices, rather than just one floor each day, as usual. After the boardroom had been declared free of bugs, its doors were locked. A guard prevented anyone from entering until half an hour before the scheduled meeting. Even then, every person going inside to prepare for it was searched and scanned, then accompanied by an armed guard to ensure they did nothing suspicious.

In his office on the ground floor, the building owner-cum-manager waited until a few seconds before the scheduled start of the meeting before opening a drawer and taking out a console. He switched it on, then pressed two keys. At the base of two of the boardroom's windows, whisker-thin antennae emerged from almost invisibly tiny holes inside the triple-paned windows. They angled toward the inner pane and pressed themselves lightly against it, where they could pick up any vibration. Any observer would have had to use a magnifying glass to detect them, particularly through the reflections on the glass – and, even then, only if he had known where to look.

The twelve members of the board filed into the room precisely at fifteen-thirty. The majority were old men, one using a wheelchair. Five were middle-aged. One, powerfully built and well-muscled, went to the head of the table. He waited until all were in their seats, then reached for a gavel, tapping it twice on the sounding block.

"In accordance with our traditions, I, Agim Nushi, selected by our Patriarch of sacred memory to succeed him as Chairman, call this meeting of the Brotherhood Council to order."

In his office, six floors below, the manager listened over an earbud as the whisker antennae picked up the slight vibration of the glass, caused by the sound of the speaker's voice. Powerful computers analyzed the vibrations, converting them to sounds, and relayed them to the earbud – and to a recording device in the open drawer.

"This is the first meeting we have had in four months. I ask your forgiveness for the delay, brothers, but I make no apologies. In the light of what we now know happened to our two destroyers in the Mycenae system last year, and what we have learned since, we must be hyper-vigilant about security."

There was a sudden stillness around the table. "You have learned more?" one demanded.

"Yes. I can now tell you that our destroyers were detected by a system surveillance satellite, or rather a constellation of such satellites. We did not believe that Eufala Corporation, as it was then known, could afford such a device; but we were wrong. The satellite detected our destroyers as they began decelerating, three billion kilometers before they reached their target.

"We also did not know that Eufala had already obtained one

modern warship, a corvette. She was, of course, much smaller and less powerful than either of our ships; but our people did not know she was there, and she was stealthy, very hard to detect. She moved into an ambush position, very slowly and quietly, and launched her missiles undetectably, at very low speed, leaving them on the line of our ships' trajectory; then she withdrew. When our destroyers reached a range from them of just one million kilometers, the missiles fired. Our vessels were taken by surprise, and did not have enough time to defend themselves. Both were destroyed. Our Patriarch died with them."

Several of the Board exclaimed in grief and anguish, but Agim held up his hand. "Do not mourn. The Patriarch told us, before he departed on his final mission, that he would rather die as a man, fighting for our Fatherland, than in bed, surrounded by the wailing of women. That is precisely what he did. Furthermore, his example must have transmitted itself to our spacers. They launched at least some of their missiles, not at their attacker, but at their primary target – the ships in orbit around Mycenae Primus Four. They damaged several, and destroyed at least one. It was named HCS *Piranha*. I understand the initials stand for 'Hawkwood Corporation Ship', the new name adopted by Eufala. We should call our enemy that in future, to avoid confusion."

"What type of ship was it?" another demanded.

"We think it was a patrol craft, a small warship. Our informant was a spacer on liberty at Constanta. Our agent plied him with food and drink, and got that much out of him, but no more before he collapsed in a drunken stupor. Wisely, I think, our agent left at that point, rather than try to pursue the matter. With luck, the spacer will not recall their conversation at all."

"Did the enemy learn anything from our ships?"

"The spacer said both were destroyed, with no survivors."

"So, they could not have learned we have two more destroyers, or other warships?"

"They will surely assume we have more armed vessels, as we would, if we were in their shoes. Do not underestimate them. They have shown courage and ability. They will be a hard nut to crack."

"Do we have to crack them at all? Can we not just ignore them, and operate in systems where they are not present?"

Agim shook his head. "They know about us. They captured at least one survivor of the ship destroyed in Mycenae earlier, that was collecting our asteroid prospector robots, and they intercepted the teams of spies we later sent to Skraill and Constanta. They may have been able to take some of them alive, and interrogate them. We do not know this with certainty, but it would be foolish to assume otherwise. They undoubtedly know of our existence, and that we have taken hostile action against them. Even though they captured no evidence, they will realize we were almost certainly behind the attack on their Mycenae base. They will not believe that we might leave them alone in future. I expect them to come after us. We must be ready when they do. Part of that is being ready to attack them, rather than wait for them to attack us."

An older man observed sourly, "We should never have persisted in the Mycenae system after losing our ship there. Because we did, we have brought this fight upon ourselves. It is unnecessary! It is distracting us from the Fatherland Project, and consuming much of what we had built up toward that end."

Agim nodded slowly. "I cannot disagree, Skender. It would have been better to let things drop. However, we did not. It seemed good to us at the time to go after Hawkwood, to teach it to leave us alone. All of us in this room voted to do so, as did our late Patriarch." He looked around the table, staring each man in the eye, daring them to deny their share of collective responsibility. "There is no point in arguing about what we should or should not have chosen. We *did* choose, and we acted on that choice. We must now live with its consequences.

"Let us get back to business. There is news concerning our preparations and our enemy's. I wish to thank Endrit and Fatmir for their invaluable assistance in helping me to coordinate everything. Without their help, we could not have achieved so much since our last meeting. Endrit, would you please begin?"

Another middle-aged man stood, taller and thinner than Agim. "Thank you, Agim." He glanced around. "It is clear Hawkwood is preparing for a major conflict. There can be no other explanation for the rate at which they are arming themselves. We have learned they have ordered a full squadron of corvettes, at least eight ships, of which six or more are now in service. They have also ordered a squadron of frigates from the same manufacturer. A frigate usually carries about twice as many missiles as a corvette."

An older man interrupted. "How can they buy such ships, when the United Planets forbids civilian-owned armed ships to carry more than two missile pods?"

"Probably in the same way we are getting around that restriction. Fatmir will speak to that shortly, if you will allow me to defer to him." The questioner inclined his head, and sat back.

"A frigate's missiles are usually of the same type as a corvette's, shorter-ranged and less powerful than those of a destroyer. That has influenced our own choice of warship, of which more in a moment. However, both corvettes and frigates are limited in the number of missiles they can carry. Therefore, our first defense, while we are waiting for our own modern warships to arrive, is to equip four fast freighters, as speedy as our old destroyers, with large quantities of missiles and modern fire control systems. Our agents have successfully obtained both."

There was a buzz of approval. "This is very good news!" another director exclaimed. "I trust those concerned have been rewarded?"

"They have," Agim confirmed with a smile. "They earned it."

"When will our new ships be ready?"

"The first two fast freighters are currently being fitted with missiles and control systems," Endrit assured him. "They will be ready for service within three months. The other two will follow about six months later. Together with our two surviving destroyers, they will be a formidable force, carrying many more missiles than all Hawkwood's corvettes and frigates put together, with modern fire control systems to use them to best effect. If we need to defend ourselves, we shall be well equipped to do so – or to attack, if need be."

"How much did all this cost?" Perparim asked.

Endrit's face fell. "It was very expensive. Our new warships will be even more so. We must pay black market prices for everything, plus bribes, plus incentives to middlemen to assist us. I daresay we will end up paying at least twice their fair market value for everything we have bought or will buy. However, there is no alternative."

Agim raised his voice over the rumble of discontent. "Fatmir, if you will please continue the report?"

"Yes, Agim." Another man stood, his gray hair and dignified mien testimony to his greater age. "We set up this security company, Kreshnik, in imitation of Hawkwood. If such a ruse worked for them, we reasoned, it will work for us too – and so it has proved. We found a shipbuilder that offers warships for sale, among other vessels. I shall not name it, for security reasons. They accepted our credentials, plus an end-user certificate we obtained from another planet with the help of two bribed Ministers of State, who will verify it if questions are asked. We have ordered a full squadron of destroyers from them, eight vessels, plus a depot ship to support them. That will instantly place our forces among the top one-tenth of all settled planets, as far as military strength is concerned. Few can afford to operate fullblown destroyers or larger warships. Most have to be content with smaller, cheaper, less capable frigates, corvettes and patrol craft, like those Hawkwood has bought."

The discontent had subsided into attentive silence. "Can *we* afford them?" another director asked dubiously. "We are paying for them out of what we have accumulated for the Fatherland Project. We have just been told we are paying double their market price. What about their operating costs? Will they slow down our ability to replenish our savings?"

"We shall only know their operating costs when we have them in service," Fatmir admitted, "but they will certainly be expensive. On the other hand, remember what Agim said after the death of our Patriarch. 'If we are defeated, the Project will go down into the dust of history alongside us. Therefore, to spend money for our own defense *is* to spend it on the Project. The two are indivisible.' His words are as true today as they were then.

"If we neglect our defenses, then either Hawkwood, or another enemy, will surely find a way to penetrate them. We must be, not just *as* strong as any likely opponent, but stronger, to ensure we prevail. Our Patriarch reminded us before his death, 'Do not let your enemies strike fear into you. Instead, *strike fear into them!* Hit back at them! Show them that for every blow they direct against us, we shall return it ten times harder!' Again, his words remain forever true. If we quibble over the cost of our defenses, we are really quibbling over his vision and his message."

Agim rose once more. "I agree, Fatmir; and I, for one, am not prepared to quibble with our Patriarch, in life or in death. His vision drew us, and bound us together, and gave us purpose. It remains our goal."

He looked around the table again, ready to answer any challenge; but none came. At least half the directors' faces showed concern or doubt, but they withheld further comment. *The question is, will they approve my request despite their fears?* he mentally reminded himself. *I cannot proceed without them. I must win over the doubters.*

"Let me remind you of how long it took us to get where we

are, and how great our success had been in recent years until Hawkwood interfered," he said. "The Patriarch withdrew from the Bregija clan more than forty years ago, when they mocked him for pointing out that unless we followed their example, we could never grow to rival the Nuevo Cartel, Cosa Nostra or Dragon Tong, the three largest criminal organizations in the settled galaxy. They said he was living in a dream world, that such greatness had long since passed us by. He refused to accept that, and set out to prove them wrong.

"It took us more than thirty-five years to accumulate enough savings to fund our initial operations, plus build our own asteroid refining ship and a space defense force to protect it and our base, develop the technology to prospect for and steal high-yield asteroids, and train our people. We have been operating for only about five years. During that time, we have raised *eleven times* more money than we did in all the years before! Is that not, in itself, proof of our Patriarch's wisdom? He said it could be done. We have proved that he was right!

"You know what resources we need to achieve our objectives. We were almost halfway toward the primary goal when we encountered Hawkwood. It will cost us about a third of what we had saved, to build up our forces to counter them; but, even as we spend it, we shall be gathering more asteroids, and rebuilding our reserves. This will be a temporary delay, a blip of no more than a year or two on the scale that our Patriarch outlined. In three to five years' time, we can still achieve our initial goal, and see the Fatherland Project take physical form for the first time. That, in itself, will convince doubters, and draw waverers to our side. Under our leadership, they will help us to make even faster progress. Look to the longer term, brothers, not just to short-term problems. Our Patriarch's vision remains our objective, and we *shall* bring it to life!"

Heads lifted, and spines stiffened with pride, all around the table. *That is better,* Agim thought. *I must remember that we all need to be constantly reminded of why we are here. We need to believe as firmly and as fervently as did our Patriarch. He must be our icon, our beacon lighting the way forward.*

"My brothers, it has been truly said that 'Three can keep a secret, if two of them are dead'. I fear that if we discuss everything in our board meetings, there will be too great a risk that something will leak to our enemies. I do *not* imply that any among us are traitors – far from it! We all had to prove our loyalty and commitment, many times over, before we were selected by our Patriarch to join the Brotherhood's inner circle. We must be equally exacting in choosing our successors, in due course. Nevertheless, we all know how easy it is for something to slip out by accident. A momentary weakness while drinking with friends, pillow talk with our wives or mistresses, a lapse in concentration... we have all suffered such things." He rolled his eyes ruefully. "Many of us have had cause to regret them later." A murmur of shared amusement ran around the table.

"For this reason, I ask the Brotherhood for permission to form an operational triumvirate with Endrit and Fatmir, for an initial period of up to three years. They will work under my direction. I will assume full responsibility, and be accountable to you for all our decisions and actions. By keeping information tightly held among us, we can ensure it does not leak, so that our enemies will not be forewarned. We shall also be able to move fast, if circumstances require it or we discover an opportunity, instead of having to wait until this Council can formally give permission for us to proceed. In fighting a dangerous enemy such as Hawkwood, such delays may be ruinous.

"I therefore ask you, brothers, to vote us the authority to proceed with this fight on those terms. We shall try to report back to you every three to six months, but sometimes even that may not be possible, given delays in interstellar travel and communication. It may also be necessary for us to withhold information about particularly sensitive projects, for security reasons. I ask your indulgence, and your permission, for all these things, in the Patriarch's name."

He noted that there was still uneasiness on some of the faces around the table. One old man asked, "Will this apply to all the work of the Brotherhood, or only to our fight with Hawkwood?"

I must concede that to him, Agim mentally acknowledged. *They will never agree to give me a dictator's authority. I must accept limits.*

"I speak only of the fight with Hawkwood," he assured the questioner, with a smile that did not reach his eyes. "In all other matters, we three shall continue to report to this board at least every quarter. I hope you will permit us to submit our reports via proxy if one or more of us is in the field, operating against our enemies."

"Thank you, Agim. That gives me greater peace of mind – and yes, of course a proxy will be acceptable under such circumstances."

"Then I ask you to vote, brothers. Will you give us the authority for which I have asked?"

For the first time in several years, the vote was not unanimous. Three of the twelve withheld their approval. Agim seethed inwardly, even as he smiled at them. *There is no room for doubters! We are at war! Either support our cause, or retire and hand over to younger men with more fire in their loins, damn you!* However, he kept his face impassive. After all, the Patriarch himself had chosen these men, proving that they were worthy – or had been, when they were younger. The fact that age might have crept up on them, tempering their enthusiasm or ability, should not be held against them. That might happen to anyone. Meanwhile, he had the permission he sought. The war could proceed.

If the doubters' obstructionism proved too great in future... well, there were solutions for that problem, too. He took comfort in the thought that the Patriarch would have understood that, and approved, if he were still here.

"IT LOOKS like their board meetings won't give us much useful information in future, then," a young man observed gloomily that evening.

"Not before the fact, anyway," the building manager replied as he piled food on his fork. The restaurant around them was filled with diners, the hubbub of their conversation, clinking glasses, and the scraping of cutlery on plates, all helping to prevent their words being overheard. "We'll still learn about some things after they've happened. Apart from that, we'll have to rely on our office bugs to pick up what they're up to."

"Yes, but that won't be enough," the third member of the group objected. "Kreshnik uses quantum-encrypted systems. We can't monitor the other side of their calls without them realizing someone's listening in. We're limited to what's said in their offices, which may not be enough to give us all the details we need. Besides, they talk outside the office as much as they do inside."

"We'll just have to do the best we can. We were lucky that the Admiral gave our mission such a high priority. Captain Lu's narrow escape must have shaken him. He sent us here with enough money to build the new block, to improve our cover story of being off-planet businessmen. It demonstrated that we meant to invest here, not just take the locals' money and run. That, in turn, meant that the Brotherhood came to us when we'd only just started construction, offering to lease the whole place provided we met their security needs and conditions. We're actually going to make a profit on this deal, if only they keep paying long enough!"

The younger man asked, "Will this go on that long?"

"It might. You heard them. If they get those destroyers, they'll be as powerful as Hawkwood, perhaps more so – unless Hawkwood has something up its sleeve we don't know about."

"The Admiral wouldn't tell us, even if they did. That's outside our area."

"Yes, it is. He's got Captain Lu to keep him informed about that. She'll still be in danger, though, if the Brotherhood decides to take the fight to Hawkwood. It'll be up to us to give the Admiral enough information to let him warn her if necessary."

"Why did the Brotherhood lease our building in the first place, rather than buy it?"

The leader shrugged. "That's been their policy ever since they arrived here. They must want to reserve all their capital for this Fatherland Project, whatever it is. Also, I suppose they can move faster if they don't have to abandon fixed property, should the need arise. If their homes and offices are rented or leased, they can just walk away from them without worrying."

"And what about their contents?"

"Stuff is just stuff. It can be replaced. They'll take only what's critical, or of sentimental value – and they're not a very senti-mental crowd, are they?"

"Unless you count hate, resentment, bitterness and anger as sentiments."

"Well... yes, there is that."

4

A THIRST FOR REVENGE

MEDUSA

"You're sure it was her?"

The speaker was clearly ill at ease in the bar on Entertainment Alley aboard the space station. The spacers thronging it were rough, tough and loud, very different from the more refined people with whom he usually worked, and the places they frequented. He couldn't know that his reaction had been anticipated. It was one of the reasons the meeting had been arranged in this setting.

"Aye, it was her. You can't disguise a repair ship. They've got too many cranes and equipment housings sticking out all over, not to mention half their superstructure being a flat deck, to work on modules and smaller craft. Besides, *Colomb* was built for the Lancastrian Commonwealth Fleet. There's something about their ships, a sort of flair, that you don't see in many others. I'll be damned if I could put my finger on it, but it's there. She still had it."

"And she still looked like that?" The businessman pointed at the picture he'd laid on the table.

"She did when she arrived." The mechanic tech sniggered. "Didn't look the same by the time we'd finished with her, o' course."

"Where did she go?"

"Now how the hell would I know that, mister? This is Medusa. Ships come in here all the time. We work on 'em, make 'em look different, then send them out to be resold. By now she's probably half the settled galaxy away, serving a new owner. Why? Didn't your insurance pay out for her?"

Not nearly enough, the questioner thought grimly. *We had to borrow a couple of hundred million from our bank to help replace her, and they gouged hell out of us on the interest rate!* He contented himself with saying, "We still want to get our hands on whoever was responsible. What about the other repair ship, the one you swapped for her?"

"She was much bigger, but empty. She had no equipment or tools to speak of. They'd have had to buy them somewhere else."

"They didn't take them off *Colomb?*"

"Her workshops and machine rooms were filled with tools an' gear when she got here, so I guess not. One thing, though – they were all pretty old and worn. I was surprised they hadn't been replaced long before."

Aha! She'd just been refurbished, and fitted out with all new tools and equipment! That means they stole all that out of her, and filled her with stuff from somewhere else that they no longer needed. If we can trace the stolen gear by its serial numbers...

"And the two fast freighters?"

"Frank an' his men brought in two brand-new million-ton fast freighters. I reckon they hadn't seen so much as a ton o' cargo yet. They swapped 'em for two used freighters half the size. Dunno where the two big 'uns came from, but they took the smaller ones to the same outfit that brought in *Colomb* and swapped her for the stripped-down repair ship."

"You mean Eufala Corporation?"

"Yeah, something like that. Weird name. Never heard the like before."

"I thought you said you didn't know where ships went when they left here?"

"Mostly I don't, but I know some o' Frank's boys. Had a beer with them one night before they left. They told me."

"I see. Well, you've been most helpful." He reached into an inside pocket of his jacket, took out a plain white envelope, and laid it on the table. "Here's the rest of what we agreed."

"You won't mind if I count it?" The tech didn't wait for an answer, but ripped open the envelope and thumbed rapidly through the banknotes inside. He looked up with a satisfied grin. "Yeah, it's all there. Thankee, mister. This'll come in right handy."

He slid the envelope into his own pocket as his visitor left the bar. He finished his tankard of beer, then stepped out himself, walking down Entertainment Alley to a diner. He found his employer seated in a booth, sipping a cup of coffee, and sat down opposite him.

"It all went just like you figured. I told him everything you wanted me to say."

"Good. Did he buy it, d'you think?"

"I reckon so. He went away with a long face."

The other produced an envelope of his own. "Here's what we agreed. Added to what he gave you, that should be better than a year's pay."

The tech tore it open and counted rapidly. "It sure is! Thankee, mister. Any time you want to put one over on someone else, just call me. I'm your man."

"I will, thanks."

The other man watched the tech leave the diner, then ordered another coffee from the automenu on the table. Provided he ordered something every half-hour, he wouldn't be disturbed.

He was on his third unwanted cup of coffee when his assistant slid into the booth. "It's done." He handed him two envelopes. "He didn't have time to spend any of it."

"Good. Endrit will be pleased that we kept our expenses low. You made sure the tech won't be found anytime soon?"

"I dumped his body down the nearest garbage chute. It's in the trash tunnel now, waiting for the next removal cycle. If no-one spots it before tomorrow morning, it'll be ground up with everything else, then vacuum-dried for disposal."

"Very well. Let's go. We've got a ship to catch."

CALLANISH

Several weeks later, the atmosphere was stormy in a boardroom in Achmore, capital city of Callanish.

"So they got away scot-free with stealing her, while we were out a quarter of a billion Neue Helvetica francs for the cost of *Colomb*'s refurbishment, plus another two hundred million to make up the insurance shortfall in her replacement value! *Four hundred and fifty million francs!*" Scott's voice was outraged.

"Not only that, they got a newer and bigger repair ship, plus two smaller freighters, in exchange for *Colomb* and our two brand-new freighters," Dunsinane observed. The Chairman's voice was dispassionate, but tight, as if he were exercising strict control over his emotions. "I think we're more than entitled, morally if not legally, to seek some sort of... compensation for that."

"Are you mad, Dunsinane?" Pentland demanded, surging to his feet. "Let me remind you that *we stole* New Orkney Enterprise's satellites around Mycenae Primus Four, using *Colomb* to do the job. Somehow, they found out that she was there, and that we'd hired her for it. They then stole her, plus the two fast freighters we'd bought using the money we got for *their* stolen satellites. We *asked* for what happened. We *started* it, dammit! After the fuss was over, NOE didn't bring charges against us. They didn't say even one word about it. They were signaling that honors were even, and they were willing to leave it at that. Why make it worse? Why start another fuss? Can we afford to lose another half-billion francs? *They* can. Don't forget, they now have legal authority to exploit the Mycenae system. Their resources must be a hundred times greater than ours, if not a thousand!"

The Chairman stared at him, drumming his fingers on the polished table-top. At last he said, his voice icy cold, "Pentland, if you ever accuse me of madness again, I... will... *break*... you. Do I make myself clear?"

The director stared at him, unintimidated. "If it comes to breaking, two can play at that game. Don't start something you can't finish."

"Oh, stop it, the pair of you!" MacNeill's voice was bitter. "This isn't solving anything. Dunsinane, I'm inclined to agree with Pentland that we've no real chance against NOE any longer. What makes you think differently?"

The chairman let out his pent-up breath in a long, slow sigh, forcing down his anger. "I don't think we need worry about NOE at all. It was their security contractor, Eufala Corporation, that stole *Colomb,* and our freighters as well. NOE had nothing to do with it, and didn't know anything about it until they found out after the fact."

There was a stiff, tense silence for a moment. Scott broke it by asking, "How did you find that out?"

"I have my own sources, ones I'm not prepared to discuss here. However, you can take that to the bank. Eufala did it, not NOE – and I'm thinking Eufala, or Hawkwood as they're now calling themselves, will be a much easier nut to crack. They don't have the mineral resources of the Mycenae system behind them. They're just a security company. In terms of corporate revenues, we're bigger than they are. That means we can fight them on better than even terms."

"They're an *armed* security company, remember? They can defend themselves with more than just money and lawyers."

"Yes, but missiles can't ward off prosecutors. What if we can trace some of the equipment aboard *Colomb* – equipment we paid for, I remind you – to Hawkwood's own repair ship? Its gear will have serial numbers, that can be compared to what we bought. That might provide grounds for a court order to seize the ship, pending criminal investigation and trial. We might even be able to swing a charge of piracy, which carries the death penalty. Also, as a second string to our bow, we can adopt Hawkwood's approach. They hired a criminal to steal our freighters – one of the best in that line of work. He's not the only one. If we hire our own, they have ships that will be vulnerable, too. I think, given time and ingenuity, we might get back all we've lost, and maybe more besides."

Pentland looked mulishly stubborn, shaking his head, but several of the other directors perked up. They were all painfully aware of their losses at Hawkwood's hands. The thought of revenge was particularly sweet.

THAT EVENING, another Albanian reviewed a recording of the board meeting with great satisfaction. Endrit would be delighted that the Callanish consortium had become their unwitting allies – or, rather, tools – against Hawkwood. Perhaps they could piggy-back their own activities on the back of whatever Dunsinane planned. That way, if anything went wrong, Callanish might be made to shoulder all the blame, with their own involvement not even suspected.

Pentland, though... he might be trouble. He led the faction that voted against Dunsinane. They lost, but they might still make mischief

– or betray Dunsinane's plans to Hawkwood, despite their promises of secrecy. Maybe we should do something about Pentland? Perhaps we could silence him in such a way that Dunsinane can take credit for 'breaking' him. He won't mind – he'll probably revel at being suspected of it, particularly since he knows there's only supposition, not real evidence, behind it – and no-one will even dream that we might have been involved.

He considered, then slowly shook his head. That was too big a step for him to take on his own. He'd suggest it to Endrit, and await his decision.

5

NEW SHIPS AND OLD

GOHEUNG

M r. Kim totted up the figures he'd tapped into his display, and blinked. "Commodore, yet again you astound me. When you placed your first order with Kang Industries, I told you I'd never before come across a private security company that could afford so many and such costly ships. This latest order will increase that total by well over fifty percent. I know you can afford it, of course – your record of timely payment with our company is second to none – but nevertheless, the scale of your operations is truly amazing."

"It's as I told you, Mr. Kim. With two more planets negotiating with us, we're going to be placed under a lot of pressure. That's why I want to accelerate our new corvette orders, even if it means slowing the frigate program, because it'll give us more ships, faster. I'm buying two more system surveillance satellites for the same reason. If we know the direction from which trouble's coming, and when it'll arrive, our smaller ships will be better able to deal with it. However, please expedite production of the frigate missile pods. We need them on hand very quickly, even if we

don't have many ships to carry them, because those that can are
going to be worked very hard. We also intend to use some as base
defense pods, in orbit around our installations. We're already
preparing the casings and auxiliary systems to allow us to do that.
The corvettes can control them."

"Pods are easy to assemble, but we'll have to put pressure on
the missile manufacturers. They seldom get such a large order,
and they'll need time to ramp up production."

"Please push them as hard as you can. I'd like to collect as
many pods as possible within six months – up to thirty, if they
can accommodate us."

Kim sucked in his breath. "That will be difficult, but I'll see
what I can do. Ah... are you willing to offer them financial
incentives?"

"If necessary, and within reason, yes."

"That will help, thank you. I'll also approach Zhang Space-
lines on your behalf. Your offer of a twenty-five percent slot fee, if
they'll allow you to buy and take delivery of the two fast
freighters we're building for them, is likely to prove very attractive. I know they're having trouble finding enough premium-rate
fast freight to fill their present ships. If they can put off their
orders until later, and earn half the price of a new freighter into
the bargain at no cost to themselves, I think they'll jump at it.
Their freighters are more than half built already. We can
complete them within three to four months."

"And the other ships?"

"It's very fortunate you placed your new order while the last
of your previous ships were still on our ways. That means we
hadn't yet allocated the corvette building way to other construction. After we finish the last two ships of your present order, we'll
set up a new production pattern of two corvettes, followed by two
frigates, and repeat that sequence until your orders are complete.
We should be able to produce two corvettes every five months,
and two frigates every seven, thanks to modular construction and

robotic assembly. The depot ships, and your other fast freighters, will be shoehorned into vacant production slots on our other ways, as quickly as we can. As for the courier vessels..." Kim hesitated. "I'd like very much to have all your business, but we have only so many building slots. If we use them for your larger vessels, we can't accommodate the smaller, and vice versa. You might be better advised to turn to another manufacturer for them."

"Thank you for your honesty. Who would you recommend?"

"Fujita of Kamamoto produce a very good design, although it's more expensive. It's slightly larger, with twenty double passenger cabins instead of our twelve, and it has a bigger hold, to carry up to five thousand tons of cargo. If you want a high-quality product for fast delivery, regardless of the price, I'd talk to them. I can provide you with a letter of introduction to my counterpart there, if you wish. We know each other."

"Thank you. That'll be very useful. As far as our freighters and depot ships are concerned, if another customer might delay their order in return for a slot fee, please let us know. If the cost is reasonable, we'll take the opening. Commander Haldane will be here tomorrow, bringing with him the crew for our first frigate, HCS *Bobcat*. After the acceptance ceremony, he'll run trials with her for three months. When they're over, you'll update our frigate design according to his findings, then modify *Bobcat* to incorporate them before we declare her operational."

"Of course. Our engineers and designers are looking forward to working with him."

"You have the reload missile pods ready for us to load aboard *Orca*, our armed freighter?"

"Yes, four of them for *Bobcat*, plus two more for *Orca*, as arranged."

"Good. All right, I'll see you in two days for the handover ceremony."

FRANK HALDANE BROUGHT *Orca* into orbit ahead of schedule, in time to come down to the planet that evening. Cochrane and Hui were surprised by his insistence on joining them at once, but at first put it down to a simple desire for a good meal at a quality restaurant. They were soon disabused when they picked him up at the spaceport terminus.

"Sir, we've got a problem," he began without preamble as he threw his carryall into the back seat of their rented vehicle, then slid in behind Hui. "Is it safe to talk in here?"

"I... I presume so," Cochrane replied, startled, as he engaged the electric motor and moved off slowly. "We chose it ourselves out of the rental lot, with no-one there to jog our elbows. I doubt they've bugged the entire fleet!"

"You never know, sir," Frank said darkly. "There are some planets... Anyway, I've got a friend, Saul. He's in the same business I was, before I joined forces with you; namely, stealing spaceships to order, or ferrying hot ones to places where they're less hot, to dispose of them. With me?"

"Uh-huh." "Go on." Cochrane and Hui spoke in unison.

"Guess whose spaceship he's just been hired to steal?"

"Not one of ours?" Cochrane demanded incredulously.

"Yes. What's more, there are two great big flashing red warning lights, sir. The first is, he's been hired by someone on Callanish named Dunsinane. Ring any bells?"

"Yes! He's the chairman of the consortium there that hired *Colomb* to steal NOE's satellites in Mycenae."

"He wants to steal *Humpback,* sir, your big warehouse freighter in Constanta orbit. He's hired Saul to figure out how to do it, raise the necessary team, and get her for him. If he can't get *Humpback,* he's to pick the next most valuable ship, and steal that. He's been told to 'inflict the greatest possible loss' on us. He says those were Dunsinane's exact words. He quibbled, citing our security as being a real danger, so Dunsinane ended up offering him double the fee. He even paid him half up front, to prove he's serious. He must want to hurt us very badly. The other flashing light is that Saul was already working for someone else, who suddenly canceled the agreement. He paid him off, and gave him a bonus to talk to Dunsinane instead. Saul said he looked scared. He knew him well enough to ask him what was going on. The man would only say that 'a guy from Patos' made him an offer he couldn't refuse."

Hui struggled around in the front seat to stare at Frank. "*Patos?* But that's –"

"Yes, ma'am. It's where that Albanian ship came from, the one that was blown up by one of our mines in Mycenae a couple of years back."

"Well, well, well." Cochrane was smiling. "How did Saul let you know about this? Do you trust him? What's the timetable?"

"I trust him enough to take him seriously, sir. I saved his ass from being sent to a prison planet one time. He'd have spent the rest of his life there, if I hadn't bribed a few guards to spring him from the transit prison. He owes me for that, and always swore he'd find a way to repay me. He knew I was working for you now, so he sent a private message to me at Constanta from another planet. It reached me just before I left to come here. He says he's drawing things out, using our good security as an excuse to delay until he's hired the best team available. He reckons he can stall another month or two before he has to go to Constanta. He wants to know whether I can fix up something that'll make him look good to Dunsinane, so he can keep his advance, but not hurt us."

"Can you have him contact me at Constanta, as quickly as possible?"

"I can send him a message from here by express interplanetary courier, sir. It'll be expensive, though."

"Hawkwood will pay for it. If he'll play along with us, I think we can make sure he not only keeps Dunsinane's advance payment, but the rest of it, too, and earns something from us into the bargain."

Frank grinned, relaxing for the first time since he'd climbed into the vehicle. "Just what have you got up that tricky little sleeve of yours, sir?"

"My tricky little arm, what else?" Frank and Hui laughed. "I think we can make Dunsinane wish he'd never been born. It seems he didn't understand our unspoken message, last time, to stay away from us. He must be a slow learner. We'll have to make it a lot clearer. Also, I think this might help us pay for a really big purchase of more missiles."

"*Huh?* How do you figure that, sir?"

"Let's wait until we've had supper, then go back to our suite. I'm going to mull over a few things in my mind while we eat. When I've got them nicely lined up, I'll tell you more about them. Oh – one more thing. You say Saul's in the same line of business you were, once upon a time. Is there anyone else you trust still doing that?"

"Ah... yeah. There aren't many as good as I was, or Saul is, but there's a couple."

"I'll want to know more after supper. We may have a use for them from time to time."

Late that night, lying together in companionable closeness, Hui said, "You really surprised me with what you planned with Frank tonight. I didn't suspect you had such a devious side."

He grinned invisibly in the darkness. "Sometimes I surprise myself, too. I think it has possibilities."

"Oh, it does – if it works. *Making* it work will be the problem."

"Yes, but then, Frank's contacts should be able to help. We'll just have to play our cards, and see how they fall. Meanwhile, there's something I've been wanting to raise with you. It's been almost a year since you last visited Qianjin, although I know you've been sending back reports to Fleet Intelligence there, and exchanging messages with your family. Isn't it time you paid them a visit?"

She sighed. "Yes, it is... but that means spending time away from you, and I don't want to do that! I'm being silly, I know."

He hugged her gently. "No, you're not. I'm going to miss you, too. I'm sure your Admiral would like to inspect *Bobcat*, to see how we've shoehorned cruiser-size missile pods into a frigate. Why don't we let Frank take her on a high-speed long-distance run to Qianjin and back? She'll need one, as part of her acceptance tests, and he could take you along too. I'm sure you can persuade your Fleet to allow her into the system. Your Admiral can look her over, and you can visit with your family. Frank won't be able to stay long, but you can take commercial spacecraft back to Constanta when you're ready, or ask the Admiral for the loan of a communications ship."

She rolled over onto her side, looking at him eagerly. "That's a wonderful idea! It would give the Admiral bragging rights if Qianjin's was the first Fleet to examine a brand-new design like your frigates. He'll probably ask permission to have several senior officers look her over, if you won't mind that, and maybe have Frank take them out for a demonstration run."

"I don't mind at all. He's let us – in particular, he's let *me* – have you as a full-time liaison officer, to exchange intelligence about the Albanians, and he's been very generous in sharing what he learns. This will be a little *quid pro quo* for that. You can take the opportunity to visit his people while you're there, and gather anything else they can provide that might help us."

"Thank you, darling. I don't know that Qianjin will want super-frigates of their own, because they cost almost three-quarters as much as a destroyer, which is a bigger and more capable design. Even so, they're bound to think hard about designs to replace their old light cruisers in due course. If you can build two of their missile pods into a frigate hull, there's no reason they can't build three or four into a destroyer hull. That might be very useful."

"Let him have a look, and tell me what he says."

"All right. What will you be doing while I'm there?"

"I have to detour via Kamamoto on my way back to Constanta, to see the Fujita shipyard about our communications vessels. Mr. Kim says their design is even better than Kang's, and he's given me a letter of introduction. We'll see what they can do for us."

"All right. With luck, you'll find a message from Frank's contact waiting for you when you reach Constanta."

"Let's hope so. Now, darling, you've been neglecting your duties. What are you going to do about it?"

"Neglecting my duties?"

"Yes. You're my liaison officer, aren't you? Why aren't we liaising?"

"Oh, *you!* Stop talking and come here!"

CONSTANTA

Cochrane wasted no time on his return to Constanta. As soon as he'd read the message Saul had sent him, in reply to Frank's message from Goheung, he summoned Lachlan MacLachlan, Hawkwood's logistics director.

"Lachlan, I want you to buy me a simple tramp freighter, a quarter of a million tons or so, certainly not much larger than that. She must be cheap, because she's disposable. I don't mind if she's old and well-worn, just so long as she's spaceworthy and not dangerous to her crew. I need her here inside a month. Can you do it?"

"A *month?* Ye Gods, sir, that's pushing it! I'll have to send one of my people to a couple of the nearer major planets, to see what's for sale, or even go myself. May I use a courier ship, to get there as fast as possible? It can carry some of our spacers as a passage crew, too, and the purchase price. We'll have no time to come back here to draw an interplanetary bearer bank draft, once we know her cost. We'll have to pay on the spot, in gold."

"No problem. If I give you all that, and the passage crew, can you come through for me? It's important."

"I... sir, you're asking something almost impossible, but I'll try. I may not be able to do it in four weeks, but I'll do my best. Would six weeks work?"

"If that's the best you can do, I suppose so, but no longer. Four would be better. Another thing. There must be no traceable connection between her and Hawkwood at first sight. Set up a shell company on the planet where you buy her, using a lawyer's office for the address, and register it as her new owner."

He mentally blessed Caitlin Ross's intelligence efforts at the height of the problems in Mycenae. The information she had gathered would now be put to very good use. He continued, "She must be insured for her full purchase price through Rendall Insurance of Callanish. Tell your people to use a local broker to do that. In addition, take out cargo insurance through Rendall, at full replacement cost, for thirty-two brand-new missile pods. I'll give you the details. They're very expensive, so the premium will be high, but that's all right. Make sure both policies meet United Planets regulations governing interplanetary payment guarantees. That's critically important, because Rendall is bonded under them. Pay both premiums in full, in gold, in advance, and have the broker send the full payment for both policies to Rendall by express courier right away. There must be no delay."

"Ah... may I ask why, sir?"

Cochrane smiled to take any sting out of his words. "If you don't ask me why, I won't have to lie to you."

"Oh. All right, sir. There's just one thing. If you make a claim

against that cargo insurance, you'll have to provide officially certified proof that the missiles were aboard. Being military hardware,
involving nuclear weapons, a simple civilian bill of lading won't
cut it, I'm afraid."

"I'll see to it."

Next, Cochrane called in Lieutenant-Commander Tom
Argyll, his Chief of Security, and explained what had happened.
"I'm planning an unpleasant surprise for Dunsinane and his
consortium. However, that Albanian worries me. If he wanted
this Saul to accept Dunsinane's job so badly, that can mean one
of two things, perhaps both. He may want to encourage the
Callanish consortium to cause trouble for us, so we have yet
another thing to worry about. That might take our focus off the
Albanians. Alternatively – or as well – he might want to try something himself at the same time. If we're blaming the Callanish
people, and trying to get our own back on them, we may not
realize that the Albanians used them to cover their tracks."

"You're making a lot of sense, sir. What do you want to do
about it?"

"I know our defensive teams are top-notch by now, after over
a year of training. What about our offensive teams?"

"The instructors say they're coming right along, sir. They tell
me that in six months, they'll be right up there with the best."

"Ask them whether they're good enough to handle a live
mission. I'm going to have our criminal contacts watch for new
arrivals on Constanta. Nicolae Albescu's people found those four
fake spacers and freight agents earlier this year, and he's been
helping us keep an eye on them. They're almost sure they're
watching us, although they're covering their tracks very well."

Argyll nodded. "That's what convinces me they're Albanian
spies, sir. They know too much tradecraft. Amateurs wouldn't be
that good."

"You may be right. At any rate, if they are Albanian agents, I daresay they'll meet whoever arrives, to coordinate action with whatever Saul is going to do. We might be able to scoop up some or all of the team, red-handed. Are our interrogation specialists ready?"

Argyll's face lost all expression. In a flat tone, he replied, "Yes, sir, they are, and they have interrogation kits patterned after those we captured from the Albanians. If we can take them alive, we can make them talk."

Cochrane grimaced. "I know how you feel, Tom. It makes me feel dirty, too! Nevertheless, we'll do whatever we have to do. Remember, they were willing to fry Frank's brain to get him to talk, and kill one of their own to stop him talking. As you said last year, if they're willing to be that ruthless, the only way we're going to stop them is to be just as ruthless ourselves."

"Yes, sir – but that doesn't mean I have to like it!"

Finally, Cochrane summoned Sue McBride, now a Commander and in charge of all engineering matters for Hawk-wood's fleet. She grinned as she entered his office.

"Och, and it's looking fit and healthy you are, sir. Hui must be agreeing with you."

He rolled his eyes. "Are you people ever going to stop teasing me about her?"

"Only when you marry her, sir!"

He sighed. "That's... never mind. I understand the nineteen defective missile cells we got with the patrol craft from New Westray are still in storage aboard *Humpback*."

"Aye, sir, they are. They're loaded with all the defective missiles, too. I was going to toss 'em into Constanta's sun, but I've been so swamped I've never found the time. It's not something I want to trust to juniors, you understand."

"I certainly do! Are their warheads still on them?"

"Most of them, yes, sir. None of them work, of course. They were in even worse shape than the missiles."

"I'm not surprised, judging by what you said when you first

saw them. All right. You'd better stand by to transfer them to another ship shortly. I have a use for them." He smiled nastily.

She looked at him narrowly. "What evil trickery are you up to now, sir?"

"Me? Evil?"

"Yes, you!" She grinned. "I've known you too long, sir. You're up to something."

"Yes, I am. I can't tell you precisely what, not yet, but it's going to be interesting."

6

HIGH AND LOW CRIMES

CONSTANTA

The Lieutenant-Commander from Constanta's System Patrol Service was the soul of cooperation, after he riffled through the banknotes in the fat envelope handed to him in the docking bay. "I'm sure there'll be no problem, ma'am," he assured Commander McBride as he slipped it into an inside pocket of his uniform jacket. "The inspection's a mere formality, designed to ensure that weapons and warheads are stored in conformity with our regulations."

"I understand. It's almost a pity to waste your time, because you know we're always very strict about safety standards. Still, the regulations must be observed."

"Yes, ma'am. I'll get right to it."

Sure enough, there were no problems at all. The officer physically counted nineteen very old missile pods in the holds of the freighter *Molly Malone*, each containing fifteen main battery and fifteen defensive missiles. Mysteriously, the inspection form on the electronic tablet listed thirty-two brand-new pods, each containing thirty main battery and thirty-five defensive missiles, plus ten penetration aids – missiles with electronic payloads replacing their warheads. Ignoring the discrepancy, he signed the document without turning an official hair, and handed back the tablet with an air of a job well done.

"I'll be back in a year for the next annual inspection, ma'am."

"And we'll have your usual welcome waiting for you."

"That's very kind of you, ma'am. Until then."

Sue watched him enter the airlock leading to his cutter, and grimaced. She didn't like dealing with corrupt officers. Too many of them cut corners on safety to save money, and that got good spacers killed. However, in this case, she was prepared to make an exception.

She uploaded a copy of the inspection form to the freighter's official document storage, glancing around the well-worn boat bay as she did so. Its paint was shabby, but every piece of equipment worked, despite its age. *Molly Malone* could serve for a few more years, until hard use finally wore her down... provided she survived whatever the Commodore had in mind for her.

"I'd better not ask any questions," she mused as she headed for her gig, carrying the electronic tablet. "Least said, soonest mended."

DURING THAT SAME DAY, two men traveled separately from the planet to the space station housing Constanta's orbital cargo and passenger terminals, Orbital Control Center, System Control Center, and the headquarters of its System Patrol Service. They were dressed in clean, unremarkable clothes that did not stand out among the crowds of orbital workers and transients. Their holdalls were examined before boarding by security personnel, but contained nothing out of the ordinary.

At the space station, the two men made their separate ways to a room in a transient hostel. It had been rented by a third man, who had arrived on the space station the week before from a passing freighter. He had stayed in the transient area of the station, and so had not had to go through customs and immigration, or endure security formalities. Neither had the big, heavy trunks and suitcases he'd brought with him.

The two shook his hand respectfully. They unpacked the luggage and began to assemble components. Before long, each of the three had twenty tubes filled with military super-explosive, a hundred times more powerful than standard commercial explosives. On the bed lay three web belts. Their pouches contained timers, detonators, glue, cord, and various fasteners in different shapes.

WHILE THE THREE were making their preparations, eighteen more men arrived at the space station from the planet, in three groups. They gathered at a bar near the shuttle bays, drinking a last beer before embarking on what was clearly going to be a working voyage. Each had a set of spacer's powered trunks, stacked two or three high, following them around like trained dogs at heel, homing on the beacons hooked to each man's belt.

"When do we leave, Saul?" one asked.

"Soon as our shuttle gets here. They'll call me. We've got a couple of hours yet. Anyone hungry? They serve a real tasty *tocana de carne* at the local eatery."

"What's that?"

"Beef stew, nicely spiced up. It's good. I had some when I got here."

"Why not? We'll be on spacer rations for a few weeks, so we may as well make the most of the opportunity."

As the spacers sat down to enjoy their meal, the three men in the hostel room were focused on last-minute preparations. One swore casually as he tried, and failed, to screw a cap onto a tube. "What's wrong with me, dammit?" he muttered, trying again, growing irritated as he fumbled with the cap, squinting at the seemingly misaligned threads.

"What d'you mean?" another asked, swaying slightly, slurring his words as if he'd had too much to drink.

"I – *it's a trap!*" the first speaker snapped, trying to stand, feeling the unsteadiness already slowing his muscles and nerves. "They're using some sort of gas!"

One of the men was already too far gone to fight. The second tried to reach for his weapon, but fell forward onto the bed. The leader managed to raise his carbine and point it at the door, but could not fumble his finger onto the firing button. He stumbled, swayed, and collapsed.

The inflow through the ventilation system died away for a moment, then was renewed with greater force. An exhaust fan in the attached bathroom spooled up to a much higher speed than normal, drawing air out of the bedroom. A baffle deployed in its outlet pipe, venting the contaminated air to vacuum rather than recycling it through the space station's filtration plant.

Five minutes later, the door to the room was slowly cracked open by armed men. They covered the prone figures while they were expertly searched, disarmed and secured. Each received a sedative injection to keep them unconscious, then they were strapped onto stretchers. Blankets covering their faces and bodies, they were carried away to a waiting cutter, and ferried planetside.

As the cutter bearing the three unconscious men left the space station, the NCO in charge of the anchor watch aboard *Molly*

Malone summoned the six spacers of his abbreviated crew. "Remember what I told you," he cautioned them. "You may have to give evidence about this under a truth-tester, so keep it absolutely straight. If you don't lie, you can't be found out."

Each man, in turn, looked intently at a terminal on the counter in the docking bay. That would allow him to swear later, in perfect truth, that he'd been working. Someone – he did not turn around, so he could affirm later that he hadn't seen his face or heard his voice, and therefore wouldn't be able to identify him or recognize him again – then pulled a thick black cloth bag over his head, tapped him lightly behind the ear – so that he'd later be able to swear he'd been struck on the head – and bound his hands and feet, not too tightly. He was gently laid on a stretcher, and carried through an airlock into a cutter.

When all seven of the crew had been loaded, the pilot of the cutter pulled away from the ship and set course for the planet. The crew would be dropped on the side of a farm road, from where they'd have to make their own way back to the nearest town. It would be an uncomfortable night, but not an unbearable one, and they would be well compensated for their trouble.

Their report of being kidnapped from *Molly Malone* by a person or persons unknown would produce a powerful reaction from Constanta's law enforcement agencies when it was filed the following afternoon. The delay would be officially described as 'unfortunate'; but everyone understood that it had taken them a lot of time and effort to make their way back to town after their ordeal. That could not be held against them.

TWO HOURS LATER, Saul led his team aboard *Molly Malone*. They looked at him with dire suspicion when he informed them that the anchor watch had already left the ship.

"Someone's gone to a lot of trouble to set this up for us," one of them said suspiciously.

"And what if they have? Be thankful we don't have to do all the hard work ourselves. Just remember your story, and keep it straight."

"Oh, I will! For what you're paying us for this gig, I can keep a dozen stories straight if I have to!"

"That's more like it. All right. Tom, park the cutter below the ship. Beacon changeover at twenty. Everybody synchronize your timepieces with the ship." There was a rustle of clothing as everyone pulled out comm units, or checked their wrists, and made the adjustment. "Tom, as soon as you're back aboard, report to me on the bridge."

"Got it, boss."

At twenty precisely, Tom, now wearing a spacesuit, flicked a switch to activate the cutter's beacon as it drifted in space, a couple of hundred meters below *Molly Malone*. It was set to precisely the same frequency and transponder code as the larger ship's beacon – which, at that very instant, Saul switched off. Nobody in OrbCon or SysCon noticed the changeover. After all, they weren't expecting anything out of the ordinary on what was a boringly normal evening, as far as they were concerned. Tom waited long enough to make sure nothing had gone wrong, then stepped out of the cutter's open rear ramp. He used a personal propulsion unit to steer himself back to *Molly Malone*'s docking bay, and her waiting airlock.

Saul took the ship out of orbit half an hour later, slipping away into the blackness of space under reaction thruster power alone, so as not to emit any gravitic drive signature. The cutter remained where it had been parked, its beacon pulsing steadily. In OrbCon, on the far side of the planet, nobody noticed anything. As far as their systems were concerned, *Molly Malone* was still in orbit, where she was supposed to be. After all, that's where her beacon was. In SysCon, they were enjoying a game of electronic poker on their watch consoles. There was nothing requiring their attention. The only patrol craft on duty was three light hours away to the galactic north. It wouldn't get back to the planet until the following evening – not that it mattered. Nothing interesting, in a criminal sense, ever happened in the Constanta system.

Molly Malone turned toward the system boundary, heading galactic south. As soon as she was far enough away from the planet to use her gravitic drive at minimum power without fear of detection, she switched to it and accelerated away.

IN A COMFORTABLE APARTMENT DOWNTOWN, a man and a woman settled down to wait. The man tuned a radio and opened a computer channel, to listen for emergency broadcasts from orbit. The woman checked that weapons were ready to hand, just in case, and poison tablets too, in case capture appeared unavoidable. Neither wanted to risk the interrogation they knew their enemies would administer, if they were taken alive. The drugs they used – derived from their own interrogation kits, captured from their predecessors here and elsewhere – would leave a human mind blasted beyond function or recognition after a few hours. Death would be infinitely preferable.

"Do you think they suspect anything?" the woman asked nervously.

"I doubt it. We have been here for several months, and no-one has taken any action against us. They would not have allowed us to operate so freely, if they thought we were spies."

"I hope you are right. I cannot forget what happened to Vasil, Besnik and Gentius a year and a half ago – and to poor Pavli, of course. I still wonder whether they were able to give him mercy, or whether those Hawkwood swine murdered him after dealing with them. I suppose we shall never know."

"Probably not, but we can avenge them all. Tonight will see our first major strike here against Hawkwood. It will not be our last!"

THE LEADER of the trio of arrested agents was the first to recover consciousness. His head was covered with a dark cloth bag, through which he could see nothing. He was strapped to what felt like a gurney, with his arms fastened to some sort of steel trays, extending outwards at an angle. He could feel a slight pain inside his left elbow, and that arm felt a little cold – sure signs that a needle had been inserted, and a drip was flowing.

He heard footsteps approaching, sounding muffled in some way. A door opened, and three people entered what was clearly his room, their footfalls much more clearly audible now. A muttered conversation, too soft for him to hear clearly, and a switch clicked. Even through the cloth bag, he was aware that a light had come on over his head. Someone tugged at the bag, and pulled it off. His eyes filled with tears as bright light, from a circular fixture above, aimed directly into his face, suddenly blinded him.

A man's voice spoke in Galactic Standard English. It was clearly directed into a microphone, because a speaker next to his head translated its words into Albanian, spoken in a mechanical-sounding voice. "You know why you are here. We need to know everything you do. I will not ask you to tell us, because we both know you will not. However, before I inject the drug, I give you five minutes to make your peace with whatever God you may believe in. After that, conscious thought will cease. You will not awaken again. Your two comrades will be treated in the same way."

He forced down the rush of panic, the urge to beg and plead for his life. He had conducted this sort of interrogation himself in the past. He knew what the drug would do to his mind. He would not be able to withhold any information at all under the interrogator's relentless questioning. The only chance to preserve secrecy would be if his interrogator did not know what questions to ask. Judging by his present circumstances, he, she or they would probably not labor under that handicap.

He wondered suddenly whether there was, after all, some sort of deity, or an afterlife of any kind. He'd always viewed those who believed in such nonsense as deluded fools, credulous idiots whose faith offered him an opportunity to deceive them, persuade them to do what he wanted on the grounds of belief, conscience or morals. Now... now, in the last conscious moments of his own life, he felt a desperate need for hope in the fight against despair. It would be very comforting to believe that there might be something waiting for him. He mentally hesitated... but no. If there was an afterlife, too many of those he'd sent to it would be waiting for him – and they would not welcome him with open arms, to put it mildly. Better by far if they had vanished forever into the void, as he was about to do.

Grimly, hopelessly, the sick, acid taste of final despair in the back of his throat, a thin white-hot wire of fear and anticipation griping his stomach, he waited for oblivion.

COCHRANE WAS WAITING in his office when Argyll entered. He looked up, saw the disgust and self-loathing in his subordinate's eyes, and gestured to a bottle on the sideboard. Tom nodded without speaking, and poured a couple of fingers of Aberfeldy into a glass. He slugged it back, coughed, and poured another before sitting down at the desk.

Cochrane lifted his own glass and sipped it moodily. "Bad?"

"Yes, sir. It was bad, but we got the information we needed."

"Tell me."

"The three were Albanian Mafia, as we figured. The leader, the man who arrived a week ago, was the one who 'persuaded' Saul's former employer to release him, so he could work for Dunsinane. He said Dunsinane accepted Saul's excuse that he couldn't hijack *Humpback,* because security aboard her was too heavy. Saul offered to steal our missile reserves instead, and Dunsinane fell for it. The Albanians planned to sabotage the space station at the same time, to punish Constanta for providing facilities to Hawkwood, and try to frighten other planets into denying them to us. They were going to plant explosives in the environmental systems, then go planetside before they went off. They wanted to vent its atmosphere to vacuum, killing everyone aboard, and make it impossible to use for a year or more until the systems could be repaired. They planned to cover their tracks by leaking information that Dunsinane and the Callanish consortium were behind the sabotage, as well as the theft of *Molly Malone.*"

"Ruthless bastards, aren't they? Did you let the Constanta authorities have a copy of the relevant bits of the recording?"

"Yes, sir. The Minister of Defense will announce that the System Patrol Service learned that 'interplanetary anarchist terrorists' planned to sabotage the space station, and intercepted them before they could get to work. Their explosives and other equipment will be put on display for the news media. He won't mention Hawkwood at all."

"He's welcome to take the credit. What about the other two planetside?"

"I suggest we leave them alone, sir. If they stay put, we can go on monitoring them and see who arrives to replace their friends. If they run for it, let's follow them and see where they go and who they meet. We stand to learn more by leaving them alone than we do by grabbing them."

"I agree. Please congratulate your team, and tell them they've earned a nice bonus."

"I will, sir. Thanks."

"I'll read your full report later, but are there any highlights?"

"Mostly a lot of information about past events, sir. The Albanians look like they're fanatical about secrecy and compartmentalizing information, just like we are. These guys didn't know much about what others are doing elsewhere right now – only their own jobs. Still, they knew a lot about how things got to this point. That might be interesting, in a 'know your enemy' sort of sense."

"It will. What about more agents here, apart from those we knew about?"

"The two local prisoners didn't know of any, sir, but the one from off-planet said there was another ring of agents. He didn't contact them, preferring to use only one ring in case something went wrong. He also named an agent on Callanish, who tried to stir up trouble for us with the consortium there. He's still there, waiting to report on whether Dunsinane's scheme worked."

"And we've no idea who the others are on Constanta?"

"No, sir, but the new man had a contact point for emergencies – a dead drop location, and a coded message to identify himself. We can use that, if you like, and see who picks it up."

Cochrane thought for a moment. "Let's monitor the dead drop location, and see whether anybody checks it. What did you do with the three agents?"

"After we completed the interrogations, we handed them over to Albrescu's people. They finished the job, then dropped the corpses where the Defense Ministry people would find them."

"I'm sorry, Tom. I know this was hard on you."

"I reckon it was hard on you, too, sir. Neither of us is cut out for this sort of thing. Unfortunately, we can't fight barbarians by the standards of civilization. The sooner we can get this filthy business over with, the sooner we can get back to being human, instead of animals!"

"I'm not sure that isn't an insult to most of the animals I've ever met. I've heard enough for now. Pass the bottle, Tom. Let's do our best to wash the sour taste out of our mouths."

CALLANISH

Two weeks later, *Molly Malone* – now renamed *Ponzey,* with every trace of her former name and registration erased – slid into orbit around Callanish. Her crew departed for another freighter waiting nearby, while their boss went planetside to report.

Dunsinane received Saul in his office. "You got her?" he asked eagerly.

"We got her, Mr. Dunsinane. She's in orbit, with her missile pods intact, as per my first report. Your own crew is already aboard her."

"Excellent!" He picked up an envelope from his desk. "Here's the second half of your payment."

Saul opened the envelope, and smiled in satisfaction to see an interplanetary bearer bank draft for fifteen million Bismarck Cluster marks, plus the five percent fee it would cost to cash it off-planet. "Thank you, Mr. Dunsinane. This will do nicely."

He headed back to orbit to join his spacers. Within an hour, the waiting freighter left orbit and headed for the system boundary.

It was two days before the skipper of Dunsinane's anchor watch crew sent him a message. He noted that the latest inventory by Constanta's System Patrol Service, as recorded in the ship's official document storage, had listed thirty-two modern missile pods. However, when inspecting the ship, he and his spacers had only found nineteen, much smaller and older than those listed. He thought Mr. Dunsinane should know of the discrepancy, and asked for instructions.

Dunsinane frowned angrily. Had Saul pulled a switch on

him? Had he, perhaps, sold some of the missing pods to someone else, on his way to Callanish? He pulled up their correspondence, and read rapidly. No, Saul had stated right from the start that there were only nineteen missile pods aboard the erstwhile *Molly Malone,* even before he stole her. Had he lied? It seemed unlikely. Was Hawkwood, then, lying about their capabilities? Did they not have as many, or as modern, weapons as they claimed?

He was still puzzling over the discrepancy two weeks later, when a fast courier vessel arrived with correspondence from an insurance broker on Mayhaven. A corporation there had filed a claim for their spaceship, which had been stolen while in orbit around Constanta. Since it had been insured for full hull value, plus full cargo replacement value, with Rendall Insurance of Callanish, the broker had submitted the claim documentation to the company for payment.

The president of Rendall paled when he saw the figures, and immediately called Dunsinane. "I... we... we can't pay it, sir."

"What do you mean, you can't pay it?"

"Sir, the cargo... the claim is for thirty-two brand-new missile pods. They're valued at over twenty-one billion kronor! The moment we got the policy notification and premium, a few weeks ago, I realized the risk was too great. I began laying it off at once in the reinsurance market, particularly with your colleagues in the Consortium, but we haven't had time to cover even half of it yet."

Sudden acid flooded Dunsinane's stomach, and he felt bile rise in his throat. "Why the devil didn't you warn me?"

"I did, sir. I sent you a message the same day the premium arrived."

Dunsinane's fingers scrabbled at his console, searching through his inbox. Yes – there it was, along with a few dozen other messages from Rendall Insurance awaiting his attention. He'd ignored them in his intense focus on what was happening at Constanta... and that now looked likely to cost him a fortune.

The executive continued, "The balance of the claim, after reinsurers cover their portion, will consume every kronor we've got, and then some. Because this is an interplanetary claim, sir, that'll put us in violation of United Planets insurance regulations, because we'll have no reserves left to cover another claim. They'll make good from the Interplanetary Insurance Reserve Fund whatever we can't pay, then they'll sue us to recover it. It'll bankrupt us, sir."

The executive's voice trembled with worry as he faced the certainty of unemployment; but Dunsinane knew he was at risk for far worse than that. The reality of the situation smashed down on him like a hammer. He was unable to speak for a moment, so great was his consternation as the other stated the obvious. "You're the owner, Chairman and Managing Director of Rendall, sir. Under Callanish law, I'm afraid the authorities may believe you've failed in your fiduciary duty to the company, because they're going to have to draw down our planetary gold and hard currency reserves to pay out the claim off-planet, in terms of United Planets requirements."

"I... ah... I'll call you back." Dunsinane's voice sounded strangled, even in his own ears, almost as if he were choking. He replaced the receiver, very slowly and carefully.

I'm trapped! I can't claim Hawkwood is lying about the missiles, because I daren't produce Molly Malone *and her cargo as evidence. She's stolen property. If she shows up in my hands, how can I explain where I got her without incriminating myself? Questioning under a truth-tester – which Hawkwood is sure to demand – will bring out the facts, and put me behind bars. She's not recorded as being here, anyway – her name is* Ponzey *now. Hawkwood can produce their own bill of lading, plus that inspection report, to prove their claim about her cargo. Interplanetary insurance inspectors are bound to accept them as valid, in the absence of any evidence to disprove them. Rendall Insurance is on the hook for the ship, plus all those non-existent missiles. They're going to liquidate my company, and take everything I own. I'm ruined!*

Dimly, through the turmoil and despair filling his brain, he recalled Pentland's advice not to start something he could not finish. The man had been right, curse him! Hawkwood had set him up! *Molly Malone's* new name was proof of that. Charles Ponzi had been one of the greatest con-men and swindlers in the history of Old Home Earth, before the Space Age had begun. Using his name for the freighter, albeit slightly misspelled, was nothing less than a deliberate taunt by Hawkwood. They must have known about his plans all along, and had waited for the right moment to bring them crashing down around his ears.

Blood pounding in his ears, eyes struggling to focus, a sudden headache filling his brain with stabbing, crippling agony, his left arm going numb, he fumbled with his comm unit... but his hands would no longer obey him. He tried to push his plushly upholstered chair back from his desk, but his foot slipped as he fell sideways. He tumbled to the thickly carpeted floor and lay there, struggling feebly, drooling, as his world faded to black amid an ocean of pain.

His secretary looked in half an hour later, concerned by his unaccustomed silence. She screamed, and frantically called for an ambulance. Her boss's comatose form was rushed to hospital, where the finest doctors on Callanish worked through the evening into the night in a fruitless effort to revive him.

Dunsinane was wheeled into intensive care, still in a coma, and connected to machines that beeped and hummed day and night by his bedside. He could not hear them.

7

PROGRESS

DEEP SPACE

A gim strode impatiently along the main passageway of the big freighter, glancing from time to time through the tiny, pressure-tested viewports letting passersby look into the massive, airless holds on either side. Space-suited figures worked to secure the last of the missile pods in the frameworks that had been erected to hold them. A carefully crafted wiring harness connected them to the fire control system built into an annex off the bridge, while thick cables plumbed them into the auxiliary reactor pod and generator installed in another hold.

"How long?" the leader demanded.

"Two more weeks, sir," the engineer replied, as firmly as his nervousness would allow. He knew the consequences of displeasing this man, particularly concerning so critical a project.

"Why so long? You promised to have the first two ships ready in six months. It is now the seventh month, and only *Butranti* is ready for trials. This ship, *Ilaria,* will take even longer. What is the reason for the delay?"

"With respect, sir, it is the supply of materials for the wiring harness. We ordered what we expected to need, but found that the bulkheads between holds had been constructed in such a way that we could not lead it by the shortest path. We had to lead it outboard of the pods, instead of inboard along the passage bulkheads. That meant we needed a lot more wire – almost a hundred kilometers more, by the time all the connections were made and spliced."

"Why did you not foresee that when you made your initial calculations?"

"Sir, with respect, we have no blueprints or schematics for these ships. We could not plan with certainty. We shall face the same problem with the next two vessels as well, because all four fast freighters came from different shipyards, and are built to different designs. We cannot simply duplicate what we have already done. Until we take off plating and look beneath it, to see where we can run our wiring harness and power cables, we can only estimate, not guarantee."

Agim paused, forcing down his irritation. He had to admit, the engineer had a point. Considering those handicaps, he had done a good job, shoehorning ten missile pods and an auxiliary reactor into *Ilaria's* central holds. He deserved commendation for that, despite the delay.

"Very well. I accept your explanation. Under the circumstances, you and your technicians have done a very good job. There will be bonuses for all of you when the work on this ship is completed, and we shall give you a couple of weeks off before you start on the next two vessels. I shall send a transport to bring your team to Patos for some rest and relaxation, and to visit your families."

"Th-thank you, sir!" The engineer's joyful relief was unfeigned. This was a better response than he had dared to hope for.

"I shall leave you now. I want to attend *Butranti's* firing trials."

"Of course, sir. Thank you for visiting us. We are honored."

As *BUTRANTI* HEADED out toward the asteroid belt in the deserted star system, Agim borrowed the Captain's office for an impromptu discussion with Fatmir, who had just arrived from Patos.

"What news?" Agim demanded, without preamble.

"The destroyer contract is signed. The shipyard has already ordered long-lead-time parts and systems for our first two warships. It is opening a disused construction way for them while it waits, and hiring more staff. It will begin constructing hull modules next month, and begin assembling them in four months, as soon as major systems have been installed. Our first destroyers should be ready seven to eight months from now, if all goes well."

"What is this 'if all goes well'? Have they not agreed to a date?"

"Yes, but they are dependent on parts and systems reaching them from other suppliers. If those are delayed, the shipyard is affected."

His boss sighed. "I have just learned that these freighter conversions will also take longer than planned, also for reasons outside the engineers' control. Sometimes I long for the magic wand wielded by wizards and witches in our children's stories!"

Fatmir sniggered. "It would be nice, yes; but sadly... Speaking of these freighters, there is another problem affecting them, and our destroyers as well."

"Oh?"

"We lack spacers to crew them all. Each freighter needs at least a hundred and twenty spacers, triple her normal crew, to maintain the missile installations, pod reactor, and wiring and power harness, and operate the fire control system when needed, in addition to normal shipboard duties. Each destroyer will have a crew of one hundred and eighty to two hundred spacers, depending on whether we plan to provide boarding and search parties or prize crews, or destroy captured vessels without seizing them for ourselves. There is also their depot ship – another two to three hundred. We also have the existing crews for our two older destroyers, rescued from the scrapyard and refurbished, plus our freighters, asteroid recovery and communications vessels, and our refinery ship. If you put all that together, we shall need more than three thousand trained officers and spacers within three to four years from now. We currently have less than a thousand. Where shall we find the rest?"

Agim cursed. "I should have foreseen this! The trouble is, I am not a spacer. I can handle almost anything planetside, but out here... all the things these people do on shipboard is a mystery to me." He thought for a moment. "We cannot possibly raise that many spacers from among our own people. We are already thinly stretched to cover all our commitments. I think, for a start, we must retire our old destroyers, and use their crews aboard our new ships when they are ready."

"I agree. Should we open spacer positions to our women?"

"Remember what the Patriarch said. Women should never be exposed to danger, because they are the future of our race. It is our privilege and duty, as men, to protect them, if necessary with our own bodies and our own lives."

"But, in that case, we shall have all our very expensive ships, and no-one to operate some of them."

Agim thought for a moment. "What of the sort of planets where Ylli got our missiles? He said most of them were backward dictatorships. Bureaucrats and officers in such places were all too eager to take bribes, that might allow them to escape to a better place. If their officers are open to such persuasion, could we use some of their spacers and junior officers on contract? We could pay the spacers a pittance, and make sure they stay out here, so they are not tempted to desert. Their senior officers back home would get most of the money."

Fatmir perked up at once. "Yes! That would give us time to train more of our people, and upgrade the training of our present spacers to make more of them supervisors. The foreigners could fill in at the lowest levels. Agim, that is brilliant!"

Agim shook his head sourly. "It is not brilliant – merely expedient. We shall send Ylli to seek out suitable planets, and discuss our needs with those who may be willing to help us."

THE FOLLOWING MORNING, *Butranti*'s commanding officer briefed Agim and Fatmir on what they were about to see.

"Our engineers have installed openings for ten missile pods in the belly of the ship, covered with sliding doors to conceal them from prying eyes that may come too close when we are in orbit. Among other things, we shall test the doors with repeated opening and closing, and see if the framework supporting the pods is sufficiently strong and stable to withstand the strain of launching our weapons.

"There is also the difficulty that our pods came from five different planets. Each used a different type of missile, with different performance. We have programmed our fire control system as best we can to accommodate that, but we have yet to test it. This we shall do over the next few days. We shall launch several of each type of missile, to see whether its parameters in the system are accurate, and modify them if they are not."

"Will that not waste a great many missiles?" Agim demanded. "They are very expensive."

"Yes, sir, they are; but if we do not know how to control them, and fire them accurately at an enemy, we may as well be unarmed. Tests are essential. What we learn here will be applied aboard all four of our armed freighters."

"Oh, very well. I suppose you are right. Continue, please."

"Thank you, sir. Finally, we need to fine-tune the fire control system and how we use it. It is a computer program that runs on hardware originally designed to scan an asteroid field, picking out potentially valuable rocks and sending mining craft to investigate them. Such systems use long-range sensor arrays, like those of warships. The new software uses them for target detection and missile control instead. It is said to be very good, and our initial tests have been promising. However, they were conducted without firing actual weapons. We shall do that this week."

"What if the missiles have different speeds or ranges?" Fatmir asked, clearly fascinated. "Surely that means you cannot fire them all together?"

"That is correct, sir. We shall assess what is best for a given target. For example, the missiles obtained from Keda are our most modern, with a powered range of six million kilometers. They will be optimum for use against enemy warships, to keep them as far away as possible. The missiles from Panatti are the oldest and slowest, with a range of only three and a half million kilometers. We should use those against unarmed targets such as enemy freighters, because we can close in on them, getting into range without fear of retaliation. We should keep our higher-performance missiles in reserve for more threatening situations."

"I see. Why not divide the missiles in such a way that one freighter has all the fast, long-range ones, and another all the slow, shorter-range ones? Each ship could then deal with a specific type of engagement, without worrying about which of its missile pods contains which sort of missile."

"Sir, what if a ship encounters a situation for which her missiles are not optimum? We cannot anticipate what will be needed, and we may not be operating with another ship better equipped to deal with the problem. Better to give each ship an equal share of all the different types of missile, so it can tailor its firing pattern to the needs of the moment."

"That makes sense," Agim agreed. He had grown interested in the technical discussion despite himself. He nodded at the captain with respect. "I can see why the Patriarch recommended you to me as a competent officer. If you continue to perform well in command of *Butranti,* I shall offer you a choice; command of either a division of all four of our armed fast freighters, or a detachment of two of our new destroyers when they come online."

"Thank you, sir!"

"Thank me when you have earned your promotion. Now, let us see how our new toys work."

PATOS

Two weeks later, Agim and Fatmir returned to Patos. They were ready to brief Endrit about the success of the missile tests, but he had more important news.

"There is word from Constanta and Callanish. Our people set up the theft of Hawkwood's missile reserves. Dunsinane's man succeeded in stealing the ship containing them, but all their modern missiles had been removed. What is worse, Hawkwood apparently knew that this was planned. They stored all their unserviceable missiles on an old, worn-out freighter, and let Dunsinane's man steal that. They may even have cooperated with him. They insured what they claim was its cargo with Dunsinane's own insurance company. They have now filed a claim for more than seven billion Neue Helvetica francs for their 'stolen' missiles. As a result, Dunsinane is bankrupt, and has suffered a stroke. He is comatose in hospital, and the word is he will not recover. His insurance company has closed its doors. The claim is now being handled through United Planets insurance regulators."

Agim cursed bitterly. "So Hawkwood will soon have more billions, with which to buy even more weapons!"

"I fear so. Worse than that, our people on Constanta set up a sabotage attack on the planet's space station. It was timed to coincide with the theft of Hawkwood's missiles, so we could blame the thieves for the attack. Instead, three of our agents were intercepted before they could attack. It is not known whether they were taken alive, but they were certainly dead when their bodies were shown on Constanta news media the following day. Wounds were visible on their corpses, as if they had been shot, but we do not know whether that was how they died, or whether the shots were fired after their interrogation and execution, to mislead us. They were identified only as 'interplanetary anarchist terrorists'. We were not mentioned."

"What of the rest of their team, and our second team?" Agim demanded, face red with anger.

"That is very strange. The other two members of their team were not harmed or arrested. They drew straws to see who would bring us the news. Drita has remained on Constanta, to monitor the situation. Flamar returned here last week. He awaits instructions, and new members of their team if we decide to send them back with him. The other team was not contacted, and should still be unknown to the Constanta authorities – but we cannot be sure, of course."

"They are still reporting on schedule?"

"Yes. Nothing appears to be wrong."

"But how do we *know* that? How do we know they have not been penetrated, or even arrested, and their places taken by Hawkwood's or Constanta's people?" Agim paced back and forth in agitation, thinking hard. "No. The risks are too great that we might be deceived. We must extract both teams, and bring them back here. We will debrief them very carefully, to make sure we understand as much as possible of the situation there; then we shall send one or two controllers there, senior people we can trust absolutely. We shall give them enough money to hire locals to spy on their behalf. If we decide to attack, or they recommend a strike, we shall send a team to join them for that purpose only, then they will get out fast. That way, our risks of losing more people will be minimized."

Fatmir and Endrit nodded in unison. "I shall send word to our people there at once," Endrit promised.

"Tell them to be careful as they leave Constanta. In their haste, they must not make mistakes that might identify them. Hawkwood is too dangerous an enemy for us to take that sort of chance."

THAT NIGHT, Agim paced the carpet in his private study at home. His mind raced as he weighed possibilities, considered alternatives, and selected options. The responsibilities entrusted to him by the Patriarch sometimes seemed like a crushing burden, weighing him down, forcing him to exert every sinew of mind and body and spirit to keep up with them.

So... our hopes for the Callanish consortium have proved fruitless. They are useless! I do not understand how they could have so deluded themselves as to think they could compete with Hawkwood as equals. They have been out-thought and out-fought at every turn!

That started him wondering. Who *was* this Captain Cochrane who had founded Eufala Corporation, later to become Hawkwood? On first investigation, some years before, he had appeared to be merely an officer in a minor Fleet who had fallen afoul of his superiors, and been axed for political rather than service reasons. That was hardly the pedigree to be expected of one who had shown so much ability over the past few years. Had he somehow been prevented from displaying his true potential, due to service politics? Whatever the reason, he had shown himself to be an opponent worthy of respect.

What am I to do about you, Captain – or Commodore, as I under-stand you are now styling yourself? Are you so dangerous to us that I dare not let you live? Are there others working with and for you who are equally capable, or more so? If I remove you, will that expose us to an even more formidable opponent? Is there anyone close to you, someone we can use as a lever against you? What about a member of your staff who can be pumped for information?

He thought for a while, then came to a decision. He had to learn more about Cochrane. He would send a personal investigator, who would work independently of any other agents and report to him alone. They would find out every scrap of information about Hawkwood and its boss that might be useful. Only when he had a more rounded picture could he decide what to do next. If the decision was for direct action, then that agent could lead a team to undertake it. They would already have all the knowledge they needed to succeed.

So... whom shall I send?

8

SETBACK

CONSTANTA

F rank Haldane's three months of trials with HCS *Bobcat*
proved to be rather more adventurous than planned. He
sent a message that he'd be returning with his crew,
leaving the frigate prototype in the shipyard's hands for modifica-
tion, but provided no further details. Cochrane was bursting with
curiosity and impatience by the time their ferry vessel, provided
courtesy of Kang Industries, pulled into orbit.

"What happened?" he demanded, almost before Frank could
take a seat in his office.

"*Bobcat* wasn't sufficiently stable, sir," Frank said simply.
"They shortened her by about thirty-five meters compared to her
parent design, the *Desroches* class destroyer. That meant her
length is very short in relation to her beam, which is still a
destroyer's cross-section. Her pitch and yaw responses at high
speeds are very quick – too quick. They'd foreseen that, and
provided additional ballast tanks to compensate; but the pipes
connecting them were standard width. When ballast had to be
transferred in a hurry, they weren't wide enough. The transfer

was too slow. We had a few moments during high-speed trials when she almost porpoised out of control. That was... *interesting.*"

"I believe you! Was the Qianjin Admiral aboard at the time?"

Frank laughed. "No, sir. By then we knew she was twitchy at high speed, so we didn't let her have her head. Even so, he and his senior commanders were very impressed with her. I suspect they're thinking about putting cruiser pods into destroyer hulls in due course."

"I'll ask Hui about that when she gets back next week. What are Kang going to do to solve the problems with *Bobcat?*"

"Three things, sir. First off, they're increasing the size of the ballast tanks and installing wider pipes between them, allowing liquid to be pumped more rapidly. Second, they're recalculating her moment of inertia in all three axes. They need to figure out how to improve her longitudinal stability. Clearly, their initial calculations weren't good enough. They're very embarrassed about that, which is why they paid for a ship to bring us home at their expense. Third, they're considering putting back a few of the frames they took out to shorten her. The designers' first-pass conclusion is that if she's several frames longer, between the missile pods and ahead of the leading pod, with a moderate weight redistribution, that should restore a lot of the stability she's lost. They're not going to do anything until they've recalculated everything, but they say that's the most likely solution."

Cochrane grimaced. "That's going to cause a big delay in building the next two frigates, isn't it?"

"Yes, sir. Mr. Kim said to ask you whether he should build four more corvettes while the modifications are being worked out and tested. He can start the first two frigates immediately after that. It'll delay their entry into service by about six months, he says. On the other hand, his designers might be able to incorporate a row of tubes for defensive missiles in the space they're adding, as part of the weight redistribution. I know you were worried that a frigate, with only seventy defensive missiles, might have to face off against a destroyer with a hundred or more offensive missiles, which might swamp her defenses. If we can raise her defensive missile count, that might be worth having."

"It won't completely solve the problem, but it'll help. I'll be very glad if Kang can make that work. Very well, I'll let him know to go ahead. When will *Bobcat* be ready for fresh trials?"

"He says five months, sir. They'll have to separate her into three sections, insert the additional frames and defensive missile tubes – they'll be stand-alone, not part of the missile pods – and then reconnect everything, including lengthening the spine, pipes, the wiring harness, and so on. It's a big job. Fortunately, their robotic constructors can do it fairly quickly."

"They've certainly made things faster compared to the old days. I'm very glad we'll have a couple of arsenal ships ready soon. In the absence of our frigates, we're going to need them to back up our corvettes, in case they run into something they can't handle."

"What's happening on that front, sir?"

"We've just taken delivery of the first two fast freighters. Grigorescu's shipyard has fabricated frames for eight cruiser-cum-frigate missile pods apiece. They're installing them in the midships holds, along with a pod-mounted reactor and generator to power their mass drivers, and a wiring harness to connect them to the ships' datalink. The corvettes will be able to talk directly to the missiles through the datalink, to program and launch them on command."

"Sounds like the extra corvettes will be really useful, then."

"Yes, they will – so much so that I think I'll retain *Amanita* for the present, rather than sell her back to Kang in part exchange for another, larger model. Until the frigates enter service, we can't afford to lose her."

"I get it, sir. Do we have enough missile pods for the arsenal ships?"

"Not yet. We have six on hand. We'll install three in each ship for now. I'm hoping to get thirty more in three months' time from Kang; and we're about to get an insurance windfall, courtesy of the Callanish consortium, that should allow us to buy a lot more."

"Come again?"

Cochrane told Frank about Saul's 'theft' of *Molly Malone,* and how he'd arranged for Dunsinane's firm to insure Hawkwood against the loss of the missiles she'd purportedly carried. By the time he finished, Frank was laughing out loud.

"I know Saul can't talk about it, for obvious reasons, but I bet he wishes he could! He could dine out on that story for years to come!"

"He certainly did a good job, from our point of view. If he'd like an opportunity to go straight, and if you can honestly recommend him, I'll give him a chance."

"Thanks, sir. I'll send word to him. I don't think he'll accept, but you never know."

"We owe you, too. After all, it was your idea to arrange for the Albanians to 'steal' our missiles. We let the Callanish consortium do that instead, but the effect was the same."

"Does that mean I get a commission on the insurance payout, sir?" Frank asked with a cheeky grin.

Laughing, Cochrane pretended to swat at him, and Frank ducked. "Greedy bugger! Still, you never know. We'll see what happens when the money comes in."

COCHRANE TOOK a couple of days off to welcome Hui back from Qianjin. He booked them into a mountain resort, far from interruptions. They luxuriated in each other's company for a few uninterrupted days.

"What are we going to do, Andrew?" she asked him one evening, lying naked and unashamed on a sheepskin rug in front of a roaring fire. "Coming back to you like this... it felt just like I was coming home – but Constanta *isn't* my home. That's on Qianjin. This isn't home for you, either. It's just a temporary base for Hawkwood. What am I going to do about you? I said I can't leave Qianjin. My whole family is there, my whole *life* until recently... but now, I'm just not sure anymore."

"If you're saying home is where I am, I'll be very flattered – and very grateful," he said quietly as he lay beside her, equally nude. "I feel pretty much the same about you coming back. Life was empty without you. I don't know what we're going to do, Hui. I love you, and I want to be with you. I don't know where that will take us, and quite frankly I'm not worried. If you and I are together, I think we could make a home anywhere, and be happy. It's not the place. It's us."

She hugged him gently. "Thanks for saying that. I guess I'm torn between who I was, and what life had made me, compared to what you're making me as we grow together. I know I'm a different woman today from what I was before we met, and that's all your fault." She stuck out her tongue at him, smiling.

They returned with the issue still unresolved, but both knew that it would have to be settled soon. Neither of them would be able – or willing – to continue in limbo for long.

Captain Dave Cousins, in command of Hawkwood's ships and operations in the Mycenae system, came back to Constanta for consultations. Cochrane took the opportunity to call together several of his core team to discuss future options. They met for breakfast, then adjourned to a meeting room.

Frank opened by discussing their present and projected fleet size. "We have seven corvettes at Mycenae: *Amanita, Banewort, Belladonna, Castor, Datura, Hellebore* and *Hemlock.* Two more, *Manchineel* and *Mandrake,* will be delivered next month, and work up their crews there. Kang Industries will build nine more for us over the next few years, as well as nine frigates – at least, those are our plans at present. We have the first two of our six new fast freighters, *Beluga* and *Narwhal*. They're here at Constanta, being fitted out as arsenal ships. Missile pods for them should be available this quarter. *Orca* continues to be our only armed freighter and training ship. She also handles special projects. We have another fast freighter, *Pilot,* to resupply the Mycenae system every month. We have two very large warehouse freighters, *Humpback* in Constanta orbit and *Bowhead* at Mycenae. There are also two depot ships there, *Anson* and *Jean Bart,* with a third, *De Ruyter,* due for delivery in a couple of months. She'll go to Mycenae to work up and relieve *Anson,* which will move to Constanta for routine maintenance, then provide basing facilities here. There are three more depot ships on order. We have three courier ships, *Agni, Hermes* and *Zaqar,* with eight more on order from Fujita. Finally, there's our repair ship, *Vulcan,* also in Mycenae."

Cousins pretended to mop his brow. "*Whew!* We never see all of them together at one time, so it's easy to lose sight of just how fast we're growing. I make that twenty-two ships either in service or about to be, and another thirty-three on order. That's a heck of a jump from having no ships at all, about four years ago!"

"It sure is," Cochrane agreed. "I'm still amazed, sometimes, to think back on it. We couldn't have done it without everyone who took a risk, and joined us early on. They've shared in our profits, of course. Thanks to that, they recommended us to their friends, who could see the money they were making and became eager to sign on. So many of them have responded that, at long last, we have more spacers than we have berths for them. That won't last, of course. In fact, we'll need to mount another recruiting drive as soon as the next ships are ready."

"What about officers, sir?" Frank asked.

"That's still a limiting factor, but the Lancastrian retired warrant officers and Limited Duty officers we hired to set up those programs for our fleet have come through for us. We now have fifteen warrant officers and seven LDO's, and there are more in prospect. We're using Warrant Officers as department heads on

some corvettes and transports, which eases the officer shortage
for those classes of ship. They're working out very well, and our
senior NCO's are glad to have a new avenue for promotion. It
wasn't often available in the New Orkney Cluster, where most of
us come from, and it's helping us to recruit more of them.

"Now, I want to discuss our deployments. We need to make
some changes. Commander Sue McBride, Hawkwood's Chief
Engineer, tells me the oldest corvettes will soon be in need of a
one-month maintenance period in a shipyard. She wants to begin
rotating them back here for that purpose. We'll use Grigorescu's
facilities, of course. He's done great work for us so far. We also
need a couple of corvettes based here for local defense, plus an
arsenal ship, and a surveillance satellite will be deployed here
later this year. The Albanians have already tried to hit us once,
and I'm sure they'll do so again. I want sufficient local defenses to
deal with that, if necessary."

After some debate, they agreed to send *Amanita* and *Banewort*
to Constanta as soon as the two new corvettes arrived in Mycenae. The older corvettes, first of their class to be delivered, would
be serviced in the shipyard. *Banewort* would then assist the new
arsenal ships to work up, because she had full-length destroyer
arrays on her longer hull, allowing her to better control their
missiles. *Amanita,* a slightly smaller ship with shorter arrays,
would go back to Mycenae to relieve *Belladonna,* which would
undergo maintenance, then join *Banewort* for local defense. As
more corvettes were delivered, the earlier ships would cycle
through the shipyard in their turn, relieving *Banewort* and
Belladonna. Each ship would offer its crew a period of extended
liberty, rest and recreation during their maintenance period.

Cochrane broached the subject of senior appointments.
"Dave has done an excellent job as Officer in Command at Mycenae. However, I haven't done nearly as good a job here! I've been
running from pillar to post, doing too many things myself,
because we haven't had enough officers to form a proper staff.

That's got to change. What's more, Dave needs a break from Mycenae, otherwise Elizabeth is going to kill me for keeping her husband so far away!" The others laughed.

"Where are you going to get staff officers, sir?" Frank asked curiously. "I don't think many of us are staff-qualified."

"That's true. Dave and I have done Staff College, but I don't think anyone else has. We'll have to offer part-time Staff College training. There are plenty of distance education materials from Staff Colleges all over the settled galaxy. I figure we can buy what we need, and set up self-study periods for our people. By working and studying at the same time, they'll take longer to learn, but they'll apply what they learn at once. That's the best we can do right now."

"Who do you want for your staff, sir?" Cousins asked.

"You, for a start, Dave. We've got to set up a proper Personnel function. We've been running that on an *ad hoc* basis since we began. You've had oversight over it, but you've complained long and loud that it's a makeshift solution at best. I want you to move back here as my combined S1, Staff Officer Personnel, and S7, Education and Training. We'll run those functions in tandem for now. I've got Caitlin Ross as my S2, Intelligence. She'll share that function with Tom Argyll, who'll be S2 for Security. Their people will work with you to screen new hires. Lachlan MacLachlan is my combined S4, Logistics, and S8, Finance. Yes, he's a civilian, but in the final analysis, Hawkwood is a civilian company, so I don't think that matters. Warrant Officer Jock Murray will handle S7, Communications and Technology. He should be at least a Lieutenant-Commander by now – his contribution to Hawkwood certainly rates that – but he says he doesn't want commissioned rank, and I'm not going to push the issue.

"I think I'll keep the S5 function, Plans, in my own hands for now, until we have more staff-trained officers. For S3, Operations, I have Commander Shearer in mind. He's currently Officer in Command of our Second Corvette Division. What do you think?"

"What about Commander Darroch, sir, of the First Corvette Division?" Cousins asked.

"I have something else in mind for him. We'll have to replace both in divisional command."

"Who's going to take their places, sir?"

"I want you to recommend the best two corvette commanding officers for promotion. If you need to consult with Darroch and Shearer before making a final selection, do that. Let's promote from within." There was a buzz of approval.

"And what about my replacement, sir?"

Cochrane smiled. "Frank, take a bow."

"*Me,* sir?" Frank's jaw dropped in surprise. "But... I've never commanded more than a single ship."

"That's why I want you as Officer Commanding Mycenae Station. You're going to command our first frigate division soon, and possibly lead a combat squadron further down the road, if things go on as they are with the Albanians. You need broader command experience of multiple units, and Mycenae will give it to you. I won't promote you to Captain immediately, because you've been a Commander for less time than some of our other Commanders, and I don't want to provoke jealousy. However, after a few months running things out there, it'll be clear to everyone whether you're ready for a fourth stripe. I'm willing to bet that you are."

Cousins grinned. "I'll second that, sir. Come on, Frank. He's put you on the spot."

"Oh, well! If I can't have *Bobcat,* and if you think I can handle Mycenae, sir, I'll take it on."

Cochrane inclined his head. "Thank you. As soon as our first two arsenal ships have passed their trials and worked up their crews, I'll send one to you. She'll need at least one corvette with her at all times, to control her missiles if necessary. You'll also have to figure out tactics to make the best use of her. You and I will liaise about that as we go along."

"Yes, sir. Ah... there's one staff position you've left out. Who's going to be your Chief of Staff, and look after your administration?"

Cochrane half-smiled, and turned to Hui. "Captain Lu," he said formally as her eyebrows shot up in surprise, "you're officially a liaison officer from the Qianjin Fleet, assigned to Hawkwood Corporation to share information concerning the Albanian threat to both our forces. However, you're also staff-qualified, and on excellent terms with everyone here. Would you please accept a temporary position as my Chief of Staff? I'd like to make it permanent, but we all know there are issues that need to be resolved if that's to happen." He winked at her, and she blushed, even as the others laughed and applauded.

"I... I don't know what to say! My Admiral might complain long and loud about one of his officers serving in another fleet."

"We're not another fleet, if it comes to that. We're a private company. Besides, if you're our liaison officer, what better way to know everything we're doing, and be able to report it to him, than to have your fingers in every one of our pies, as Chief of Staff?" The others laughed again, clearly amused by Hui's confusion.

"Won't your people resent taking orders from an outsider?"

"Not if I officially order them to do so, and make it clear your rank is as valid inside Hawkwood as it is in Qianjin's Fleet."

"Well... I..." She glanced around the table. "Thank you all very much for being willing to have me in so critical a position. It's very flattering. I accept, subject to the condition that I write to my Admiral to obtain his permission. If he agrees, good. If he objects, I'll have to step down. Is that acceptable?"

"It is to me," Cochrane assured her, and a chorus of approval from the others showed they felt the same.

"All right. I'll make a start, and we'll see what happens."

9

RECALL

PATOS

Agim looked up from his terminal, bleary-eyed with weariness, as his secretary knocked at the door. "Jehona Sejdiu is here to see you, sir."

"Thank you, Vesa. Send her in, please, and bring coffee for us."

"At once, sir."

His eyes glowed as the woman was shown into his office. She smiled warmly as she saw him, her eyes meeting his frankly. He ushered her to the group of chairs in the corner of the office, and waited until the secretary had poured coffee and left them alone.

"It is very good to see you again, Jehona," he began. "I hesitated before asking your husband's permission to see you, because... well, I have never forgotten what we once were to each other. You changed me, helped me to become a man rather than a foolish, headstrong boy."

She blushed, and looked down at her cup. "We were... different people then, yes. Even though things did not work out between us, I have never forgotten, either. When Pal used to get jealous, in our early years together, I reminded him that the woman he married was, in some measure, the product of what you and I had shared, and that he should be grateful for that. After our children came along, that cleared the air, and we've never had that problem again."

"I am very glad to hear that. He gave me permission to see you readily enough. That was good of him."

"Why did you want to see me?"

Agim sighed. "I... I need you to serve our cause once again, as you did before."

Her eyes widened with shock and surprise. "Agim, *no!* Surely, you're joking! I haven't practiced tradecraft in two decades or more, and I'm almost fifty! There's no way I can compete against youngsters, with all their energy and drive!"

He shook his head. "I am not joking." He ticked off points on his fingers. "You were one of our best agents, if not the best in our year. You achieved great things for our cause. The Patriarch congratulated you personally, and held you up as an example before subsequent classes. I cannot believe that such talent simply disappears with age. Next, you do not look like a typical agent. We know the type well, because we are on our guard against our enemies sending them against us. Young, fit, strong, keen-eyed, observant, always on the alert. The best can disguise all that, and perhaps fool us, but lesser agents cannot. You are entering middle age as we reckon our years, and are carrying a little more weight than is good for you." He flushed. "So am I, if truth be told." They laughed softly together. "You do not look like someone to be feared, or suspected.

"Then, there are your qualifications. You are an accountant. You obtained a post-graduate degree from a Neue Helvetica university. Such skills and qualifications are in great demand by businesses on every planet. They may offer you a way to infiltrate our enemies that less qualified agents cannot match, because they will be less likely to suspect you. Finally, there is your commitment. You know what we are striving for, and you believe in it with all your heart. After all, you are the Patriarch's grand-daughter. Who better to serve his vision and bring it closer to fulfilment, by helping to remove the obstacles in its path?"

She hung her head in silence, clearly thinking hard. At last she looked up. "What about my children? Yes, they are grown now, but they are not yet wise. Fjolla has been married for less than a year, and is expecting her first child. She will need her mother's help. Alban is a Sub-Lieutenant in our space forces. I see him only occasionally, when he comes home on leave, but I would miss that altogether if I were on assignment. As for the twins, Lindita and Pjeter will graduate this year. Am I to miss that, too?"

"I understand. I am a father, and I know how much I missed being able to be there for all the highlights in my children's lives. However, the Patriarch asked me to sacrifice that, for the good of the Cause. You know how hard he worked me, during the years before he appointed me to succeed him as Chairman of the Brotherhood. He was testing me during that time, as he tested many others. Only I passed all his tests, to become all that he wished me to be. Sacrifice was part of that, and it was a price I paid willingly for the sake of his vision, which has become ours. I am asking you to do no less.

"Our enemies are strong and capable. You do not know much about them yet, because we have not spoken of them outside the inner circle of the Brotherhood; but they are the ones who killed your grandfather, getting on for two years ago. They grow stronger by the day. I desperately need information as to what motivates them. If I can find that key, perhaps we can find a way to deal with them without all-out war. However, we also cannot back down. You know the Patriarch's dictum; if we are struck, we must never accept it, but instead strike back ten times as hard. We have been faithful to that.

"If we are to avenge your grandfather's death, we must know

how and when and where to strike our enemies most effectively, and what their defenses are, and how to avoid them. I need you to get that information for us. I know nobody else with your dedication to our cause, and your skills, which I remember so well. I am sure you can regain them, with a little refresher training and some practice. I do not pretend the job will be either easy or safe. Our enemies have demonstrated that they will interrogate our captured agents as ruthlessly as we interrogate theirs. If it looks like they will capture you, you will have to make sure they can learn nothing from you." She flinched, but he held up his hand. "Yes, I know you cannot bear the thought of leaving your husband a widower, and your children orphaned. However, you accepted the danger with fortitude during the years we worked together. You understand the need. Will you accept the challenge?"

She sat in silence for a long time. He thought he saw the gleam of moisture in her eyes, but said nothing. He could not coerce her in this. She had the right to make up her own mind, without undue pressure. He owed that, not just to her, but to her grandfather.

At last she said, "I cannot give you my answer now. I must speak with my husband about this. You know that, if I am in the field, it may be necessary for me to... behave in ways that might – no, *would* – violate our marriage oath, in order to obtain the information you seek." She looked up at him, her face taut, forcing herself to face reality. "I do not want that – the very *thought* is repulsive, much less the deed! – yet you know as well as I that it may become necessary. You and I both used our bodies to entrap our targets, when we were in the field. It is all too common. There is also the very real risk that I may not return. He must understand both dangers clearly, and give me permission to risk them."

He nodded slowly, feeling despair creep into his heart. What man would freely allow his wife to commit adultery, even if it was for the Cause? He quailed mentally at the thought of his wife asking him that question. He managed to say, "What if he will not agree?"

"Then I will not do this. He is my heart, and my life. I will not go against his wishes."

"I... I applaud your commitment. Of course, given who your grandfather was, I am not surprised. I can only hope and pray that his example, and his ultimate sacrifice of his life for our Cause, will help your husband, and you, to consider an equally great sacrifice. I do not ask it lightly."

Her eyes softened. "I know you are sincere, Agim. I would never expect less from you."

"Thank you," he said simply.

"Let us speak of more practical matters. You say I shall need some refresher training. I agree, of course. How security-conscious are our enemies?"

"They are getting better by the day. Agents who were recently withdrawn from the field say they have hired experts to upgrade their skills and knowledge. They now have very well-trained security guards, and a strike team as well, for action against individuals and groups they want to take out before they pose a threat. They use crawling nanobugs and flying flitterbugs, as well as larger drones, to secure their premises, including inspecting every cable and environmental duct at least once per week. Their electronic defenses against bugging were lacking in the early years, but have greatly improved, to the point that they may rival our own. I do not think we will be able to penetrate their security by technical means alone. It will require the human element – which is why I asked you to come here today."

She was frowning at him. "All that you have described... my husband is Head of Security for our asteroid refining operation, as you know." He nodded. "He has told me about some of our defensive measures. That is not a breach of security, of course – you and I used to penetrate such defenses as part of our job. He wants me to use that background to help him make sure no-one else will do that to us." He nodded again. "What you have just told me mirrors our own efforts. Where did our enemies learn about them?"

"What do you mean?"

"You said they would not hesitate to interrogate me. Have they interrogated others of our people?"

"Yes... yes, they have." He did not have to add that they had not survived. That went with the territory, in their profession.

"Then I think we know where they got some of those ideas. Have they, perhaps, used their knowledge of our techniques against us? Are you sure these offices are as secure as you think?"

His jaw dropped. He was speechless for a moment. At last he ground out, "Thank you, Jehona. You almost gave me a heart attack... yet, still, I thank you." She giggled as he went on, "I shall discuss this with our security team. Perhaps I should bring in your husband, to shake them up a little. They may have grown too accustomed to their task, too complacent after years of not identifying any threats. You are right. What our enemies learned from us, and now use to defend themselves against us, they can also use to attack us. We must redouble our alertness."

She nodded as she rose to her feet. "Then at least I have been able to render you some service today. I shall speak with my husband tonight, and let you know what he says."

He stood, and took her proffered hand, bending to kiss it very gently. "Thank you, Jehona. If it is given to our Patriarch to be aware of such things, may his spirit guide you and your husband to make the right choice. Let me walk you out. I shall then visit our security team, and start the process of... shaking things up."

"OH, *SHIT!*"

The 'building manager', seated several floors below in his

office, had listened with care to the conversation, picked up by whisker feelers against the inner panes of glass in Agim's office and relayed to him through computers that translated its vibrations into sound. Now his eyes widened with shock. He pressed a buzzer.

Within seconds, another man hurried into the office. "What is it, Abis?"

His boss hurriedly explained Agim's reaction to the woman's concerns. "I think he means it. I reckon they're going to go through this building with a fine-tooth comb. Our window whiskers may not survive that close an inspection."

The new arrival swore bitterly. "What are we going to do?"

"We're going to strip out everything in these offices that might incriminate us, right now, before they can start looking. I want all the recorders and special gear out of here. Take them to our van in the basement parking. Carry them in boxes and bags that don't show what's inside. Go to the usual place and leave them there, using every precaution against being followed. Go home after that, and wait for my call. If things look bad, I'll send word."

"What are you going to do?"

"What else can I do but work here until closing? This is my job. If I walk out halfway through the day, it'll look suspicious. That's the last thing we want right now."

"I... all right, but *be careful!* I don't want to have to explain to the Admiral what happened to you!"

"I always am, Fihr. I always am."

As his subordinate hurried out, Abis took a small box from his desk drawer and opened it. Inside nestled several strange-looking white objects, almost like half a molar tooth. He reached into his mouth, unscrewed something, and removed an almost identical object, then replaced it with one of those in the box. He had to suppress a slight shiver as he did so. If the tenants suspected anything, and took him alive, he knew what the inevitable end would be. Death would be infinitely preferable.

As Fihr came back with a cardboard box, to clean out the gear in his office, he handed him a half-tooth. "Put this in now. I hope and pray we never need them, but..."

"Yeah. But."

As Fihr went out with the laden box, Abis picked up his comm unit and sent an innocuous five-word message to another comm code, one that was not identified in his contacts file. No-one replied, but he knew those who monitored that code would now be on the alert, just in case. As soon as the message had gone out, he erased it from the comm unit's memory, as if it had never been sent.

AGIM STUDIED the surveillance vid from the basement garage, hissing slightly between his teeth. "When did this happen?"

"He left only a few minutes before you finished speaking to us. We do not know what was in the boxes and bags he loaded."

"They do not know we have installed our own concealed cameras down there?"

"They have never given any sign of it, sir."

"Very well. That may have been routine, for all we know; but it may not. You did well to inform me. Now, join the others in checking the building. If we find anything, it may be an indication that they heard my conversation with Jehona, or what I said to you after she left, and are taking precautions against being found out."

"Yes, sir."

Agim replayed the vid as the security guard turned and left the room. He scratched his jaw, thinking hard. *Perhaps we should put a tracer on that van when it returns, to see where it goes every day. On the other hand, if they are enemies – although they have given no sign of that since we moved in – then they may find it, which would reveal that we suspect them. What to do?*

He was interrupted by a buzz from his comm unit. He scooped it from his belt. "Yes?"

"Sir, would you please come to your office at once?" The voice was the head of the security detail on duty.

Agim ran nimbly up the stairs, and arrived at his office panting only slightly. "What is it?"

The man gestured to one of the triple-paned windows. Two guards were kneeling beside it. They had torn away the paneling beneath it, and were peering at two thin wires that ran from the window frame down between the studs. "Mirela checked the window frames with a magnifying glass. She noticed two tiny holes at the base of the frame that should not be there, between the inner and center panes. She called me, and I told them to look beneath it. We think the holes are for whisker vibration sensors. We have cut the wires, in case they are."

Agim's blood ran icy cold. If the enemy had been listening to his conversations since he moved in... "What about other rooms?"

"We are checking every window frame, sir. I –"

Another guard appeared in the doorway. "Sir! The board-room! We think we have found another one!"

Agim wanted to throw back his head and scream in frustration. *"How could we have missed this?* Your people scanned the building in depth, before we moved in! How was it they did not detect these whiskers?"

"I... Sir, I have no excuse. I can only say that it is almost impossible to detect such things if one does not know they are there, and looks for them specifically. You know this from your own time in the field, sir."

Agim breathed hard. The man was right. This *was* an almost foolproof setup. He had used something like it against their enemies, in years gone by. If Jehona had not raised the issue of security...

"We shall discuss that later. Right now, we need to know who is behind this. I think the building manager can perhaps help us."

"Yes, sir. You wish us to secure him?"

"At once. Make sure he is able to talk."

"I shall go myself, sir."

The man spun on his heel and ran out, shouting for some of his guards to join him.

ABIS HEARD the click over the line as the wires were cut, and closed his eyes as dread seeped into his very bones. *How quickly today's gone to shit! Just half an hour ago, everything was fine... and now this. They'll be coming. Sure as hell, they're going to come for me.*

He hurried into the anteroom. His secretary, a local woman who knew nothing of their secret activities, had asked for the afternoon off. He was suddenly grateful she would not be there to see this. He closed and locked the door leading to the corridor, then went back to his office.

He activated his terminal, and brought up the security cameras covering the corridor outside the building manager's offices. It was deserted. He kept a careful eye on the display as he took up his comm unit, and activated a pre-programmed routine with a single keystroke.

The unit automatically dialed six comm codes, all set up long ago for one-time emergency use, and transmitted a three-word signal. The codes would forward it to others, where he knew recipients would be waiting for it with something of the same fear he felt right now. As soon as it had sent the message, the comm unit wiped its memory clean, using a military algorithm to ensure no data could be recovered. Abis locked it in an inconspic-uous drawer, to give it time to complete the procedure before it could be interrupted.

He knew he had no chance to escape. The guards had spread

throughout the building almost as soon as Fihr had left the parking garage. He had seen them on the security cameras, and hoped against hope that this was just a routine check. Now he knew that it was not. He wasn't religious, but was suddenly almost devoutly grateful that the younger man would be spared this. He tried to suppress the panic bubbling just below the surface of his self-control. It was too late for that now. He'd known the risks when he signed on the dotted line. Now he had to accept the consequences... and, ghastly as those consequences were, they still beat the alternative a hundred times over.

As four men appeared in the corridor, walking briskly toward the entrance to his office suite, Abis reached into his mouth and twisted the fake tooth a quarter turn, rocking it back and forth. A small pin emerged from the crown, sticking up about a millimeter. He kept his teeth carefully apart as he watched the terminal display.

The men tried the handle of the door. It did not open. One of them looked questioningly at another, who nodded. The first man took a device from his pocket, one Abis recognized. He held it against the lock and pressed a button. From inside his office, Abis could hear the electronic lock's sudden *ting!* as the picker traced its combination and entered it. The door clicked open.

Abis' last thought, as he bit down hard on the pin, was of the small country house where he had grown up. As pressurized spray burst out of the tooth, he swallowed hard, twice, then inhaled deeply through his mouth to absorb the last of the vapor.

I'm sorry, Mom and Dad. I won't be coming home this time. If the prophets were right, I'll be waiting for you when you arrive.

By the time the guards, pulsers drawn, reached his desk, Abis was jerking and twitching on the floor behind it in a final spasm.

~

HER COMM UNIT rang as Jehona and her husband were eating supper. She excused herself to answer it, and frowned when she recognized Agim's voice. "Why are you calling me?" she hissed. "Can't you give me privacy with my husband tonight?"

His voice was grim. "You should know that your warning was entirely correct."

She froze. "You mean...?"

"Yes. There were listening devices. The building manager was part of it. He killed himself before we could take him. His employees have all vanished from their homes, except for a local secretary who knows nothing. They all destroyed their residences by fire before leaving, presumably to get rid of evidence we could use, and slagged their electronic devices to prevent any data being recovered. We presume they have a plan to get off Patos, just as our people have when they are on an enemy planet. We shall watch for them, and alert the authorities, of course."

"I... I see. Thank you for telling me."

"No, Jehona; thank *you* for your timely warning. But for that, they would still be listening to us."

"Did they learn much of importance?"

"Of course they did!" He breathed heavily for a moment. "I apologize. I should not snap at you. Yes, they learned much. Fortunately, my two lieutenants and I discussed many issues at other places, rather than talk about them where even our own people might overhear us. That will protect us to a certain extent. Nevertheless, they will have learned a great deal."

"You have no idea who they were?"

"Who else could they be but Hawkwood, or agents working on its behalf?"

"I suppose you're right. What now?"

"Speak to your husband. You have my permission to tell him what I have just told you, to illustrate our peril. Let me know tomorrow what he says."

There was a click as Agim terminated the call.

She laid down the comm unit, and walked slowly back to the table, her face pensive.

"Who was it, dear?"

"It was Agim. Darling... we need to talk. Right now."

"But we're still eating!"

"I'm sorry. It can't wait. Will you sit down with me in the living-room?"

"Yes, of course."

She told him of Agim's request, and the reasons he had advanced for it. Pal was thunderstruck. "How *dare* he ask this of you? More to the point, how dare he ask it of *me?*"

"He asks because our enemies are growing bolder." She described the afternoon's events. "He sounded really worried when he called. He told me I could tell you what had happened, so that you understood the danger we are in."

His face turned pensive. He thought for a long moment. She started to speak, but he held up his hand. She waited in silence.

At last he turned to her, and gathered her into his arms. "Darling... everything in me, as a man, screams that I should forbid this. I can't bear the thought of placing you in such danger. However, Agim is right. Our peril is great. I need to know... what do *you* want to do? Are you truly willing to place yourself in such peril, knowing what you risk?"

She laid her head on his shoulder, tears trickling from her closed eyes. "Pal, I am my grandfather's descendant. You know what he would say. How can I do otherwise?"

He sighed, long and low. "Yes, you are; and yes, I know what he would say." Silence. "Very well. If you see no other way, you may do this. I ask only one thing. I want a way to communicate privately with you, a channel that is ours alone, and does not go through Agim or any other part of the Brotherhood. If... if things go badly... I need you to tell me, before the end, so that I can tell our children. I cannot simply pretend that you have vanished without trace. I owe that to them."

Her tears came faster. "I... you know that is against all tradecraft?"

"Yes, I know – and I don't care. That is my condition."

"In that case... yes. I'll do it. It will be for us alone."

He kissed her, very tenderly.

THE FOLLOWING MORNING, Agim sighed with heartfelt relief when Jehona told him her husband's decision. "I can never thank you enough, either of you. How soon can you be ready to start refresher training?"

"Give me a month to wind up my involvement with several groups of which I'm a member. I'll tell them I'm going off-planet, on behalf of my husband. They will be intensely curious, but not suspicious. I shall also start exercising. I must get back in shape as quickly as I can."

"Good. I shall make the arrangements." He grimaced. "I, too, should start exercising." He heard her chuckle mischievously, and could not restrain his own rueful smile.

He ended the conversation and sat back in his chair. His eyes fell on the torn paneling beneath his office windows, and he scowled. There was still no sign of the rest of the agents he presumed had been working with the building manager. They would continue to scour the planet for them, but if they were as good as his people, they would be hard to find.

I must answer this affront! I must show Hawkwood that we are not afraid of them. I must show them that the discovery of their spies has made us more determined, not less. I must hurt them, in response to the hurt they have done us – but how? What should I do?

The germ of an idea came to him. He mulled it over, examining it from all angles. It would be risky, and potentially costly too: but if it succeeded, it would cost the enemy much more.

He called Endrit. "Meet me in the foyer. Let us go for a walk. I have a plan for a retaliation attack against Hawkwood for this spying outrage. I want to discuss it with you."

As he walked to the stairs, he thought to himself, *I must make a habit of discussing critical issues in different locations, so that our enemies never know ahead of time where they should listen. If we keep them guessing, we gain an edge – and we need one. They have shown themselves to be just as capable as we are. We must never underestimate them again!*

10

NEXT STEPS

CONSTANTA

Hui tapped at his office door. "Do you have a moment?"

Cochrane looked up from his terminal. "Of course. Come in."

She walked over to the desk, holding a couple of sheets of paper. "Admiral Kwan replied to my message, approving my request to serve as your Chief of Staff temporarily. Instead of an electronic signal, he sent an old-fashioned letter, and included a personal message."

"He did? What was it?"

"You'd better read it." She handed over the papers.

Cochrane laid them on his desk, and scanned through them. The message came in the last few paragraphs.

You have been open and honest with me about your relationship with Commodore Cochrane. For this, I thank you, but I must also caution you. You are an officer in the Fleet of Qianjin. That is not just your primary professional loyalty; it is, or should be, your only professional loyalty. I do not fear that your relationship with him will lead you to betray us, because he is not our enemy. In fact, in terms of the threat we both face from Albanian Mafia infiltration, he is presently our de facto ally, which is why I shall allow you to serve as his interim Chief of Staff. Nevertheless, this may place you in an awkward position in the longer term.

You are not the first person to experience this difficulty. I have come across it before, and seen the damage it can do to both parties. To avoid that, I strongly advise that you regularize your relationship with the Commodore, either by reverting to a purely professional association, or by formalizing the bond between you. If you do neither, you will continue to be torn between your conflicting loyalties. That will undoubtedly affect both your relationship and your career in the longer term.

I suggest you discuss this with the Commodore. He sounds like a very good man, from what you and others have told me about him. I am sure he will understand your dilemma. Between you, I trust that you will resolve this conundrum. I sincerely hope you will do so as soon as possible, and I wish both of you every success.

Cochrane nodded thoughtfully as he handed the papers back to her. "He sounds like a good man himself."

"He is. What do you think of his advice?"

"I think he's right. I've said as much to you, you'll recall."

"Yes, you have. I know where you stand, and I love you for it. You're so uncomplicated! Sadly, I'm not. I'm still torn between my family, and my home planet, and you. I want them all, but I can't *have* them all!" Her voice was sad.

"Surely you can have them all, but in a different way? I mean, if you and I get married, you won't be abandoning them. We can visit your family, and they can visit us. It's just that you'd be living somewhere else. What if your Fleet appointed you as a military attaché to, say, the United Planets? You'd be living and working on Neue Helvetica, and might not see them more often than every couple of years. Living with me would be like that in some ways."

"Yes, it would, but at Neue Helvetica I'd always know that sooner or later, I'd be going back. If we marry, I won't. *You'll* be my home, wherever we end up."

He nodded. "That'll apply to me, too, you know," he reminded her softly. "You'll be *my* home."

She wiped a tear from the corner of my eye. "Now look what you've made me do!" she said, half-crossly. "I know, darling. I think, for a man, it's a lot less complicated than it is for a woman. We think differently, we *feel* differently. I... I don't know what to do! They talk about feeling 'torn'. That's exactly what I feel like right now! Part of me – a big part – wants nothing more than to 'regularize our relationship', as Admiral Kwan put it, and spend the rest of my life with you. Another part, though... that's the memory of another man I once thought of in that way, and after five years, he dumped me. It's the fear that says I'll be burning my boats and my bridges, and there'll be no way back. I'm sorry, darling. You don't deserve this from me."

He shrugged. "Let's at least set a term to this. You know I want you to be my wife. I know a big part of you wants that, too. Why don't we agree that in not more than one year from today, we must make a choice? If it's to get married, let's not dither about it any longer. If it's that we can't marry, for whatever reason, then let's cut the knot and separate, for both our sakes. Either way, we know there'll be a limit to worrying about it. One way or another, the uncertainty *will* end."

She stared at him for a long moment. "You really mean that?"

"Hui, I love you. Nothing's going to change that; but I can't rest easy with the way we are now, any more than you can. I want both of us to be able to look ahead and know that there *will* be a solution, one way or the other. If nothing else, it'll force us to reevaluate our priorities and our relationship, and really work at figuring things out, instead of just drifting along, letting events dictate what happens next."

Her shoulders slumped slightly. "That's... that's not what I had in mind when I brought you this letter, but... I suppose you're right. I guess that's what the Admiral was getting at."

"I think it is."

"All right." She took a deep breath. "One year."

A FEW DAYS LATER, a message arrived from Mr. Kim of Kang Industries. The industrialist informed Cochrane that modifications to *Bobcat* were well under way, and asked him to make a choice. "We can install a row of ten tubes for cruiser-size defensive missiles, with a powered range of five million kilometers," he wrote. "Alternatively, in the same space, we can install eighteen tubes for corvette-size defensive missiles, with a powered range of three million kilometers. The latter option would increase the ship's defensive barrage by ten percent over the former. Please advise which option you would prefer us to install."

Cochrane grinned. The more defensive missiles, the better, as far as he was concerned. He began tapping out a reply, telling Kim to install the second option, and standardize on it for all future frigates if trials proved it to be satisfactory.

He was interrupted by his secretary. "Sir, a Mr. Pentland has sent a message. He's just arrived from Callanish, and would like to speak with you. It's very strange, sir; he asked me to assure you that he isn't your enemy."

Cochrane frowned. "Give me a moment." He called up a list of the members of the Callanish consortium. Sure enough, Pentland was listed among its directors. *Why would he want to see me? I thought the consortium was defunct, after the savaging we gave*

Dunsinane. He shrugged. There would probably be no harm in finding out.

He raised his voice. "You can make an appointment for him when convenient. Thank you."

"Yes, sir."

Pentland arrived the following morning. Cochrane looked at him curiously as his secretary ushered him in. The man looked older than his years, and tired, as if he were worn out from carrying a heavy burden for far too long. Nevertheless, he shook hands firmly, looking him right in the eye.

"I suppose the first order of business is for me to apologize," Pentland began as he took his seat. "I'm no saint, and I know you aren't either; but when Dunsinane began his insane quest for revenge, I should have warned you. I tried to warn him, but he wouldn't listen."

Cochrane said coolly, "It would have been much better for him if he had."

"Better for all of us! You brought him down right properly, and in the process brought down most of the consortium with him. We all had fingers in the insurance or reinsurance market pies, and all of us got burned. I suppose I was lucky. After realizing how demented Dunsinane was about you, I stopped reinsuring Rendall Insurance policies, and told my people to steer clear of any company that did. That shielded me to some extent. I didn't lose everything. The other directors were much worse off. I daresay they brought it on themselves, but most of them were bankrupted. One shot himself the day before I left Callanish to come here. He left his wife, three grown children, and several grandchildren. She's got nothing left. She'll have to move in with one of her children.

"Dunsinane's wife is in similar straits. Her husband will never recover. He'll be in a coma until he dies. In the unlikely event he regains consciousness, there are civil lawsuits and criminal charges lined up waiting for him. It might be more merciful, for her sake and for his, to switch off the machines keeping him alive, and let him go."

"Criminal charges, you say?"

"Yes. There's a spaceship in Callanish orbit, crewed by his people, who say he sent them aboard her to take over from a passage crew. Turns out she has a false name and registration. All traces of her previous name and registration have been erased. No-one knows who brought her to Callanish, or why, but the authorities presume she's stolen. She's carrying old missiles and their pods, including nuclear warheads, for which Dunsinane had no permit. I found that odd, in view of your claim against Rendall for a lot of missiles aboard a stolen spaceship. I don't suppose you'd care to comment?"

"No. The missiles that were stolen from us were modern units, as shown on both the bill of lading, and the inspection report from Constanta's System Patrol Service. It was dated the same day she was stolen. Clearly, those old missiles can't be ours. Have you tried to trace them?"

"Callanish's System Patrol Service tried. The manufacturer had records saying they'd been sold to New Westray decades ago, but the authorities there deny any knowledge of them. They say all their old missiles were expended some time ago, along with the patrol craft that carried them – those were used as targets. They seemed almost embarrassed to be asked. Again, I don't suppose you'd know anything about that?"

"Why should I? Hawkwood doesn't own any patrol craft. We never have."

"Hmmm. I seem to recall that its predecessor, Eufala Corporation, did. Those were handed over to the New Orkney Enterprise, weren't they?"

"That was a couple of years ago. You could ask NOE about them, but they probably won't be interested in helping you, not after your consortium stole their satellites. What's more, Callanish's government allowed you to use its repair ship to steal them, so NOE isn't exactly feeling charitable toward your planet in general."

Pentland's face split into an unwilling grin. "I've got to hand it to you, Cochrane. You're a cool bastard, and a canny one. I think we both know the truth, but you're never going to admit it. Why should you? You've covered your tracks so well, I doubt anyone could make anything stick if they tried." He sighed. "However, you spoke of 'feeling charitable'. That's why I'm here."

"Oh?"

"Dunsinane's wife has been left penniless. When his father set up Rendall Insurance several decades ago, he registered it as a family corporation. Under Callanish law, there are certain tax advantages to that. Unfortunately, it also means that all the family assets are pledged as security against the company's debts. When Rendall was bankrupted by your claim, the authorities seized everything Dunsinane owned. His wife would be on the streets, if I and a couple of others hadn't helped her. Her children live off-planet, so unless she goes to join them – which would mean abandoning her husband in a nursing home – she can't live with them. As for Flett, the man who shot himself, his wife is in similar straits. I thought... well..."

Cochrane said, "You thought that, since Rendall's money ended up in Hawkwood's bank account, along with more from reinsurers and the Interplanetary Insurance Reserve Fund, I might be feeling generous?"

"Well... yes, that's about the size of it. The ladies were never your enemies, Cochrane, and probably never knew what their husbands were doing. They're innocent victims. I don't think they deserve what's happened to them."

"I daresay you're right. If I help them, what's the best way to get the money to them without awkward questions being asked? I mean, if their husbands' assets have been seized, won't the Callanish authorities try to seize anything I send them, too?"

"Aye, they might. Best to put it in an off-planet account, and have a regular monthly stipend sent to them, with the right to draw capital if they need it to buy a home or something like that."

"Do they have an agent on Callanish who can disburse the money?"

"I doubt it. I'd offer to act on their behalf, but you wouldn't trust me, and I don't blame you."

Cochrane looked at him thoughtfully. "Under normal circumstances, no, I wouldn't, but I think this is different. You didn't have to come and see me on their behalf. That speaks well of you. Besides, if I ever find out you've played me false, or them, I'll deal with you as you deserve. I'm sure you know I'm not joking."

Pentland couldn't suppress an involuntary shiver. "I think you mean every word. I've learned the hard way that you don't threaten – you promise. What's more, you keep your promises."

"That I do. Very well. I'll arrange with a lawyer on Neue Helvetica to set up two trust funds. Give my secretary the details of each woman, and she can prepare a letter for my signature. To tide them over until the arrangements have been made, I'll give you the equivalent of two hundred thousand kronor, in cash, to take back with you. I'll send it to your hotel this afternoon by messenger. That should be enough for their needs for a few months."

"Aye, it will. Thank you, Cochrane. I didn't know whether you'd care enough to help, but I took a chance. I'm glad to see my hopes weren't in vain."

"I may be ruthless to my enemies, Mr. Pentland, but I'm not a monster. As you said, the ladies weren't part of Dunsinane's stupidity or your consortium's criminal activity, and they don't deserve to be punished by association." He stood. "Please give their details to my secretary on your way out, and your contact information as well. You'll be hearing from my lawyer."

"I will." Pentland came to his feet, and made as if to offer his hand, but Cochrane merely stood there. "Ah. Well. I'll say goodbye, then."

"Goodbye, Mr. Pentland. Thank you for bringing this to my attention."

THE FOLLOWING DAY, Cochrane sent for Henry Martin, Jock Murray and Tom Argyll. "There's a big project we need to discuss," he began. "Before we do, Henry, do you have enough people in your security team, and do you trust them with your life? If not, you need to get rid of those you doubt, and replace them right away. Tom has a team of operatives that he and I trust completely. You can discuss your needs with him. Tom, let him have anybody he needs."

"Aye aye, sir."

Henry replied, "I trust those I have, sir, but I could use a small team of hard men to do whatever may be necessary to keep the rest of us safe. That may include taking care of the opposition's hard men, sir."

"Ours can do that," Tom assured him.

"Then I'll take a small team of them, please, with all the equipment they may need."

"How long will you need them?"

Cochrane put in, "At least three to four months, maybe as long as a year. If any of them can speak Greek, so much the better. I'll ask you to go and set that up, Tom, while I discuss the operation with Henry and Jock."

"Aye, sir."

After Tom let himself out, Cochrane got down to business. "We've learned from confidential sources that the Albanians have ordered a squadron of destroyers and a depot ship from Metaxas Shipyards on New Skyros." He'd decided he couldn't share the fact that Hawkwood was receiving intelligence from Qianjin spies on Patos. If that information leaked out, the agents would be as good as dead.

"They've set up a security company to buy them," he continued, "much like we've done with our ships. To get fully-fledged warships, rather than civilian-licensed armed vessels, they're using a fake end user certificate. They got it by bribing a couple of cabinet ministers on another minor planet, which is the buyer of record. Their security company will supposedly take delivery on behalf of their client, and operate the ships while training the planet's own spacers to take over. Since that planet can't afford even one destroyer, much less a squadron of them, I think we all know what the reality will be."

Henry nodded. "It won't be the first time something like that has happened, sir. It's always done through a shipyard on a minor planet, probably using several cut-outs. They won't get the best or most sophisticated ships that way, but they're not more than a generation or two behind those of major powers, in terms of their technology."

"You're right. Our frigates will have better technology, and more powerful and longer-range missiles, but they won't have as many of them. Two of those destroyers could probably go up against three of our frigates on roughly even terms. I don't want that to happen."

"So, what are we going to do about it, sir?" Jock asked.

Cochrane smiled. "Henry, you're going to New Skyros. I want you to contact the local underworld. Arrange whatever introductions you need first, but try to get things moving as quickly as possible. I want you to do three things. First, use them to slow down construction of the destroyers. You know the sort of thing we need; shipments of material and parts going astray, industrial action by workers, maybe a problem with welding quality, all the usual troubles. Second, find out when and where the Albanians will send their passage crews to take delivery. I'm assuming they'll put them up on the space station while they get to know the ships. They'll then deliver them, ostensibly to the planet that's bought them, but really to the Albanians' base, wherever that is. I think we might cause a lot of difficulties for those passage crews; food poisoning, double-booked hotel accommodation, passport problems, and so on. With me so far?"

"I am, sir." Henry was grinning evilly. "I can see I'm going to have fun with this. You might also look for a cooperative United Planets weapons inspector, sir. I know a couple of names, and they can suggest others. If he or she were to ask why the destroyers made for the purchasing planet didn't arrive there, and where they've gone instead, that can make a lot of trouble for the shipyard. The inspector can slap a stop-work or no-delivery order on it, prohibiting the rest of the destroyers from leaving – or perhaps even being built – until the UP figures out what's going on. It'll take a while for the Albanians to find someone senior to the inspector, who's willing to take a bribe to shut him down. That'll cost them a whole lot of time and money."

"That's a stroke of genius, Henry! We'll do it."

"It'll be expensive, though, sir. My work on New Skyros will cost a pretty penny, too. You can't arrange all those problems without paying some hefty bribes."

"Thanks to a very large insurance payout we've just received, money won't be an issue. The third thing I need you to do will involve Dave. Find out where the shipyard assembles missiles before loading them on newly built warships. It may be a New Skyros government arsenal, or on the shipyards' own premises. Wherever it is, security is sure to be heavy. If possible, I want you to get Dave in there, and out again."

"What do you want me to do, sir?" the electronics specialist asked.

Cochrane spent several minutes explaining his idea. "Think you can do that?"

"If Henry can fix the security problem, yes, sir, but how are you going to keep any New Skyros people from being affected?"

"I can't say for sure, not from this far away in distance and in time. You and Henry will have to learn more about the setup there, and how the Albanians plan to take delivery. When you've done that, it'll be up to you to decide whether it's safe to proceed. If it isn't, don't. I don't want to hurt innocent people. I'd rather abandon that part of the plan. However, if you can do it without affecting innocent people, we might be able to adjust the odds against us in our favor."

"I'm all for that, sir. I'll do my best."

11

RETALIATION

MYCENAE SYSTEM

BROTHERHOOD SHIP BUTRANTI

The Plot crew stared in almost hypnotized fascination at their three-dimensional display, as the Mycenae binary star system unfolded inside it. Even at their velocity of one-quarter of the speed of light, it seemed to grow only slowly. Three billion kilometers still separated them from the smaller of the two suns, Mycenae Secundus.

"Their ships seem concentrated in two places, sir," the Executive Officer noted in a quiet voice, almost whispering. "There are a number of gravitic drive signatures around Mycenae Primus Four, and more at Mycenae Secundus Two. Why those two planets, I wonder?"

The Captain explained, "Primus Four was where Hawkwood had its ships. We believe it is now the hub of the New Orkney Enterprise's operations. Hawkwood moved its base to Secundus Two."

"What ships do they have there, sir?"

"We are not sure. We know they have taken several new vessels into service since the Patriarch's martyrdom, but their exact number and type are uncertain. Before now, it was considered too risky to send our ships into an unknown, but certainly high-threat situation. With our high speed and heavy armament, we can take risks that our older vessels cannot; but even so, we must remain undetected. Our mission is reconnaissance only. We shall leave retaliation to *Ilaria*."

The younger man sniggered nastily. "With luck, by the time *Saranda* follows *Ilaria*, she will have rather fewer enemy ships to count!"

"Let us hope so. We shall wait until we get much closer before we send back details of what we can see. We must give *Ilaria* every opportunity to choose the best target and head toward it."

Coasting under total emissions silence, her gravitic drive shut down, not even reaction thrusters in use, *Butranti* arrowed onward.

~

BROTHERHOOD SHIP ILARIA

Ten hours' travel time behind *Butranti*, moving at only one-tenth of the speed of light instead of her consort's one-quarter, *Ilaria* coasted toward Mycenae. The atmosphere on her bridge, with its adapted Operations Center consoles, was even more tense. Below, in her holds, her auxiliary pod reactor and generator were operating at redline as they prepared all the contents of her ten missile pods. One hundred and eighty main battery missiles, and the same number of defensive units, would be ready to unleash fire and destruction on their enemies.

The operator at the Communications console suddenly jerked upright. He listened intently, then punched at his keyboard. "Communications to Command! Tight-beam signal coming in from *Butranti,* sir!"

"At last!" Captain Vrioni exclaimed from his command chair. He jumped to his feet and strode toward the Plot display. "Put it straight through."

He gazed eagerly at the display as icons began to appear. The plan had worked! *Butranti* had entered the Mycenae system in total silence, at maximum speed. Her only task had been to identify where all the ships were in the system, and if possible whose they were, and what type of vessel. She had signaled that information back to him, using a tight-beam transmission that could not be intercepted or overheard by any vessel more than a degree or two off the beam. He could see two concentrations. The smaller, around the planet Mycenae Primus Four, he dismissed. Those were New Orkney Enterprise ships, and of no concern. The bigger concentration, though, around Mycenae Secundus Two... those must be Hawkwood's!

The operator studied the icons, and the gravitic drive signature characteristics *Butranti* had sent back. "Ready to report, sir."

"Ignore everything except the Secundus side of the system. What are those ships?"

"Butranti says the signatures indicate, in orbit around Secundus Two, three light warships or courier vessels; two probable depot ships; and three freighter-type vessels, one very large, two smaller. The large freighter has a small craft in close formation, probably, from its low power signature, a big cargo shuttle. It may be transferring stores to the other ships. There are four more of the small ship signatures on inner and outer system patrol, sir."

Vrioni nodded slowly. "The smaller signatures are probably corvettes," he said absently. "We know Hawkwood has ordered a number of them. They are no match for us, particularly since they have no idea we are coming. I am surprised there are three freighters, though. That is an unusually high number. I wonder...

They had a repair ship earlier. It may be one of those signatures."

"That is possible, sir," the operator agreed. "Its gravitic drive would be that of a fast-freighter-type vessel."

The captain rubbed his hands together eagerly. "Navigator, calculate our course change to pass within firing range of Secundus Two – let us say three million kilometers."

The Navigating Officer was already hard at work on his console. "Just a moment, please, sir... We need sixty percent thruster power for seventeen minutes. That will change our trajectory without emitting large light signatures from the throats of our thrusters. I know nobody is likely to detect them this far away, so in theory we could change course faster using full power; but why take a chance, sir?"

"I approve of your caution, Navigator. The fewer chances we take, the better. Very well. Change course, get us on trajectory, then report to me our estimated time of attack."

"Aye aye, sir!"

Privately, Vrioni regretted not being able to blaze toward his victims at top speed, but he understood the reason. *Butranti* had needed to get in and out of the system as fast as possible without being detected or identified. Her early target identification had given him time to alter course toward them. His sensors and fire control systems would be capable of far greater accuracy at one-tenth of light speed than at higher velocities. His job was to cause as much death, damage and destruction to the enemy as he could. For that, accuracy far outweighed speed in importance.

BROTHERHOOD SHIP SARANDA

Fifteen hours behind *Ilaria,* the courier ship *Saranda* loafed through space at one-tenth of light speed, far slower than her maximum velocity of four-tenths Cee. Lieutenant-Commander Malaj chafed under the unbearably sedate rate of progress, but he understood why it was necessary. Once *Ilaria* signaled her estimated time of attack, he would chase after her, accelerating fast. He would time his arrival to pass through the Mycenae system at maximum velocity, with his drive shut down to avoid detection. In passing, he would note every ship in the system, and later compare notes with the two vessels that had preceded him. By subtracting his count from what they had detected, they would be able to see how much success her attack had achieved.

I hope she will avenge the Patriarch in the blood of our enemies, he thought bitterly to himself. He had lost friends aboard the two destroyers that had attempted to attack the system two years before. Soon, very soon now, they would be avenged as well.

HCS JEAN BART

Newly-promoted Captain Frank Haldane walked into the Operations Center aboard the depot ship that currently served as Mycenae station flagship. The duty officer called, "Station OC on deck!", and began to rise, but Frank waved his hand.

"Relax," he called genially. "I'm just checking what's going on out there." He crossed to the Plot display. "What can you tell me?"

"Everything's routine, sir." The operator highlighted each icon in the display as he named it, changing the range scale from short to long as required. "Here in orbit around Secundus Two we have this ship, plus the corvette *Manchineel* giving half her crew liberty aboard us; *Bowhead,* our big warehouse freighter, plus her defensive missile tender in close formation; *De Ruyter,* our sister ship, working up; the repair ship, *Vulcan;* the arsenal ship, *Narwhal,* plus her attached corvette, *Datura;* and the courier vessel *Zaqar.* On patrol in the inner system are corvettes *Castor* and *Hellebore,* and in the outer system, *Hemlock* and *Mandrake.* NOE has their depot ship, *Amelia,* in orbit around Primus Four, along with a replenishment freighter, plus two of their patrol craft. A third patrol craft is half a light-hour out from that planet on local patrol, while the fourth is guarding their asteroid mining installation one light-hour from us, sir. They have several small asteroid mining boats near her."

"Good report, spacer. Thank you." He studied the pattern of icons, each reflecting the current position of a ship as denoted by its identification beacon and gravitic drive signature. "Is the system surveillance satellite on line?"

"It is, sir. That display is next door, if you'd like to check it, but we've got the datalink working now, so it feeds all its information to this smaller display for quick reference. We only use its larger display if we pick up an unexpected long-range target, and we want to track it more accurately."

"That's good. I must thank the techs for their hard work." He glanced at the duty officer. "Any word from *Narwhal* and *Datura* about the datalink upgrade?"

"*Vulcan* reported last night that she'd finished the installation aboard *Narwhal,* sir. They're testing it in orbit today, and tomorrow they'll go out to the far reaches of the asteroid belt to practice against multiple targets. *Vulcan* says *Narwhal* should see a threefold improvement in remote programming speed for her missiles, sir."

"Excellent! If it works, the tech who thought of it is going to be a lot better off. Commodore Cochrane pays well for good ideas like that."

"Yes, sir. I haven't met anyone who doesn't like our incentive program."

"Send a signal to *Vulcan.* Invite Commander McBride to join me for lunch, and bring that tech with her. I'd like to know more about how he came up with the idea."

"Aye aye, sir." The Duty Officer turned to the Communications desk.

Frank gave a last glance at the Plot display, then turned and headed for his office. He had plenty of headaches awaiting his attention. As he walked down the corridor, he grinned ruefully to himself. The Commodore had said he needed 'broader command experience of multiple units', but he'd assumed that meant tactical command – not administration.

"Oh, well, they do say there's no peace for the wicked," he muttered to himself as he entered the anteroom. Unfortunately, his Chief Petty Officer assistant heard him.

"You got that right, sir! These requisitions need your approval, and I..."

BROTHERHOOD SHIP ILARIA

Sub-Lieutenant Alban Sejdiu cursed beneath his breath as the clumsy, poorly-trained Kedan spacer fumbled, dropping the expensive powered torque driver on the deck instead of placing it in his extended hand. He bit his lip to hold back a volley of oaths.

It wouldn't help to yell at the trembling spacer, who was already convinced that Albanians in general hated him. Too many of them defaulted to screaming and intimidation, instead of teaching by example and being patient with these men. After all, they hadn't asked to be here. They'd only just been taken aboard *Ilaria* in their home system, without so much as a word of explanation. They had no idea they'd be serving far from home for at least a year or two, if not longer. Most of the wages they earned, plus a 'commission' for their services, would go into their senior officers' pockets, not their own. In their shoes, he would hate to be treated like that. Therefore, it would be better to give them reason to like him, and come to him with their problems.

The more they did that, the better the results he'd get out of them.

He spoke slowly, so the translation software in the computer strapped to his arm could turn his words into the Malay dialect spoken on Keda. "My friend, that was clumsy. Those drivers are expensive, and need to be treated with care. Have you got grease on your hands?"

The hapless spacer turned them palm-up. Sure enough, both were smeared with grease from the framework on which they'd been working.

"You see, my friend? That is why we give you those rags." He pointed to the shop rag tucked behind the belt of the spacer's utility coveralls. "Wipe your hands constantly, to keep them as clean and dry as possible. When that gets too dirty, throw it away," gesturing to the disposal slot in the bulkhead, "and take another from the box. That will help you hold on to your gear. Understand?"

"Yes, sir!" The man's gratitude at his soft-spoken words was almost pathetic.

Alban smiled at him. "Good. Now, let's try that again. Pass me the driver, please."

The spacer hurriedly wiped his hands, then bent, picked up the tool with exaggerated care, wiped it clean, and passed it to him as if it were an egg in danger of breaking. Alban took it from him equally carefully, and checked it quickly. Fortunately, it seemed to be still in working order.

"Thank you, Mahmud."

He applied the driver's socket to the recalcitrant nut at the base of the lifeboat. A few quick bursts of power, and the release mechanism was set to the correct tension. He backed carefully out of the narrow space, handing the tool to another member of his eight-strong work party.

His Albanian petty officer assistant looked on, mouth curling in disgust, but said nothing. He'd already been sharply corrected, more than once, by this jumped-up young sprog, for treating these idiots as they deserved. He wasn't going to risk another shouting match. The Chief had already warned him he'd be disrated, if it came to that. This one had influence beyond his rank.

Alban opened his mouth to speak, but was interrupted by the sound of the power pack in the base of the hulking missile cell in the hold next door, spooling up to a high whine. He hurried over to the capacitor ring console, followed by the rest of the Kedan spacers under training. This might not be the most important job aboard *Ilaria,* but it was *his* job, and he was going to do it to the best of his ability. After all, he had the example of his illustrious great-grandfather to follow. As a direct descendant of the Patriarch, he could do no less.

HCS JEAN BART

"It just seemed logical to tie the datalink function into the battle computer, sir, rather than the communications system." The Petty Officer Second Class technician shrugged his shoulders, uncomfortable at hobnobbing with two senior officers over a meal. "The battle computers are a whole lot faster and more powerful, and they're not usually so busy they can't handle another program or two. That speeded up signal processing, which in turn allowed greater throughput. I don't know that it was any sort of special insight, sir. It just seemed logical when I thought about it."

"It was," Commander McBride assured him. "Once we've tested and debugged it under operational conditions, I think it's going to get you a nice fat incentive award from the Commodore." She poked her fork into another slice of meat, cut off a suitable portion, and began to load it with mashed potatoes and gravy.

"I'm getting more and more impressed with those corvettes'

systems, the more I learn about them," Frank said as he sipped his glass of water. "They seem a whole lot more capable than most of the other small warships I've come across. I think Kang must have standardized on a powerful battle computer across their range, rather than have a small, medium or large version depending on the class of ship."

"Yes," Sue agreed. "I –"

Alarms shrieked atonally throughout the mess hall and down the corridor. "General Quarters! *General Quarters!*"

Afterwards, Frank could never remember the mad dash down the corridor to the OpCen. He burst through the door, panting, and lunged for the Command console. The duty officer had already vacated his seat, and was standing next to it, staring at the Plot display.

"Tell me!" Frank ordered crisply as he slid into the chair.

"Eighty-plus missiles launched three million clicks out, sir, still launching," the Plot operator reported crisply. "No ship gravitic drive signature, but a probable single source."

Eighty-plus launches? Still launching? Frank thought as he reached for his microphone. *That's got to be a destroyer, or something larger – and he's come out of nowhere. He must have coasted in from far outside the system, never using his gravitic drive, otherwise the satellite would have detected him.*

He pressed the button. "System Command to all ships. All defenses to automatic. Weapons free! *Weapons free!*" He knew his command was unnecessary, because every ship would already be preparing to fire; but at least he'd done something to justify his existence.

Even as he spoke, a starburst icon suddenly appeared in the Plot, at almost exactly the point where the missile traces originated. The operator exclaimed, *"Nuclear explosion near launch point!* It must be one of the mines, sir!"

Only then did Frank remember the hundred-odd autonomous space mines, deployed in a random, constantly changing pattern around Mycenae Secundus Two. They were leftovers from the early days in Mycenae. They had been bought to defend NOE's asteroid prospector robots. No longer needed for that task, they now maneuvered independently within a three-million-kilometer radius of the planet, except for the approach and departure lanes, which they were programmed to avoid.

One less mine now, he thought, his mouth twisting with satisfaction as another icon appeared on the plot. The operator almost screamed, *"Bogey!* Unknown gravitic drive signature at launch point!"

~

BROTHERHOOD SHIP ILARIA

Alban listened to the Captain's voice, crackling over the compartment speaker. "Commanding Officer to all hands. We are about to avenge the Patriarch! Do your duty, and do it well! *Stand by to fire!"*

He felt a thrill of pride. He, a direct descendant of the Patriarch, would have a hand in exacting retribution for his death. How fortunate he was!

His thoughts were interrupted by a rapid sequence of whining sounds from the compartment next door, as each missile tube's mass driver abruptly fired its heavy weapon out of the pod into the black vacuum of space. As soon as each missile moved far enough away from *Ilaria* to be clear of her gravitic drive field – even though it was not in use at present, the precaution was automatic – he knew it would power up its own drive, swerve onto its pre-programmed course, and accelerate toward the enemy, its warhead ready to wreak destruction upon them.

The eight Kedan spacers huddled in a group, not understanding the ear-splitting whines coming from next door. They stared intently at their officer. Alone among those on board, this one really seemed to care about them. They had better jump at his command, and do everything he told them, for fear they might be reassigned to someone less sympathetic and understanding.

THE MINE HAD BEEN DRIFTING in space for years, interrupted only by regular visits from a cargo shuttle to replace its fusion micro-reactor cartridge and check its systems. It kept tireless vigil, seeking any gravitic drive signature lacking an authorized beacon to indicate that the ship was friendly.

Suddenly, only about half a million kilometers away, missile gravitic drive signatures began to blossom. It could not find any ship signature, but its electronic brain knew that if missiles were being launched, they had to be coming from something larger. The mine's computer instantly brought up its array in active rather than passive mode, flooding nearby space with radar emissions. Almost at once, it found the launching vessel, and locked onto it as it drew nearer. The computer calculated at blinding speed. Yes, it would pass within extreme range.

A cartridge kicked out a laser cone assembly containing twenty-five rods, very carefully aligned to cover a destroyer-size ship from bow to stern at a range of twelve thousand kilometers. The instant it had deployed, a five-megaton thermonuclear warhead blew the mine and the laser cone assembly into radioactive molecules. In the instant of their destruction, each laser rod emitted a powerful beam, streaking across space.

The cone was almost twice as far from the target as its designed range; but its target was much, much larger than a destroyer. More than half the laser beams smashed through *Ilaria*'s hull. They did not destroy any critical systems, but they penetrated compartments, shattered equipment, and killed crew members.

The attack, coming out of nowhere, completely unexpected, stunned *Ilaria*'s bridge crew. One moment, they were exulting in the destruction they were unleashing on an unsuspecting enemy; the next, the enemy had turned the tables.

Captain Vrioni screamed, *"Evasive action!* Hard-a-port! Drive to full power!"

At the Helm console, the operator instantly thrust the power slider from zero to maximum. The giant gravitic drive in the stern began to spool up, radiating its unmistakable signature from the drive field antennae carefully spaced along and around the ship's hull.

SUB-LIEUTENANT SEJDIU SPUN around as a laser beam smashed through the outer hull of the compartment next door, sending a loud boom through the plating. It speared through the missile pod from one side to the other. Its remaining missiles froze in their tubes as the pod's power pack was destroyed. Fragments of wreckage flew in all directions.

Three of them were large and heavy enough to penetrate the bulkhead separating the missile compartment from the capacitor ring control room. One punctured a neat hole, but did no further damage. A second punched into the shoulder of the Albanian petty officer, almost severing his left arm in a gush of blood. He collapsed to the deck, screaming. The third fragment knocked a section of pipe loose from the bulkhead. It flew across the compartment, and struck Alban's head a glancing blow as he tried to duck. Bright lights seemed to burst in his brain as he fell forward, out cold.

The eight Kedan spacers heard the shriek of air as it vented to space through the holes in the bulkhead, drawn into the missile compartment and then out through the damaged hull plating. They knew they had only seconds to live – but salvation was at hand. The lifeboat they had just been working on stood ready. Without a second thought, they ran for it. They had to pass the console as they did so, and two of them caught the young officer beneath his arms and dragged him with them. The others ignored the screaming, struggling, writhing petty officer. Anyone who treated them like that did not deserve rescuing, as far as they were concerned.

They rushed through the airlock and sealed the inner portal, threw themselves into the lifeboat, closed its hatch, and hurriedly strapped themselves in. The senior spacer, not much better educated than his fellows, peered at the pilot's console. There were dials and switches and controls he did not recognize; but all spacers knew what the red button marked 'EMERGENCY LAUNCH' meant. All lifeboats used it, by interplanetary convention. He reached out, flipped up the safety cover over the button, and slammed his fist down on it.

With a thumping impact, as if its fragile hull had been hit by a hammer, the lifeboat was shoved away from the hull by two powerful hydraulic pistons. It rocked, suddenly weightless in the absence of the ship's artificial gravity field, as *Ilaria*'s gravitic drive jumped to full power, accelerating the big vessel past it and away. Its own power pack still dormant, its internal gravity inoperative, the bright orange lifeboat bobbed in space, its automatic emergency beacon emitting a plaintive plea for rescue.

MYCENAE SECUNDUS TWO ORBIT

The incoming missiles were far too numerous, and moving far too fast, for the weapons officers of Hawkwood's ships – none of whom had yet arrived at their consoles – to manually do anything about them. Fortunately, Kang Industries' designers had automated many defensive functions. Once activated by the

Officer of the Deck, the ships' battle computers were able to react independently, prioritizing available targets according to the threat they posed, and launching missiles to intercept them. Under the circumstances, they responded very well indeed; not perfectly, but a valiant effort.

HCS *Datura's* datalink flexed its new-found speed through the ship's battle computer as it poured data to the missiles in the eight pods aboard HCS *Narwhal,* the arsenal ship with which she had been paired for operational testing. There was a fifteen-second pause as instructions, intercept positions, and courses were passed. It was enough time for *Datura's* commanding officer, sliding behind his command console as he arrived in her Operations Center, to curse bitterly at the realization that his was the only corvette assigned to *Narwhal.* His weapons system could control a salvo of up to one hundred and twenty offensive and one hundred and twenty defensive missiles. However, the two capabilities could not be linked, to control two hundred and forty missiles of a single type. *Narwhal* carried two hundred and eighty defensive missiles, but he could control only forty-three percent of them at any one time. A second corvette in company could have doubled that.

The arsenal ship began to vomit her first salvo. One hundred and twenty defensive missiles went screaming out to face one hundred and fifty-seven main battery weapons. Unfortunately, the attacking missiles had spread out, to avoid interference between their gravitic drive fields. This forced the defensive weapons to do likewise to intercept them. The gaps between the outgoing missiles produced voids in the defensive barrier, through which attackers could thread their way. What's more, the thermonuclear blast warheads on the defensive missiles often took out their fellow defenders as they detonated in blinding, kilometers-wide fireballs. Fratricide and voids meant that a hundred and fifteen attacking missiles made it through the first wave of defenders.

Datura's battle computers wasted no time. They instantly launched another hundred and twenty defensive missiles. By now *Manchineel* had begun to fire her own weapons, and *Beluga*'s missile tender, an old patrol craft converted for the purpose, added its fifty rounds to the mix. The depot ships each carried a pod of thirty defensive missiles, and began to launch them under local control as their crews reached their action stations and sprang into action. A second wave of well over two hundred defensive missiles slashed at the threats... but the fratricide became much worse as the incoming weapons approached their targets. Their increasing proximity meant that the defending missiles were, of necessity, also closer together. A single thermonuclear detonation might take out up to half a dozen of them, before they could target an incoming enemy.

A rolling blast front of defensive thermonuclear explosions erupted only a few hundred thousand kilometers from Secundus Two orbit. Another fifty-two of the incoming weapons were destroyed, and twenty-eight more were taken out of the fight as their sensors or guidance systems were overloaded and fried by close-range radiation. They zoomed on, but no longer posed a threat. Their control systems would self-detonate their nuclear warheads after a pre-programmed period without guidance input or a visible target.

The surviving thirty-five missiles charged in to point-blank range. As they did so, the point defense laser cannon, four aboard each corvette and depot ship, opened fire. By now the incoming weapons were moving at better than four-tenths of light speed, making tracking them very difficult. Under the circumstances, the lasers did very well to nail eighteen of them.

The remaining seventeen missiles struck home.

Four targeted *Bowhead,* the huge two-and-a-half-million-ton warehouse freighter. Each missile's laser cone fired twenty to thirty beams. More than seventy of them laced her hull. A ship so large was very hard to kill; but her gravitic drive was destroyed, one of her two huge reactors went into emergency shutdown, and her wiring harness was severed in two critical places. Her logistics computers were fried by a power surge so great, it overwhelmed their protective systems. Many of her holds were pierced, the supplies within them suffering damage and destruction.

Nine missiles went after *Vulcan*. The corvettes' systems had given top priority to defending their own vessels, and only then worried about the ships in company. As a result, they allowed too many missiles to get through to her. The half-million-ton repair ship, crammed with vital tools, essential equipment and critical spares, staggered in her orbit as over a hundred and forty laser beams slashed through her hull. She vanished in a thermonuclear ball of fire as one of the beams took out her central fusion reactor, unleashing its fury upon her. Everybody on board died instantly.

HCS *Manchineel* had been caught woefully unprepared, with half her crew absent on the depot ship. Those left aboard raced to their action stations, but could not do everything that would have been done by their colleagues. As a result, her defensive fire began later than the other corvettes, and was not as effective. Three missiles screamed toward her, rolled to aim their warheads, and fired. They got close enough to connect with almost all their laser beams.

Hit more than sixty times, the relatively tiny *Manchineel* reeled. Every system aboard went into emergency shutdown. Most of her internal atmosphere voided to vacuum through the holes piercing her hull. Except for a lucky handful who were in the few remaining airtight compartments, every man and woman aboard died. She floated in space, an almost lifeless hulk.

The last incoming missile targeted *De Ruyter*, the brand-new depot ship. Its laser beams pierced two holds and three crew compartments – but they were all empty. She was still working up, so the holds were not yet filled with supplies, and her crew had raced to General Quarters. Airtight doors slammed shut automatically as alarms sounded, sealing off the damage. Her people would have to find other places to sleep until their accommodation could be repaired, but she would live to reach a shipyard.

Even as the last enemy missiles exploded, the battle computers on HCS *Datura* reached a firing solution for the gravitic drive that had suddenly come to life at the enemy's launching position, and was now accelerating away from the planet. Without waiting for orders, still in automatic mode, the weapons system issued instructions to the main battery missiles aboard *Narwhal*. Fifty of the big weapons flew from their tubes, turned onto their pre-programmed courses, and sped after the fleeing vessel.

∼

BROTHERHOOD SHIP ILARIA

Captain Vrioni watched the Plot display intently as *Ilaria* swerved to port, then straightened on her new course. She did not appear to have been critically damaged by whatever had targeted her. He left the gravitic drive at full power, building toward maximum velocity to make his escape as quickly as possible. The entire attack was reflected in the display, the diminishing number of his missiles persevering through a double barrage of defensive weapons before striking home. He let out an undignified yell of triumph, echoed by the entire bridge crew, as *Vulcan* vanished in the starburst icon of a thermonuclear explosion.

The operator suddenly called, "Third missile barrage! Third barrage! They're... sir, they're aimed at us!"

Vrioni scoffed. "Let them! Those corvette missiles have a powered range of only five to six million kilometers. We're opening the range with every second that passes. They'll run out of reactor fuel before they can reach us!"

But the arsenal ship's main battery missiles were designed for cruisers, not corvettes. They were almost twice as large as the smaller units, with a powered range of twelve million kilometers, faster acceleration, and a much bigger and more potent warhead. They streaked closer, showing no sign of slowing down or running out of fuel.

Vrioni felt panic clutch at his heart for the second time that day. "Defenses to automatic! *Weapons free!* Helm hard-a-starboard!"

Datura's battle computers had made allowances for evasive maneuvers. The incoming missiles were spread out in a wide pattern, so that whatever way *Ilaria* dodged, some of them were bound to reach her. Vrioni had left his defensive fire too late. It knocked down more than two-thirds of them, but the remainder dodged, twisted and maneuvered their way closer.

Each warhead carried fifty laser rods in its cone. They arrived with shattering force, spearing through *Ilaria*'s hull from stem to stern and spine to keel. Three smashed into the bridge, killing Captain Vrioni and every member of the operations crew, leaving the ship leaderless in her most critical moment of need. A follow-up volley of twenty more missiles, which she could neither defend against nor evade, finished the job. *Ilaria* vanished in a bright, spherical actinic flash.

In the absence of orders to abandon ship, none of her crew had taken to the lifeboats. They died with her.

HCS JEAN BART

Frank watched with bitter triumph as the attacker, whoever she had been, joined *Vulcan* in thermonuclear obliteration. He picked up his microphone – then noticed Sue McBride standing stock-still beside his command console. She was staring into the Plot display, at the place where *Vulcan* had been. Her right hand, clenched into a fist, was thrust into her mouth, and she was biting its knuckles so hard that blood was trickling down her wrist.

He dropped the microphone, stood up, and tentatively touched her shoulder. "Sue –"

"Don't touch me!" she screamed hysterically, drawing every eye in the OpCen to her like a magnet. "They're... they're all *dead!*" She burst into tears.

He suddenly realized that for all her years of service, Sue had never seen battle. She'd been, first a technician, then an engineer, but never a combat officer. She'd just witnessed her pride and joy, the repair ship she'd set up from scratch, blown out of space, along with every spacer, technician and officer aboard her – many of them people she'd personally selected. A lot of them had been, not just her subordinates, but friends of many years' stand-ing, who'd been aboard because of her. The sense of loss and guilt she must be feeling right now had to be utterly over-whelming.

"Sue, I... I'm sorry." He looked around, and caught the eye of the Navigating Officer. *"Get her to the doctor!"* he mouthed silently, indicating Sue with a sideways jerk of his head.

The Navigator nodded, and came over to them. He said, very gently, "Commander, you're needed in the Sick Bay."

"What? I – *sick bay?* What do you mean?" Her voice trembled. Tears flowed down her cheeks, her body shuddering and shaking as if she had a sudden, violent fever.

"This way, please, ma'am."

Frank watched them go, immense aching sadness for Sue, and everyone else they'd lost, in his heart. He wondered for a moment whether she would ever return to her old self... but he had no time to worry about that now. There was too much to be done.

He picked up the microphone once more. "System Command to all ships. Well done, everybody. A sneak attack like that, launched with no warning, might have destroyed us all. Our losses are deeply painful, but we'll have to wait to mourn our dead.

"All ships in Secundus Two orbit are to dispatch small craft with rescue parties to *Manchineel* and *Bowhead*. Render assistance to other vessels as required. *Zaqar* is to head for the lifeboat beacon left behind by the enemy ship near her firing position. Recover any survivors, and bring them back to the flagship for medical treatment and interrogation. Mark my words – *bring them back alive!* We need answers, and they're the only people around here who can give them to us. No revenge, no summary justice, no violence unless they offer it first. I want them *alive!*"

The depot ship's commanding officer asked, in a low voice, "Is that why you chose *Zaqar* to go get those survivors?"

Frank nodded grimly. "Yes. She's an unarmed courier ship. She can't just blast them out of space. After what we've just been through, I can't be sure a corvette would be so restrained."

12

ASSESSMENT

CONSTANTA

"They've damned near crippled our operations in Mycenae." Cochrane gave his one-sentence assessment crisply, grimly, as he put down the tablet from which he'd been reading Frank's initial dispatch. "We're going to have to invest a hell of a lot of time and money just to get back to where we were, let alone continue to expand our activities."

Around the conference room table, the members of his abbreviated staff still showed their shock and astonishment. *Zaqar* had emerged at Constanta's system boundary less than three hours before, to transmit the first report of the engagement at Mycenae. She was approaching orbit, bringing more detailed accounts.

Cochrane pushed back his chair and stood, his mind whirling as he weighed up options. He strode back and forth as he snapped orders. "All right. Lachlan, I need you to look for ships right away. We put too many of our eggs in one basket aboard *Bowhead*. Not only is she effectively a write-off, but many of the supplies aboard her will have been damaged. Even worse, we've lost her logistics system. There are backups, of course – we have the grandfather versions here – but it'll take a while to get a working system going again. Until that happens, those in Mycenae can't be sure where to locate the stores they need, even assuming they're not damaged. Sheer lack of supplies is going to restrict our operations there in the short to medium term. We're going to have to ship a lot more stores from here to there, to keep them going.

"I want you to find two freighters to replace *Bowhead,* one to one-and-a-half million tons apiece. If you can't find them in a hurry, I'll take three slightly smaller ones. We'll set up the stores in Mycenae across them, divided equally, so that the loss of one ship won't mean the loss of all stores for that station. I'd like them to be as new, and in as good a condition, as possible. The need is critically urgent. Price is not as important as getting the right ships in the shortest possible time. I'll pay a premium if I have to."

"Got it, sir," Lachlan replied, head down as he made rapid notes. "What about repairing *Bowhead,* and what about *Humpback* here, sir? Do you want to replace her too?"

"I'd like to replace *Humpback,* for the same reasons, but not right away. Let's deal with Mycenae's problems first. We can't repair *Bowhead.* It'd take a repair ship – which we no longer have – several weeks at least to fix her up enough to proceed to a ship-yard under her own power. It might take a lot longer, depending on how much damage she's suffered, and what parts need to be ordered and shipped to her. After that, it'd take the yard several months, maybe longer, to do a thorough rebuild and refurbishment. We can't afford the delay. As soon as *Bowhead* has been emptied of all usable supplies, we'll drop her into one of Mycenae's stars."

There was an incredulous rustle around the table. "But, sir," Lachlan protested, "we've got a lot invested in her. We can't just throw that away!"

Cochrane gave him a tight smile. "The enemy threw it away

for us when they crippled her. If we let them tie us up in even more knots to fix her, rather than moving on and getting ourselves fighting fit as quickly as possible, they'll win again. No. We'll cut our losses and replace her. You won't be happy to hear we're going to do the same with *Manchineel.*"

"But, sir! She's a brand-new corvette – one of the latest two to arrive!"

"She was. Now she's a derelict wreck. It would take as long, or longer, to get her back into running condition as it would *Bowhead,* and we'd be wasting more time and money in a shipyard to repair her. We'll recover any usable weapons, stores and equipment from her, then she can follow *Bowhead* into the star. We'll order two more corvettes from Kang to replace her."

"Two, sir?" Dave Cousins asked.

"Yes. One will be *Manchineel II.* The other will replace *Amanita* in our operational lineup – as you know, she's the prototype, and smaller than the others in our fleet – but we'll keep *Amanita,* rather than trade her in on a bigger model. If we suffer more losses, we'll use her to help make up for them while we order replacements. Meanwhile, she can help to train new spacers."

"I get it, sir."

Cochrane turned back to his logistics staff officer. "Lachlan, I want two repair ships to replace *Vulcan.* She was half a million tons, and stuffed to the gunwales with everything she might need. We've lost all that with her – probably the equivalent of a billion francs or more, in terms of replacement value." Another rustle of astonishment ran around the table.

He went on, "We can't do without a repair ship, but when we got *Vulcan,* we assumed we'd have to do even major shipyard repairs ourselves. Time has proven us wrong. Grigorescu's shipyard here has done stellar work for us, and its capabilities have grown to match our needs. A shipyard can do bigger jobs faster, easier and cheaper than a repair ship. Therefore, we'll have one repair ship on station in Mycenae to do routine maintenance, and put damaged ships into good enough working order to make the trip to a shipyard. However, we won't plan on using her as a mobile service and engineering base to do everything, as we did with *Vulcan.* She won't have to be as sophisticated.

"A second repair ship will be here at base, partly to train our own technicians and spacers, partly to supplement what Grigorescu does for us. While the shipyard is working on a vessel's hull, for example, the repair ship can work on some of her systems. That should speed things up. If we lose the repair ship in Mycenae, or she needs to come back here for her own maintenance, the repair ship here can relieve her there."

"Got it, sir. Ah... repair ships are as expensive as major warships, thanks to all their sophisticated robotics and systems and tools. If we order two new ones, even less sophisticated than *Vulcan,* they'll cost us up to a billion francs each, fully equipped, sir." Another rustle of dismay.

"I understand, but we don't have a choice. Spend the money, and get the best ones you can. If nothing satisfactory – by which I mean top-quality – is available on the used market, order them as new construction, and we'll just have to wait for them. Let's see if we can lease one in the short term, while waiting for ours to be built. If Sue can return to duty – Frank says she's almost catatonic at present, so that may not be possible – she can advise us on what to put aboard them. If she isn't, I'll ask Captain Lu," and he nodded to Hui by his side, "to approach Qianjin's Fleet to send us a few of their engineering officers as consultants, to help us make that call."

Hui nodded soberly. "I'm sure that won't be a problem, particularly if you offer a consultancy fee."

"Consider it done. Let me know what would be appropriate."

Cousins' brow furrowed. "Sir, you're throwing money around like it's confetti. How are we going to pay for all this?"

"Don't forget, we recently received a seven-billion-franc insurance payout. What's more, our previous asteroid mining – or, rather, 'stealing' – ventures netted us a lot of money. Even after paying for every ship and missile we currently have on order, we still have several billion francs in reserve. Now that we face a lot more expenses, I'm going to mount some more asteroid ventures. You and I will discuss that. We captured over two hundred prospector robots when we started work in the Mycenae system, and we'll use them all." He paused, then grinned suddenly. "In fact, we'll put them back in the Mycenae system. We know that's a very rich asteroid belt, and we already have ships there to do the work."

"Won't the New Orkney Enterprise object, sir?" Dave queried, startled.

"We'll tell them we're setting a trap, to try to lure back the people who just hit us, and we're going to make it look as realistic as possible. Don't forget, their people saw the whole fight from Mycenae Primus Four, and their patrol craft came over to help our recovery effort. There's no doubt they understand the Albanians are a threat to their operations as well as ours, so I daresay they'll let us go ahead. It's in their interests, after all. We just won't tell them we're going to keep the asteroids we find, to pay for our expansion."

"Ah... if you say so, sir. Who's going to tell NOE?"

"I'm going to Mycenae at once, to see the state of affairs for myself. I'll drop in at Rousay on the way, and tell NOE what we intend to do. *Orca* will be back next month, after her most recent training trip. By then you should have received word from me to go ahead. If so, load the bots aboard her and send her to Mycenae. If not, wait for my message. I'll go on to Kang Industries after visiting Mycenae, so I'll be gone for several weeks. You'll be in charge during my absence.

"Your most important job is to recruit more spacers, particularly technical specialists and engineers for our new repair ships. We lost just about all we had, except for the maintenance crews aboard the depot ships, and we can't spare them. We'll need two to three hundred, maybe more, and good ones are very hard to find. Start looking right away, even before we have ships for them to serve on, but don't relax our recruiting standards. We can't afford that. You might consider offering paid training and bonuses to any of our existing spacers who want to make a career change into that field. They'll have to sign contracts to serve for several years after being trained, of course."

"Yes, sir. It's a question of aptitude, though. Not everyone has it."

"True. We'll also consider robotic and artificial intelligence options. Frank says the automated weapons systems on our corvettes did a much better job than he'd expected. Let's find out whether something as good is available for repair ships. I'll talk to Kang, and we'll look at other shipyards."

Hui asked, "What about the prisoners?"

"That's a good question. The young officer suffered a depressed skull fracture. *Jean Bart's* doctor operated, with the help of one of its Medicomp systems, to relieve the pressure on his brain; but at the time Frank wrote, he was still comatose. The spacers, oddly enough, were from Keda. It's a small backwater planet, a couple of hundred light years from Mycenae. Why the Albanians are hiring there, I have no idea. I daresay that officer can tell us more, if he survives."

Tom Argyll's face twisted in distaste. "Are you planning to interrogate him the way we did those captured agents, sir?"

"No. We'll treat him as a prisoner of war. He wasn't spying on us – he was engaged in combat. If we give him better treatment, he might be willing to talk to us. At the very least, we may need to exchange him for one of our own, someday. We can't do that if he's dead."

"You'd better let them know we have him, then, sir, otherwise they won't know it's worth keeping our people alive for an exchange."

"Good point! I'll do that. We know the names of some of their top people." He didn't look at Hui as he said that. No-one else knew that Qianjin had its own agents keeping an eye on the Albanians, and was sharing intelligence with Hawkwood. "I'll send word to them, discreetly."

~

PATOS

At almost the same time, Agim summed up the situation for Endrit and Fatmir. "It looks as if we got three of their ships – at least, that is how many of their gravitic drive signatures and beacons were no longer operating when *Saranda* went past, an hour after the strike. Sadly, we have no idea what happened to *Ilaria*. *Saranda* could detect no wreckage, and no Hawkwood ships were mounting any obvious search and rescue attempt along her projected course. There was one lifeboat beacon near Secundus Two, but that might have been from a Hawkwood ship. I fear *Ilaria* must have been destroyed by their counter-fire."

"But how?" Endrit demanded. "She was not using anything emitting a signature that could be tracked! The most they could have detected was when she fired her missiles, and they would have been too busy defending against them to bother with her at that moment. By the time our missiles had struck, *Ilaria* should have disappeared into space once more!"

"I do not know. We may never know, unless we learn something from Hawkwood spacers who were there. Unfortunately, we had to withdraw our teams of spies from Constanta, due to the risk of infiltration. I have another plan to gather intelligence there. It will soon go into effect. Let us see whether that can glean us any more information."

"What is it?" Fatmir asked, but instantly looked chagrined as he waved his hands in negation. "I apologize. That was a foolish question. I do not need to know."

"No, you do not," Agim said severely. "Remember, the more we compartmentalize our operations, the less the risk of betrayal or compromise."

Endrit said slowly, "Was it worth it? Was losing one of our new fast freighters, with all its missiles, and over a hundred of our spacers, worth what we achieved?"

"Yes," Agim said unhesitatingly. "Do not forget, its value is not only in the destruction we wrought. That was not even our primary purpose. We were sending a message to Hawkwood that their spying would not intimidate us. We killed one of their spies – or, rather, he killed himself – and disrupted an operation that must have taken them a lot of time, trouble and expense to set up. By striking back as soon as possible after we detected it, they will understand our meaning. If they do that again, we will hit them again, even harder next time. That was a message worth sending, even at the cost of losing *Ilaria*. The damage she inflicted was a bonus."

Above their heads, as they stood beneath a tree in the park, what looked like a brown moth clung to the bark. Its antennae vibrated slightly as it hung there, motionless.

"What will we announce about *Ilaria?*"

"I have already told others, including the Brotherhood Council, that she is on a special mission. It will take several months to a year to complete. Our other ships on the Mycenae mission did not see her destruction, so their crews cannot question it. I have ordered their commanding officers to stick to our cover story at all costs. We shall have to announce it at some stage, but not yet. We must prepare our people for the shock. I think, if we have some new destroyers to show them before then, it will help to cushion the blow."

"Let us hope so. What are our other ships doing now?"

"They are back at base. They will need several months,

perhaps as much as a year, to educate and train their Kedan spacers, who have proved woefully inadequate. We may have struck a
bad bargain there, but we must make the best of it. At least, once
we have trained them to our standards, they can replace our own
people, who can then take more responsible positions on the
armed freighters, and crew our new destroyers as they come off
the building ways."

The three concluded their business, then walked away in
different directions. The moth waited until they were out of sight,
then flew off toward a nearby parking lot, where a small van
waited, its side window half-open.

As he drove home that night, Agim pondered. Should he tell
Jehona and Pal that their oldest son was missing, believed killed,
aboard *Ilaria*? He thought about that for a long time before decid-
ing, *No. I need her to be completely focused on her mission, not
mourning her son; and her husband is vital to us, as Head of Security
for our refinery ship. We cannot afford either of them to be distracted. I
shall simply tell them the cover story, and warn them not to discuss
their son's absence with anybody.*

He told them as much the following morning, when he
attended the small private ceremony for Jehona's graduation from
her refresher training. The head of the small, highly secretive spy
training center had assured him that she was as good as ever –
perhaps even better than when she was younger. "She is more
mature, more discerning," he had said. "I wish I could keep her
here as an instructor. She would be invaluable."

"You cannot have her. I need her too much in the field."

"Well, sir, you have in her one of the best agents I have ever
seen. She will do well."

Jehona and her husband looked disappointed when told that
Alban was on detached service with his ship. "May we know
where?" Pal asked.

"I am sorry. As your wife's grandfather always reminded us,
three can keep a secret..."

Grinning, they joined him in the final, chorused phrase, "If two of them are dead!"

Jehona turned to her husband. "That is why I cannot tell you where I am going – not that I know myself, yet!"

"I understand. Security is my business, too." He kissed her. "Be safe, my darling. Come home to me."

"I will do my best. I promise."

Agim drew himself up. "And I, for my part, promise that I shall not place Jehona at unreasonable risk. I shall always be honest with both of you about our needs, and I shall never lie to you about anything concerning or affecting your mission."

Pal stood there, waving, as his wife drove away with Agim, feeling as if his heart were already breaking. Would she ever come back?

13

LESSONS LEARNED

NEW MYCENAE

"**A**nd the New Orkney Enterprise bought your fake-asteroid-mining plan, sir?" Frank asked as their pilot guided the gig toward the wreckage that had once been HCS *Manchineel.*

"In the words of the old fisherman's proverb, they fell for it hook, line and sinker," Cochrane said. "They weren't too happy at first, but when I pointed out that since we don't know where the Albanians are basing their ships, the only way to get at them is to make them come to us, they saw the sense in what I was proposing. They've agreed, provided we set up our asteroid operation at least one light-hour away from theirs. They'll have their people avoid it like the plague."

"That'll work, sir. I'll send a corvette to do some preliminary scouting. Their systems can detect different densities of asteroid, if they get close enough. I'll try to find an area with a lot of M- and S-type asteroids, then the prospector bots can take a closer look."

"Good. Thank you, Frank." He peered out of the window as the gig passed slowly along *Manchineel*'s starboard side. "Ye Gods, that's not a ship any longer – that's a colander in space!"

"I'm afraid so, sir. There are only three compartments that didn't vent their atmosphere to vacuum, and only five survivors from them. Everyone else aboard didn't make it."

"You've recovered the bodies?"

"Yes, sir. They're stored aboard *Jean Bart,* awaiting your orders. That's not a problem, by the way. Exposure to vacuum desiccated them all."

"Space fatalities usually end up like that. What's the general feeling about funerals and memorials?"

"They were spacers, sir, so a traditional spacer's funeral, dropping their bodies into the nearest star, will work for most of our people. They'd like to have some sort of memorial, though."

"I'll be glad to provide one. We'll put it on Constanta for now, but build it so we can dismantle it if we move from there, and take it with us."

"I think they'll appreciate that, sir."

"I – good grief!" Cochrane pointed at the stern, where the docking bay was blown wide open by what had obviously been an internal explosion. "What did that?"

"The cutter was carrying volatile cargo, sir. She'd just docked, but hadn't been unloaded when a laser beam went through her. That's the result."

Cochrane shook his head in dismay. "I've never seen damage like that before. Well, it reinforces my earlier decision. We won't even try to repair *Manchineel;* we'll simply replace her."

"I think you're right. If you're finished here, may I tell the pilot to go over to *Bowhead,* sir?"

"Yes, go ahead."

As the gig left the shattered wreckage of *Manchineel* behind, and started on the long hop to where *Bowhead* orbited the airless, lifeless planet below, Cochrane asked softly, "What was it like, being under that big an attack? There were – what? Over a hundred and fifty missiles coming at you? That's a hell of a barrage."

"Yes, sir, and our counter-barrage fired over three times as many missiles back at them, including those that destroyed the intruder. It was like hail, going out from us toward them. It looked just like that in the Plot display – a hailstorm in space, an airless storm."

"I've no doubt it was impressive. Speaking of destroying the intruder, how are our prisoners doing?"

"The Kedans are just happy to be alive and safe, sir. They have no idea who they were working for, or why they were there. I think their officers just shoved them aboard through the airlock, then went off, counting the money they'd been paid to provide cheap labor. I suspect the Albanians don't have enough of their own spacers. I reckon they're trying to make up the shortfall by hiring more from planets that won't ask awkward questions."

"And the officer?"

"He's conscious, sir, but still very weak. The doctor says he's lucky to be alive. So far there doesn't seem to be any long-term neurological damage, which is good news."

"Is he talking to us about anything?"

"He won't, sir. He seems to think it's his duty to be silent."

"If he was in a regular armed force, during time of war, it would be. Working for Albanian thugs hardly qualifies! Still, let's leave it at that for now. Once he sees we're treating him well, and as his condition improves, he may open up. When are you sending him back to Constanta?"

"I wanted to ask about that, sir. Can we legally keep him a prisoner on Constanta? It's neutral territory, so to speak."

Cochrane blinked. "You know, I didn't think about that, but you're right. Here in Mycenae, there's no local authority to care.

Back at Constanta, it'll be a different story." He thought for a moment. "Can you keep him here for the time being, and the Kedans too?"

"Yes, sir. You built a brig into the depot ships, so there's enough room for all of them. He's still in sick bay, of course. I think it might be worth converting a berthing unit into a makeshift prison, though. It'll be more comfortable than the brig, and you said you wanted them treated well."

"I'll leave that up to you, as long as they can't threaten the ship's security or try to escape. Give me photographs and personal details of all of them before I leave, including their DNA profiles, in case I find a use for them. Has there been much resentment toward them from the crew?"

"Some, sir. After all, they helped kill a bunch of us in a sneak attack."

"Let's hope it stays at low level. If you get any troublemakers trying to stir things up, tell them we need these people to talk, and they aren't helping. If they won't shut up, send them back to Constanta aboard the monthly freighter, and we'll fire their asses when they get there."

"Will do, sir. Now, to change the subject, I've been putting a lot of effort into analyzing what happened. There are several lessons we can take away from Mycenae Two, sir."

"Mycenae Two?"

"The Second Battle of Mycenae, sir – the first being the fight with the two destroyers, a couple of years ago."

Cochrane gave a mirthless chuckle. "I see. All right, what are they?"

"First off, sir, we had only one corvette with the arsenal ship, because they were still working out the kinks in a new, faster datalink setup. That worked like a charm, by the way. I'd like to recommend the tech who came up with the idea for a thumping great incentive award. We might have suffered more casualties, if it weren't for *Datura* being able to program the missiles aboard *Narwhal* so much faster."

"It'll be a pleasure. I'll see him later today, and announce his award publicly over the intercom. That should make the rest of the ship's company sit up and take notice."

"I think it will, sir. The thing is, one corvette can control a salvo of only one hundred and twenty missiles of each type, offensive or defensive. That meant *Datura* could control less than half *Narwhal*'s defensive missiles in each salvo. If we'd had two corvettes assigned to *Narwhal,* they could have doubled the throw weight of the first salvo. We need to make sure that happens in future. Also, we should ask Kang Industries whether their battle computers can be reprogrammed. At present, they can control a hundred and twenty offensive missiles, and the same number of defensive weapons at the same time, but not two hundred and forty of a single type. Why is that?"

"It's probably because their fire control software is designed for destroyers, of which Kang's design has exactly that number of each type of missile. They probably never figured on one ship controlling another vessel's missile load, to exceed that number. I'll talk to them."

"Thank you, sir. The initial weight of fire is important, because analysis of our defensive missile fire reveals several interesting things. We used almost four defensive missiles for every incoming weapon we stopped. Fratricide was a big problem, getting bigger the closer they got, because one of our missiles sometimes took out several more defenders in the blast of its warhead. We should consider a launch pattern that spaces them out better, to avoid that. It may even mean launching fewer defensive missiles in a salvo, because if we reduce fratricide, we increase the number of enemy missiles we can target."

"You're making a lot of sense. Go on."

"We never knew they were coming until they opened fire. They must have sneaked into the system with everything shut down, so our surveillance satellite cluster couldn't spot them. We wouldn't have been able to fire back at them without the explosion of that mine. It forced them to power up their drive, to turn away from any more mines that might be nearby. That gave us an emission signature we could track and target. Without it, they'd have got clean away. I recommend we get a lot more mines, sir, and maybe sow the field as far out as five million kilometers around the planet, except for arrival and departure lanes. They'll help keep sneaky visitors honest."

Cochrane guffawed. "That's one way to put it. Mines we can get. I'll see to it."

"Next, sir, they came right to where we were. They didn't have to maneuver at all – at least, not using their gravitic drive – to get to us. That means they must have scouted this system, and sent back information to the attacker about where to come. How long that was before the attack, I couldn't say. They might even have sent a third ship, sometime after the attack, to count the number of ships we had left and see how well they did. If all of them were emission-silent, we wouldn't have known, sir."

"No, we wouldn't. The only improvement we can make is to have orbital radar telescopes, which are pencil-beam rather than wide-array. They can pick up radar targets way out yonder, but unless they know where to look, they'll miss them. There's really no defense against an enemy, particularly one with a stealthy hull, who can come in without any emissions at all. Even a passive surveillance array spread over an entire star system is only effective out to four or five light-days, and even that won't catch an intruder who's emissions-silent."

"Yes, sir. Another lesson learned is that it's far better to take out the launching platform before it can fire its missiles. While they're aboard, we can concentrate on a single target. Once they're in space, we have scores or hundreds of targets, each smaller and more difficult to hit than a spaceship. I know that, if we can't spot the ship, we can't target her, sir, but we need to figure out some way to improve that situation. If we fire offensive missiles at her the moment she starts launching, we might force her to concentrate on defending herself, rather than launching the rest of her offensive salvo. If we hit her, we hit all the missiles still aboard her, too."

"That's an age-old problem in fleet and wet-water naval warfare. I'll see whether there are any new technologies or tactics that might improve our odds."

"Thank you, sir. Next, we come to the volume of fire. The enemy put over a hundred and fifty missiles into space. Interestingly, they had different rates of acceleration. I think they bought missiles from several sources and put them all aboard one ship. She must have been an armed freighter, sir. A destroyer only carries a hundred to a hundred and twenty main battery missiles. She launched a lot more than that."

"There couldn't have been two ships, you suppose?"

"Not from the plot tracks, sir. All the missiles came off one course line, in rapid succession. If there were two ships, some of them would have shown up as offset to port or starboard, or ahead, or behind the others. I think this was one big ship, with lots of missile pods – rather like our arsenal ship, except she could clearly control her own weapons."

"Point taken. If we can arm big fast freighters, so can they – and they can get them into service faster than ordering a purpose-built warship from scratch. Next?"

"Sir, we need to spread our standard orbital formation over a wider area, and use decoys. The enemy could focus their aim on a few targets, relatively close together, and pound each of them with lots of weapons. If our ships had been spaced further apart, and we'd had decoys spread out around them, broadcasting realistic beacons and gravitic drive signatures, they'd have had to target all of them. We could have concentrated our counter-fire on missiles whose trajectories showed they were aimed at real ships. Wider formations would make that clear, because the spacing between the missiles would increase as they closed in. Their targets would become more obvious. We could have ignored the other weapons, and let them hit the decoys."

"Another excellent point. I'll ask Kang what they can offer as space vehicles to carry the decoys. It may be something as simple as cargo shuttles, or we may need something more complex. I'll push that as a top-priority project."

"Thank you, sir. Finally, there's the question of hitting back. The Albanians know where we are, but we have no idea where their base is. The navigation data we recovered from their asteroid collection ship, the first time we encountered them, and then from their destroyer after Mycenae One, were quantum-encrypted. We haven't been able to crack it. How can we find out where they are, so we can dish it out as well as taking it? A lot of our spacers are on a slow burn about that. They want to hit back."

"So do I! All I can say, and all you can tell them, is that we're doing our best. That officer you captured is probably too junior to be entrusted with the coordinates, but you never know. If we can persuade him to talk at all, we may be able to get something out of him. We'll also look at... let's just say, other avenues of information. I won't say more at present."

"I read you loud and clear, sir. Just so it doesn't take too long."

"I'll see what I can do." Cochrane glanced out of the window. "We're coming up to *Bowhead*. Have you managed to recover anything from her holds?"

"Yes, sir, but it's very difficult without a real-time inventory. We're working from printouts of a backup copy. Also, a lot of stuff was damaged by the laser beams. I reckon we lost at least a third of her cargo, if not more. It's going to take months to sort it all out. Are you getting us a replacement warehouse freighter?"

Cochrane explained his plans for multiple, smaller warehouse freighters. "You can put them in different orbits, so that if you lose one, you'll still have the other. It'll be less convenient to have to spread things around, but I hope it'll be less costly if we lose another one."

"I guess so, sir. Sometimes logistical efficiency has to give way to tactical reality."

"Hmmm... I think I'll quote that line to Lachlan MacLachlan, if only to see him wince!"

14

INFILTRATION

CONSTANTA

The immigration officer slipped her passport chip into his reader and scanned the pages rapidly. "You're from Onesta? I don't think I've met anyone from that planet before. Welcome to Constanta, Ms. Funar."

"Thank you."

"What brings you here?"

She feigned a blush. "Well... I met this man, and he lives here, and he's invited me to visit him to meet his family."

"Oh, I see. What's his name?"

"Andrei Constantin."

"Ah, yes." The officer glanced at her out of the corner of his eye as he checked her passport, wondering if he should ask her to be more precise. Constantin was, after all, the most common surname in the phone directory – not surprising, since the planet had been named for the family that had organized and led its colonization – and Andrei was the most common man's name. There were probably scores, maybe even hundreds of men with that combination. *No,* he decided. *She looks harmless enough.*

"Do you intend to work while you're here?"

"Ah... I don't intend to right now, but I suppose that depends on how well things go. If that changes, who should I see about a work permit?"

Sounds honest, too, he thought. "You'll find our Immigration Department very helpful, Ms. Funar, particularly since you're an accountant. We issue short-term work permits for up to two years, with very little formality, to people whose qualifications will be useful to the planet."

"Oh, good! Thank you."

He made a quick entry into the system, then removed her passport chip and returned it to her. "Have a pleasant stay on Constanta, Ms. Funar. You can collect your baggage through there, then go through Customs on your way to the planetside shuttle."

"Thank you, sir."

She's a bit old for me, he mused as he watched her walk away, *but she's kept her looks. She's still got it, and then some. If her boyfriend doesn't watch out, he'll have a lot of competition for her.*

Customs proved to be as little obstacle as Immigration had been. As she walked down the space station's passage toward the planetside shuttle, her luggage obediently following her on a powered cart, Jehona thought to herself, *Remember, your name is Antonia Funar, from Onesta. You've never heard of Patos, or Jehona Sejdiu, or the Fatherland Project, or anyone or anything else from your past. Live your new character,* believe *that you're her, and you'll become* her. *Anything less, and they'll find out about you, sooner or later – and that'll be a horrible way to die!*

Over the next few weeks, she polished her command of the local dialect, drove and walked all over the city to internalize the details of the maps she'd committed to memory, rented a small but comfortable apartment, and bought a used car in good condition, a common model that would not arouse comment or be out of place anywhere. She paid extra to have a service tech go over it in detail, to make sure it was reliable and worth its price. She also bought several seemingly innocuous items from local suppliers, paying cash wherever possible. When taken home, disassembled, and reassembled or combined into new configurations, they were transformed into equipment she would find very useful, but could not have brought through customs without questions being asked.

She also joined a weight training gymnasium that offered self-defense classes. The instructor who signed her up took her through a preliminary round of exercises, angling to have her sign up for his professional services at an additional fee, but soon admitted defeat. "I think you know more about this than I do, ma'am. I can see you won't need any help."

She smiled sweetly at him. "I've been doing it for a few years, so I'm used to it."

Looking at her rippling, well-toned muscles and smooth, polished execution of squats, lifts and presses, the instructor couldn't help thinking that she could give pointers to most of the staff, if she wanted to. Later that week, watching her deliver expertly timed kicks and full-power punches to a training bag, he silently decided that he'd rather be her student, if the opportunity ever arose.

After a month, which she judged would seem long enough to any investigator for a budding relationship to turn sour and end abruptly, she went to Immigration and applied for a two-year work permit. The clerk promised that it would be ready within a week. "I've never met anyone before with a post-graduate degree in accounting from Neue Helvetica, or your work record. With those qualifications and experience, every business in town will want to talk to you."

∾

NEW SKYROS

Several hundred light years away, other infiltrators were also at work.

Jock looked up from the stove, where he was cooking supper, as Henry opened the front door and walked into their efficiency apartment. It was in a working-class area of the city, unremarkable and just like thousands of others all around it. They dressed and acted to match the surroundings.

"What's the news?" he asked.

"They finished the final round of builder's testing yesterday, and the purchaser's representative signed off on them. The passage crews have been trained and are ready to go."

Jock grinned. "They got over that attack of food poisoning?"

"Yes, although it disrupted their training for a week until they'd all recovered. The restaurant where they ate was shut down by the space station sanitary department. It issued a big fine to the owners. They're appealing it, because the Patos spacers were the only ones to get sick. None of the other diners there that night showed any symptoms, which they say proves the spacers must have got sick from their own poor hygiene, not the restaurant food. The shipyard jumped in on the side of the spacers, of course. There's a big fuss brewing up about it."

Jock laughed. "That'll give them something to think about."

"It sure will. Add that to the industrial action, breakdowns, power failures, and parts that didn't turn up on time or in the right place, and the first pair of destroyers is four months late. The purchaser's rep is blowing steam out of both ears, and threatening to invoke the penalty clauses in the contract, but the shipyard is claiming the delays are due to *force majeure,* which excuses them. It may end up in court, although I doubt it. Both sides have too much at stake to risk a big fight. They don't like each other very much right now, but they'll figure out a way to get on with it."

"Uh-huh. When do we get moving?"

"Tomorrow. The weapons release form will be signed at the Orbital Arsenal, which will slide the missiles into pods as the last act before delivery. The two destroyers will be loaded with their six pods apiece next week, and the freighter that brought their passage crews will carry twenty-four more pods – two reloads for each destroyer – in its holds."

"That's thirty-six pods in all. Sounds like the Albanians want to be ready for trouble."

"Either that, or they plan on using some of the spare pods on another fast freighter, like the one that hit Mycenae a few months ago."

Jock swore. *"Bastards!* I knew a lot of the electronics techs aboard *Vulcan,* and Sue's a good friend. I hear she still hasn't managed to get over it."

Henry shrugged. "She may never get over it. Some people can't. I'm sorry, Jock. It's not that I don't care. It's just the way it is."

Jock heaved a sigh. "You're right, unfortunately. All right. We'll do what we can to hit back at them for her."

"That's for sure! Anyway, once the release form is signed, a local firm will ship two range safety packages per missile pod up to the Arsenal. They'll be inserted into one offensive and one defensive missile in every pod, to allow for future firing trials. That's where you come in."

"I'm ready. Let's see... with thirty-six missile pods, that'll mean seventy-two range safety packages. I'll need at least an hour to work on each one, so I doubt I'll be able to do more than five or six before we have to leave."

"If we distribute them carefully through the shipment, that should be enough for one or two ships; maybe all three, if we get very lucky."

"Here's hoping!"

THE FOLLOWING NIGHT, as they approached the factory, Jock said, "I've got to hand it to you, Henry. Here I was, I was beating my head against a brick wall, trying to figure out how to penetrate the security of the arsenal – and all the time you were working on an angle with no security to speak of. How the hell did you come up with this idea?"

Henry chuckled. "You've just got to learn to think like a crook, Jock. I mean, think of your average rich man in his home. He's got possessions he wants to protect, his wife's jewelry, maybe a lot of cash, that sort of thing. He buys a decent safe, or maybe builds a vault into his house. He also installs high-security doors front and back, so it's harder to break into his home. Now it's all safe, right? No, it isn't. You see, he's focused on the nice shiny door, and the secure lock, and how plush the safe is inside, and all that sort of thing.

"A thief ignores all that. He looks at the windows, and the spaces between the studs in the wall, and the exterior siding, and the interior surfaces – even the roof. He can remove siding, cut out a panel between studs, pull or cut out the insulation, and punch through the interior surface in less than five minutes on a good day. If he's in a hurry, and doesn't mind making a noise, he can do it in twenty to thirty seconds, using something like a stolen backhoe. That bypasses all the high-security features. Alarms are only as good as their wiring and their monitoring service. Both can be bypassed, or just ignored if he can get in and out fast enough – he'll be gone before anyone can respond. If he does a little research, he can figure out exactly where the owner's shiny new safe or vault is, and come in right next to, or behind, or above, or underneath it. One pass with a thermal lance around the vault door frame or one of its walls, or an explosive charge, and it's open. If it's a safe, he can pass a chain around it and pull it right through the wall, or blow or cut the floor and wall out from under and behind it, so it falls out of the house. He can pick it up and take the whole thing with him, to open it somewhere else."

Jock quipped, "Lends a whole new meaning to smash-and-grab."

"It sure does! The same principle applies to stealing spaceships, like the patrol craft we got from New Westray when the Commodore set up this whole thing. You figure out a way around the defenses. Hardly anyone ever actually sees a spaceship with their own two eyes, not unless they go right up to it in a cutter or cargo shuttle. To most people it's a blip on a radar screen, or an icon in a Plot display. Most times, the blip or icon isn't the ship at all; it's a transponder beacon. You don't have to worry about people seeing you get away with the ship, if the beacon doesn't move. Switch off the beacon in the ship at the same moment as you switch on another one right next to it, and Orbital Control or System Control probably won't even notice. You can sneak away quietly in the ship, with them none the wiser. Only when your replacement beacon runs out of battery power, or someone goes to visit the ship and finds it gone, will they realize something's wrong."

Jock had listened, fascinated, to the former criminal's exposition of his craft. "Sounds like you were really good at that sort of thing, Henry."

"I made a living."

"I bet you did! What if someone got clever, and tied up their stuff in so much security that you just couldn't break in?"

"That's a common error. People set up all these smart systems that only they can operate, and figure no-one can get in now. Sure, they can. A ruthless criminal will kidnap him, or maybe his wife or son or daughter, and give him a choice. Open up, or have one of his, or their, fingers, or ears, or noses removed. Still dithering? Have another one! It normally doesn't take long. I was never in that line of business – I don't have the stomach for it – but I know others who were. I've even used a couple of them from time to time, if I was dealing with other criminals who were just as bad."

Jock couldn't suppress a shiver. "Remind me to stay on your good side!"

"I will. Tonight, we're getting in the easy way. Missiles and nuclear warheads have security crawling all over them. They're weapons, which means they're scary. People want to keep scary things secure so they can't bite them, so they put layers of security around them. Range safety packages, on the other hand... it's like their name says. They're *safety* packages, not weapons. It's basic psychology. A safety package isn't dangerous, by definition, so they don't need much protecting, right?"

Now it was Jock's turn to laugh. "Unless someone like me gets at them."

He was still amused as Henry led the way into the deserted factory, after slipping a sheaf of folded banknotes to an appreciative night watchman at the entrance to the yard. The seventy-two boxes containing the safety packages were lined up in rows, waiting to be collected the following morning and taken up to the Arsenal. He and Henry selected six, taking them from widely spaced locations in the rows, and laid them on a table.

Henry unboxed the first package. Jock unscrewed its access panel and disconnected the capacitor that powered the device at all times, even when ship's power was switched off. He lowered a jeweler's visor over his eyes, and began unplugging and unscrewing tiny components and cables to get to the heart of the device. He referred constantly to a schematic diagram as he worked. It took him almost twenty minutes to uncover the chip that contained the critical circuits.

He used a special tool to liquidize the sealant holding the chip in its socket, and eased it out onto the table. Reaching into his toolkit, he took out an identical-looking chip, one of several Henry had obtained, along with the schematics, through a little judicious bribery and corruption a month ago. Jock had reprogrammed them using some specialized equipment, also obtained by Henry through local contacts. Holding the chip carefully in the jaws of an insertion tool, he planted it in the newly vacated socket and re-sealed it in place; then he began the tedious task of replacing everything he'd removed to get at it.

Twenty-five minutes later, he watched the last light turn green on the self-test display, and nodded with satisfaction. He screwed the access panel back into place, and handed the device to Henry to be re-boxed and replaced in the waiting lines; then he turned to the next one.

It was after four in the morning before Jock finished the fifth device. Eyes blurring with tiredness, the result of focusing fiercely on tiny connections at close range, he shook his head. "I'm done, Henry. I just can't see clearly enough to manage a sixth."

"Five will have to do, then. That should be enough for at least partial success."

"Let's hope so."

They made sure everything looked the same as before they'd arrived, then slipped out to where their van was parked. They drove back to their apartment, collected their already-packed luggage, returned the van to the rental agency, then took a cab to the spaceport. By evening they'd completed planetary exit formalities, and boarded the grimy tramp freighter that had been loafing in orbit for three weeks, 'making repairs' while waiting for them. By midnight, it was heading for the system boundary. Its officially filed flight plan was to the Bismarck Cluster, but that would last no longer than its first hyper-jump. From there, it would turn toward Constanta.

～

CONSTANTA

Mr. Grigorescu flipped through the screens of information on his terminal. "You've worked in some very interesting places, Ms. Funar. I must admit, I'm surprised that someone with your qualifications and experience has ended up on a smaller planet like Constanta. We don't normally attract visitors of your caliber."

She seemed to blush. "Ah... it's a little embarrassing, sir. I met a man, and things got... involved. He invited me to come here, and I did; but after a while, he began to get very possessive, very controlling. I wasn't prepared to put up with that, so we broke up – on rather bad terms, I'm afraid. I'm looking for a job for a year or two, to rebuild my savings and re-establish myself. I'd rather do that first, then go home, rather than appear to crawl back like a failure."

Grigorescu nodded approvingly. "That's a very sound approach, if I may say so. I like people with self-discipline and determination. Ah... may I ask who he was?"

"That's a private matter, sir."

"I'm sorry. I didn't mean to pry." He seemed embarrassed as he turned away from the terminal, back toward her. "I can certainly use you, Ms. Funar. With the expansion we've enjoyed over the past few years, the shipyard really needs to overhaul its accounts department and put better management systems in place. If you can help us do that, you'll go on your way with my grateful thanks, and a nice bonus to ease your return home."

"Thank you very much, sir."

They spent a while discussing salary and other details. Grigorescu warned, "You'll be based planetside most of the time, but there will be times we'll need you to go up to the orbital shipyard. We have visiting staff quarters there, not great, but adequate, and you won't be there for more than a few days at a time. I trust that won't be a problem?"

"Not at all, sir."

"Good. When can you start?"

"Would Monday be in order, sir?"

"It certainly would! I'll tell Personnel to make the arrangements." He offered his hand. "Welcome to the family at Grigorescu Shipyard, Ms. Funar. You'll soon make friends here."

She shook it firmly. "Thank you, sir."

15

LOSSES

NEW SKYROS

The final briefing before departure from New Skyros was relaxed. The three Brotherhood commanding officers were relieved to get away from a planet where so many things had gone wrong over the past few months. They'd made sure to document every one of them, to prove to an increasingly irascible Agim that none of the incidents had been their fault. He was not taking the delays well.

"We'll travel in company to the system boundary," Captain Hoxha told the others. "After that, of course, it'll be impossible to stay together until we reach base. We'll rendezvous at the system boundary there at eleven on the second of next month, due galactic south of the fleet beacon, at a range of one-point-two billion kilometers. Try to be there on time, so we all look good. Make your arrival signal individually, as you emerge from your last hyper-jump, then wait for the rest of us. We'll travel in together, in close formation." The two destroyer commanders nodded their understanding.

Mr. Metaxas and his shipyard executives muttered more than

a few prayers under their joint and several breaths, as they watched the icons of the three ships head away from the planet toward the system boundary. Never in their experience had a contract run into so many difficulties, almost from its inception. It was as if it had been jinxed by a malevolent spirit – not that they were superstitious, of course. There were still six more destroyers and a depot ship to be constructed and delivered. Despite the record profit they were making on each ship, they did not look forward to the further troubles that they were sure would await them.

AT THE NEW Skyros system boundary, the three ships exchanged final signals of farewell and good wishes for the voyage, then separated to make their first hyper-jumps. The destroyer *Aries,* named for the first of the historical signs of the zodiac, was the first to depart, followed by her sister ship *Taurus.* Last to leave was the fast freighter *Rades.*

In two of the missile pods aboard *Aries,* range safety packages inserted into individual missiles sensed the unmistakable gravitational shift pattern of a spaceship's hyper-jump, picked up by their accelerometers. The chips installed by Jock Murray compared the accelerometer readings to their preprogrammed routines, and added one to a zeroed-out counter.

On board *Rades,* three more range safety packages, in three more missile pods carried in her cargo holds, did the same.

COMMANDER GJONAJ SETTLED into his command chair aboard *Aries* as the time grew near for her fifth hyper-jump of the voyage. He was growing less tense, less stressed, as New Skyros fell further and further behind them. Perhaps they had left their bad luck at the planet? He hoped so. The sooner he could pick up the bulk of his crew at base, and train them to make the best use of this shiny new modern warship, the sooner they could all help to avenge the Patriarch. That was something to look forward to!

He listened to the reports coming in to the OpCen from his abbreviated passage crew. Satisfied at last, he sounded the hyper-jump alarm. For one minute, it echoed through the passages and compartments, warning everyone on board to secure themselves against any sudden movement as the ship was launched through space and time in a single powerful transition.

Right on time, the ship's computers triggered a massive power dump from the capacitor ring into the gravitic drive. Instantly, a gigantic toroid-shaped gravitic field formed around and ahead of *Aries'* hull, pulling the warship into it. Time and space warped as the toroid spat out the vessel, twenty light years ahead of its previous position, that much closer to its destination.

Jock's reprogrammed chips in the range safety packages compared readings from their accelerometers, confirmed that this was, indeed, another hyper-jump, and added one more digit to their counters. They clicked over to read '5'. That instantly triggered an automatic subroutine, one normally only initiated if a missile had gone out of control during a test flight, and now posed a danger to other traffic, and had to be destroyed.

Instructions blazed from the range safety packages to their missiles' payloads. Safety features were automatically bypassed or neutralized in such an emergency. With a blinding flash, visible for many thousands of kilometers – if anyone had been so far into deep space as to witness it – two five-megaton thermonuclear warheads detonated. *Aries* and all aboard her were utterly consumed in their actinic fire.

∾

TEN DAYS LATER, *Taurus* emerged from her final hyper-jump, almost exactly in the right position in relation to the secret base in the otherwise deserted star system. Commander Prifti nodded in satisfaction. "Well done, navigator! You put us right on the button."

"Thank you, sir."

"Communications, make our arrival signal, and advise we will wait here for *Aries* and *Rades.*"

"Aye aye, sir."

They waited, growing more and more impatient. Prifti glanced at the bulkhead timepiece again and again, but saw only the inexorable passage of time. What could be keeping the other two ships? He had arrived precisely on time. Surely, they could not have fallen that far behind him?

Six hours had passed before his impatience grew too great. "Communications, signal to base. *Taurus* is proceeding to rendezvous. We can wait no longer for *Aries* and *Rades.*"

"Aye aye, sir."

"Navigator, put us on course to enter orbit at base as quickly as possible. Max cruise speed."

"Aye aye, sir."

Turning her back to the void, *Taurus* set out on the last, lonely leg of her journey.

∾

PATOS

"What could possibly have happened? Did our enemies intercept them?" Agim's voice trembled with fury.

Captain Toci shook his head emphatically. "We have no idea what happened, sir, but I can assure you, our enemies did *not* intercept them. That would be impossible – against all the laws of physics and mathematics – for the same reason that we cannot travel in formation between our departure points and our destinations."

"Why? *Why?* I do not understand!"

The captain suppressed a sigh. "Sir, one light year is almost nine and a half trillion kilometers. Freighters cover ten to fifteen light years in a single hyper-jump; warships and courier vessels, up to twenty. Twenty light years is so great a distance that the human mind cannot comprehend it. It has no yardstick against which to measure it. Suffice it to say that if our astrogators make an error of one hundredth of one degree in their calculations – which is not uncommon, due to sensor margin of error – then our ships can be trillions of kilometers out of position, up or down, left or right, or before or behind where they planned to emerge from a twenty-light-year hyper-jump. A power fluctuation in the capacitor ring can accomplish the same thing, building on navigational errors. That is why we spend hours recalculating our position after every hyper-jump, while our capacitor ring recharges. When we are as sure as we can be of our location, we hyper-jump once more, and so on.

"Such enormous margins of error make it flatly impossible to plan an interception of a ship in transit. Not only would an enemy have to know exactly where she was planning to exit her hyper-jump, he would also have to calculate exactly where any error was going to place her in relation to that position. It cannot be done. Once a ship has left a system, she is effectively invulnerable until she reaches another system, where she can once again be precisely located and targeted. The only exception is if she should hyper-jump by accident into range of an enemy ship she did not know would be there."

Agim nodded reluctant understanding. "But, if your error potential is so great, how do you ever arrive where you want to be?"

"When we draw near to our destination, we make our penultimate hyper-jump to a point about half a light year from it. That way, we can calculate the final jump much more accurately, over a much shorter distance. The same error of one hundredth of a degree, over half a light year, will put us at most about a hundred and thirty million kilometers out of position. Given that the average system boundary is plus-or-minus one billion kilometers from its star, and we aim to arrive well outside it, that is a sufficient safety margin for us to make that jump with confidence."

"I see. So, you are telling me there is no way Hawkwood could have intercepted our ships *en route?*"

"No, sir. It is absolutely impossible." The Captain's assurance was total.

"I must take your word for it. What, then, could have happened to them?"

"There are natural hazards, sir. If we jump too close to a black hole or a star, we might emerge so close to it that we cannot escape its gravitational pull. If we jump into the path of an oncoming planet or asteroid, we might not be able to take evasive action in time. There might have been a malfunction of a critical system on board, for example, the gravitic drive, leaving the ship stranded in deep space. Every year, one or two spaceships vanish without trace, so those hazards are real; but given the number of spaceships in operation, and the incomprehensibly vast distances they cover, the odds of them happening are vanishingly small. For two out of three ships to disappear on the same delivery voyage, from the same starting point, is unheard of in my experience. It is statistically impossible that both losses could be due to such circumstances. I can only suspect sabotage."

"*I knew it!*" Agim raged. "I *knew* those bastards would not give up! They do not listen to warnings, it seems. Well, there will be no more. We shall find a way to finish them once and for all!"

"Yes, sir. I should point out, sir, that we now have just three armed fast freighters, plus one modern destroyer with no reloads for her missiles. Our two older destroyers have already been taken out of service, and are not worth reactivating, because they are no longer capable of facing modern warships. That means our forces are far too small to engage in all-out battle against Hawkwood. We do not know precisely what they used against *Ilaria,* but I am sure it was more than mere corvette missiles. She carried more defensive missiles than all the corvettes in orbit around Mycenae Secundus Two, combined, carried offensive missiles. I cannot imagine their weapons could have prevailed against her without another, more powerful factor on their side."

"I... I must concede your point," Agim said stiffly. "Thank you for taking the initiative to come here so swiftly to report to me. I do not need to tell you to keep absolutely quiet about this. Order the officers and spacers under your command to do likewise. Hawkwood must never know that their attempts at sabotage succeeded. Let them live in fear that we found out about them, and prevented them, and are now planning to strike them again."

"Yes, sir. May I make a suggestion, please?"

"Of course."

"Sir, why not send regular reconnaissance missions through the Mycenae system, and through Constanta too? We did so twice during the battle where *Ilaria* vanished. Neither was detected by the enemy. If we send a ship through at high velocity, in complete emissions shutdown, she should be able to pass close enough to our enemy's bases to count their ships, and get some idea of what they are doing. If we could do this every month, or at least every quarter, it would provide a valuable baseline of intelligence when we have enough ships to strike them at last. At that time, we could ramp up our intelligence-gathering efforts to obtain more recent information."

"That is an excellent idea, Captain!" Agim looked at him with approval. "Kindly dispatch a suitable vessel to make such a reconnaissance at once. Can she reach both planets on the same voyage?"

"Yes, sir, although that will take longer. She will be gone for up to a month."

"I understand, but we must conserve our available fast ships against future need. Send a ship every second month for now. Keep me informed of what they find."

"I hear and obey, sir."

"Thank you again. You may return to our base. I will send more orders to you in due course."

~

THAT AFTERNOON, walking slowly among the trees in the park, as had become their habit, Agim told his lieutenants, "I received a letter yesterday from the Consulate of Neue Helvetica. It said they had a message for me from their Consul on Constanta, via their Foreign Ministry on Neue Helvetica itself."

Endrit drew in his breath with a sharp hiss. "Who sent it?"

"Need you ask? It was personal from Commodore Cochrane, addressed to me by name."

"But – but how did he know who you are?" Fatmir demanded, aghast.

"He has captured enough of our people, and interrogated them, to learn that. Also, we know his agents have been busy here for some time."

"What did he say?"

Agim sighed. "He says that Sub-Lieutenant Alban Sejdiu and eight Kedan spacers survived the destruction of *Ilaria*. They are now prisoners of war, as he terms them. He assures me that they will be well treated, and not harmed in any way. Apparently Sejdiu was severely injured, and underwent surgery to treat a depressed fracture of the skull, but is expected to recover fully."

There was a moment's silence as his aides absorbed the news. "We have not announced *Ilaria*'s loss," Endrit pointed out. "What if they do so, and produce their prisoners as proof?"

"They have not done so yet, as far as we know. Given that, I do not know why they should announce it now, so long after the fight. Perhaps they hope to exchange their prisoners for any of their people we capture."

"That makes sense," Fatmir agreed eagerly. "Will you allow such a swap?"

"I... I do not know. I shall have to think about it."

"Is it not time to announce *Ilaria*'s loss ourselves, to forestall any statement they may release?" Endrit asked.

"I am considering it. What do you think?"

Endrit squared his shoulders. "It will undoubtedly hurt our people's morale. On the other hand, if it is presented properly, it will also stiffen their sinews, and lead them to greater commitment and dedication. What if you announce she was ambushed while on a secret mission to learn the enemy's plans against us, but destroyed three of the enemy's ships before she was lost? That stretches the truth only slightly. You can extol her crew's bravery against impossible odds."

"That... that could work. Yes, I think you have it. I shall prepare an announcement."

"I suggest you do not mention survivors," Fatmir cautioned. "We order all our spacers to fight to the death. If they learn that an officer, and a direct descendant of the Patriarch, has surrendered, they might waver in their resolve."

"A good point. It would have been better for all of us if he had died. I shall not mention him."

Agim repeated what Captain Toci had told him about the odds against the two ships' disappearance being happenstance. "I think our enemies sabotaged them. There is no other reasonable explanation. However, the Captain warns that our forces are too weak at present to mount any meaningful revenge strike. We must wait, and build up our fleet, and look to a climactic battle later."

Endrit asked, "Can we not mount quick raids? We might destroy a ship here or there, and we can surely keep Hawkwood's people under stress, not knowing when or where we shall strike next."

"That may be possible. I shall consider our options. I shall be happier when we have at least four new destroyers on hand, to supplement our remaining armed fast freighters."

Fatmir said eagerly, "Could we buy another fast freighter, and load her with the missiles from our old destroyers? That would give us four of them, plus several modern destroyers, within two years from today. Such a force should be able to defend against anything Hawkwood can throw at it. Once the rest of the destroyers are here, we shall be powerful enough to settle our account with them once and for all."

"That is a good idea. I shall consider it. However, between *Aries* and *Rades,* and the missile cargo the freighter carried, we have lost over seven billion Neue Helvetica francs, thanks to the ruinously inflated prices the shipyard charged us. We had no choice but to pay them, of course; and we shall have to pay as much again to replace what we have lost. Another fast freighter will be an additional expense." He sighed. "I had hoped to avoid drawing down the Fatherland Project's reserve funds even more, but I fear we have no choice."

After a few more issues were settled, the three men separated. Agim walked slowly back to the new offices they had recently occupied, replacing their old premises that had been so thoroughly bugged. His head was down, deep in thought, so he didn't notice the moths that flew from tree to tree, keeping up with him, or the one that flew away from where they had met, heading for the parking lot.

I must *make the announcement. It is now more dangerous to conceal Ilaria's loss than to reveal it – but what about Jehona and Pal? I cannot tell them their son is alive, and a prisoner. Pal will be distraught at Alban's death. He will insist that Jehona must be told, but her mission is too important to allow her to mourn. I shall have to tell him that I have sent word to*

her, *even though I dare not. I must also reply to this Commodore Cochrane,*
acknowledging receipt of his message, but not committing us to anything
or asking any favors. I wonder if I should send agents to locate and kill
young Sejdiu, so he cannot be used for propaganda purposes against us?

He physically flinched as another thought came to him. *What*
if his mother should see him on Constanta? God forbid! We cannot
allow that. Her mission is beyond critical for us. It is vital. Her son
cannot be allowed to distract her from it in any way. No, he must *die.*
It is the only possible solution!

As for our ships... Captain Toci is right. We must build up our
strength until we can be sure of victory. Let us see what his reconnais-
sance shows. If we notice an opportunity, by all means let us take it. If
not, we shall watch, and wait, and plan. Sooner or later, our time will
come.

16

NEW TOOLS

CONSTANTA

"But what good are they without cargo compartments?" 'Antonia' asked, staring in bewilderment through the viewport of the orbital shipyard's corridor. Three cargo shuttles were ranged along the maintenance way. Workers directed robotic constructors as they cut away the ten-thousand-ton-capacity holds that took up most of the small crafts' hulls, leaving only an abbreviated stump containing the engineering systems and crew quarters. They were adding some sort of clamps around the front of the stump, and a new compartment at the rear of the hull.

"I'm told they're going to mate with cargo pods," Grigorescu informed his accountant. "It's a new idea. Instead of loading and unloading cargo from big containers in freighter holds into the cargo shuttles, the big containers will be loaded with pre-packed pods. They'll be taken out of the container and floated out of the hold into space, where one of those things will latch on to them and take them to wherever they're needed. They'll be tethered there using tractor and pressor beams, and unloaded at leisure while the cargo shuttle goes back to fetch another cargo pod."

"That's an interesting concept. What about ballast? I mean, their center of balance and flight characteristics must be messed up without a cargo compartment. I don't see how they can move unless some sort of counterweight is installed up front, where it used to be."

He looked at her with new respect. "Not many people would think about that. Are you sure you don't have any background in space?"

Mentally she cursed herself. *Don't show too much knowledge, you idiot!* Aloud she said merely, "Oh, I've sailed a little on small boats. Center of balance and ballasting are critical to that. You can't alter one of them without all sorts of problems, so it seemed logical that the same would apply to these."

"Yes, it does. We'll get around it in two ways. We'll build ballast tanks fore and aft underneath the rear hull. Reaction mass can be pumped between them to lend at least some stability. That won't be enough to fully solve the problem, so we'll modify their flight software to take account of their unbalanced state. They'll need to use their maneuvering thrusters constantly at low power when they're unloaded, to keep them stable while moving. We'll reposition the thrusters, and install a couple more at their extremities, to make that work."

"That sounds like it'll be expensive, wasting all that reaction mass."

He laughed. "Trust an accountant to look at that angle! Yes, it will, but like everything else in space, it's a trade-off. It wastes money to have cargo shuttles and their crews sit idle while they're being loaded and unloaded. If they can keep busy, taking containers to and fro, they'll have less idle time, so the investment in craft and crew will be used more efficiently."

"I get it. I'd like to see a cost-benefit analysis on that. May I ask Hawkwood for their figures?"

Her boss shook his head. "I'm afraid not. They're extraordinarily vigilant about security. We need to know quite a lot about them, by the nature of the work we do for them, but they absolutely insist that anyone getting access to any of their files must first go through their security clearance procedures. They include a very intrusive truth-tester examination. I undergo it every year, just like all their officers and senior personnel, from the top down. Junior employees and spacers do it every two years. I wouldn't like to put you through that for no good reason."

She made a *moue* of distaste. "That's an unpardonable invasion of privacy! I mean, it's not like they're some sort of government agency. I'd never allow a private company to rummage through my deepest, most private, most intimate thoughts. The very idea is repellent!"

"They may be a private company, but they conduct themselves as if they were a military fleet. Given the opponents they've come up against, I'm not surprised."

She tried to look surprised. "What sort of opponents?"

"Oh, smugglers, pirates, that sort of thing." Her boss tried to look and sound casual. "I've seen the damage to some of their ships – but I'm not supposed to talk about that at all. Forget I said anything."

"All right."

As they continued down the passage, she thought to herself in frustration, *I daren't go through Hawkwood's security procedure. Any competent truth-tester operator – and theirs are bound to be competent – will realize something is wrong, and then it'll be all over for me. I'll have to find another way. I wonder how much information the shipyard has in its confidential files on Hawkwood and its ships? We need to know how many they have, and of what type, and how they're armed and equipped. I don't have access to those files as an accountant, but... maybe there's a way. I must try to get an inside look at the shipyard's computer security system.*

"Hello, darling," Hui said as she walked into Cochrane's office.

He looked up with a smile. "Now that's a greeting I've never had from any previous Chief of Staff!"

"That's because I'm the first Chief of Staff you've ever had," she said unrepentantly, sticking out her tongue at him.

He laughed. "You've spoiled me for any others. Good morning, darling. What's up?"

"Quite a lot, actually. Do you have a few minutes for me?"

"This can wait." He blanked his terminal screen, and stood. "Let's sit in the comfortable chairs." They walked over to the group of armchairs in the corner and sat down. She activated her tablet and scanned it as she talked.

"First off, Admiral Kwan says he owes you an apology. It seems the Second Battle of Mycenae was sparked by the Albanians discovering one of our spy rings on Patos. The lead agent was killed, but he was able to warn the rest of his team in time for them to use their escape plan. They got off-planet safely, and brought back their latest intelligence with them. The Albanians don't know about our involvement, so they blamed Hawkwood for the spy ring, and wanted to send a message by hitting back, hard."

Cochrane's face fell. "They certainly did that. I'm very sorry your people lost an agent. I hope the Albanians didn't take him alive, to interrogate him before he died."

"I hope so, too. The Admiral is still sending us intelligence, so I daresay that wasn't the only ring we had on Patos. I won't speculate, for obvious reasons."

"I should say not!" He hesitated. "Would you please tell Admiral Kang that if the dead agent left behind a family, or anyone who needs help, Hawkwood will be honored to contribute to their support? I'm not putting an upper limit on that. He can let me know, and I'll send the funds to him for onward transmission."

"Thank you, darling. I know he'll appreciate it very much. I'll tell him." She reached forward and placed her hand on his knee for a moment. "Just so you know, I appreciate it very much, too."

He shrugged. "It's the least we can do. He was helping us, too, after all."

"Yes, he was. All right, next thing. Kang is working hard. They're testing a new battle computer, more powerful than the previous model. Its software has been upgraded to use our revised datalink interface. It'll be able to control up to three hundred missiles of any type in a single volley. It's a big job, and they say they'll need another three or four months to test it thoroughly, but it should be a plug-in retrofit for all their ships, up to and including destroyers."

He exhaled in relief. "That's great news! If we can remove that bottleneck, it'll give us a lot more capability, offensively and defensively."

"Next, they're building your new defensive missile pods for the cargo shuttles. Mr. Kim says, if you keep coming up with good ideas like that, he's going to have to start paying you design royalties." They laughed. "He'll have thirty-six of them ready for collection in two months. Each will carry fifteen of their corvette-size defensive missiles, plus an auxiliary reactor and generator to power them up and launch them on command via datalink, just like the arsenal ships' missiles."

"Good. Those cut-down cargo shuttles will have decoy beacons built into their new rear compartments, and missile pods up front. They'll simulate our ships in orbit around Mycenae Secundus Two, and thicken our defensive barrage if necessary."

"That's what you and Dave were working on a couple of years ago, wasn't it?"

"Yes. We've been noodling over it ever since then. Earlier this year, we sent our final design proposals to Kang. They agreed to build the pods, and we're modifying cargo shuttles here to carry them. We're concealing their purpose by telling the shipyard they're to move cargo pods."

"So that's why you went and bought all those extra cargo shuttles! You didn't tell me about this, darling?" Her voice was questioning.

"Compartmentalization, dear. There's a lot I don't tell you – not because I don't trust you, but because you don't need to know. You know how serious we are about that."

"Yes, I do. I suppose it's the conflict between being both your Chief of Staff, and your lover!"

"Well, guided missiles and suchlike aren't exactly pillow talk, are they?"

"No, although you seem to guide your missile awfully well." She let out a peal of laughter as he flushed slightly. "You're embarrassed!"

"A little, yes." He strove to regain his composure. "All right. Next?"

"*Beluga*'s datalink has been upgraded at Grigorescu's shipyard to incorporate the same improvements that were made to *Narwhal*'s at Mycenae. The next two arsenal ships will arrive next week, and Grigorescu will build it into them, too, while making the other modifications. We have enough missile pods for both new ships, and Kang will have another thirty-six ready for collection along with the cargo shuttle missile pods."

"If you keep giving me good news like this, I may declare a half-day holiday and take you out for a long, liquid lunch!" He scratched his chin. "I think we're going to have to rename our arsenal ships. We've been using the names of whale species from Earth, but we need to distinguish between freighters that are freighters, and freighters that carry missiles."

"Why not leave freighters as whales, and reuse your old patrol craft names for the arsenal ships? NOE renamed the patrol craft after you handed them over, so there won't be any confusion."

"That's a great idea! All right. We had five, all named for predatory fish of the Amazon River: *Piranha, Payara, Trairao, Arapaima* and *Bicuda*. We'll reuse those, with the suffix 'II' added, plus a sixth, *Sorubim*. I had that name in mind for another patrol craft, but we never got it into working order. I'll assign the names to our existing and new arsenal ships, and notify Mycenae."

She nodded. "Some more good news from Fujita. The first two communications vessels from our order of eight, *Hermoth* and *Iris,* will depart next week. They'll go straight to Mycenae, of course, to work up there, far from prying eyes."

He shook his head. "I'm not so sure about that. We think the Albanians reconnoitered the system before, and probably after, Mycenae II. I daresay they'll go on sending spaceships through at high speed, under tight emissions control, to keep an eye on us. They won't see what we're doing from day to day, but that'll give them a regular snapshot view of the ships in the system, where they are, and so on. I hope they spot our new asteroid prospecting site, and try something there."

"They've already lost one ship trying to collect asteroids in Mycenae. Do you think they'll be fooled again?"

He shrugged. "We can only hope."

"All right. Fujita also says they've started work on the first of our new repair ships, *Vulcan II*. She'll be ready in a year. They hope to start the second ship, *Hephaestus,* in about six months, as soon as there's an opening on their building ways." She shook her head. "A billion francs apiece for two repair ships! That still seems like an awful lot of money to me."

"It is, but we can't do without them, so we'll just have to grin and bear it."

"If you say so, darling." She blanked the tablet screen. "That's all I have for you this morning. Now, what was that about a long, liquid lunch?"

He laughed. "All right. Let me finish what I'm doing. I'll come to your office in half an hour to collect you."

MYCENAE SYSTEM

Frank Haldane looked up from his command console as Commander Darroch was shown into the OpCen. He jumped to his feet. *"Angus!* It's good to see you again."

The Commander saluted, a broad smile on his face, then shook Frank's proffered hand. "And you, sir."

"How's my baby?" Frank gestured toward the Plot, where HCS *Bobcat's* icon was now shown parked very close to *Jean Bart's*.

"She's as good as she could be, sir. We're still running trials, of course, but it looks like the instability you found has been completely cured. She handles like a champion."

"I'll have to make time to come out with you for a high-speed run, to feel the difference."

"Any time, sir. There seem to be an awful lot more ships in the system since the last time I was here. I'll have to be careful not to run into any of them."

"There are. Come over to the Plot." He walked over with his guest. "Operator, who's doing what, with which, to whom?"

The NCO on duty grinned, and pointed to icons as he named them. "Around *Jean Bart* we have *Bobcat,* the courier ship *Agni,* and the brand-new corvettes *Monkshood* and *Nightshade,* both just arrived and starting their workup period. The arsenal ship *Narwhal* – sorry, sir, I mean *Arapaima II;* I keep forgetting her new name – is accompanied by the corvettes *Belladonna* and *Hemlock.* The two new warehouse freighters, *Bowhead II* and *Dolphin,* are parked next to the original *Bowhead,* unloading her holds into their own and re-cataloging everything. The new communications ships, *Hermoth* and *Iris,* are running around the inner system, working up, and we have three corvettes on inner and outer system patrol, *Amanita, Hellebore* and *Mandrake.* Finally, the freighter *Pilot* is on her way out of the system, heading back to Constanta to pick up the next load of supplies."

Darroch smiled. "Seventeen ships! That's a much better picture than a few years ago, when we had only a single corvette, a few old, outdated patrol craft, and a converted freighter serving as a makeshift depot ship."

"It sure is! It's going to get a lot busier soon. You know about the new decoys?"

"Yes, I heard. They'll make it a lot harder for any sneak attacker to know what to shoot at."

"They'll help us shoot back at his missiles, too. We've sown a hundred mines around our asteroid prospector bots, and another hundred around this planet, and there are more coming. We'll let them orbit out to five million kilometers, as soon as we have enough of them to warrant that. We're going to program a few of them to emit active radar pulses from time to time, then move immediately, so an intruder can't fix their position. If someone's sneaking around at the wrong moment, we might get a radar reflection off her hull, and be able to do something about her."

"I hope I'm here when that happens, sir. I'd like to have a live target for *Bobcat*'s missiles."

"So would I!"

THE COURIER SHIP *Saranda* scorched through the Mycenae system at her maximum velocity of four-tenths of light speed. Her gravitic drive was shut down, along with every other item of equipment that emitted a signal of any kind. She coasted in complete electronic silence.

In her Operations Center, Lieutenant-Commander Malaj fumed. At this velocity, *Saranda*'s sensors were almost overwhelmed by the complications of time dilation, relative motion and the Lorentz-Fitzgerald contraction. It was hard to make out exactly what was being portrayed in her Plot display. The recording of her headlong rush through the system would have to be replayed on faster, more powerful computers than her own, to make more sense of it. Even so, he could see that the Hawkwood ships in orbit around Secundus Two had been reinforced. There were several more gravitic drives emitting their characteristic signatures, including many more smaller vessels, corvettes or courier ships.

The Plot operator said, concern in his voice, "What's this one, sir?" He pointed to an icon near what they presumed was the local depot ship. "That looks like a destroyer-class gravitic drive, but Hawkwood doesn't have any destroyers."

"They have not had any up to now," Malaj agreed, his voice grim, "but that does not mean they cannot get any, does it?"

"Ah... no, sir, it doesn't."

"Mark that one for future reference. We must alert Captain Toci as soon as we get back. He will want to analyze that signature in as much detail as possible."

"Aye aye, sir."

Trouble is, Malaj thought, *it will take us two and a half weeks to get back to base. They should have sent another ship to Constanta, instead of making us do the round trip. We could have got back much faster, if not for that. They should not have to wait that long for this intelligence... but there is no help for it. I think I shall slow down to half this speed to survey the Constanta system, and see whether our sensors get better results. If they do, next time we come back here, we shall do the same, and learn more. Speed is safety, but we came to collect intelligence, not run a race.*

17

KILL TEAM

PATOS

As he turned into the driveway leading to the farmhouse, Agim dragged his mind away from the latest reconnaissance report submitted by Captain Toci. It certainly looked as if the damage they'd inflicted on Hawkwood had been speedily put right, and new ships had replaced those they had lost. He ground his teeth in frustration. Not only was the enemy's fleet growing, but their sabotage attack had damaged the Brotherhood's fleet as much as theirs – proportionally more, in fact.

As he got out of the car, he thought of the briefing he was about to give. He wished beyond words that he did not have to deliver it... but wishes were dust and ashes in the face of hard reality. He shivered as he remembered the desolation, the torment, on the face of Pal Sejdiu as he had told him of *Ilaria*'s loss, and the supposed death of his son, and the explosion of grief from the young man's brother and sisters.

"Have you told Jehona?" her husband had demanded brokenly.

"I... I have sent word to her. She will get it as soon as possible."

"I must see her!"

"That is not possible. She is already deployed. It would destroy her cover, and imperil her mission."

"Do you think I care? Do you think *she* will care? Alban was our firstborn!"

"I am sorry. It cannot be done. As soon as she has succeeded, I shall bring her back. You will have to wait until then."

Despite the family's entreaties, he had remorselessly stuck to his position. Their calls and correspondence were now all under rigorous surveillance, in case any of them tried to do anything foolish, or sought to blame the disaster on Agim or any of the Brotherhood's other leaders.

The head of the training school met him at the door. "Good morning, sir. The team is assembled and ready for you."

"Good. Let us begin right away. I cannot stay long."

"Yes, sir. This way, please."

The team, four men and a woman, were in one of the classrooms at the rear. Agim greeted them as he walked to the lecturer's podium.

"You know why you are here," he began without preamble. "Yours is one of the most vital missions I have ever had to entrust to a group of our agents. It is a measure of our trust in you that you have been selected for this task."

He displayed an image of a young officer on the screen behind him. "This is Sub-Lieutenant Alban Sejdiu. He was a junior officer aboard our armed freighter *Ilaria*. Despite our instructions to our spacers that they should fight to the death, Sejdiu cravenly chose to surrender rather than die. As a result, the enemy learned much from him. What is more, he is preparing to help their propaganda efforts against us. They can produce him, in uniform, along with other proofs of his service, including the lifeboat he used to escape his ship before she was destroyed. He will be a powerful tool against us in their hands.

"Worse, his mother is one of our most distinguished agents. She is presently in the field, engaged in a most sensitive intelligence operation *on the very same planet where he is being held*. Tragically, she cannot help but be affected if she learns of her son's treachery. No matter how professional she is, she is his mother. We all know the depth and power of that bond, from our own experience." His audience nodded.

"Your task is threefold. You will go to Constanta, and find out where Alban Sejdiu is being held. You will find a way to infiltrate that place and kill him, so that there is no possibility that our enemies can use him against us, and to punish him for his treachery. Do not interrogate him, do not even speak to him – just kill him. He deserves nothing more." Nods of agreement, bitter anger in their eyes at their comrade's betrayal.

"You will also try to locate his mother, Jehona Sejdiu." He threw her picture onto the screen. "She is on Constanta, using the cover name of Antonia Funar. If she has not learned of her son's treachery, all well and good. However, if she *has* heard about his defection... that may change things. You will have to assess the situation for yourselves, because I cannot anticipate what you will find. If there is even the slightest chance that she may be cooperating with our enemies, for the sake of her son, then she must die too. Her son has damaged us badly enough. She could damage us far more, with all she knows. If there is any doubt at all, kill her." More nods.

"Those two are your top priority. Kill Alban Sejdiu, and if there is any doubt at all about her loyalty, kill his mother. After that, if it is possible – and it may not be, if the enemy's security for its leaders is as good as ours – you should try to locate their leader, Commodore Andrew Cochrane." Another picture appeared on the screen. "He is a very intelligent man, who has been able to respond to all our efforts against him and Hawkwood with telling blows of his own. If you can find a way to kill him, or those closest to him, particularly his advisers and staff, do so. The more of them we can take out of the picture, the easier it will be to move against their successors when the time comes. However, as I said, that is secondary to disposing of Alban Sejdiu and, if necessary, his mother. At all costs, those two are your imperatives!

"I will not hide it from you that yours is a high-risk operation. You have all volunteered for this mission, knowing and accepting those risks. For that, for your courage and commitment, I honor you, and I thank you for your dedication to our cause." He bowed to them, and they bowed back in mutual respect.

"Without men and women such as you, we should not have got as far as we have, and the triumph of our cause would not be as near. Rest assured, thanks to your efforts, and those of others like you, we *shall* triumph, and soon!"

As AGIM DROVE AWAY from the farmhouse, Pal Sejdiu entered a small shop in a suburban mall. His face was still tight with the pain of his grief. The shopkeeper hurried forward to greet him, but stopped short. "Pal! What is wrong?"

"It is... I cannot speak of it yet, Afrim. It is a personal matter."

"I am sorry, my friend. How are things at the ship?"

"They are as they should be. I am back here for another regular administration session. Did you get that module for me?"

"Yes, I did. It is in the back."

"I'll come with you."

The two men walked companionably to the rear of the store, and through a door in the back wall. The agent watching unobtrusively from the mall outside wondered for a moment whether he should go into the shop, to keep a closer watch, but almost instantly decided against it. Pal came to this store regularly, to buy components for his youngest son's hobby of amateur robotics. This was surely just another routine visit.

The shopkeeper showed Pal a box containing a control module. "I am sorry it took so long, but I had to order it from off-planet."

"That is no problem. Let me pay you for it." He fumbled in his pocket, and pulled out a slim chip case. "Oh, damn! I forgot I had to upload this file for my daughter. It's a copy of some study material she wants to send to a friend. May I please use your shop terminal?"

"Of course." He waved at the desk in the corner as the front door chimed for attention. "I'll attend to that customer while you send it."

"Thank you."

Pal sat down at the terminal and entered a call code. A mailbox was displayed. He uploaded the contents of the chip into it. It looked like a school report about a poem, a line-by-line analysis of text, rhyme and meaning. However, it disguised a carefully crafted message, one that would be intelligible only to someone possessing the necessary key to decode it. He entered an anonymous sender address, and a destination code that would automatically reroute the message to a different system. Coming from the shop terminal, it would be just another anonymous communication, with no easily traceable link to Pal.

He pressed the 'Send' key. The message would now be transferred to the off-planet queue, to be collected by the next weekly dispatch vessel. From there, it would be routed to an interplanetary message repository, copies of which were circulated to all settled planets every week. Within six to eight weeks, Jehona should be able to read it.

You must think I am deaf, dumb and blind, he mentally snorted at Agim as he cleared the terminal and pocketed the chip case. *You forget who and what I am. I routinely monitor everyone's communications at the refinery ship. Did you think I would not recognize the signs when you did that to me? That is why I insisted Jehona should set this up before she left. I feared something like this might happen. You will not prevent me from sharing our grief with my wife, damn you!*

"No! *NO!* You ask too much!"

The speaker glared at Agim. Age had weakened his body, but not his mind, and his voice was determined. "We authorized the use of the patrimony collected for the Fatherland Project, because you told us that spending on our security *was* spending on the Project. However, today we have less security *and* less patrimony! One of our new and very expensive warships has vanished without trace, and one of our freighters too, laden with missiles. You blame that on our enemies, but advance not one shred of verifiable evidence to prove it. Furthermore, one of the four armed fast freighters we authorized has already been lost. You claim she destroyed three enemy ships in her last fight, but where is the evidence? Missing gravitic drive signatures are not proof. Those ships may have been damaged enough that their drives were shut down, but not destroyed; or they may have moved off at low power, which cannot be easily detected. *No,* Agim. I shall need far stronger evidence that what we have already authorized has been well spent, before I vote for even more of our patrimony to be diverted. So far, I have seen none." There were several grunts and exclamations of agreement.

Another old man spoke up. "You have said we should trust you because the Patriarch personally selected you for your office, so that to have faith in you is to have faith in him who chose you. That is all very well, but he chose all of us except our three newest members, all of whom we voted for unanimously. It seems to me that the Patriarch would have expected all of us to put faith in each other, because he trusted all of us. Instead, you, Endrit and Fatmir have become a triumvirate. We seldom know where you are or what you are doing. We receive limited reports, only as often as you see fit to make them. This is not what our Patriarch established as our model of government. I believe it is time for this Brotherhood to reassert its authority and govern as a Council, not delegate our powers indefinitely." This time, the open approval was even stronger.

A third man raised his hand. Suppressing his anger and frustration with difficulty, Agim nodded to him, conceding the floor.

"I do not believe the three of you are wasting your time or our money," the speaker began. "We have known you for too long to doubt your integrity. However, part of the problem for you, and for all of us as a Council, is that we are remote from the reality of this conflict. We sit here on Patos and pull strings, while others dance at the end of them, and sometimes die. That is a problem for all our people. If we lose too many of them for no visible progress, they will come to doubt our ability to lead them. If they doubt that, they will eventually begin to doubt the Patriarch who developed the vision that leads us all, and who hand-picked almost all of us. That would be a disaster.

"I submit that we are all frustrated because, deep down inside, we know this. We feel the weight of loss when our people die, but we cannot reveal it to those around us, because we must maintain a façade of confidence and determination. The Patriarch suffered loss among his loved ones, yet never showed emotion. We strive to follow his example – yet we are not him. We do not have his indomitable, remorseless strength of will. That, perhaps, is why he chose a Council to take over the leadership of the Fatherland Project. He knew that none of us, individually, could match him; but perhaps all of us, collectively, could do so. By surrendering our collective judgment to a small minority, I believe we have departed from his vision. Our anger and resentment should be focused, not on Agim, Endrit and Fatmir, who I believe are truly doing their best, but on ourselves, because we have failed to live up to the Patriarch's trust."

"Well said, Gjon!" another said, and there was a general murmur of approval.

Agim allowed the discussion and recriminations to continue a while longer as he thought fast, trying to put together an argument that would convince the doubters. He sensed Fatmir and Endrit were growing frustrated enough to throw up their hands and quit. He could not allow that. He needed them too much.

At last he stood. "I have listened to you, brothers, and given you the chance to speak your minds. I have not attempted to silence those who dispute my competence, nor have I tried to impose my will on yours. To do either would be to dishonor the Patriarch who appointed me. Yet, I submit, you are not being fair or just.

"We are not running a business. We are fighting a war. We did not seek this conflict. If Hawkwood had not interfered with us, we should never have engaged in hostilities with them. Never forget, *they fired first*. They stole our asteroid prospector robots and the asteroids they had beaconed for recovery, and destroyed the ship we sent to collect the latest batch from Mycenae. Our Patriarch himself approved striking back against them, and accompanied our destroyers. Tragically, we lost both him and our ships. After such a disaster, there could be no turning back. To do so would be unfaithful to the man who told us, 'Do not let your enemies strike fear into you. Instead, *strike fear into them!* Hit back at them! Show them that for every blow they direct against us, we shall return it ten times harder!' He reinforced that lesson during his life, and in his death. That is precisely what Endrit, Fatmir and I have been preparing to do.

"I think you fail to grasp the nature of war in our age. We are separated from the scene of conflict by many light years – unimaginable distances. It will take weeks for a request for guidance or orders to be sent from a battle front to Patos, be debated in this Council, and our reply sent back. During that time, the situation will inevitably have changed. The enemy will have acted, or withdrawn; our forces will have had to be resupplied, or reassigned elsewhere to respond to an enemy initiative; or any one of many other things. It is simply impossible to exercise tight central control. Instead, we must select the best possible commanders, and trust them to lead the fight locally in accordance with our overall guidance.

"In asking your permission to lead the fight myself, with the help of Endrit and Fatmir as my lieutenants, I was following that principle. Sometimes news comes in, or events occur, that require a rapid response. If I must summon this Council every time, and brief you all, and wait for your decision, then work out how to implement it in practice, that will add days to our response. That is too long in wartime – and make no mistake, we *are* fighting a war, for our very survival as a people!

"The same applies to using the patrimony of the Fatherland Project to fight this war. I have not concealed from you how we have used it. You approved that in advance. However, you have not allowed for the fact that, in war, there are casualties. We have suffered them, as well as the enemy. It is to replace those casualties that I seek more funds. This is not throwing good money after bad. It is, if you like, throwing good money after good, because in war, one *must* expend one's resources to win. One must equip one's forces with the tools they need to triumph, and replace the tools that will inevitably be broken in the process. The side most willing and able to do that, usually wins."

The debate went back and forth for over an hour. Eventually, Agim used his most powerful argument. "Brothers, if you wish, I shall resign my position as Chairman. You may elect someone else, better able to exercise the responsibility the Patriarch vested in that position. You have but to say the word."

That silenced much of the opposition. Most of the Council were older men, no longer able to take an active leadership role. If they replaced Agim, it would have to be with Fatmir or Endrit, the most able of their members; but they were already associated with him. Slowly, bitterly in some cases, the councilors were forced to accept that they had no real alternative. By a narrow majority, they renewed Agim's mandate, and his assistants', and gave him what he had requested; the right to draw on the patrimony of the Fatherland Project for more funds to replace their losses.

He knew the Council would not continue to support him indefinitely. He had to produce results, or face the real risk of being replaced. Time was not on his side.

Perhaps, if the kill team can dispose of Commodore Cochrane, that will be a sop to their concerns, he thought as he drove home that evening. *If not him, then perhaps some of his staff. I must meet with them before they leave tomorrow morning and re-emphasize that part of their mission, perhaps give it a higher priority. If we kill the equivalent of the Council on the enemy's side, surely our Council must recognize that as a victory?*

18

CONSULTATION

CONSTANTA

C aitlin Ross returned to Constanta at last, traveling in company with a civilian from Qianjin named Chen Huan. She brought him with her to report to Cochrane about her activities.

When the initial formalities were over and they'd settled into comfortable chairs, each with coffee or tea according to preference, Caitlin began, "It's a long story, sir, and I can't yet report full success; but Mr. Chen and I have covered a lot of ground between us. We figured it was time we briefed you about it, before going on to the next step."

"By all means. Which Qianjin agency or department do you represent, Mr. Chen?"

"Ah... I don't, Commodore. I work for a different organization."

"I see." Cochrane understood at once that Chen must be a member of the Dragon Tong. "How did you make contact with Lieutenant-Commander Ross?"

"Your official request for assistance in researching the background of the Albanian Brotherhood, in the light of the problems they're causing, was forwarded to my organization. Since we deal with such issues on a more regular basis than our Fleet, it was felt we would be better suited to work with the Commander."

"I see."

Caitlin took up the thread. "I spent months going through all available records on Qianjin, sir. There weren't many of them, and a lot of connections had to be made by inference rather than by a trail of evidence. The Brotherhood are very secretive about themselves and their operations. That's made worse by the fact that our particular problem children broke away from the larger Albanian Mafia over forty years ago. No-one was sure why. I decided the best way to figure out what they're up to would be to find out what brought them to where they are today.

"While I was doing that research, Mr. Chen was going through interplanetary criminal records, trying to locate convicted criminals or expert witnesses who might be able to tell us more. I'll let him tell that side of the story."

"Thank you, Commander." Chen sipped his tea, then set down the cup. "The Albanian Mafia is made up of clans, family groups. It seems the breakaway faction was originally part of the Bregija clan. Over the years, we'd run into enough Bregijas and their allies to have heard about the split, but not why it happened. The man behind it was Bashkim Bregija. He came up with an idea so out of the ordinary that the rest of the clan refused to consider it."

"What was it?" Cochrane asked.

"He called it the 'Fatherland Project'. He planned to build up funds by stealing high-grade asteroids and processing them for precious metals and high-value minerals. When he'd accumulated sufficient money, he wanted to buy a planet."

"Buy... oh, I get it – at one of the regular United Planets auctions?"

"Yes, sir. Exploration companies find a planet or star system potentially offering a good return on investment, whether through exploitation of natural resources, or colonization, or both. They do a full survey, post the results for interested buyers, then auction it off to the highest bidder. That's usually done through the UP, which grants title to the planet or star system to the buyer. The purchaser gets exclusive exploitation and settlement rights. Bashkim planned to buy a planet, then settle his own clan there. He would probably have thrown it open in due course to settlement by other Albanians who were prepared to accept his leadership."

Cochrane nodded. "That's somewhat like how the New Orkney Enterprise – or, rather, its parent planets – gained the rights to the Mycenae system. The First Families from the New Orkney Cluster found and explored the system, then set up NOE to exploit it. All right. Please go on."

"Yes, sir. After a lot of searching through criminal records, I found that a dozen Albanian asteroid smugglers, members of the breakaway faction, were arrested in the Kagamit system about twenty years ago. They were all sentenced to life imprisonment with hard labor, to be served in the asteroid mining and processing industry there. That seemed like a lead worth pursuing for more information. Fortunately, we have some... influence... in that system, so we were able to get permission to speak to them." He gestured politely to Caitlin to take over once more.

"Thanks, Huan. Sir, we traveled to Kagamit aboard my courier ship, and spent a couple of days reading through court records of their trial, looking for anything we could use. They'd refused to testify in their own defense, and wouldn't answer questions. The court eventually ordered the use of truth-testers, but even then, they revealed as little as possible. That counted against them when sentence was passed. Instead of getting a shorter sentence, they were classified as unrepentant habitual criminals, and imprisoned for life.

"We arranged to go out to the asteroid mining project to talk to them, and got permission from the authorities – with the help of a hefty bribe, disguised as a good-behavior bond – to offer them a deal if they'd cooperate. It took a lot of persuasion..."

∽

KAGAMIT

"If you help us, we'll help you." Caitlin looked around the five convicts seated on the other side of the table. All were hand-cuffed and in leg-irons, visible evidence of their official status as 'incorrigibles' and 'troublemakers'. They stared back at her, their eyes impassive in their lined, prematurely aged faces, showing the hardships of twenty years' brutal labor aboard an asteroid processing and refining ship.

"We've made a deal with the Kagamit authorities," she went on. "If you tell us what we need to know, they'll transfer you to a medium-security prison planetside. It'll be a lot easier and more pleasant than this place. Provided you don't make trouble, you can stay there; and if you serve five years there with no discipli-nary infractions, they'll consider promoting you to a minimum-security facility. You can serve out the rest of your sentences there, in as much comfort as you can expect from a prison system. You'll have to earn that through good behavior – but you won't get the chance unless you help us."

The oldest prisoner spoke. He was gray-haired, iron-faced, his voice gravelly and hoarse from an old injury to his larynx, evidenced by a jagged, uneven scar on his throat. "How do we know you speak the truth? What is to stop them sending us back here after you leave?"

Caitlin looked at the tall, craggy figure of the Warden of the convict facility aboard the refinery ship, seated at the head of the long conference table. "Sir?"

The Warden's face twisted in distaste. "As far as I'm concerned, all five of you can stay here until you die or rot. Such chances should only go to those who've behaved, and you haven't! Unfortunately, that's out of my hands." He brought up a document on the screen against the bulkhead. "That's the official letter these two brought me from the Ministry of Justice. It guarantees what she said, as you can read for yourselves. Why they'd be so stupid as to trust you in a soft prison planetside, I don't know. I suspect they'll find out the hard way that they were wrong about you. Still, that'll be their problem, not mine – until they send you back here, that is, because I don't think you've got enough sense or self-control to stay out of trouble down there."

Caitlin couldn't help smiling quietly to herself. The Warden's attitude in telling the prisoners about it was probably a better guarantee of the letter's authenticity than anything else.

The five prisoners all nodded. One said quietly to the others, in Albanian, "I don't trust them, but if we refuse this offer, we know our fate. We shall die here, just like our seven comrades who have already died working on this hell-ship." He clearly did not know that translation software on Caitlin's and Chen's comm units was interpreting his words, relaying them to their earbuds.

"Why not remain silent, and follow their example?" their leader asked, also in Albanian. "If these people are lying, we have nothing to lose by not talking." He turned to Caitlin, reverting to Galactic Standard English. "Why should we cooperate? More than half of us are already dead. Why should Kagamit change how it treats us, and why should we believe that they will?"

"I can't persuade you of that, and I won't be here to guarantee it," she said evenly. "However, I've done my best to ensure that the arrangement will be honored. I should also point out that my patience is not inexhaustible. There are four other groups of Albanian asteroid thieves and raiders, imprisoned on other planets." There weren't, but the prisoners didn't need to know that. "We came here first, because you've spent the longest time behind bars. If you won't talk, we'll try the next planet. I'm willing to bet that out of the five, we'll find at least one group willing to talk to us.

"Also, consider this. We already know enough about Bashkim Bregija and his 'Fatherland Project' to be sure you were part of it. We don't need you to tell us *what* he was doing; we know that. We need to know *why* he was doing it; to understand his motivation, which drives the Brotherhood to this day. If we know that, we might be able to resolve our conflict without too many more casualties. The Brotherhood's made so many enemies that, unless we find a way to end this conflict soon, all the clans of the entire Albanian Mafia may find themselves targeted. Do you want that much blood on your hands? – because that's what your refusal might lead to."

Chen added, "There's another thing. Your Brotherhood commenced full-scale operations about six years ago, after spending four decades building up the resources it needed to do so with smaller operations, such as the one during which you were captured. In the last few years, it's taken in at least a hundred billion Neue Helvetica francs." The five men on the other side of the table sat up straighter, eyes widening as they heard the figure. "That's all come out of the pockets of people, corporations and planets from whom it stole asteroids. You can understand why they're angry about that, and want to stop it any way they have to – if necessary, by wiping out the Brotherhood altogether. All of you must still have family members in the Brotherhood, even though they've had no contact with you. Do you really want your entire line to be wiped out, root and branch?"

Caitlin put in, "You might also ask why the Brotherhood hasn't spent any of that money to help or support you. A few bribes in the right places might have made your lives a lot easier – maybe even saved the lives of some of your comrades. Money paid into your prison commissary accounts might have helped you live more comfortably. None of that happened, because Bashkim Bregija insisted that every single franc had to be hoarded for his 'Fatherland Project'. You're irrelevant, as far as he's concerned. Your sacrifice here means nothing to him. That's proved by how he and the Brotherhood have ignored you, ever since you were caught.

"As to why I think Kagamit will treat you better, if you cooperate..." She took three small, hard objects from her pocket and rolled them idly onto the table. The prisoners' eyes widened as they saw the gold *taels,* small oblongs of yellow metal stamped with their weight and the mint that had produced them. "I've always found that honey attracts more flies than vinegar, and these get more cooperation than threats. Wouldn't you agree, Warden?"

He half-sneered. "If the Minister lets you post a bond against the good behavior of some convicts, that's his concern. I don't imagine you'll get it back, even if they don't disobey regulations again – which seems to be a sport with them, so you're even more sure to lose your money."

"So, either way, the Minister gets his money; and in return, you get your chance at a better life," Chen told the convicts. "Don't be so foolish as to throw it away. You'll never get an opportunity like this again."

"All right. What's it to be?" Caitlin challenged them as she scooped up the *taels* and returned them to her pocket.

The leader glanced at the others. "Can we talk alone?" he asked.

Caitlin stood. "We'll come back in ten minutes."

She and Chen followed the Warden out of the room. He closed the door, and stood glowering at the chained convicts through windows in the partition as they turned to each other and broke into animated conversation. "You know they're going to ask for more," he pointed out bitterly. "Scum like this always try for everything they can get."

"If they give me what I need, I'm willing to bargain with them," Caitlin replied. "I daresay a deposit to their commissary accounts might be arranged, or something like that. You can handle that for us, can't you? I'll pay any processing fees involved."

The official perked up at once. "Processing fees? They might be expensive."

"I expect so. Do you think ten *taels* might cover them?"

The Warden licked his lips. She knew the gold's value on the local black market would be pretty close to his annual salary. "I think that would be sufficient, yes."

I just bet you do, she thought, amused. *Funny how, as soon as you're cut in on the bribes, you change your tune!* "Then consider it done. I'm sure we can rely on your cooperation and support."

"Oh, yes! Yes, of course!"

~

CONSTANTA

Cochrane tried to frown disapprovingly, but couldn't suppress a grin. "So you've been spending my money like water, have you?"

"In a manner of speaking, yes, sir."

"And did you get value for it?"

"I think so, sir. They gave us a great deal of background information – all minor in itself, but it helped to fill out the picture of what motivates the Brotherhood and makes them so fanatical. I've included it all in my report, which I transmitted from the ship as we approached. Briefly, Bashkin Bregija seems to have been an unusually gifted demagogue, a hypnotic speaker who could motivate his audience to believe in, and attempt, what would seem impossible, even insane, to any normal person. He set them on fire with his vision that only if they had their own planet would they be able to reach the same level of influence and power as the Big Three criminal organizations."

Cochrane shook his head. "That's crazy! A physical base is only one requirement for that sort of thing, and probably not the most important one, at that. An adequate skills base, commitment and loyalty, cohesiveness, motivation... there's a long, long list. We're learning a lot about that ourselves, as we try to mold Hawkwood into what we want it to be."

"Yes, sir."

"I presume the Dragon Tong is one of the 'Big Three'?" He glanced at Chen. "Who are the other two?"

Chen replied, "The Cosa Nostra and the Nuevo Cartel. All three organizations began on Old Home Earth before or at the start of the Space Age. Both of the others are similar in size and power to ourselves, although we like to think we are larger and better. They would probably make the same claim, of course." His audience laughed.

"Don't you get crossways with them sometimes?" Cochrane asked.

"We tend to steer clear of each other's planets of influence, sir. That's an unofficial arrangement, but in practice it's proved very stable. On planets where we all have interests, we try not to interfere with each other."

"And how do you deal with conflicts when they arise?"

"It's funny you should ask that, sir, because I think the Brotherhood's activities have escalated to the point that they're infringing on all of our spheres of influence. I discussed this with my superiors before we left Qianjin to come here, and they agree. In fact, they've authorized me to discuss the matter with the other two members of the Big Three. With your permission, I'd like Lieutenant-Commander Ross to come with me as Hawkwood's representative, because you're as involved in the whole Brotherhood mess as any of us. I think her expertise and breadth of knowledge will be very convincing."

"Caitlin?"

"I'd like to go, sir. This will be a unique experience."

"It will be necessary for Lieutenant-Commander Ross, and Hawkwood Corporation as well, to guarantee confidentiality," Chen cautioned.

"I think we can agree to that," Cochrane acknowledged. "Where will this meeting take place?"

Chen half-smiled. "Have you ever heard of the planet Bintulu?"

Caitlin sat bolt upright. "The underworld playground?"

"Oh, it's more than that – a great deal more."

"I'd heard of it, but only vague rumors," Cochrane noted.

"I think Lieutenant-Commander Ross will be able to tell you a lot more about it when we return, sir."

"I'll look forward to that. When will you leave?"

"If you'll let us use the Commander's communications vessel, we can be on our way in a few days. She should be fully fueled and stored, and her crew given a chance for liberty if possible, sir. We've worked them hard, and there's more of that ahead."

"All right. I'll arrange that. Meanwhile, both of you catch up on some rest and relaxation planetside. Oh – one more thing. Caitlin, you've done a great job so far. I think you've more than earned a promotion. While you're on R&R, get yourself the insignia of full Commander's rank."

She flushed. "Thank you, sir! That'll give me even more to celebrate."

19

REHABILITATION

MYCENAE SYSTEM

Frank looked up from his desk as Lieutenant-Commander Moncrieff knocked at the door. "What is it? Oh – it's you, doctor. Come in and sit down."

"Thank you, sir."

"What's this about our prisoners in your latest report?"

"Sub-Lieutenant Sejdiu is as medically recovered as he'll ever get from his head injury. I'd say it's left him with a propensity for headaches, but nothing much worse. However, he needs more rehabilitation than we can provide in Mycenae. The eight Kedan spacers with him are getting space-happy, too. He says their previous work never had them in space for more than two or three months at a time, but they've now been off-planet for over a year. They're getting a bit loopy, sir. I think all of them need time planetside, for psychological as well as physical health reasons."

Frank sighed. "I see your point, doctor. I know I get to the point, after too long in space, that I want to go planetside, find a nice storm, and stand outside in the wind and the rain, just to remind myself how nice it is to experience even bad weather occasionally!"

She laughed. "Me, too, sir. I'm looking forward to doing exactly that when my relief arrives next month."

"That gives me an idea. It'll be better for Sejdiu to make the transfer under medical supervision, right?"

"Well, yes, sir, although I think he's recovered enough that routine medical care could handle his needs."

"I daresay the Commodore would want us to be careful. I'll forward your report to him, and suggest that he find secure quarters where we can keep the prisoners planetside for a month or two. The officer can receive therapy, and the spacers can wander around outside and soak up some sun. They can travel to Constanta with you, so you can keep an eye on his condition."

～

CONSTANTA

Two weeks later, Cochrane read Frank's report and frowned. He skimmed through the doctor's recommendations, then summoned Tom Argyll and described the problem. "What can we do about this? Technically, Constanta is neutral territory. We've no legal right to hold prisoners here – hell, we've no legal right to hold them anywhere! It's not like we're a sovereign nation at war with another. We're just a private company, in the eyes of the law."

"Yes, sir. It might help if we became a sovereign nation. We could get away with a lot more!" They laughed softly together. "We bought that farm outside the city to house our security training camp. The off-planet instructors lived in the farmhouse, some distance from the training grounds. They've all left now, after bringing enough of us up to their level. Our own instructors don't live out there. Why don't we convert the farmhouse into quarters for our prisoners? We could extend it with temporary buildings, and put up a security barrier around it to keep the prisoners in and snoopers out. We could even treat it as a training exercise. I'll rotate our security teams through it to guard the prisoners, and warn them that our offensive teams will try to sneak past their guard or mount an attack, at least once every week. I'll offer a bonus to the offensive team every time they succeed, and to the defenders every time they spot them and keep them out. It'll keep both sides on their toes."

Cochrane grinned. "I like it! All right, get that set up. You've got about a month before the prisoners arrive. We'll bring them straight down to the farm in a cutter, bypassing customs and immigration. I'll square that with the Defense and Foreign Ministries. They take enough money in bribes for our armed vessel license each year that I don't think they'll turn a hair at a few temporary, unregistered visitors."

"What about that Sub-Lieutenant's medical care, sir?"

"I'll send his file over to Elizabeth, Captain Cousins' wife. She can recommend therapists to help with his rehabilitation. We'll send them out there to do it, rather than bring him into town. I won't take the risk that he might escape. That would be very embarrassing, not to mention very awkward if he got clean away. He hasn't told us anything about his own people, but he's always watching what's going on, according to Frank's reports. He's probably learned enough about how we do things to be valuable to them."

"All right, sir. I'll start getting things organized at the farmhouse."

Cochrane pulled up Sub-Lieutenant Sejdiu's file, including his medical records, and assembled the necessary details to be forwarded to Elizabeth Cousins. He was scrolling through the last few pages when Hui came in.

"What was that?" she asked curiously. "It looked like an X-ray."

"It was. It's our prisoner's skull after surgery, showing the repair. He was lucky to survive." He flipped back to the first page. "Here's what he looked like when we captured him." The image showed a limp, unconscious figure, blood running down his face from a depressed fracture above one eye. "Here he is a few weeks later, once he'd regained consciousness." The second picture showed a much-improved patient. His hair had been shaved around the operation site, but his eyes were clear, looking straight out at the lens, almost defiant in their expression.

"He's so *young!*" she exclaimed.

"Old enough to help kill our people, when it came to that. He's damned lucky Frank sent a courier ship to collect the survivors. After that sneak attack, I think our warships might not have bothered. One shot from a laser cannon, and that lifeboat would have ceased to be a problem." Cochrane sounded exasperated, but shook his head even as he spoke. "That would have been wrong, though, no matter how tempting. Someday some of our people may be in the same situation, and need rescuing. That's why I told the head of the Albanians that we had him. I want them to take prisoners, too, if they can, rather than kill our people out of hand, in the hope of an eventual exchange."

"Do you think they will?"

"I have no idea, but at least I tried."

Two weeks later, Hui walked the few blocks between Hawk-wood's premises and those of the Grigorescu Shipyard. She was expected, and ushered into the owner's office.

"Good morning, Matei. It's such a lovely day, I decided to hand-deliver the final payment for the conversion of those eighteen cargo shuttles, rather than just do an electronic transfer."

"Hello, Hui. It's good to see you again." He accepted the envelope from her. "We had a lot of trouble getting them to stay balanced in flight without their cargo compartments, but I think we got it right in the end – just as long as they don't run out of reaction mass. As soon as that happens, they'll be uncontrollable. You'll have to tow them to another ship to refuel their tanks."

She laughed. "I doubt they'll be flying anywhere without pods unless it's between ships, so they should never be far from a fuel source if they need one. You did good work, and quickly. Your shipyard's developing a well-earned reputation for quality."

"That's thanks to you. We were just a sleepy little backwater business, looking after local orbital craft and the occasional visiting freighter, until you came along. First there were those old patrol craft to be modernized, then all the modifications to commercial freighters, and maintenance work on your corvettes... you're becoming like a military Fleet in miniature, you know – and not so miniature, at that. We've had to grow fast, to keep pace with your needs. That's helped us attract business from off-planet, too. I've just signed a contract to modernize two old freighters for a cargo line on Jaelle, only a few light years away. They like the thought of keeping the work in the family, so to speak – our planets were colonized at the same time, both by Romanian groups."

"That's good news. I notice you're hiring a lot more people planetside, as well as aboard the shipyard in space. You've taken over two more floors of this building."

"Yes, we've had to. Our administration wasn't keeping pace with our growth. It was getting more and more difficult to keep track of everything. Fortunately, a few months ago, I was able to hire a very highly qualified accountant who'd recently arrived here. She's already transformed our management systems, giving us much better control. I'd be lost without them now."

"Sounds interesting. I must meet her. We might ask to borrow her for a few months after she revamps your systems, to look at our own."

Grigorescu shook his head. "I don't think she'll do it. I

mentioned you required anyone accessing your files to undergo your standard security screening, including truth-testing. She said something about that being 'an unpardonable invasion of privacy', and that she'd never allow a private company access to that much information about her. She found even the thought repellent."

"I can't say I blame her. It is repellent, in one sense. On the other hand, we're in a very high-risk business, with lots of security requirements that a typical company doesn't have. We've got to have those measures in place to protect ourselves."

"I suppose you do. Would you like to meet her, anyway? Her office is just down the corridor."

"Why not, while I'm here?"

Grigorescu ushered her down the passage and knocked at a half-open door. "Antonia, I'd like to introduce Captain Lu Hui. She's Hawkwood's Chief of Staff. Captain, this is Antonia Funar."

The attractive woman behind the desk looked up from her terminal, then rose to her feet. "Good morning, Captain. I've heard a lot of good things about you from Mr. Grigorescu."

"And he's said a lot of good things about you," Hui replied as they shook hands. She tried not to look too interested as she covertly scanned the accountant. She'd got to her feet in a smooth, effortless manner that hinted at strength and flexibility – not necessarily what one would expect in a business executive who looked to be in her late forties or early fifties. Her face was attractive, and her eyes particularly striking, with a rare gray-green coloration. Somehow, they nagged at Hui's subconscious. *Have I met her before?* she wondered. *Her eyes seem familiar.*

'Antonia' studied her visitor just as intently, if equally covertly. According to Agim's briefings, this woman was a senior officer in Qianjin's Fleet. Qianjin was home to the Dragon Tong, one of the Big Three criminal organizations the Patriarch had cited as the prime reason he'd begun the Fatherland Project. Not for the first time, she wondered what sort of ties could possibly exist between it and Hawkwood. Perhaps she could find out.

"What brings you to Constanta, Captain?" she asked. "I wouldn't have thought there was any reason for official contact between this planet and yours."

"A number of planets have problems with criminals interfering with asteroid mining activities. Hawkwood provides security to one operation like that, and it's negotiating with others to do the same. That's of interest to us from a professional point of view, so we exchange information with them, and keep each other informed. My position as Chief of Staff at Hawkwood is part of that. It helps me keep an eye on what they're doing, and helps them at the same time, because they don't have many staff-qualified officers, although they're training a number of them now."

"Do Hawkwood and your Fleet operate together?"

"No, it doesn't go that far – at least, not yet. If we both had sufficiently serious problems dealing with the same criminals, I suppose we might join forces to take care of them. That decision would be taken far above my pay grade, of course."

"I see." Inwardly, the spy felt a sudden chill. The Brotherhood was having enough trouble dealing with Hawkwood alone. If it had to face the armed forces of the Dragon Tong's planet as well, that might be too much to handle. This information, irrespective of anything else she learned, was enough to justify her mission. Agim would be seriously alarmed when he heard it. He would have to deal with Hawkwood before it could ally itself more closely with a more powerful enemy.

"I'd like to invite you to look at our management systems, as well as the shipyard's, but Mr. Grigorescu informs me you aren't willing to go through our security checks."

"No. I was raised to value my privacy. The thought of some truth-tester operator being able to rummage through my most intimate thoughts is very disturbing."

"But he can't. He can only detect whether or not your answers are true or false, not what you're thinking."

"That's not exactly true, Captain. If he establishes a pattern of questioning, true or false answers will reveal a lot. Say he wanted to know about my love life. He could ask questions about past partners, my attitudes, my experiences, and so on. If I didn't want to answer, or evaded a direct answer, that would show up as a lack of truthfulness. If he asked enough questions, he'd be able to pin down the subject, or event, or relationship, that was bothering me. That's going too far, in my opinion."

Hui nodded. "I see your point. Well, it's a pity, but we won't be able to use you, then."

"I don't think you'll be losing much. I've more than enough to keep me busy here for several months yet. I don't think I could take on more responsibilities right now."

As Hui walked back to Hawkwood's premises, her mind kept returning to the accountant's eyes. Something was bugging her about them. She shook her head as she walked into her office, trying to put it out of her mind and focus on the work that awaited her... but it kept coming back to her over the following days. Somewhere, she'd seen those eyes before.

TWO WEEKS LATER, the freighter *Pilot* slid into orbit around Constanta, after another monthly resupply run to Mycenae. Doctor Moncrieff met Tom Argyll and his security team in the docking bay. After the usual greetings, she assured him, "Sub-Lieutenant Sejdiu is doing fine, considering what he's been through. His mental functioning is at least ninety-five percent of what it was, and there's still slow improvement. Therapy, and a couple of months of breathing good, thick planetside air, and some long walks on grass and dirt instead of steel decks, will do him the world of good."

"And the Kedan spacers?"

She laughed. "They can't wait to get outside, either! They're like puppies or kittens, if you ask me, always playful and looking for fun. It's hard to regard them as enemies. In fact, I don't think they regard us as enemies at all. I think the Albanians hired them through their senior officers, without telling them they'd be fighting anyone or who their opponents were. I've grown to like them. They're simple people, uncomplicated."

"I'll brief our security people accordingly. We won't get far with a harsh approach. That would just alienate them. Gentle treatment is more likely to get us the cooperation we want."

"Exactly. The same goes for the Sub-Lieutenant. He won't speak of his service at all, but that's more of an attitude of a prisoner of war. He doesn't want to give away secrets. He doesn't strike me as a bad man."

"All right." Tom glanced over his shoulder at the guards who'd accompanied him. "You all heard that. Treat our prisoners gently, with as much kindness as possible. Make sure you pass that on to your reliefs planetside."

"Yes, sir," the Staff Sergeant in charge of the escort acknowledged, as his guards muttered their understanding. "We'll treat them like they were babies, and we were their mothers."

"Don't take that too far, or they might expect you to breast-feed them."

Doctor Moncrieff blinked, while the guards guffawed. "If your people manage that, I'll personally get your name into every medical journal in the settled galaxy! We'll make history – and our fortunes!"

The prisoners had no idea why the guards who escorted them aboard a cutter were laughing so much. They took it in their stride, though. Their anticipation at feeling sunshine on their skins, and smelling fresh, unprocessed air after so many months in space, was almost tangible.

LATER THAT AFTERNOON, Tom reported back to headquarters planetside. Hui was with Cochrane when he knocked at the door.

"Come in, Tom. Are our prisoners safe and sound?"

"Yes, sir. They're out at the farm. They were so excited to be planetside again, it took the guards almost an hour to herd them the hundred or so meters between the cutter landing pad and the farmhouse. They just wanted to stand there, kick off their boots and socks and walk barefoot on the grass, smell the flowers, all those things you just can't do in space."

"I hope you let them?"

"I didn't have the heart to pull them away, sir. Those Kedans really are like children, just like Doctor Moncrieff said. It's hard to dislike them. The officer's a bit more stiff and stand-offish, but he was enjoying himself just as much – he just didn't allow himself to show it."

Hui suddenly smacked her forehead with her palm. *"That's it!"*

The men stared at her in astonishment. "That's what, ma'am?" Tom asked.

"The eyes! That accountant's eyes, that Antonia Whatshername that Matei Grigorescu hired! I *knew* I'd seen them somewhere before!" She turned to Cochrane. "Can you bring up that prisoner's picture again – the one taken a few weeks after his surgery?"

"Sure."

They walked over to the desk. With a few keystrokes, Cochrane brought up the Albanian officer's file on his terminal. "Is that the one you meant?"

"That's it! Now, go to Grigorescu Shipyard's site on the planetary network."

"Just a moment." A few more keystrokes, and it was done.

"Right. Navigate to the pictures of corporate officers, and find that accountant."

Another couple of keystrokes. "Is this her? Antonia Funar?"

"That's her. Bring up her picture, and display it next to the picture of that officer."

Cochrane did as she had asked – then goggled at the screen. "What the *hell?*"

Tom said slowly, clearly as stunned as his boss, "If that's not a family resemblance, I've never seen one, sir."

"That's for sure. He's got the chin and jawline of a strong man, determined, set, but his eyes... they're so like hers, it's uncanny. That color, too, a sort of gray-green. That's not very common."

"There's something else you should know," Hui told them, her voice vibrating with excitement. She told them of the accountant's reluctance to undergo a truth-tester examination. "I thought at the time it was just a strong desire for personal privacy, but what if it was something more? What if she has something to hide? Could this be it – that she's related to the prisoner?"

They stared at each other wordlessly for several moments. At last Tom asked, his voice filled with concern, "If she's related to him, why would she have come here? Could it be she heard he was our prisoner, and thought she'd find him here? If so, why would she be working as an accountant, instead of looking around? There are so many questions, I don't know where to start asking them."

Cochrane said, "Let's do things a step at a time. Have some of your people keep her under surveillance. She may be trained – in fact, let's assume she's a highly trained agent, right from the start, to avoid making mistakes. Your people will have to watch her very discreetly, if necessary at a distance. Others can start checking her background. When did she arrive here, and why? What did she do after that? When and why did she start working at Grigorescu? Meanwhile, send a couple of your investigators to Onesta – that's where her bio says she was born and raised. I'll give them a courier ship to make a fast trip. Make sure her flight plan doesn't mention Onesta at all, in case this 'Antonia' is watching for that. Tell them to find out everything they can about her there, and to work fast. I want them back here as quickly as possible, certainly inside a month."

"What should we do about the prisoner in the meantime, sir?"

"I think he's safe enough out at the farm. She won't know he's there, and your surveillance team can alert the guards if she drives out that way. That'll give them time to get the prisoners under cover and out of sight."

"Aye aye, sir. I'll get right on it."

20

INTRUSION

MYCENAE SYSTEM

Frank was at *Jean Bart*'s docking bay to greet Commander Darroch as he boarded the depot ship from his gig. "Welcome back, Angus!" he called, as *Bobcat*'s commanding officer came through the airlock.

"It's good to be back, sir." They shook hands firmly.

"Come on down to my office." As they headed for the high-speed walkway, Frank added, "I take it *Bobcat* didn't need to go back into the dockyard for any more modifications?"

"No, sir. You seem to have identified all the problems during her first tests. They fixed everything you found while they lengthened her. She's passed every test with flying colors, and the Commodore has approved the start of frigate production using her modified design. The next two corvettes, *Wolfsbane* and *Aconite,* will be delivered soon, and two frigates, *Caracal* and *Jaguarundi,* will take their place on the production line. You should see them here to work up in about nine or ten months from now, sir."

"It can't come too soon for me! Once they're ready for service,

I'll be the new Officer in Command of Hawkwood's First Frigate
Division."

"That's great, sir! Who'll take your place here?"

"I don't know yet, but there are a couple of candidates. A lot
depends on whether we sign another system security contract. If
we do, that'll need another senior officer to command that
station. He'll have a depot ship, a courier vessel and four
corvettes under his command."

"Sounds like Hawkwood's going to be expanding even more,
sir."

"It does. Those of us on board now can look forward to lots of
hard work, and good prospects to make lots of money."

Darroch snorted. "What was the old toast in the wet-water
Royal Navy before the French Revolution? 'A bloody war or a
sickly season', I think it was. They had far too many officers as the
result of previous wars. A lot of them were put ashore on half-pay,
because there were no berths for them, what with so many ships
being placed in reserve. The only openings for advancement, or
even just a seagoing appointment, were if a more senior officer
died or retired."

"I hadn't heard that one. I'm glad we don't have that problem.
Is *Bobcat* ready for duty?"

"She is, sir. Her crew had already gained a lot of experience
under your command during her first trials, so we combined the
second series of trials with working-up exercises. We're fighting
fit and ready to go."

"Good. I'll start you on patrols tomorrow, to let you practice
working with the system surveillance satellite and the minefield
around Secundus Two. We've got almost three hundred in place
now, patrolling out to five million kilometers from the planet, but
leaving the approach and departure lanes clear."

"We'll be ready, sir."

BROTHERHOOD SHIP SARANDA

The courier vessel *Saranda* was moving relatively slowly on this
pass through the Mycenae system. Her previous visit had yielded
some worthwhile intelligence, but her maximum velocity of four-
tenths of light speed had made it very difficult for her sensors to
take accurate readings. This time, she was forgoing the greater
security of speed in favor of the higher precision of slower
movement.

Lieutenant-Commander Malaj called the ship to general
quarters as it approached the planet known simply as Mycenae
Secundus Two. He took his seat at the command console, and
prepared to supervise the collection of every emission from every
ship in orbit around, or on patrol near, the Hawkwood base. He
concentrated on that, to the exclusion of almost every other
activity on board.

In the Engineering Department, Lieutenant Belushi hovered
over the dials and gauges on his monitoring board. The gravitic
drive was, of course, shut down, to avoid emissions that the
enemy could track. However, if sudden maneuvers were needed,
it would have to be brought up without delay. What's more, the
gravitic shield, also produced by the gravitic drive and designed
to deflect debris in the path of the ship, was still in operation. It
would be far too dangerous to proceed without it at any speed
worthy of the name. Even a pea-sized piece of debris might penetrate *Saranda* from end to end, if struck head-on at a significant
fraction of light speed. What the colossal kinetic energy released
by that impact would do to the ship, and everyone aboard her,
didn't bear thinking about.

He scowled across the room at the four Kedan spacers – 'technicians' in name only, as far as he was concerned – who stood
against the bulkhead, ready to act on his command. He turned to
the Petty Officer beside him at the console. "Keep an eye on those
monkeys. Make sure they don't do anything except what we tell

them. I don't want them screwing up this pass, and us having to carry the can for it!" He didn't bother to lower his voice.

"I will, sir," the NCO assured him.

The senior of the four Keda men bit his lip to stop himself making a very rude remark in Albanian, learned the hard way from the NCO's who'd bullied and prodded his men into learning their jobs over the past year. It hurt to be treated like an animal, dismissed contemptuously as worthless or uncivilized. However, there was nothing they could do about it... yet.

He glanced at the entrance to the ship's minuscule docking bay, where a cutter and a gig waited. It offered a potential reprieve from the stifling atmosphere in the engineering control room. He asked, in broken Albanian, "Sir, should we clean out the cutter while we have nothing else to do? I noticed it was dirty, the last time we were inside."

"Then why didn't you clean it right away? You know where the cleaning gear is. Get on with it!"

"Aye aye, sir."

As the officer watched the four men hurry out, he said to no-one in particular, "At least they've learned enough to take the dirty work off our hands, even if they haven't got the sense to do it without being told."

The NCO grunted. "Suits me, sir. I'll save my time and energy for more important stuff."

THE ELECTRONIC 'BRAIN' of an autonomous orbital mine cannot be said to 'think' at all. If it could have felt emotion, it would have been utterly astonished to find a spaceship bearing down on it, and shoving it rudely out of its way as it rushed by.

As *Saranda* passed close to Secundus Two, keeping five million kilometers away from the planet to avoid even the slightest risk of detection, its gravitic shield deflected one of the outermost of the mines protecting the vessels orbiting the planet, that had strayed too close to its path. The ship broadcast no emissions at all, so the mine could not 'see' what had disturbed its peaceful vigil; but its onboard computer knew that only one thing could have done this. The mine instantly switched its array from passive to active mode, bathing surrounding space in a torrent of radar energy.

Saranda was well past the mine by the time it detected her, and out of range of its laser cone. That did not stop the mine broadcasting the position and course of the intruder at full power to every other mine nearby. Its warning was also picked up by the mine control console in the Operations Center aboard *Jean Bart*. The message was instantly relayed to every Hawkwood ship in the Mycenae system. Light speed delay meant that many ships would not receive it right away... but it was propagating at ten times *Saranda*'s velocity.

As more mines received the signal, they, too, switched on their active sensors. Several of them also obtained readings of *Saranda*'s course and speed, and relayed them to the OpCen. Now the intruder's trajectory and velocity could be plotted more accurately, and more precise warnings issued – along with orders to intercept her.

THE CONTACT between the mine and *Saranda*'s gravitic deflection shield was very light and very fleeting, over almost before it had begun. Nevertheless, it shook *Saranda* hard, taking everyone on board completely by surprise. Those not strapped into chairs or bunks were sent flying as the deck heaved beneath their feet. Several were injured as they slammed into bulkheads, furniture, and each other.

The ship's hull whiplashed slightly as the energy of the deflection was passed down her length, like a ripple passing through water. The sliding cover over the docking bay, presenting a smooth, stealthy surface to protect against radar or lidar detection, buckled as its frame twisted around it. It popped out and flew away from the ship, moving outwards as it began to diverge from her base trajectory. It would leave the system in due course on its own path, to be lost in the trackless wastes of deep space and never seen again.

The ship's gig and cutter, secured by locking bars holding them against the airlocks in the docking bay, were rocked back and forth. The smaller, lighter gig withstood the flexing of the hull, and remained in place. The larger, heavier cutter did not. Her inertia snapped all but one of the locking bars securing her. In an automatic reaction to the suddenly unsafe condition of its connection, the concertina tunnel extending from the ship's hull to her rear ramp withdrew into its housing. As its sensors recognized that the tunnel was unlocking from around it, the ramp's emergency system kicked into action. It slammed closed and sealed itself with a sudden hiss, preventing the cutter's internal atmosphere from escaping.

The four Kedan spacers were tossed about inside the small craft as if they were rag dolls. One broke his neck against a storage cabinet as he slammed into one of its sharp corners at just the wrong angle. The others were knocked unconscious as their heads struck the inside of the hull. The cleaning materials they were using splashed and splattered all over the interior.

As *Saranda* sped onward, the cutter swayed and tugged against the restraint of the sole locking bar still holding it in place.

～

LIEUTENANT-COMMANDER MALAJ CURSED VIOLENTLY as he struggled to make sense of what had just happened. *Saranda* had clearly suffered a near-miss with something big and heavy, but what? There were no gravitic drive emissions anywhere near her. Worse, there were now small active radar emitters lighting off from several point sources nearby. He knew they would obtain reflections from his ship's hull. If the enemy could track them and work out his course and speed, they might be able to intercept him.

He hit the release buckle of his harness, thrust himself to his feet, and hurried across to the Plot, where the operator – who had not fastened his harness – was groaning on the floor, holding his right arm. "Stand up, man!" he snapped as he stepped over him. "Return to your duties at once!"

"My arm, sir – I think it's broken!"

"Then call for a relief at once! You can't go to sick bay until someone's taken over your post."

"Yes, sir." The man struggled to his knees and crawled over to the Communications console.

Malaj scanned the three-dimensional plot carefully. Anything behind him was no longer a concern. It would take them too long to catch him, and even if they tried, he could always increase speed and outrun them. The problem was the three ships ahead of him, on inner and outer system patrol. Could any of them possibly change course in time to reach him, before he could leave the system?

Muttering in aggravation at having to do it himself, he instructed the Plot computer to calculate the odds of interception. Almost at once, it highlighted an icon in the display. Only one enemy ship, with a gravitic drive signature resembling that of a destroyer, could get close enough to *Saranda* to threaten her. He made up his mind at once. He would have to take evasive action. Fortunately, a destroyer could achieve about one-third Cee at best. He could exceed that comfortably. Combined with a ten-degree change in trajectory, it would be enough that even her missiles, building upon her base speed as she drew closer, would not be able to reach *Saranda*.

He hurried back to his command console and checked his calculations. Satisfied, he called to the Helm console, "Drive to full power! Change course to 090:100!"

"Drive to full, course 90:100, sir!"

The Helm operator was still startled and shaken by the sudden jolt of the near-collision with the mine. He didn't operate the controls as smoothly as usual. Instead, he slammed the power slider all the way from 'Stop' to 'Full Ahead' in a single swift motion, even as he tipped the course control joystick over to one side.

The courier vessel jolted again, hard, as her drive cut in with unaccustomed abruptness. The remaining locking bar holding the cutter to the ship sheared under the stress. The cutter was ejected cleanly from the wide-open docking bay, floating away on the ship's original course as the larger vessel's trajectory began to change. It drifted, without power or beacon or anything else to indicate its presence, as its mother ship accelerated away.

~

HCS BOBCAT

Commander Darroch settled into his chair at the Command console as *Bobcat*'s crew charged to their action stations. He glanced at the Plot, and bared his teeth in an aggressive grin. The unknown contact had gone to what looked like full power, and was accelerating at a rate that proved she must be a courier vessel. No other type of spaceship could move that fast; but *Bobcat* came close, thanks to having a full-size destroyer power plant and gravitic drive in a hull at least twelve thousand tons lighter than that class of ship. She had touched point-three-seven-five Cee on her trials. What's more, her missiles were cruiser sized units, with twice the range and power of corvette weapons. Judging from their minor course change, the enemy clearly did not expect or understand either factor.

"Command to Navigator. Give me a course to intercept, or at least put us within missile range. I think we can do it from here at max power."

"Navigator to Command, wait one, sir... calculating... got it!" A course appeared on Darroch's console. "Steer that, sir, at full emergency power, and we'll be within missile range in about half an hour. She can't change course much further without running afoul of either *Monkshood* or *Datura* in the outer system."

"Helm, make it so. Full emergency power. Let's get 'em!"

The OpCen throbbed with anticipation as *Bobcat* accelerated in pursuit of her prey.

BROTHERHOOD SHIP SARANDA

Lieutenant-Commander Malaj left the Navigator in temporary control of the OpCen, while he went to investigate the sudden lurch as *Saranda* had begun to accelerate. He excoriated Lieutenant Belushi in harsh, intemperate language when he discovered that the cutter was gone, and the docking bay open to space. "Why didn't you find this out earlier, and report it to me?"

"Sir, I – we were busy with –"

"I don't care what you were busy with! You're the Engineer Officer, damn you! It's *your* job to stay on top of your department, *not mine,* you useless sonofabitch!"

He stormed back to the OpCen, fuming. He'd highlight every line of Belushi's next fitness report in red, he decided silently, and see to it that he never commanded anything larger or better than a sanitation scow for the rest of his career. He was so preoccupied with his anger and frustration that he failed to notice the movements of the nearest enemy vessel for some time. The OpCen crew, sensing his fury, were reluctant to draw attention to themselves by mentioning it. It was, after all, his responsibility to stay on top of the overall situation, not theirs.

At last the Plot operator said, hesitantly, "Plot to Command. The nearest enemy vessel is accelerating very fast, sir."

"What?" Malaj was jolted out of his preoccupation. He scanned the display swiftly. "You *fool!* Why didn't you report her earlier?"

"Sir, it's not clear that she's a threat. Corvette missiles don't have the range or speed to catch us from her nearest possible approach."

The commanding officer ran some rapid calculations, and mellowed slightly. "You're right, but you should still have warned me. Besides, her gravitic drive's more powerful than a corvette's – more like a destroyer's. Their missiles can't reach us, either, but I'd prefer more of a safety margin. She can't be a destroyer, though. She's already moving faster than they're capable of. What the hell *is* she?"

He made sure they were recording every detail of their escape. Captain Toci would want to know as much as possible about this new ship. As for the other ships, *Saranda* couldn't change course much further without risking interception by the two corvettes further out in the system, which were already charging toward her predicted trajectory at full power.

"We'll remain on this course," he decided. "It's the safest option open to us."

∾

HCS BOBCAT

"She's almost in range, sir."

Commander Darroch smiled in satisfaction as the Weapons Officer gave him the good news. "Hold on, Lieutenant. Let's get closer. Once she realizes our missiles are much longer-ranged than a ship this size should be able to carry, she's going to take evasive action. I want to get close enough to fire a pattern wide enough that some of our missiles will catch her, no matter which way she dodges. We can follow that up with a second pattern, if necessary, to nail her down."

"Aye aye, sir. I'll prepare a firing plan along those lines."

"Do that, Lieutenant. If you miss her, I'll cancel your commission, disrate you to Spacer Third Class, and have you on latrine duty out here in the Mycenae system for the rest of your career!" A chuckle ran around the OpCen.

It took no more than a few minutes for *Bobcat*'s powerful battle computer, newly upgraded to Kang Industries' latest and much-improved design, to work out the details. The Weapons Officer reported, quiet triumph in his voice, "She'll be in range of our wide pattern in seven minutes, sir. After that, it won't matter what she does. We'll have her by the short and curlies."

BROTHERHOOD SHIP SARANDA

"Vampire! *Vampire!* Missiles fired, sir!"

Lieutenant-Commander Malaj jolted erect in his command chair, utterly astonished. "But they're out of range! There's no way their missiles have enough powered range to reach us as we flash past them! They're wasting an entire salvo!"

Even as he watched, the incoming missiles diverged, spreading into a wide pattern. He knew what that portended. They wanted to make sure he couldn't dodge fast or far enough to avoid them all. He thought uneasily, *What have they got up their sleeve? They must know their missiles don't have the range or speed to reach me from there!*

Within a minute, it became obvious that these were no ordinary corvette or destroyer missiles. They were accelerating too fast. They had more power than they should have had, and probably more fuel, too. His stomach knotted in sudden fear as he hammered at his keyboard. The ship's computer calculated an optimal course to evade, and threw it onto his and the Helm's console. "Command to Helm! Get onto that course, fast as you can!"

"Aye aye, sir!"

It was no good. The thirty missiles screamed closer. He knew that at least two-thirds would miss... but six to eight might reach him. His only hope was that they would be at such extreme range that their laser cones, designed for a range of ten to twelve thousand kilometers, would spread so wide that *Saranda* could slip between their beams.

Unfortunately for his hopes, *Bobcat*'s big missiles carried cones stuffed with twice as many laser rods as those on corvette weapons... and they were long-ranged enough to get within effective firing range before unleashing them.

~

HCS BOBCAT

"Approaching engagement range, sir," the Weapons Officer called sharply.

The OpCen crew stared in absorbed fascination at the Plot display as *Bobcat*'s missiles closed in. Seven of them made it to firing range, swiveled to point their laser cones at the target, and detonated in giant circular thermonuclear fireballs. Out of each explosion, no less than fifty laser beams slashed and tore at the fleeing vessel.

Saranda shuddered and shook as beams pierced her every compartment. More than half her crew, including Lieutenant-Commander Maraj, were already dead by the time a laser smashed through her fusion reactor, venting its fury on everything around it as it died an actinic death. The courier vessel vanished in a fireball to match those of the missiles that had destroyed her.

Darroch exhaled, a long, slow sigh of satisfaction. "Well done, Weapons! Looks like your commission is safe for now. Let's –"

He was interrupted by an urgent call from the Plot. "Sir! Unknown beacon activated, far back along the target's former trajectory. It's not a lifeboat, or a ship – or if it is, it's like no ship's beacon I've ever seen. It may be a small craft, sir."

"What the hell?" Darroch wondered aloud. "Let's find out. Navigator, give me a course to close on that beacon. We'll approach it carefully, and see what it is. Weapons, work up a firing solution as we approach, but do not fire, I say again, *do not fire* without my express authority."

"Navigator to Command, aye aye, sir."

"Weapons to Command, aye aye, sir."

THE SENIOR KEDAN spacer staggered to his feet aboard the drifting, slowly tumbling cutter, holding his aching head. He shook the two men lying near him, but they were still out cold. His eyes filled with tears as he saw Putera lying in the corner, not breathing, his head at an impossible angle to his body. Clearly, he had not survived whatever had happened.

He dragged himself over to the pilot's console. He knew nothing of how to control a small craft, but he knew enough to recognize many of the dials, gauges, switches and levers. His eyes fastened upon the communications panel, and gleamed as he spotted the controls for the small craft's identification beacon. He reached out and flipped a switch, then sat back. He did not know how long help would take to arrive, but surely someone, somewhere in the system, would detect it and come to investigate.

Softly, mournfully, he began to recite the prayers for Putera's soul.

IT TOOK several hours for *Bobcat* to slow down, change her trajectory to rendezvous with the drifting cutter, and have her own small craft tow it back to her docking bay. Efforts to dock it were hampered by the snapped-off docking bars still attached to its hull, preventing the use of normal methods. In the end, an emergency airlock of flexible tubing was hurriedly jury-rigged, extending from the ship's hull to the cutter's rear ramp while the small craft was held suspended by tractor and pressor beams. Armed spacers opened the ramp, to find the hapless Kedan crew members inside. They were more than happy to surrender peacefully.

By then Commander Darroch had been in communication with Captain Haldane on *Jean Bart*. Following instructions, he treated the rescued spacers with kindness, communicating with them through commercial translation programs that had been refined through experience with the spacers captured from *Ilaria* some time before. By the time *Bobcat* returned to orbit around Mycenae Secundus Two, the Kedans were beginning to relax, reassured that their days of unending harsh treatment were over.

Frank met *Bobcat's* cutter in the docking bay. Darroch exited first. As Frank shook his hand and congratulated him, the prisoners and their escort emerged, to be met with a relaxed martial formality.

The senior surviving Kedan spacer drew himself up and looked at the obviously senior officer speaking to Darroch. He clearly wished to speak. Frank noticed, and turned to him. "You wanted to say something?"

The spacer saluted formally, and Frank returned it. "Sir, our fallen comrade. It is our custom to bury our dead on the day they die, or at least as quickly as possible after that. Can... can anything be done to allow us to honor him?"

Frank listened to the computer translation, and frowned. "You said 'bury'? We can't bury anybody in space."

"No, sir. We have had to accept the usual space custom of dropping the dead into the nearest star, when there is no other way; but there is a planet below us. May we bury him there, please?"

"You realize it's an airless, lifeless planet? I don't know that any human being has ever set foot on its surface."

"That will not matter to God, sir. He created all things, including that planet. Even though our brother may be the only human ever buried there, and his grave remain deserted for the rest of time, his soul will know we did our best for him, and God will too."

Frank was nonplussed for a moment. It would mean extra time and trouble for *Jean Bart*'s crew to escort the prisoners planetside, dig a grave, and bury the dead man; but it would give the captives peace of mind, and perhaps an incentive to provide information more willingly. On balance, it was worth trying. He nodded. "Yes, you may do that. How do you prepare your dead for burial?"

"We wash them, and wrap them in white cloth. Could we...?"

"I'll give orders that you be supplied with the necessary materials. Prepare him, then a cutter will take you planetside, along with an escort."

The spacer's knees suddenly felt wobbly with relief. "Thank you, sir! *Thank you!*" Clearly, their captors were going to treat them far better than their employers had ever done.

The following morning, as time was recorded aboard Hawkwood's ships in the system, a cutter descended toward the unnamed, airless planet. The Kedan spacers peered through the pilot's viewscreen as it descended, and unanimously picked a small, flat peak in the foothills of an impressively soaring mountain range, looking out over a seemingly endless, dusty plain, pockmarked with craters. The small craft landed to one side of the summit, and its space-suited occupants got out, carrying with them small, improvised explosive shaped charges and other tools.

The charges made quick work of loosening the rock and hard-packed dirt, and shovels scraped it aside to produce a usable grave. The three surviving Kedans laid the body tenderly in the grave, and helped their escort cover it once more with the soil and shattered rock excavated to make room for it. A simple metal sheet, cut to resemble a gravestone, was inserted at its head, with the dead spacer's name, and dates of birth and death, painted on it. The senior Kedan led his comrades in the traditional funeral prayers, after which the escort fired three volleys over the grave from their bead carbines. There was no sound in the airless void as the shots were fired. They aimed toward the mountains behind the grave, serving as a monumentally large backstop for the first and almost certainly the only time in their existence.

When the cutter returned to *Jean Bart,* the senior Kedan asked to speak to the guard commander. What he said led the NCO to make a hurried call, which led to more calls, which led to a visit to the brig by Captain Haldane.

"You wanted to see me?" he said to the spacer.

"Yes, sir," came the reply through the translation computer. "You have treated us well, and helped us to render final honors to our fallen brother. For this, we thank you, and are willing to help you in any way we can. Do you need our services as spacers?"

Frank thought fast. "I don't think I can do that, although if you're prepared to give your word that you won't make any trouble, we can give you better and more comfortable accommodation, with fewer restrictions. What we really need is information. We don't know enough about the Albanians who hired you – how many people they have, how many ships, what their plans are. We don't even know where their base is, for heaven's sake! Anything you can tell us may be helpful."

"We shall do that, sir. Ah... you said you don't know where their base is?"

Frank felt a wild hope surge within him. "No. Do you?"

"Not exactly, sir, but I may be able to get close. You see, after our first trip to this system, our ship journeyed to a planet called Patos, and then back to our base again. I was in the Engineering crew the whole time. On the console there, they showed our course, plus the distance covered in each hyper-jump. Due to the age of her capacitor ring, restricting its storage capacity, *Saranda* jumped eighteen-point-four light years at maximum charge, rather than her designed twenty. I remember her course both ways, and how many times she jumped on each journey between departure and arrival. Would that help?"

"It sure would! I'll have you talk with our Navigator, and we'll see what we can figure out."

⁓

HCS JEAN BART

The following morning, Frank and *Jean Bart*'s Navigating Officer, Lieutenant Fullerton, met at the Plot console. "How did it go?" Frank asked.

"Sir, I have the approximate – but not exact – dates of *Saranda*'s trips to Patos and back from her base, and the courses she followed each time, reckoned from departure from each point to the system boundary, which I've presumed to be in a straight line to her destination. I know how many jumps she made, and I've been able to extrapolate approximately how many light years that covered each way. I know the movement of the stars, so I've been able to make some allowance for that, although without knowing exact dates for her trips, it's impossible to pin down her starting and ending points with high precision. Putting all that together, I think I can place their base inside a sphere with a radius of about one hundred light years. I can't be more precise than that, sir."

"That's still a hell of a lot closer than nothing! Show me."

The Navigator changed the Plot display to reflect a star map, and highlighted a region. "There, sir. It's about six hundred light years from here."

Frank studied it. "There are no inhabited planets marked within it – the nearest is about twenty light years outside the sphere. I make it fifteen... no, sixteen deserted star systems inside that circle."

"Actually, sir, there are seventeen. One's a minor system, hidden from this angle behind a larger one."

"All right." He heaved a sigh. "Like I said, this gives us something concrete for the first time. I'll report this to Commodore Cochrane. Well done, and thank you."

As Frank headed for his office to write his report, he couldn't help thinking that the Albanians might have brought nemesis upon themselves. They'd virtually shanghaied the Kedan spacers into their service, without their consent or understanding. They'd treated them almost like slaves. Now, those 'slaves' might have contributed to the undoing of their hated and resented 'masters'.

He grinned to himself. There was something very fitting about that.

21

CONFERENCE

BINTULU

A s soon as the communications vessel had made its arrival signal to Bintulu System Control, Chen sent another, encrypted signal to the Qianjin embassy on the planet. "I've asked them to clear our path through Customs and Immigration," he explained to Caitlin Ross as the ship arrowed toward the planet. "That'll avoid unnecessary delays."

She frowned. "You've been very mysterious about Bintulu all the way here. Isn't it time you told me what's going on?"

"I suppose it is, but please remember what I said to the Commodore when he approved your coming with me. This is all confidential. A lot of it's an open secret, but we still don't talk about it, because having undue attention drawn to it would be... awkward... for all sorts of people and organizations."

"I'll be the soul of discretion."

"Thank you. I suppose I should begin at the beginning. Do you know where the name Bintulu comes from?"

"I can't say I do."

"It was a town in the Malayan state of Sarawak on Old Home Earth."

"Sarawak? Oh, yes!" She couldn't help a giggle. "I remember, as a teenager, reading a blood-curdling romance about it – a swooning virgin kidnapped by swarthy pirates, then rescued by a heroic heavily-muscled figure full of dash and derring-do. She married him, and they founded a dynasty together. It was called 'The White Rajah of Sarawak', and claimed to be the 'true story' of someone named James Brooke."

"I'm impressed! You're better informed than I thought. There really was a James Brooke, and he was the first so-called 'White Rajah'. It's also true that Sarawak, his fiefdom, was infested with pirates. They only gave up that way of life when he threatened to exterminate them unless they did. He had to make brutal examples of a few villages before they learned he wasn't joking. He never married, so that romance you remember didn't get everything right, but he was a very impressive man, by all accounts.

"When the Scramble for Space started, some businessmen from Sarawak could read the signs of the times. They leveraged their hydrocarbon revenues to buy a prospector ship, and sent some of their sons away to look for a planet where they could settle. They knew Old Home Earth was in a downward spiral, and didn't expect things to improve anytime soon. They were right, of course. The ship found this planet, and claimed it. Over the next century or so, the families of the discoverers moved here. They named it for the city most of them came from.

"It's said that a lot of their early revenues, before they got a local economy going, came from space piracy. That's not unlikely, given their ancestry, but it's hotly denied by the present government, and it's very politically incorrect to mention it. In due course, Bintulu adopted a strict policy that no outside criminal activity would be tolerated within its system. They wanted to avoid reprisals from the victims of piracy elsewhere, by claiming that no such crimes had ever been committed here. They developed a pretty strong System Patrol Service to make sure their new enthusiasm for law and order took hold. Some outsiders didn't want to listen, so they were used as examples to show others what happened to idiots like that."

"If the place was settled by pirates, and they had the example of the White Rajah to inspire them, I imagine the punishments were vivid enough to drive home that point."

"Very much so. I understand one crew was literally made to 'walk the plank' out of an airlock of their spaceship, into vacuum, without benefit of spacesuits. It was filmed and broadcast."

"Doesn't sound like entertainment to me."

"I daresay it didn't to the guests of honor, either. Anyway, over time, Bintulu's role expanded. It's now considered neutral ground and a 'safe haven' by every major criminal organization. They come here to relax, hold discussions, or do legitimate business, but never to plan or commit crimes. The punishment for that is still extreme, and there are no exceptions, no matter who's involved. All the Big Three have 'embassies' here, to liaise with each other. Several smaller groups do the same. It's a clearing-house for information for all of us."

"A sort of criminal United Planets?"

"I suppose you could call it that. Interplanetary arrest warrants aren't honored here, so unless you commit a crime locally, you won't be detained or extradited. The reverse of that coin is that Bintulu has 'arrangements' with people like us. If someone offends here and tries to flee off-planet, he'll be found and brought back, dead or alive. It tends to keep everyone on the straight and narrow.

"Because of that freedom from arrest, the Bintulu system's become a center for the transshipment of cargoes. The planetary government leased out to local merchants the entire orbitals of the fourth planet from this star. It's airless, and not needed for anything better. Anything that goes on there is legally the responsibility of the leaseholders, not Bintulu itself, and planetary

police don't operate there. The merchants built vast orbital ware-
houses and freight handling facilities. They accept cargoes from
incoming ships, and trade them for goods already here. No-one
asks any questions, meaning that stolen goods might wind up
hundreds of light years from where they came. That makes them
almost completely untraceable."

Caitlin frowned. "But surely, if you know all this, so does
interplanetary law enforcement? Why don't they come looking
for stolen goods here? Why doesn't the United Planets just shut
the place down?"

"You don't get it. Bintulu is as useful to law enforcement as it
is to criminals. For a start, you can't take action without evidence.
It takes time for news of a crime to circulate to other planets.
Until that happens, who's to say that certain goods in transit
through the Bintulu system were stolen? By the time word
reaches here, the goods will be long gone, so where's your
evidence? Also, it's become common to list stolen items of importance on a local network, offering a reward for their return.
Sometimes, the reward is higher than the thieves could make by
shipping it elsewhere, or high enough to bring it back from wherever it went. In such cases, private arrangements are made. It's all
very discreet.

"What's more, a lot of law enforcement agencies from all over
the settled galaxy have offices here, keeping their fingers on the
pulse, so to speak, to try to figure out what big-time criminals are
doing. The local authorities don't mind, as long as no-one makes
trouble of any sort. It's a kind of unofficial truce, and oddly
civilized."

"How do those merchants make their money, if they aren't
selling goods of their own?"

"They charge premium rates for the use of their orbital facilities, and a percentage on the value of exchanged goods. Bintulu
takes ten percent off the top in taxation. That doesn't sound high,
but when you consider the volume and value of goods passing

through this system, it adds up to a very nice sum. On top of asteroid mining fees, customs tariffs and business levies, it brings in enough that the planet doesn't need income or consumption taxes."

Caitlin grinned. "Sounds like a good place to live."

"They probably wouldn't let you in. They're very restrictive about immigration, although tourists are always welcome. If you have enough money to buy a protective residence permit, and promise to behave, they'll make an exception, of course.

"Anyway, let's get back to business. The Qianjin Embassy will notify the authorities that we're above board, so we won't be delayed during arrival formalities. When we get planetside, I'll ask the Embassy to set up a three-way meeting with the embassies of the Cosa Nostra and Nuevo Cartel, so you can make your presentation. There may be proposals for action following your briefing, or everything may be referred to higher authority. I daresay there'll be follow-up meetings in due course, if everyone thinks it's appropriate."

"I suppose I won't be involved in those."

"You never know. Hawkwood's impressed us with its capabilities. If the others feel the same way, they might want you to remain involved. We'll have to wait and see."

KAMPUNG, Bintulu's capital city, was divided by the Batang River. Its two halves were a study in contrasts. West Kampung was a fairly standard medium-size city, with a spaceport, a built-up business district, a smaller entertainment and shopping area, and several residential suburbs. East Kampung was another matter. It was centered around a thriving entertainment hub, with hotels, casinos, nightclubs, theaters, restaurants and other diversions. On the hillside above were several imposing buildings housing embassies and consulates, spreading out to residential suburbs with luxurious homes set in spacious grounds, heavily patrolled by a private police force.

"That's the area for visitors," Chen pointed out as they flew over it in the shuttle bringing them down from the orbiting space station. "East Kampung is basically set aside for them. Regular planetary laws and rules are relaxed there. If you've come for a good time, that's where you'll find it. West Kampung is for the locals, although many of them go across the river to have a good time. It's the seat of government, too."

"And the houses in East Kampung?"

"They're for people who choose to settle here, for health or other reasons. If you've been in a line of work where rivalries tend to be settled in blood, it can be difficult to simply retire in peace and quiet. Also, there are takeovers and mergers, just like in the business world, but they tend to be rather more aggressive. If someone comes out on the losing end, or wants to drop out of a criminal lifestyle for whatever reason, they can move here. They've got to have money, of course; a protective resident permit costs millions, and those houses and estates aren't cheap, and the security provided for them costs a lot. On the other hand, nobody's going to bother them here, because – well, this is Bintulu."

"I see. Surely they must get bored, though?"

"Perhaps, but at least they're still alive. A lot of them begin more regular careers here, investing in the entertainment industry, or helping their children to make a fresh start, here or off-planet. It may not be safe for those born off-planet to leave here, but their offspring usually can, provided they stay on the straight and narrow. Their parents' enemies will still be out there, ready to deal with the second or third generation if it tries to take after the first."

The Qianjin Embassy accommodated them in a guest house in its grounds, luxuriously furnished and equipped. The envoy who collected them from the spaceport explained that the meeting they'd requested had already been set up for the following morning. "We'll use a room in the East Kampung Conference Center," she explained. "It's the usual procedure. Security is good there, and the place is swept for listening devices every week."

The conference center proved to be a modern, well-equipped building with very heavy security. Guards patrolled the grounds, a security desk denied entry to all but authorized persons, and a counter in the central lobby on each floor further ensured privacy and confidentiality. They were shown to a room on the third level, where a central table was flanked by eight chairs. Audio-visual equipment was provided for presentations, and Caitlin set up her personal data system while they waited for the other delegates to arrive.

Augustu Cravotta represented the Cosa Nostra. He was a short, rotund, florid man, with sharp, bright eyes that never stopped flickering from person to person. He was accompanied by an aide who was not introduced, but sat behind his chair, recording the discussion. The Nuevo Cartel emissary, Hernando Torres, was tall and thin, almost cadaverous, his sunken cheeks and pitch-black eyes seeming to pierce right through whomever he was looking at. Caitlin was sure he was wearing dark contact lenses to disguise his true eye color. His aide, a buxom young woman, also was not introduced.

As soon as everyone was seated and brief introductions of the principals had been made, Chen got proceedings under way. "Thank you for attending this meeting. We asked for it in order to tell you of an interplanetary problem that has affected the Dragon Tong, and which we know is affecting your organizations as well. Commander Caitlin Ross represents a company, Hawk-wood Security, that has spearheaded the investigation of and fight against a breakaway faction of the Albanian Mafia, an offshoot of the Bregija Clan calling itself the Albanian Brotherhood. They're stealing asteroids to fund a particular project. I'll let her outline what's been going on."

Caitlin took almost an hour to explain the sequence of events that had led Hawkwood into conflict with the Brotherhood, her investigations, and what they now knew about their enemy. At each stage, she used photographs, records and other evidence to substantiate her claims.

"All of the Big Three are losing money to the Brotherhood, through their targeting of your resources," she finished. "The Dragon Tong suggested to us that we should brief the Cosa Nostra and the Nuevo Cartel as well, so that all three organizations can consider the problem and discuss potential solutions. That's why I came here. I'm grateful to you for listening. I'll try to answer any questions you may have."

There weren't many questions, to her surprise. The most important one had been anticipated. Cravotta asked, "You say this Albanian Brotherhood is stealing from us, too. I have no knowledge of that, or evidence for it. Can you prove it?"

In answer, Caitlin reached for one of two boxes she'd placed on a sideboard, and handed it to him. "This piece of asteroid, veined with precious metals, came from a mining operation in the Riesi system, in which your organization has a major interest. If you'll have it analyzed, its chemical composition will provide evidence of its origins. It came from a Brotherhood spaceship." She reached for the other box, and set it down before Hernando Torres. "This contains a piece of asteroid from the Janos system, in which your cartel has an interest. Analysis will prove that. It was obtained from a similar source."

"What source? How did you get your hands on one – no, presumably two – of their ships?" the Nuevo Cartel man demanded.

"We destroyed one in the Mycenae system, and searched its wreckage. The other was intercepted elsewhere." The Dragon Tong had obtained the second specimen, rather than Hawkwood, but she and Chen had agreed that their audience didn't need to know that.

Chen added, "We know for certain, from discussions with imprisoned Brotherhood members and other sources, that they've cleared over a hundred billion Neue Helvetica francs from their asteroid theft operations in just the last five to six years. They're doing this on an industrial scale. They're accumulating funds to buy a planet for themselves. They think that'll be the key to becoming as large and as influential as our organizations."

The other two envoys snorted disdainfully. "Lizards boast they are descended from dinosaurs," Torres sniffed. "Nevertheless, once a lizard, always a lizard – and this breakaway offshoot is a very small lizard."

"At present, yes," Chen agreed. "However, what if it grows to be a large one? And what about the money they are stealing from us? We operate on a very large scale, more so than the economies of most planets, but even so, a hundred billion is a very substantial sum. If one group gets away with stealing that much, particularly from us, more will be encouraged to try their luck. It is our opinion that this should be nipped in the bud, and an example made of all concerned, to prevent that."

"A very good point," the other conceded.

"You say they are based on Patos?" Cravotta asked.

"Ah... not exactly," Caitlin demurred. "That seems to be where they live, and from where they plan and control their operations. They also have a fleet of ships, some armed, some merchant vessels, including a refinery ship. Those are based elsewhere, probably in a deserted star system. We're looking for their base right now."

"So there will be two prongs to this; dealing with their ships, and dealing with their people. I presume you plan to handle the first?"

"We're considering what we can do. It will depend on a

number of things, including the size and scope of their defenses, the number of vessels involved, and whether we have sufficient ships and weapons of our own to take them down. They've hurt us badly, but we think we've hurt them even more. I can't speak for our boss, but I'm sure he'll act if he sees a way that offers a reasonable chance of success. However, we almost certainly won't be able to do anything about the Brotherhood on Patos. That's a sovereign planet, after all, and we're just a space security company."

"What support does Hawkwood expect from our organizations?" Torres asked.

"So far, we've paid for all our operations out of our revenues from the Mycenae system and elsewhere. Our expenses have been very high, with tens of billions of francs already spent and committed for future warship purchases and operations. If your organizations can help defray some of that, in cash or in kind, I'm sure my boss would be grateful. On the other hand, that's not the primary reason I'm here. I came because Mr. Chen and his organization invited me to brief you on the size and scope of the problem. If your organizations plan any sort of joint response, I guess that's up to you, but I don't know whether or not we'll have any role in that."

Chen spoke up. "The Dragon Tong would like to propose that we leave the Brotherhood's ships to Hawkwood, while providing them with appropriate support. If they can take care of that problem, we submit that all of us will be well served, so it will be to our advantage to help them. As for Patos, Hawkwood cannot act there, but we have resources they do not. Perhaps we can find a way to neutralize the Brotherhood there. This will, of course, require further consultation."

"None of us are active on Patos, as far as I recall," Torres pointed out. "That means we can cooperate there without offending each other, or getting in each other's way."

"A good point," Cravotta conceded. "I daresay some of our

people will have had dealings with criminals there from time to time, even if only through cut-outs. We might be able to persuade some of them to help us, in exchange for future favors."

"And for the loot they might get from the Brotherhood," Torres said with an unpleasant smile.

"There is also the thought that, if the Brotherhood tries to leave Patos, we can be watching and waiting for an opportunity," Chen added, to murmurs of approval from the others.

They eventually agreed to report back to their respective organizations, and meet again at the same place in four months, to discuss possible joint action. Caitlin was authorized to report back to Hawkwood about what had happened. The company would be informed in due course whether support would be forthcoming for its space-based operations, but it would not be expected to participate in any action on Patos.

With that, Caitlin had to be content.

22

ASSASSINS

CONSTANTA

Aferdita hurried up the stairs to the apartment. She took the time to hastily, perfunctorily knock on the door, using today's tap code to alert those inside, then punched in the combination to open it. Pushing it wide, she was shocked to find the team leader aiming his pulser at her head.

"*Flamar!* It's me!"

"I see that." His voice was savage. "Why the hell are you in such a hurry? You know we're at risk every second we're on Constanta. Anything out of the ordinary is a possible danger sign. Slow down and act normally, damn you!"

"I – I'm sorry. It's just that we've found them!"

"Who? The prisoners?"

"Yes! Halil and I were outside town, flying a drone along the foothills, looking at every farm, as you told us. There's one that looks like it's been set up as a training ground for a military or police unit. It's got firing ranges, a shoot house, all the usual facilities. The farmhouse is in a secluded hollow some distance away. Portable buildings have been set up in the yard, and a fence has been put up all around – a tall one, at least two meters high. We saw four men with brown skins exercising in the yard, guarded by a couple of men carrying carbines. Halil says he thinks they're some of the Kedan spacers!"

"Did you bring back vid?"

She reached into her pocket and handed him a data chip. He hurried over to a terminal and plugged it in, scanning the images carefully. "I think he's right. If that's the place, there should be eight of them, plus Sub-Lieutenant Sejdiu – unless Hawkwood has moved him into town, to be more easily available to work with them. I... no, on second thought, scratch that. He's still a prisoner, and they won't want to take a chance that he might escape them and make his own way home. He'll probably still be out there."

"What are we going to do?"

"Is Halil still there?"

"Yes, as you ordered. You said that if we found anything, one person was to keep watch over it, and the other come back to report."

"Good. We'll set up a hide on one of the closest foothills, looking down onto the farmhouse, and keep watch until we're sure how many people are there, and who they are. We'll take it in turns."

"Not too close," she warned reflexively. "They may have sensors, too."

"They're sure to. All right, help me pack what we need into a couple of rucksacks. We'll take it out to Halil and find a good place to set up."

Two DAYS LATER, two men were perched on a hilltop, three kilometers from the farm, looking down at it through military-grade digital binoculars. The senior of the two remarked, "It's going to be tough sneaking in there. They've cleared the underbrush from around the fence, so we can't crawl up to it under cover and cut it. What's more, those look like normal fence posts, but I'm willing to bet they're stuffed full of sensors."

"So how are we going to do it, sergeant?"

"We'll have to find an approach route that won't expose us to the guards' sensors. Scan the countryside between here and there. See if you can find a gully, or a series of low-lying hollows, that we can use to move in."

"Yes, sergeant."

The operator began to study the terrain, while the sergeant made notes about what he could see of the farm. None of the other direct-action teams had managed to penetrate it so far. He wanted his to be the first. The thought of spending Lieutenant-Commander Argyll's promised bonus for success on a riotous party, and flaunting it in the faces of their colleagues, was irresistible.

His junior spoke up. "Sergeant? See that tall tree flanked by three smaller ones, on the hillside about twenty degrees to our right, half a kilometer down slope?"

"Yeah, I see it."

"Take a look at its base. Do you see what I see?"

The sergeant focused his powerful binoculars. "Well, well, well. And who might you be?" The figure of a man was clearly visible, lying very still, looking down at the farm through what appeared to be commercial hunting binoculars.

"He's not one of our team," the private said unnecessarily.

"No, he's not. We can't see his face from here, but I'm sure he's not from the other teams, either. His clothes and gear are all wrong."

"Do you think..."

"Yes, I do. I'm going to call the boss. He'll want to know about this ASAP."

He reached into his jacket for his satellite comm unit.

"WE DON'T KNOW who they are, sir, but I reckon it's most likely our Albanian friends, up to mischief."

Tom Argyll finished his report and sat back, waiting. Cochrane nodded slowly. "I daresay you're right. What do you think they're planning?"

"Sir, the way I see it, they can only be after one of two things. Either they want to free our prisoners and spirit them off-planet, or they want to silence them, to prevent us producing them as proof that we destroyed one of their ships. Given the difficulty they'd have getting the prisoners up to orbit, then boarding a ship and getting out of the system, in the face of the warships we've got on hand, I just don't see how it can be a rescue, sir. Besides, they tried to murder the survivor from their asteroid ship, a couple of years ago. If they tried to kill their own once, why not again?"

"We're thinking along the same lines. How will you stop them?"

"Right now, sir, we're trying to find out how many of them they are. We've already tracked one of them back to an apartment in town. There appear to be at least three people using it, two men and a woman. However, we've only been watching them for two days. There may be more, and they may have another hideout somewhere. I'd like to go on watching them until we're sure.

"After that, sir, it's up to you. If they're Albanian agents, it'll be very difficult to take them in their hideouts. They'll be trained to a hair, equipped to defend themselves, and determined to die rather than be taken alive. I think we'll have a better chance of success if we take them when they're away from home. That means waiting until they're all out and about. We daren't try to take them down one or two at a time. If any warning gets back to the others, they'll scatter before we can round them all up. I presume you want prisoners for interrogation, sir?"

"I most certainly do. I never expected this. I can only assume their leader sent them after I told him about our prisoner. That says all sorts of things about him, none of them good. Let's learn all we can about him from them. I daresay we'll have to deal with him in due course."

"Yes, sir. I've already warned the teams to take extreme precautions against being spotted. We can't afford to take any chances with these people. They're too good."

"I hope you're doing something nice for the people who spotted them?"

Tom grinned. "Yes, sir. The sergeant is now a staff sergeant, and the private is now a corporal. They both have nice bonuses to celebrate their promotions, too. There's nothing like a little professional envy to motivate the others to try to outdo them."

"I'm sure you're right. Please thank them from me, personally."

THE FOLLOWING WEEK, the two investigators Tom had sent to Onesta returned. He brought them straight to Cochrane's office to make their report, bringing Hui along as well.

"There's an Antonia Funar on Onesta matching every detail she provided, sir, except for one thing," the lead investigator reported. There was a smugness in his voice that suggested he was very pleased with himself. "Date of birth, parents, schooling, university education, the lot – everything matches what the Antonia Funar here said about herself."

"So, where's the catch?" Hui asked suspiciously

"Antonia Funar was killed in a car crash on Onesta eleven years ago, ma'am. We've included a picture of her gravestone in our report."

Cochrane nodded. "Someone did only half a job picking out a cover identity for her. They'd have done better to pick someone living, but whose present whereabouts were unknown. That would have been harder to disprove."

"Yes, sir. We also brought back the medical records of the Antonia Funar from Onesta."

Hui's head snapped up. Her eyes glowed eagerly. "Do they include her DNA profile?"

"Yes, ma'am, they do."

"Excellent! We can compare it to this woman's. That should prove beyond any doubt that she's not who she says she is. How can we get a DNA sample from her?"

"She'll have had to provide one in her medical profile as part of her application for a work permit," Cochrane pointed out. "I'll ask our contacts at the Defense Ministry to pull it for us. We should have it by tomorrow."

"I'll run a comparison right away, sir," Tom promised.

"Thank you. While you're doing that, take the DNA profile of Sub-Lieutenant Sejdiu – it's in his medical records – and compare it as well. If there's a match between his mitochondrial DNA and the woman calling herself Antonia Funar, that'll prove the relationship between them. I should have thought to do that earlier."

"You can't think of everything, sir. I should have thought of it, too."

THAT NIGHT, 'ANTONIA' sat down at the desk in her small apartment, and called up an interplanetary message database. There had been nothing for her ever since she started checking it; but tonight, there was mail. She smiled as she saw the innocuous-seeming literary report. Eagerly, she plugged in a chip containing a decoding program, and read its output line by line as it appeared.

Dearest Jehona,

My heart is still broken at the news of Alban's death.

She goggled at the display, feeling a wave of sick shock and horror wash over her.

I am devastated at the thought that he will no longer come running through the door with his cheerful laugh and his sunny smile. He was our firstborn, and can never be replaced in my heart. I am sure that for you, his mother, to whom he is flesh of your flesh and blood of your blood, it must be even worse.

The tears began to flow as she read, feeling an icy numbness sweep through her body.

Agim has told me he sent word to you about Ilaria's loss. It seems she was engaged in a spying mission against our enemies, but was detected. She took three of their ships with her before she was destroyed. Agim tried to comfort me with the 'consolation' that our son died heroically in the service of the Fatherland Project. That is the official line. You and I know better the true cost to those aboard, and to all their families. Words are completely inadequate.

She nodded dumbly. There were no words adequate to describe such loss, such pain.

I was extremely angry that Agim refused to pass on a message to you from me over Alban's death. He said it would not be safe, because you were already deployed. He did not want to tell you at all, but I insisted that you be informed. Nobody has the right to withhold such news from a mother or father. He resisted, but I would not yield, and eventually he gave in.

She wondered bitterly, through her tears, whether Agim had

indeed 'given in', or only pretended to be persuaded. She had had no word from him since this mission began, even in response to the two reports she had submitted thus far. His message might have been delayed, of course; but given that Pal's would have been even longer delayed due to the roundabout route it had taken to reach her, that seemed unlikely.

Agim even went so far as to put our entire family's messages, of any and every nature, under intercept. He forgot that I would recognize the tell-tale signs. I am therefore sending this to you from an outside terminal, one that will not be traced back to me. I shall look for your reply using similar methods.

Even through her grief, she fumed. How dare anyone, even Agim, suspect the loyalty of direct descendants of the Patriarch?

I wish I were with you, dearest love, to offer what comfort I may. I fear there is little to be had at present. I long for your return from whatever your assignment may be. Until then, know that I hold you close in my heart. You have my whole love. I shall cherish our children, and help them to remain steadfast in Alban's memory, even as they grieve.

She reached out with a shaking, trembling hand, and shut down the terminal. Standing up, feeling like the weight of the entire universe had settled on her shoulders, she tottered down the passage to the refresher.

She hung over the toilet bowl for what seemed like an endless age, vomiting until it felt like her stomach would follow its contents up her throat. At last, when the bile had spent itself, she rinsed out her mouth, then staggered into the bedroom. Clutching a pillow to herself, a pale imitation of her husband's comforting presence, she cried for what seemed like half the night.

At first light, she got up, showered, and made herself presentable. She forced herself to eat some breakfast, and gathered her things together. She could not bring back her son... but she could make those who had killed him pay a price for his death. That was now doubly her duty, both as an agent and as a bereaved mother.

She set off for work with renewed resolve.

"THERE'S no doubt about it, sir. This 'Antonia Funar' isn't the one on Onesta, but she is the mother of Sub-Lieutenant Sejdiu. The DNA comparison is conclusive."

"All right," Cochrane replied. "Why do you think she's here? My first reaction is that she's got to be an Albanian agent, but is it possible she came here to look for her son?"

Tom shrugged. "She can't be an amateur, sir, not with such a carefully constructed cover story. That's the mark of a professional. I'd say she came here to spy on us. Getting a job at the shipyard we use for all our maintenance and repairs fits that very well. As for her son, we know she arrived here well after he was captured; but we don't know whether Agim told his family about that. He may have kept that to himself. He may not even have announced the loss of his ship."

"You're right," Hui agreed. "The question is, what do we do about her? We can't ignore her."

"No, we can't, but do we have to act right away?" Cochrane asked. "She may have others helping her. I think we need to watch her, and see who her associates might be. We may uncover another ring, to go with those who are – *hey!* Wait a minute! Agim may not have told *her* about her son being captured, but he must have told the other team that's watching the prisoners. Unless he had, they wouldn't be watching them, would they? Why not her, too? Doesn't he trust her? Does he think she'll go all maternal, and try to save her son by giving herself up?"

Tom shook his head. "We can't possibly know that yet, sir. I think you're right; we need to take our time, watch her very carefully, and keep tabs on that other team. There are five of them, by the way; we found two more in another apartment. They meet the others regularly, and share reconnaissance duties with them at the overlook they've constructed on the hillside above the farmhouse. We may find some convergence between them and Ms. Funar, or we may not. At least, by waiting, we can keep our options open."

"Do you have enough people to follow everybody?"

"It'll be tight, sir, but I think we'll manage. I'll pull some of the guards from the farmhouse, and have the others work longer shifts, to free up extra people for surveillance."

FLAMAR WAVED a printout in the air as he sat down. The others were already gathered in the living-room, eating supper from plates on their laps.

"It's her. 'Antonia Funar' is listed as the management accountant for Grigorescu Shipyards. The photograph on their corporate site was evidence enough, but I sat at a café outside their offices this afternoon, and waited until she came out. There's no doubt about it."

"Did she have anyone with her?" one of his agents asked.

"She was talking with her boss, who I recognized from his picture on the corporate site. They got into a cab together. I don't know where they went, but it doesn't matter right now. The main thing is, we've nailed down both of our primary targets."

"Yes, we have," Aferdita said proudly. "I took this from our overwatch position this morning." She handed over a picture. "It's Sub-Lieutenant Sejdiu, all right."

"Well done! This is a good picture, nice and clear. Yes, that's him all right, and we've seen eight different dark-skinned men in the compound, all under guard. Those must be the Kedan spacers. What about other arrivals?"

"No-one's come to stay. The guards are changed every twenty-four hours, and they bring in rations and other supplies with them, so there are no other deliveries. The only other regular visitor is a therapist from a local private hospital. She goes there three times a week. They make her park her car outside the fence, and collect her in some sort of electric cart to drive her up to the farmhouse. When she finishes with whatever she does inside, they drive her back to her car. There are always at least two guards, one to open the gate for her, the other driving the cart."

"That's interesting." The leader picked up the plate that had been laid ready by his chair, and began eating. Through a mouthful of food, he asked, "Do you think there's a chance we could use her arrival or departure to get in?"

"Perhaps. Two days a week she goes during the morning, but on Monday she arrives in the late afternoon. The nights are drawing in now. Winter is coming. It'll be darker at that time before long. If we wait until then, and take out her guards, and rush in through the open gate, we can bypass all the perimeter defenses we've identified and make straight for the house. The path isn't booby-trapped, as far as we can see."

The leader chewed, and swallowed hard. *"Urp!* All right. We'll carry on watching, and wait for the evenings to get darker. At the same time, we'll mount surveillance over Antonia Funar. Better to think of her by that name, in case anything happens." The other four nodded. "We'll try to find out whether she's been turned. If we aren't sure, we'll have to decide among ourselves what to do. If we are sure, we'll have to hit her when we take out the Sub-Lieutenant. We can't risk news of one attempt alerting our other target."

"And the Commodore, and his staff?"

"Leave them to me. I've found the apartment building where most of them live, and we know where their offices are. If I can figure out how to get a big enough bomb into either building, or both, we can kill all their important leaders at once. That'll have to coincide with our attacks on the other targets, of course."

"How will we get away afterwards?"

"I don't know yet. We'll have to think about that very carefully. Remember, this mission is more important than any, or even all, of our lives. It may not be possible for us to get away; but if we accomplish all our objectives, that will make our deaths worthwhile. The Patriarch gave his life for our cause. If necessary, we can do no less."

23

PLANNING

CONSTANTA

Cochrane scrolled through Frank's latest report, reading swiftly. His eyes lit up at the news that the fourth shipment of asteroids from Mycenae since they'd restarted prospecting operations there had just been dispatched to the refinery ship at Barjah aboard HCS *Orca,* their armed freighter. She'd loaded thirty-five high-grade rocks, averaging over two thousand tons each, after the prospector bots had hit a particularly fruitful patch of asteroids. The richest in concentrated precious metals and rare earth minerals, at least in the Mycenae system, tended to be smaller than average, which made handling them considerably easier.

He did some quick mental calculations. *We've cleared over six billion Neue Helvetica francs out of each of the three shipments so far. This one should be more – probably eight to nine billion. That means we'll have covered all our new ship and missile orders, with something to spare.*

It was good to realize that the company was once again on a sound financial footing, despite its losses at Mycenae II and all the expenses involved in recovering from that battle. He said as much to Hui over lunch.

"It's odd to think that the same system that cost us so much money, Mycenae, has also provided the money to recover from those costs," she pointed out with a twinkle in her eye.

He laughed. "You're right. I hadn't looked at it that way."

"Are you going to stop now?"

"Not at all. This has shown me that we might run into serious losses, and have to recover from them, at any time. I'm going to build up our reserves until we're sure we can rebuild after even the worst disaster, no matter how much it costs us."

"Isn't that greedy? I mean, I don't know any private company in the settled galaxy that can boast reserves that big."

"It may be greedy in the purely commercial sense, but we aren't a purely commercial company. I founded Eufala, which became Hawkwood, to offer a way to escape the New Orkney Cluster, for the benefit of all the good people I knew there. It wasn't just for me, or just about money. Several thousand have now taken advantage of that. I must keep faith with them, and their families, too. I want to make sure we never leave them in the lurch. Keeping the company going, no matter what, is part of that.

"Also, we're facing greater risks than any normal company. If the Albanians hit us again, with better ships and weapons and more of them, we might lose half our fleet in a single battle. I'm not willing to fight with one arm tied behind my back, while we raise money to afford replacements. While we're scrabbling for funds, they may hit us again and finish us off. No, I want as much financial security as we can accumulate, literally for the sake of our survival."

"I see. I don't suppose your people will complain. You've been generous with profit sharing."

"Yes. Those on our payroll are going to make a lot more from their profit share than they do from their salaries. They'll get less, of course, once the asteroid income dries up; but while it lasts, they can make the most of it."

"Your original team must be millionaires many times over by now."

"Yes. They've kept their initial payout invested in the company, where it's making even more for them, and periodic profit distributions have increased it even further."

She grinned. "I'm feeling left out! I'm the only one of your senior advisers not on your payroll! That's not a hint, by the way – just teasing. I'm content with my Qianjin salary."

He smiled. "You don't have to hint. When you became my Chief of Staff, I put you on full Captain's salary with us, too, with profit share to match. It's accumulating in a bank account on Neue Helvetica, in hard currency. With the asteroid profit share, I won't be surprised if it'll reach seven figures soon."

"*Andrew!* You shouldn't have! I can't accept it!"

"Why not? It's not as if you're being disloyal to Qianjin by accepting it – and you're certainly earning every franc, by your hard work for us."

"But – but what if Admiral Kang objects?"

"If you like, we'll formally ask his permission to pay you at least a profit share. I bet he'll allow that. Besides, if you marry me and we set up our home somewhere else, you'll need a nest egg of your own." His eyes laughed at her.

She blushed. "I... Andrew, I've thought long and hard about that since you gave me a year to make up my mind. That's almost over now, isn't it?"

"Yes, it is, but I've been trying very hard not to nag you about it."

"You still want to marry me?"

"Yes, I do."

"And you're willing to find a new home with me where we can both be happy?"

"Yes, I am. Constanta's just our temporary base. We can afford to live anywhere in the settled galaxy. I want to finish our fight with the Albanians. After that, if you really want, we can make a new start somewhere else. By then, Dave and the others will be able to run Hawkwood without me, so I can leave the company in good conscience."

"Oh, I won't ask you to do that! I like the company, and the people you've gathered around you. I hope you can base it somewhere nicer, though, a place where it's more fun to live."

"As our client base grows, I'm sure we'll need to do that as a matter of simple business sense."

She sighed. "All right. I suppose I had to wake up to the fact that it's not a matter of whether you can live with someone. It's whether you can live without them. I've got an Andrew-shaped hole in me now, one that only you can fill. I can't change that even if I want to. I'll marry you, darling – but will you mind if we make regular trips to see the rest of my family on Qianjin?"

He beamed, a huge smile lighting up his face. "Of course not. We'll have to build a house with a guest wing, so they can visit us, too."

Her eyes twinkled mischievously. "Build a wing for the children, too."

"A *wing*? Do you have plans I should know about?"

"Oh, you'll definitely be involved in them! With today's medicine, I'll be fertile for another thirty years or more. I reckon I can make up for lost time in having a family, and you're far too nice a man not to make more of you."

"Oh, well. Practice makes pregnant, they do say!" He ducked as she threw her dinner roll at him. "When should we set the date?"

"Would you mind if we married on Qianjin, so all my family can be there?"

"Not at all – but let's do it soon. I've waited long enough!" He hesitated. "What about your career in Qianjin's Fleet?"

"I've chosen you, darling. You're more important to me than

that. I'm not abandoning my career, of course; I'll simply continue it in Hawkwood, instead of at Qianjin. Being your Chief of Staff has proved to me I can be happy here, too."

He reached across the table and squeezed her hand. "Thank you, dearest. You've made me very happy. May I kidnap you from the office this afternoon, and take you home, and show you just how happy?"

"Pay the bill and let's go. I want dessert, and you're it!"

THEY MET next morning with Dave Cousins, Tom Argyll and Caitlyn Ross, who'd just returned from Bintulu. She opened proceedings by reporting on what had happened there.

"It looks promising," she concluded. "We won't be involved in whatever they plan to do on Patos, but they'll probably leave the space-based fight to us, hopefully contributing to that effort. I get the impression they don't want to take overt action, because all of them deliberately maintain low profiles in the public arena. They'll act as discreetly as possible."

"That squares with the official attitude of the Qianjin Fleet," Hui confirmed. "The Tong and Qianjin's Government are very firmly kept apart. I've never been involved in any joint project with the Tong at all, except for Hawkwood, where I was asked to assist as a Fleet professional, reporting to the Fleet. I've never been asked, and I'd refuse, to do anything criminal as part of that."

"Well, if we're able to deal with it, I'm willing to," Cochrane declared firmly. "We'll have to know a lot more about what we're facing, though. Let me tell you what Frank just figured out." He described the evidence provided by the most recent Kedan captives, and how *Jean Bart*'s navigation officer had figured out the region of space in which the Albanian base was likely to be found. "There are seventeen stars in a two-hundred-light-year-diameter sphere. Any of them might contain what we're looking for. If they don't, there are another fifteen to twenty stars within close range of that sphere. We're going to have to check all of them until we pin them down."

Captain Cousins made a *moue* of distaste. "That'll be a very big search job, sir. It'll take several ships, and several months, to do it properly. I'm not sure we can spare that many vessels right now."

"Perhaps we can't, but we still need to do it, and soon. In a year or two, we'll have enough warships with experienced crews that we may be able to do something permanent about the Albanians, unless they turn out to be more heavily armed than we expect. If they are, we'll just have to get reinforcements from somewhere."

"Aye aye, sir."

"Remember, sir, it's not just their ships," Caitlin warned. "It's their tribal nature. They've got a solid core of true believers. They won't be deterred if they lose their ships; they'll just start rebuilding all over again. Our name will be number one on their list of enemies when they're once again able to take revenge. We'll just be postponing the inevitable, unless we can deal with all of them at once."

"I agree, Caitlin. That's your hot potato. I want you to start thinking about how to deal with their 'true believer' core. We can't solve that problem in a military manner. Frankly, if the Big Three don't take care of it, I don't know how we can – but one way or another, it *must* be solved. That's your baby – or, rather, one of your babies."

"Gee, *thanks,* sir!" They all laughed at her hard-done-by expression and tone.

Cochrane looked at Tom. "What do you have for us?"

"Some interesting stuff, sir. Those five agents appear to be operating in two teams. Two people, sometimes helped by a third who seems to be the overall leader, are keeping watch over the prisoner compound. Two more, again helped by the leader, are watching 'Antonia Funar'. That concerns me, sir. They seem obsessed with following her wherever she goes, and they take note of anyone she meets. It's almost as if they suspect her of something, and they're looking for proof."

"Disloyalty, perhaps? What would they regard as evidence of that?" Cousins asked.

"I'm not sure, sir. As an example, if I saw my agent meeting a known enemy agent or officer without a good reason I knew about in advance, that would seem suspicious to me."

"Then why not arrange something like that, and see what they do?"

"What if they try to kill her?" Cochrane asked. "We can't endanger whoever she meets from our side."

"I don't think they'd do it right then and there, sir," Tom assured him. "If they're planning to do something about the prisoners, too, they'll have to coordinate their attacks. I reckon we should be able to stop them."

"What if they plan to attack Hawkwood, too?" Hui asked. "I mean, if they're going to make two separate attacks already, why not a third?"

"We've already considered that, ma'am, and we're watching everything they do. They've bought four vans, two fairly new, and two older, cheaper models. They're parked in an old warehouse they've rented down in the industrial area. They've taken the seats out of the older vans, and installed boxes of some sort. We think they may have converted them into bombs."

"So, if I can arrange to be seen in public with this Antonia Funar, they might take that as evidence that she'd been turned?"

"I would, in their shoes, ma'am."

"In that case, I'll wander over to the shipyard's offices tomorrow, invite Mr. Grigorescu to lunch, and persuade him to bring her along. I'm sure I can think of a suitable excuse. That'll give them plenty of time to see us together."

"I'll have a team covering you, ma'am."

"Thanks. I appreciate that."

FLAMAR WEAVED AS QUICKLY and unobtrusively as he could through the lunchtime pedestrian traffic. His eyes scanned his surroundings constantly, trying to detect followers, or people watching him, or anything out of the ordinary. He found nothing.

At last he spotted Gentian, seated at a table in the outdoor area of an upmarket café. His team member noticed him and waved enthusiastically, as if spotting a friend, then gestured to the chair next to him. Flamar walked over and sat down. A hovering waiter instantly appeared, so he ordered a coffee he didn't want.

As soon as the waiter had left, he said in a low voice, "I got your call. What is it?"

"Look over there, to the right, at the outdoor seating area of the restaurant across the walkway."

The leader did as he was bid, and felt his blood turn to ice in his veins. 'Antonia Fumar' was sitting at a table, with her boss and the Qianjin captain who served as Hawkwood's Chief of Staff.

He sat silent for a couple of minutes, thoughts racing through his brain. Gentian did not interrupt him. He knew the signs by now. At last his boss said quietly, "You did well to call me. We've been looking for evidence like this ever since we got here, and never found any. I wonder what made them break cover at last?"

"Perhaps they've heard something we haven't. Something may have happened that they know about, but we don't yet."

"That's probably it. All right, keep watch as normal for the rest of your shift, then come back to the apartment. We'll all meet tonight. It's time to end this."

24

ATTACK

CONSTANTA

The therapist parked her car outside the gate, and picked up her comm unit to let the guards inside know she was there; then she collected her shoulder bag full of equipment, and locked her vehicle. As she walked to the gate, she could see the utility cart heading down the drive toward her.

From the hide on the mountainside above, a man watched as she got into the cart, while another guard locked the gate behind her. The vehicle drove back to the farmhouse, and the three disappeared inside.

The man picked up his comm unit and made a call. "They're inside. She'll be busy for at least an hour."

He heard Flamar's voice. "Very well. We'll move in and stand by outside the gate. You have overwatch. The moment she comes out, weapons free. Time it to give the rest of us the best possible chance."

"Understand weapons free when she comes out. Good luck."

"And to you."

The man ended the call, then reached for the bulky, heavy

rucksacks that had been brought up the mountain over the past three days by himself and his comrades. He set to work assembling three tubes, and tripod mounts for them.

GENTIAN PAUSED at the door of the old van. "I suppose this is goodbye," he said, almost sadly.

Aferdita nodded. "If we are successful, yes." She had to swallow hard to get the words out. Even though the risks and demands of the mission had been made very clear before they volunteered for it, and again before they departed, the thought of what lay ahead was daunting.

"Strike hard and strike sure, sister. In the Patriarch's name!"

"In the Patriarch's name."

Gentian got into the van, plugged a cable into a test unit hanging down from a switch on the console, and pressed a button. He grunted in satisfaction as a light glowed green. The circuit to the explosives and detonators was in working order.

Aferdita watched him drive the van out of the warehouse, its power pack laboring under the weight of its deadly cargo, then climbed into her own van, this one not burdened with a heavy load. She tested the detonator circuits of the explosive vest waiting for her in the passenger seat, then put it on. She gave Gentian time to get well ahead of her before she left, driving carefully in the evening traffic. An accident at this point might ruin everything.

The two vans made their way across the city. The first headed for the apartment building owned by Hawkwood Corporation. Several of its senior officers were already at home, preparing supper. Others were on their way there. Gentian parked the van in an alley close to the building, then settled down to wait.

Aferdita pulled her van into an open parking spot in the alley running next to the building containing Antonia Funar's apartment. As she sat, waiting, sweat broke out on her forehead, and her stomach churned at the thought of what lay ahead. Despite her dedication to their cause, the prospect was daunting.

At last she could stand it no longer. She opened the door, scooted over to a bush growing in a planter at the entrance to the alley, and was violently sick.

A watcher pressed a microphone button. "She's out of the van, sir. We can take her now, without killing her. Over."

"Negative, I say again, *negative*. It's too soon. We don't know whether she'll have to call anyone, or someone will call her. If she doesn't, or doesn't answer, it would give us away. Over."

"OK, sir. We'll wait. Standing by."

The watcher looked on as Aferdita stood upright again, her head swimming, and staggered back to her van. She climbed inside and closed the door, then lowered the window, hanging her head out into the fresh air outside. He said to his partner, "That'll maybe let Mack and Sammy do this the easy way, rather than us having to do it the hard way."

"Works for me, boss. She looks so damned *young!* I know she's an enemy, and a well-trained, dangerous one, but I can't help thinking of my little sister when I look at her."

"Watch those attitudes. They can get you killed in a hurry. She'd do it herself in a heartbeat, if it would further her mission."

"I know, but even so... Guess I'm just a softie at heart."

"Then you're in the wrong job." The leader's voice was hard, uncompromising. "Don't let that stop you, if we have to kill her."

"Oh, don't worry, boss. I won't lose any sleep if we do. It's just that..."

"Yeah. I know."

Grimly, the leader thought, *It's a good thing you don't know we'll interrogate them using their own techniques, if we take them alive. It's the only way to make them talk. Damn them for making us behave like them!*

IN THE FARMHOUSE, the watch commander checked a time display, then clicked a switch on a jamming unit on the table next to him. A directional aerial on the roof, aimed at the hillside above, began to transmit as he nodded to the three figures near the front door. "It's time."

Without saying a word, they opened the door and filed through it, heading for the utility cart parked nearby. The two guards were dressed in what looked like their normal uniform; but this version had been made from ballistic cloth, offering much greater protection against incoming fire. The 'therapist' was another member of the security team, disguised to look enough like the real practitioner to pass muster in the rapidly deepening gloom of evening.

They settled into their seats, and the driver started the vehicle toward the gate. When he got there, he remained behind the wheel, but unfastened his seat belt, ready for an instant dismount. His partner and the woman got out of the vehicle. The guard picked up the lock and fumbled with its keypad. The inner gates began to swing open.

THE MAN on the hillside squinted through the light-intensifying scope next to the missile launcher. He saw the guard pick up the outer gates' lock, enter a code, and push them back. As soon as they began to move, he pressed the first firing button. To his utter shock and dismay, no missile leapt from its tube. He stiffened in sudden panic, even as he felt a sharp sting in his jaw, and another through the collar over his neck. As he dropped the button and reached for the pulser lying ready on the ground beside his head, he felt a wave of dizziness sweep over him.

He knew at once what must have happened. He'd been

targeted by nanobugs or flitterbugs, firing needles tipped with a
paralyzing neurotoxin. His enemies, whoever they were, had
somehow jammed his missiles' wireless remote-control firing
circuits. They would wait until he was unconscious, then secure
him before administering the antidote. He knew what awaited
him when he woke up. They would undoubtedly interrogate him,
just as he would do to them if the tables were turned. He dared
not allow that. Besides, he would not be conscious long enough
to reach the comm unit and call Flamar – but he had to warn him
somehow.

Desperately fighting the dizziness, using his last moment of
controlled thought and movement, he raised the pulser barrel,
placed it against his ear, and pressed the firing button.

FLAMAR WAS SITTING in the driver's seat of the second explosives-
laden van. His window was open, to let him hear more clearly. He
was ready to drive through the gates, knocking their remains out
of the way if necessary, as soon as the missile had blown them
both open; then he would head for the house, to crash into it and
detonate his lethal cargo, killing most of those inside. His team
would follow up, with more missiles from the hillside and gunfire
from his comrade on the road. They would make sure there were
no survivors.

He heard the faint sound of a shot, echoing down the hillside.
His partner did, too, from his position next to a culvert, fifty feet
from the gates, on the other side of the road. The man reared up,
lining his carbine at the guards at the gates. He moved so fast that
the hovering flitterbugs missed his head and face. Their needles
hit the rucksack on his back. They were too low-powered to penetrate such barriers. That left the watching security team no
choice.

Two carbine shots exploded, then two more. The man was

flung forward into the side of the culvert by the impact of the hypersonic beads. He dropped his weapon and collapsed to the ground in a crumpled heap.

Flamar's thoughts had been focused on the imminent attack, and on his comrades back in the city, and their preparations to take out the leadership of Hawkwood Corporation and the traitor spy. He took just too long to shake his mind free of those distractions. Even as his head jerked around toward the nearby shots and he reached for his pulser, he felt the stabbing pain of a needle penetrating the back of his neck. He spun back toward his window – only to have another needle spear directly into his left eye. Agony roared through him as he involuntarily clapped his hands to his face.

He realized at once what had happened, just as his subordinate up the hill had done, and tried to end his life before it was too late... but he had hesitated just too long, and the neurotoxin in his eye was just too close to his brain, and his hands had just too far to travel. Worse, he'd fastened his seatbelt, so that if he'd had to use the van to ram the partially open gates aside, the impact would not have jolted him out of his seat. Now the belt got in his way as he tried to lean over and grasp his pulser, laid ready on the passenger seat. By the time he began to raise the weapon, his motor control was too far gone. The pulser fell from his nerveless fingers as he crumpled, unconscious.

The guards at the gate had flung themselves flat as the shots sounded. Now they rose, and ran down the road toward the attackers. Others emerged from the bushes to help them. They gathered up both bodies and all the equipment, and took everything back to the farmhouse. On the hillside above, another team checked the dead man, then collected his gear and weapons and carried everything to a utility transport, waiting on a dirt track winding through the forest below.

Within a few minutes, there was no visible evidence to

suggest that anything untoward had ever happened on the mountainside, or near the farm below.

THE WATCHERS in town heard Tom Argyll's voice. "The farm went down as scheduled. No casualties to the good guys. We'll give it five minutes, to allow enough time for a call from there to alert the Commodore, then we'll start moving. That should draw them in. All teams, stand by."

The observers settled themselves behind their weapons and consoles, and prepared for action.

Gentian tensed as he saw a sudden flurry of movement in the ground-floor garage beneath the apartment block. Two indistinct figures, about the same size and height as Commodore Cochrane and Captain Lu, ran from the elevator toward their vehicle. As its lights came on, the door to the garage began to slide open.

Gentian gulped, reached for his comm unit, and punched in Aferdita's code. "It's time." He didn't wait for a response, but heard her gasp as he dropped the unit on the seat beside him. He gunned the van's powerpack and began to pull out of the parking bay, ready to force his way through the opening door into the garage and detonate his bomb, bringing down the entire building above him. Everyone in the basement would certainly be killed, and most of those in the apartments, too.

The van's cargo was too dangerous for the Hawkwood security team to even consider using less-lethal methods such as nanobugs or flitterbugs. They dared not risk an explosion. The vehicle's first centimeter of movement triggered a laser sensor, focused on the corner of its front bumper. A military particle beam rifle, a sniper's weapon, was aimed at the driver's head through the closed window. In the instant the vehicle began to move, the rifle fired automatically. The beam shattered the window as if it did not exist. Gentian never felt the blow as his skull and its contents were shredded by flying glass fragments and the massive energy transfer from the beam. Shattered fragments of bone and droplets of moist red-and-gray matter splattered all over the interior of the van. The vehicle jerked as his lifeless foot slipped off the accelerator, and automatically stopped as its safety sensors applied the brakes. The detonator switch in the cab, and the multiple activators built into the front of the van, never had a chance to perform their lethal function.

A kilometer away, Aferdita tried to control the fear surging up inside her. She knew her death was necessary, and that it would further the cause... but everything inside her cried out against losing the life it seemed she had only just begun to savor. She sternly commanded her trembling legs to obey her as she got out of the van, closed its door, and began to walk toward the entrance to the apartment building. She carried a box, labeled from a well-known delivery firm, plus an electronic clipboard to obtain the recipient's signature. Her pulser was in her waistband, hidden by the box, and her explosive vest looked like just another puffy outer garment, warm against the chill of the early evening. When the recipient came to the door of her apartment to sign for the package, she would be able to visually identify her for certain. She would then detonate the vest. Her prey would not be able to escape the blast and spreading shrapnel at arm's length.

She came to the end of the alley, and turned toward the entrance – then cried out involuntarily as four short, sharp stinging pains hit her, one just below each ear, the other further down either side of her neck. She turned her head to glimpse a small, flying 'insect' hovering beside her. Her eyes widened as she recognized the twin tiny tubes mounted immediately below its 'head'... but she did not have time to do more than register their presence before dizziness swept through her. The team assigned to take her down had used double the recommended minimum dose of darts, to ensure she did not retain motor control long enough to activate her bomb vest. Her reactions already slowed by her physical discomfort, she couldn't drop her box and the clipboard to reach her vest's detonator switch before she slumped to the ground. She struggled briefly, but slipped into unconsciousness.

Once again, cleanup teams took care of the evidence. Within moments, everything had returned to normal. At that hour of the evening, with few passersby, no-one noticed anything out of place.

COCHRANE AND HUI were seated side by side on the sofa, waiting. He grabbed his comm unit as it pinged. "Cochrane."

"Sir, it's Tom. Complete success. We had to kill the driver of the bomb van outside your apartments. Two died at the farm, one hit by our security team on the road, one suicide with his own pulser. We've got the team leader, and we're taking the woman out there to join him for interrogation. What are your orders, sir?"

Cochrane thought rapidly. "Interrogate the team leader. I want to know everything – who sent them, their mission, what they were told, anything and everything that might prove useful. Keep the woman under wraps. Don't let her see or hear anything, and make sure she's under constant guard. She must not be allowed to commit suicide. Bring me the recording of the leader's interrogation as soon as it's over, along with the highlights we'll need to convince this 'Antonia Funar' that she was a target, too."

"Aye aye, sir. Do you want us to bring her in as well?"

"I don't know yet. It'll depend on what we learn from the leader. Don't forget, she'll be at least as well trained as they were, so we'll have to take her just as carefully if it comes to that. I want her alive, and able to understand."

"Aye aye, sir. I'll see you in the small hours of the morning."

FLAMAR AWOKE to find himself lying on his back, strapped to some sort of gurney or stretcher. His arms extended from his sides at about a thirty-degree angle to his body, securely fastened to metal extensions. His left eye hurt with a dull ache, and he could feel a bandage over it, fastened around his head. His right eye was obscured by a dark cloth bag over his head, preventing him from seeing anything. He could feel a slight pain in his left elbow, and a coolness running from it up his arm. He knew at once what that meant. As his narcotic-sodden brain woke up more and more, he realized that his hair had been clipped so short it was no more than fuzz. Some sort of gel had been applied to his head, and a neural net stretched tightly over his scalp.

He struggled and writhed and tested his bonds for several minutes, but they did not give way. He desperately willed himself to die, but his body obstinately clung to life. He knew his enemies had him at their mercy. He also understood what they were about to do to him. He'd done it to others often enough to be sure about that. All he could do was conduct himself during his last conscious moments with as much courage and dignity as he could muster.

At last he heard two sets of footsteps coming down a corridor. The door to his room opened, a switch clicked, and a circle of light suddenly appeared dimly through the dark cloth of the bag over his head. A hand whisked it away, and he cried out involuntarily as the bright lights blinded him, bringing tears to his sole working eye.

A voice said in Galactic Standard English, "You know why you are here, and what we are going to do. You have five minutes to make your peace with whatever God you believe in." A computer translated the words into Albanian through its speaker, to ensure he understood. He did not dignify them with a reply, just blinked the tears from his eye, then stared straight up into the darkness beyond the lights. He forced stillness upon his body, refusing to allow it to tremble with fear.

At last the voice spoke. "Let us begin." A second person lifted the tube running into the needle in his arm. He knew they would be inserting a hypodermic syringe into a port and injecting a complex blend of narcotics. He felt it as a stinging warmth, surging up his arm. He tried to cling to his soul, to who he truly was... but he felt himself slipping away into a mental haze.

It felt as if he was swaying, like standing on the deck of a boat being rocked by small waves, or cradled in the arms of his mother as she swung him from side to side. The world grew foggy, strangely translucent. The person who had been Flamar knew – he had absolute, blind, infallible faith – that he was safe with these people. They would look after him. He need fear nothing if he did what they asked.

The voice asked, "What is your true name?"

"I... I am Flamar Hajdari."

"What are the true names of the members of your team? Who sent you? What were your orders? When did you leave Patos? When..."

It was four hours before the voice was satisfied. By then, enough of the drug had been injected that Flamar had begun to lose his faculties forever. Within two more hours, the irreversible deterioration of his brain would push him into a vegetative state, from which he would never recover. That was an unavoidable side effect of what was otherwise the most effective interrogation drug cocktail ever developed.

"What do we do now?" the second person asked.

"There's nothing more he can tell us, and no way to bring him back. Inject this." Another syringe changed hands.

Within two minutes, Flamar had taken leave of life as well as his senses.

～

It was four the following morning before Tom Argyll finished briefing Cochrane and Hui. They all looked tired and stressed after listening to key portions of the interrogation.

"How could this Agim be so plain, damnably *evil* as to send killers after one of his officers who'd done nothing wrong?" Hui asked, almost in a whisper. "Does he have no loyalty to his own people?"

"That's a question I plan to ask Sejdiu's mother as soon as possible," Cochrane replied, frowning. "There are so many wheels within wheels here that I'm not sure I've got it all straight, even now. What do you think, Tom?"

"Sir, I reckon the only thing that might break open the logjam, and find out exactly what we've got, is to let the different parties confront each other. Let's arrange a meeting between Sub-Lieutenant Sejdiu, his mother, and that female agent."

"What if one or the other of them tries to harm themselves, or each other?" Hui asked. "Don't forget, the younger agent is still under orders to kill both the others."

"That's a good point, ma'am. I'll divide a room into three holding areas with plasglass partitions between them, plus a fourth area for the interrogator."

"That'll be me," Cochrane informed him. "It's time I got involved. Make sure both agents, Sejdiu's mother and the younger woman, are physically restrained as well. They're too well trained to take any chances with them. The officer is probably also willing to fight, but he won't be nearly so well trained. I think I'll have him restrained as well, at least at first, just to be on the safe side."

"Aye aye, sir. When do you want to do this?"

"As soon as you can arrange it. Let's take down Sejdiu's mother as she leaves for work in a few hours' time. Your flitter-bugs can do that without causing too much of a fuss. Take her out to the farm, and set up that interrogation room as you described. While you're doing that, have one of your teams go through her apartment with a fine-tooth comb. I'll be interested to see what they find. We'll excuse her absence to Grigorescu. I'll come out to the farm after work. Let's play the cards, and let them fall where they may."

"May I come too?" Hui asked, her eyes flashing as if to say, *You'd better not try to keep me out of this!*

He sighed. "Could I stop you?"

"No, not really."

"Then you can come. It's not going to be pretty, love. I'm probably going to have to get tough with them, and display my ruthless side."

"Since you're my husband-to-be, and they wanted to kill us both, I'm feeling a little ruthless toward them myself – so you go right ahead!"

Tom got to his feet. "All right, sir. I'll be ready for you by tonight."

"Thanks, Tom. Meanwhile, I'm going to consider very carefully what we'd like the Albanians to think. If we can feed them misinformation, using these agents' channels of communication, it might pay dividends later. I'll think about that, and put my head together with Dave and Hui, and we'll see what might work."

25

CONFRONTATION

CONSTANTA

For what seemed like the hundredth time, Jehona wriggled and twisted on her bed, but could not dislodge the hook-and-loop bands that held her wrists and forearms together, as well as her calves and ankles. The straps securing her to the bed would not allow her to roll onto the floor, to move about in search of anything that might cut or loosen her bonds. She had been bound by experts. What's more, they had almost shaved her skull, leaving only a thin fuzz of hair. She tried to ignore the dull despair she felt at having been captured, and focus her entire being on remaining alert to any opportunity her captors might allow.

She heard footsteps coming down a passage outside her room. The door opened, and two men entered. One said, "Ma'am, we're moving you down the passage to an interview room. This isn't a forced interrogation. You're going to learn why you're here, and what we know. We think a lot of it is going to surprise you."

"What's the meaning of this?" she blazed indignantly. "How

dare you kidnap me? Mr. Grigorescu will have informed the police by now! He'll –"

"Stow it, ma'am," the second man said bluntly. We know you're really Jehona Sejdiu, and why you're here. Now it's time for you to learn the rest of the story."

Shock silenced her as she heard her real name spoken aloud for the first time in months. She remained silent as the two men lifted her, placed her gently in a wheelchair, and pushed her down a long passage. Doors to either side were closed, offering no clue as to what they contained.

She was wheeled into a room at the end of the corridor. The rear half had been divided into three narrow sections by vertical plasglass sheets, thick and tough, fastened to wooden frames in the floor and the ceiling. Each of the first two sections contained a wooden chair with arms and a padded seat, fastened securely to the floor with brackets. Her escort wheeled her to the center section and lifted her into the wooden chair, securing her to it with hook-and-loop straps.

"Just wait here, ma'am," one advised her. "We'll be bringing in one more person, then someone who'll explain to you what's going on. There'll be a fourth visitor soon – and that's going to be the nicest surprise you've had for a long time." He was smiling as he said it, but not maliciously, she thought.

"What do you mean?"

"All in good time, ma'am."

The two men went out. A few minutes later, they wheeled in a much younger woman, secured in the same way as herself, also with her hair trimmed to a thin fuzz. She stared in astonishment at Jehona, clearly recognizing her. *"Traitor!"* she blurted out furiously in Albanian. "Did you betray them, as well as us? Is that why you are tied?"

"What are you talking about?" Jehona asked in astonishment, then forced herself to stop. Her enemies would do anything they thought might persuade her to talk, just as she would have done if their positions were reversed. Silence was the best response. It betrayed nothing. Her instructors had re-emphasized that, time and time again.

Her accuser appeared to have learned a similar lesson. She pressed her lips tightly together, and refused to look at Jehona as the men fastened her to the chair in the leftmost cubicle. That left the one on Jehona's right. She wondered for a moment who was to occupy it, then pushed the thought from her mind. *Focus!* she commanded herself. *This may be the end for you. If it is, sacrifice your life proudly for our cause, just as Grandfather did.* For a moment, she allowed herself one despairing thought about her husband and surviving children... then she shook her head, and straightened, and put them out of her mind.

The two men separated. Each took a neural net out of his pocket, and placed it securely on the head of one of the women; then they plugged thin cables into sockets at the rear of the nets. They led the cables to the back of the room, and plugged their other ends into sockets attached to the wall. Wires ran from them along the baseboard, exiting at one side of the room.

"These are truth-testers," one of the men explained to both women as he moved back into their view. "We need them to know when you're being truthful. You'll see in due course that they'll help you understand each other better, too."

As the men walked out, Jehona tried to figure out what they could possibly mean. She failed.

Cochrane looked up as the young officer was led into the living-room of the farmhouse. He rose to meet him. "Good evening, Sub-Lieutenant."

The young man instinctively stiffened to attention at the sight of the single broad ring on the black sleeves of Cochrane's winter uniform. "Good evening, sir."

"I had you brought here because I have to solve a problem tonight. You see, some of your own people have come here, to this planet, under orders to kill you, because you're a traitor to their cause."

Alban's eyes widened in shock. "You – you can't be serious, sir!"

"I'm in deadly earnest. I'm prepared to prove that to you. However, there's a condition. To introduce you to some of those involved, and let you satisfy yourself that I've told you the truth, I need to be certain that none of you can harm any of the others. That means you'll have to be secured hand and foot, and brought into the room in a wheelchair." He held up his hand to stifle the younger man's instinctive protest. "That's not because I distrust you. You've behaved honorably as our prisoner, and earned our respect. I'm doing this because the situation is so volatile, and the dangers so real, that I don't want to leave the slightest opening for anything to go wrong. I won't force this on you. If you refuse to be bound, I'll return you to your room, and conduct the rest of this evening's proceedings on my own. I'll play you a recording of them later. If you accept being bound, I promise that, as soon as I'm satisfied any danger is past, I'll have you released. It's your choice."

"I... I don't understand, sir."

"I know you don't. I'm sorry to put you in such a quandary. However, please accept my word that this is necessary. I don't know how tonight is going to go down. I'm trying to make it as safe as possible for everyone. There's only enough space for two guards in that room, along with three prisoners, including you if you choose to participate, plus myself. Bonds are necessary to keep things under control."

Alban thought for a moment, then stiffened to attention. "Sir, we are enemies, but you've treated me with respect, and never tried to force me to disclose anything. I must believe that you're being honorable in this, too. Even though I resent it, I will submit to being bound, sir."

"Thank you. I don't think you'll regret it when this is all over. I'll have these two men secure you, then they'll stand by until I call them to bring you in."

"Yes, sir."

Cochrane left them to it, and walked down the corridor. He paused outside the makeshift interrogation room, and took a deep breath. Tonight's events might save lives... or destroy them. He devoutly hoped to avoid that. There had been too many lives ruined already.

He pushed the door open and walked in. The two women looked at him warily, clearly expecting trouble. Their faces were determined, pushing away fear as they confronted what might well be a short and painful future.

"Ladies, my name is Commodore Andrew Cochrane. I'm the head of Hawkwood Security, against which both of you have been spying. Allow me to introduce you to each other.

"Mrs. Jehona Sejdiu, you are a spy in the pay of the Albanian Brotherhood. You were sent here by Agim Nushi to find out all you could about Hawkwood and myself, including identifying ways in which we might be attacked. Mr. Nushi did not lie to you at the time, but he has lied to you since, largely by omission. He has also actively lied to your family.

"Ms. Aferdita Tahiri, Agim Nushi sent you and four others to Constanta to kill Mrs. Sejdiu's son, Alban, a Sub-Lieutenant in your forces whom we had captured. He –"

"You *captured* Alban?" Jehona burst out, unable to control her astonishment and sudden, wild hope. "I –"

Cochrane held up his hand. "All in good time, Mrs. Sejdiu. Ms. Tahiri, Mr. Nushi told you that Alban had turned traitor, that he was helping us by providing information and producing propaganda against the Brotherhood. He lied. Sub-Lieutenant Sejdiu did nothing of the kind. He –"

"Of course you would say that!" the young woman burst out. "You are trying to deceive me, to turn me against our leader!" She spoke in lightly accented Galactic Standard English. Her face was twisted in anger and hatred.

"I hope to prove to you tonight that you're wrong. Let me finish, please. You were also ordered to spy on Mrs. Sejdiu. Mr. Nushi told you he was afraid she might have turned against the Brotherhood after finding out that her son was our prisoner. He told you to find out the truth, and if she had been turned, to kill her too."

Jehona twisted her head to stare at the woman alongside her. Her face showed anger, bewilderment and shock.

"Finally," Cochrane continued, "your team was ordered to locate me and Hawkwood's senior officers, and attack us if possible, but as a secondary objective to Sub-Lieutenant Sejdiu and his mother. Last night, you tried to accomplish all three objectives. You failed. We killed two out of three attackers at this farm, and captured the leader of your team, Flamar Hajdari. We killed another member of your team, Gentian Gashi, when he tried to drive a van loaded with explosives into the parking garage of the apartment block where I and most of my staff live. Finally, we captured you as you walked toward Mrs. Sejdiu's apartment, carrying a parcel that you were going to deliver to her. You were wearing an explosive vest, that you planned to detonate as soon as she opened the door to sign for it."

Jehona's face was a study in mingled outrage and incredulity. "What – why – I –"

"If you'll wait a very short while, ma'am, I think you'll understand," Cochrane said to her, not unkindly. "Ms. Tahiri, have I summed up the situation truthfully?"

"I'm not telling you anything! Why not ask Flamar?"

"Oh, we did. We interrogated him last night, using the same drugs and techniques your people had used against us in the past. That's how we learned about them." Both women visibly flinched. "You'll understand that he has since died, but we recorded everything he told us. I'll be playing you excerpts from that in a short while. Right now, though, I want to bring in the third actor in tonight's little drama. Mrs. Sejdiu, I understand you've been informed that your son was killed in action. We found a message from your husband to that effect in your apartment."

"Y – yes."

"He was not killed. He was gravely injured, and knocked unconscious. Some spacers from Keda, hired by your people, escaped from the damaged compartment where he was, and took him with them when they boarded a lifeboat. We rescued them, then operated on him to relieve a compression fracture in his skull. He's made a full recovery, although he's still undergoing therapy."

Tears were pouring down Jehona's face. "You – you're lying! This *cannot* be! Agim would not have lied to my *entire family* about this!"

"He did, ma'am – and he knew it was a lie, too, because I'd been in contact with him, to tell him your son and the Kedan spacers were our prisoners. I'm going to prove it to you, by bringing your son into this room." He turned, put his head out of the door, and called, "Bring in the Sub-Lieutenant, please."

Cochrane had anticipated an emotional scene, but even he was surprised by the outburst when Alban was wheeled in. Jehona, already in tears, shouted his name aloud, and struggled desperately to free herself so that she could run to her son. Alban did the same, turning to Cochrane with tears in his eyes. "Release me, damn you! She is my *mother!*"

Cochrane had to raise his voice in a powerful shout. *"Silence!"* He waited until the two, shocked, were staring at him. "Sub-Lieutenant Sejdiu, I cannot release your mother, because she's a very highly trained agent. Her unarmed combat skills are exceptional, as we've learned through watching her exercise them. These two men are equally skilled, but I'm not. I can't take the risk that she might injure any of us once she was free, or force us to injure her to keep the rest of us safe. Whether or not she's ever free again will depend on what happens here tonight." He turned to the two guards. "Please wheel Sub-Lieutenant Sejdiu into the third partitioned space."

They did so, then took up positions in the front corners of the room, from where they could reach any of the pinioned prisoners quickly. Cochrane waited until movement had ceased, then went on, "Mrs. Sejdiu, I said I'd prove you'd been lied to by Mr. Nushi. This is the first evidence of that. There's more. I'm going to play selected excerpts from the interrogation of Mr. Hajdari last night."

He turned to a player on a table behind him, and started it running. For several minutes, they all listened to Flamar's voice, soft and dreamy under the influence of the interrogation drug, confirm the orders that Agim had issued to the team, what they had done since arriving on Constanta, and what they had planned to do the previous evening.

"Who was that?" Alban demanded when the playback had finished.

"That was the late Flamar Hajdari, leader of the team of agents. He died last night, after we interrogated him."

"You mean you killed him!"

"Yes, we did." The young officer appeared shocked by Cochrane's calm admission. "We killed him because the interrogation drug we used on him had by then irreparably scrambled his brain, leaving him a vegetable." His voice became icy cold. "We learned about that drug from *your* Brotherhood, Sub-Lieutenant. They used it against our people. The lethal injection we used to kill him in the end came out of a hypodermic syringe carried into a nursing home on this planet by another of *your* agents. I seem to recall his name was Vadil."

"It was Vadil Berisha," Jehona said hoarsely. "I did not know him, but I was informed of his mission during my refresher training."

"Thank you, Mrs. Sejdiu. He tried to murder another of your people, a survivor of an asteroid-gathering ship that was destroyed by an orbital mine in the Mycenae system. We'd brought him here to receive long-term medical care that we couldn't provide in space. We hoped he would recover one day. Vadil intended to make sure he didn't, by injecting him with a fast-acting lethal poison. We shot him before he could do so, and recovered three syringes of the poison from his body. We used one of them last night to end Mr. Hajdari's life, after interrogating him."

Alban was staring at Cochrane as if he were some horrifying, disgusting insect. "And you admit to cold-blooded murder?" he almost spat. "So much for your honor as an officer!"

Cochrane's voice was frosted steel. "Didn't you hear me mention that your mother is also a trained agent? How many people has she interrogated, then murdered, in the same fashion? How many people has Ms. Tahiri killed like that?"

Jehona's voice was soft, but the pain in it was clearly audible. "I... I have never killed anyone like that, Commodore. I was always involved with intelligence-gathering, not interrogation. However, I know the methods and poisons of which you speak." She turned her head to look at her son. "The Commodore is telling the truth, my son. We do use such techniques, and I know of several occasions on which they were used. I... I am sorry, Alban. You never knew who and what I was before I married your father."

Tears were pouring down her face once more. Her son goggled at her in astonishment as Cochrane nodded. "Thank you, Mrs. Sejdiu. Young man, consider this. We would never willingly have used such methods, but they're so devastatingly effective that we saw no other way to learn what we were up against. We had no wish to be your enemies. We knew nothing about you –

we'd never even *heard* of the Albanian Brotherhood – until your people tried to steal asteroids from a system we'd been hired to protect. We tried to stop you, as we were legally entitled to do; but instead of backing down and looking for easier pickings elsewhere, you escalated the fight against us."

His voice became biting, angry. "You, the Brotherhood, are *criminals,* plain and simple. You have no legal or moral justification for your fight against us. However, you've forced us to defend ourselves against you. Since you hold nothing back in your attacks, we can't afford to hold anything back in our defense – but that's *your* fault. We learned that ruthlessness from *you,* and last night we used *your* techniques to learn what *your* spy team leader knew about us and planned to do to us. Don't you dare call *me* dishonorable for trying to protect my people in the only way possible, against criminal thugs who wouldn't recognize honor if it reared up and spat in their faces!"

The young man's face showed his inner struggle. "I... I am *not* a thug! I have never been a criminal!"

Cochrane cocked his head for a moment, looking thoughtfully at him. "I daresay you, as an individual, are correct, Sub-Lieutenant. You've behaved honorably in captivity, and never betrayed your cause or your superiors, even though both are unworthy of you. I accept that you're a man of honor, who's been brainwashed almost from birth into supporting a cause that's morally and intellectually bankrupt. In fact, I wish you were in my service. Someone with your obvious talent and ability would rise quickly through our ranks, and go far. It's a pity that isn't possible. Nevertheless, in general, your Brotherhood's behavior has been nothing less than criminal, right from the start. Your Patriarch began it that way, and the rot set in right from the start."

"My great-grandfather was no criminal! He left the Bregija clan because it would not allow him to pursue his dream!"

"Your great-grandfather? You mean you're directly descended from Bashkim Bregija?"

Jehona put in, "He was my grandfather."

"What were you told about how he split from his clan?"

"We... we were told he tried to persuade the Bregija elders of his vision. When they refused, and mocked him, he broke away, taking with him those who shared his ideals and were loyal to them. We have built our own clan around them."

"That sounds nice, ma'am, but it's not true – at least, not according to the Bregijas. They claim Bashkim insulted the Bregija elders, calling them cowards and weaklings for refusing to adopt his vision of an Albanian homeworld, from which they could build a criminal empire to rival the Big Three – the Cosa Nostra, the Nuevo Cartel and the Dragon Tong. He started plotting to kill some of his opponents on the clan leadership council, and have them replaced by his sympathizers. He made so much trouble that the clan eventually expelled and proscribed him.

"He got off-planet one step ahead of an execution squad, and gathered around him malcontents and dissidents from other Albanian Mafia clans. They eventually settled on Patos, where, as you say, they've formed their own equivalent of a clan. However, they weren't there because of his idea. They followed him because he was a strong leader who could weld their disparate elements together into a cause. They had nothing better to live for, after being expelled from their own clans. They wanted the security of a clan structure, something they'd been used to since birth. In him, they found a leader who promised that. It took him a long time to convince them to commit everything they had to his vision. I'll give him this, he must have been one hell of an orator and politician.

"We know all about how he laid the foundations. We've spoken to several people he used, then discarded or abandoned, as part of the process. It took him almost four decades to put everything in place. It was going well, too, except for one thing. The entire project was built upon crime – stealing asteroids that didn't belong to you, and to which you had no right at all. You ran into us when we stopped one such theft. There have been other setbacks in other systems, and more will come, because people are now aware of what you're doing, and mobilizing against you.

"We aren't the only enemy you've made. You're making the situation worse by hitting back against everyone you perceive as having opposed you, even though they have every right to protect their property and defend themselves against you. The Big Three are now talking to each other, discussing joint action against you."

That drew exclamations of surprise from all three. Alban was clearly at a loss for words. Jehona sat with her head bowed, fighting the realization that Agim had broken his promise, to her and her husband, that he would never lie to them about anything to do with this mission. For her part, Aferdita was numb inside. All her upbringing, training and formation had been based on the vision of Bashkim Bregija as the Patriarch, the wise leader who had led his people into the galactic wilderness to find a new home, a refuge – in due course – for all the Albanian clans.

At last Jehona looked up. "How can I be sure Agim knew my son was alive, at the time he told my family he was dead? What if he truly believed him to be dead, lost with his ship?"

Cochrane shook his head firmly. "Ma'am, I wrote to him in care of the Neue Helvetica chargé d'affaires on Constanta. He forwarded my message to the Foreign Ministry on Neue Helvetica, which forwarded it in turn to their chargé d'affaires on Patos. She delivered it to your boss, and certified to the Foreign Ministry that she'd done so. In due course, Agim acknowledged receipt of it through her, nothing more. The chargé d'affaires on Patos sent that back to Neue Helvetica as well, which sent it to the chargé d'affaires here, who delivered it to us.

"I can show you all those messages. You can compare their dates with the date he told your family that your son was dead. If that isn't enough to convince you, I'll arrange for you to speak with the chargé d'affaires yourself. You can identify him from the diplomatic corps page on the planetary net, so you'll know we aren't trying to fob you off with someone in disguise. You can even write to the Foreign Ministry on Neue Helvetica, if you wish, sending them copies of the messages and asking them to confirm that they're real. They will.

"What's more, there's the briefing he gave to the assassination team. He told them, months after informing your family that the Sub-Lieutenant had been killed, that he was still alive, and that he was a traitor – yet another lie. The team leader confirmed that during his interrogation last night, and I'm sure Ms. Tahiri will do the same, if you ask her."

Aferdita, sitting dumbstruck in her chair, could only nod mutely as Jehona glanced at her. The Commodore's certainty was so clear, his words so convincing, that there was no room left for either woman to doubt what he had told them. Jehona's heart was torn with anxiety for her husband and their other children. Agim had deliberately lied to them that their son and brother was dead, and to her fellow agents that he was a traitor. *What kind of monster would do that?* she asked herself desperately. She could find no answer.

Alban asked, "What are you going to do with us?"

"With you, nothing, Sub-Lieutenant. I don't hold you responsible for spying on us, like your mother and this other woman have done. You will continue as our prisoner of war, unless something happens to justify a change in that status. As for your mother, she's a spy. I have every right to treat her as one, including interrogating her to find out what she's learned about us, and what she's told her boss. The only reason I haven't yet done so is out of respect for you. You've comported yourself in every way as an officer should. I'd hate to repay that by killing your mother – but I will, if I must. That's up to her, not me."

He turned to Aferdita. "As for you, ma'am, you're also a trained agent. You have no right to expect mercy. You were taken in the act of attempted murder, even though it was one of your own people you were trying to kill. You were part of a team that tried to kill the Sub-Lieutenant last night, and me, too, and my fiancée, and many of my staff. I have every right to treat you as the spy and assassin that you are. The only reason you haven't already been interrogated is that I wanted to give the Sub-Lieutenant and his mother a chance to hear what we know. If they don't or won't believe it, I'm going to make them attend your interrogation, so they can hear and witness you confirming everything I've told them about you and your team. After that, you won't have a brain anymore, so you'll end up as dead as your late team leader."

He tried to keep his voice as harsh and unfeeling as he could, to appear more convincing. It seemed to work. Aferdita flinched, and stared down at the floor, shoulders hunched as if against a blow.

Jehona said, tonelessly, "What do you want from me?"

"I'm not expecting to convert you from the beliefs in which you were raised, although I hope you have the intelligence to realize how flawed they are. I need to know what you learned about Hawkwood, and what you've told your boss about us in your reports, and what his intentions are toward us. If you tell me that much, I'll allow you to live, and confine you as a prisoner with your son. It won't be on a planet, because the risk of someone like you escaping is too great. You're too well trained for me to take that chance. You'll be held aboard one of our ships, under close security. It'll be as comfortable as we can make it."

"So we might be stuck in space for years?"

"I think this will be over, one way or another, within a couple of years. Like I said, the Brotherhood has made a lot of enemies recently. Once that problem has been solved, I think we can at least confine you less strictly, if not release you, provided we can be sure you no longer pose a threat to us. That remains to be seen, of course."

"And... if I tell you, what about this woman – Aferdita Tahiri?"

"I hadn't given her any thought yet. Why?"

Jehona took a moment to marshal her thoughts. "Commodore, if I help you, I'd like to make three requests. I can't make them demands, because I have no leverage to insist on them. Nevertheless, I ask them of you as favors."

"Name them."

"First, let Aferdita Tahiri live. She's an agent, yes, and she was taken in action against you; but she was also brought up, as I was, in the shadow of the Patriarch and the legend that has grown up around him. I'm still not convinced that's entirely false, although you've given me a lot of food for thought. I'd like to see the records of what you've learned, to understand him better."

"I can arrange that."

"Thank you. She... she needs time to make up her own mind. I can't hold her trying to kill me against her. She was obeying orders she believed to be justified and appropriate. As the Patriarch's granddaughter, I don't want another death in his name on my conscience."

Aferdita stared at Jehona as if she were some exotic species of animal that she'd never seen before. Her eyes brimmed with unshed tears, and she had to force down a sudden wild hope. Might she yet live through this, with her mind unimpaired?

Cochrane nodded slowly. "That's very considerate of you, Mrs. Sejdiu – and far more merciful than Ms. Tahiri has any right to expect. Next?"

"I want to send a message to my husband. I have a way to do that. He can't go on believing that Alban is dead. He must be told."

"What if he can't keep the knowledge to himself? He's bound to be so overjoyed and relieved that it'll be almost impossible to conceal."

"I trust him to do so. I know him."

"I'll think about that, too. If I agree, I'll want to read the message before you send it, and know the full details of how you'll encrypt and transmit it. We'll do that for you. Next?"

Jehona struggled to find words. "I... I want to keep my family safe against... against whatever may happen. You say the Brotherhood has made more enemies, and that they are talking to each other. I have heard of clan wars among the Albanians. They tend to be bloody, merciless, and absolute. More than once, an entire clan has been killed, to prevent its descendants ever again making trouble for the victors. I... I do not want that to happen to my family. Can you find a way to keep them safe, if it comes to that? Will you?"

"I don't know if that will be possible, ma'am. I'm prepared to try, if you give me all the information I need, but I can't promise success. For a start, we have no agents on Patos at all, and I don't know how we'd get any there. Without them, I don't see that we can do much."

She jerked upright. *"No agents?* Then who has been spying on us?"

"Not us. Remember what I told you about the Big Three? Draw your own conclusions."

Her face went white as a surge of apprehension flooded through her. If enemies of that caliber were already working against them... She shook her head. There was nothing she could do about that now, and no chance to warn even her husband, much less Agim, about it. She could only try to salvage what she could. Slowly she said, "If you will try, that is the best I can hope for. I may be able to help you get some of your people to Patos, if I can set that up with my husband."

Cochrane's eyebrows rose. "I'll... I'll consider that. That's as far as I can go at present."

Aferdita raised her head and said, almost timidly, "Commodore, may I say something?"

"What is it?"

"I can tell you what I know, too, if you will try to help my family also. I, too, know the results of clan feuds. I want to keep them safe."

"I already know most of what you can tell me from the interrogation of your team leader."

"I know you do. I cannot offer what I do not have. I can only hope that what little I can add may persuade you." Her eyes blinked rapidly as she tried to hold back her tears.

Cochrane thought for a moment. "I'm willing to proceed on that basis, but there's a condition. I know I can trust the word of Sub-Lieutenant Sejdiu. He's been an honorable officer ever since he fell into our hands. However, I need the word of both you ladies that you will accept captivity until the issue is decided, and not offer any resistance, and not try to escape, and make no trouble whatsoever. I warn you that if you break your word, or even give us grounds to suspect you may have broken your word, the penalty will be immediate – I repeat, *immediate* – drug-induced interrogation, followed by death. There will be no second chances. Are you willing to give me your word about that? I remind you that you're under truth-tester examination, so any lie will show up at once."

Jehona nodded. "I give you my word, Commodore."

Aferdita struggled with herself for a moment, then submitted. "I give you my word."

Cochrane raised his voice. "Truth-testers, confirm, please."

A disembodied voice sounded through a speaker. "Both truth-testers confirm, Captain. They meant it."

Alban spoke up from his chair. "Sir, I thank you for your trust in me. I'd like to add my own parole. I will not try to escape, or do anything incompatible with my status as a prisoner of war, so long as these women are held as captives under the conditions you've laid down."

"Thank you, Sub-Lieutenant. That wasn't necessary, but I'm glad you made the offer. It makes the next step easier." He

glanced at the guards. "Please release all three; the Sub-Lieutenant first, then his mother, then Ms. Tahiri."

The two men glanced at him, then at each other, but moved
to obey. Alban stood up, waiting impatiently while they released
his mother, then swept her into a huge hug. She wept as she laid
her head on his shoulder. As they clung to each other, the men
released Aferdita's bonds. She stood up, rubbing her wrists.

Jehona turned to her. "Aferdita, you did not know me. You
were following orders when you tried to kill me. I will not hold
that against you. I have heard enough tonight to make me question... many things of which I was once certain. I hope you will
join my son and I in doing that, and finding out the truth. Help us
to help each other."

"I will, ma'am. Thank you... thank you for speaking up for
me. I think, without that, I would shortly have been dead." She
glanced at Cochrane.

"Yes, you would," he assured her. "However, you've made your
commitment, so I'll trust you to keep it. All three of you will be
confined to this house, except for exercise periods outside under
close guard. You'll be interrogated tomorrow – without drugs –
concerning what I need to know from you. After that, I'll arrange
to have you sent up to orbit, and transferred to a spaceship. I'll
see you again before you leave, to discuss your requests
concerning your families, and consider what might be done
about them."

As he walked to the door, he added, "Guards, return Ms.
Tahiri to her room. Give Mrs. Sejdiu and her son some time
together before you return them to theirs. If they want to sit
somewhere more comfortable, and share a snack and some tea or
coffee, let them."

"Aye aye, sir," the senior guard replied.

Cochrane let himself out, and headed for the guardroom.
There he found Hui, who'd watched the proceedings on closed-
circuit vid. She hugged him as he walked in.

"I was proud of you tonight," she said softly, her eyes shining. "You were utterly convincing – and a lot more merciful than I thought you were going to be."

"I hadn't planned on that," he admitted, "but it occurred to me that if I behave as badly as the enemy all the time, how can I claim to be any better than him? Sometimes I'll need to be as brutal as he is, but not always."

"You're right. I'm glad you realized it in time to avoid that trap tonight."

"So am I. Come on, darling. Let's go back to the apartment."

26

WHAT NEXT?

CONSTANTA

L ong after Hui had fallen asleep, Cochrane lay awake, staring up at the ceiling of their darkened bedroom. His mind would not let go of all that had happened over the last two days, and what it implied for the future.

We've got four big problems to solve. We've got to find out where the Brotherhood fleet is based, and how big it is. After that, we've got to figure out how to destroy it, and its base, so that there isn't anything left to rebuild. That's complicated by what to do about the Kedan spacers they've hired. They didn't ask to be there – they were sent by their senior officers without so much as a by-your-leave. They're the equivalent of slave labor. We can't just kill them all out of hand – but what do we do with them? If we return the ones we already have, will they be allowed to rejoin their families on Keda, or shot to hide what their bosses did?

The third problem is the Brotherhood itself. They're mostly on Patos, which is neutral territory. They don't run the planet; they're not even one percent of its people. They've probably bribed the authorities to turn a blind eye to their presence, and what they're doing, but that doesn't mean we can hold the entire planet responsible. Hawkwood certainly can't touch their people there – so what can we do? Can the Big Three deal with them? Do we have to kill them all? The Big Three may not hesitate to do that, but I won't. If we get the ringleaders, and the most committed and involved people, will it be safe to let the rest live, or will they want revenge someday?

The last problem... we're the last problem. Hawkwood's grown too large for the work we have on hand right now. That's because of the Brotherhood threat. We've paid for our growth by doing the same thing they did – stealing asteroids – but we can't go on doing that. Sooner or later, we'll get caught. I'll build up our reserves as much as I can while the going's good in Mycenae, but within a few years, that'll be over. What then? Can we find enough asteroids in unclaimed systems to keep ourselves going? Can we find enough work to sustain our fleet and our numbers? If Dave's idea about lower fees plus asteroid rights works out, we might... but we can't guarantee that. We don't even know if we'll still be based here at Constanta. Where will we go? What will we become?

He mulled over the issues long into the night, unable to stop his mind worrying at them like a dog with a bone. At last, he mentally shrugged. *I don't know the answers yet, and I won't find them tonight. Those are tomorrow's problems, and next week's, and next month's, and next year's.*

He rolled over, snuggled closer to Hui's comforting warmth, and settled down to try to get some sleep.

EXCERPT FROM "THE PRIDE OF THE DAMNED"

Here's an excerpt from Book 3 of the "Cochrane's Company" trilogy. "The Pride of the Damned" will be published in July 2018.

Captain Pernaska sat on the hard, narrow bunk in his cell, closed his eyes, and prepared himself for death.

Remember our Patriarch, he thought forcefully to himself. He dared not speak aloud, because the enemy would overhear him through the microphones they were sure to have hidden in this confined space. *Even in his dotage, afflicted with disease, he went on a combat operation, to prove to our people that he would never ask them to risk anything he was not prepared to risk himself. What an example he set! He died in action, and inspired all of us to avenge his loss in the blood of our enemies. Today is my chance to do that. It is not a tragedy – it is an honor! May I prove worthy of it, and may my death be worthy of his!*

He had to act before his captors could transfer him to an interrogation facility. He knew all the Brotherhood's plans for the next few years, and all about their ships. Most important of all, he knew the coordinates of their secret base, information entrusted only to the Commanding Officers, Executive Officers and navigators of their vessels. Hawkwood absolutely could not, under any circumstances, be allowed to learn that secret... so he had to die. It was as simple as that.

His kidnappers had been almost unbelievably, even criminally inept in giving him access to the ship's entertainment library, via the screen on the bulkhead beyond the bars. He was still puzzled by that. Hawkwood had proved to be a formidable opponent in space combat, worthy of the Brotherhood's steel. Why had they made such an elementary error? Perhaps this ship was the exception that proved the rule of their efficiency and effectiveness, the weakest link in their chain. Please God, let its crew not be alone in being so sloppy! Of course, it might not be a Hawkwood vessel at all: but it had brought him as a prisoner to Hawkwood's home planet, so that was irrelevant. He would treat its crew as the enemy.

He had taken advantage of the screen and its voice-activated controls – which his oh-so-stupid captors had obligingly demonstrated to him – to access the courier vessel's layout, provided as part of the entertainment library so that passengers could find their way around if necessary. He knew where the brig was in relation to the rest of the ship, and where the airtight bulkheads and doors were that would separate the vessel into pressure-tight compartments in an emergency.

In Galactic Standard English, he called, "Display orbital approach." The screen obediently flickered, then resolved into a radar-like display of the planet ahead. Several spaceships' orbits were outlined in yellow, while this ship's approach to its own assigned trajectory was shown in red. The vessel looked to be no more than a few minutes away from entering orbit. He took a deep breath. It was almost time.

He'd asked for a couple of pairs of utility overalls, to wear instead of his Captain's uniform. He'd sent that to the ship's laundry, to be restored to pristine freshness in readiness for this day. Now he took off the overalls, folded them, laid them on his

freshly-made bed, and put on his uniform. He tied the old-fashioned laces, critically observing his reflection in the shoes that
he'd polished to mirror brightness, just like when he'd been a
cadet officer all those years ago. He settled the jacket over his
shoulders, and buttoned it. He had no mirror in which to
examine his appearance, but knew it would be as close to perfect
as possible under the circumstances.

He heard approaching footsteps, and smothered a savage grin
with his hand. He'd been on his best behavior with the spacers
who brought him meals twice a day, and escorted him to and
from the shower twice a week. He'd tried very hard to give the
impression of a man resigned to captivity, wanting no trouble,
willing even to grovel before his guards in order to avoid conflict.
He knew some of them regarded him with scornful contempt as a
result... which was exactly how he had hoped they would react.

He reached beneath the mattress on the unused top bunk,
and withdrew the pen that one of the spacers had indulgently
lent him 'to write a letter to my wife'. When he'd handed over the
letter – addressed to a non-existent woman, and filled with mean-
ingless platitudes – it had been to a different spacer, who hadn't
asked for the pen to be returned. He had taken full advantage of
that mistake. It had given him a weapon.

He palmed the pen, with the point up his sleeve, as two
spacers entered the brig compartment. Both were armed with
pulsers, but only one had his weapon in his hand. The other's
was in the flap holster at his waist, which was unfastened,
allowing the butt to peep out from beneath the synthleather
cover.

"All right," the armed spacer said in Galactic Standard
English, using what he presumably intended to be a
commanding tone of voice. "Stand back from the door while we
unlock it, then we'll cuff your hands and take you to the docking
bay."

"Yes, of course," the captain answered subserviently, stepping back, half-turning away, hunching his shoulders as if to avoid a blow. The two spacers exchanged contemptuous glances, then the second, empty-handed man unlocked the barred door and swung it open.

"Turn around and put your hands behind your back," he ordered as he stepped inside.

The captain made as if to obey, but instead of stopping with his back to the spacer, he continued turning, all the way around, moving suddenly faster. Before the startled man could react, he reached out with his left hand, grabbed his collar, and pulled him powerfully forward as he thrust with the pen in his right hand. Its point speared deep into the spacer's left eye. He screamed in agony.

"WHAT TH–" the second spacer began to yell, eyes bulging in surprise – but Pernaska did not stop. His left hand, still grasping the injured man's collar, twisted him half-around while his now-empty right hand snaked out and grasped the butt of the holstered weapon, drawing it and releasing its safety catch. He violently shoved his writhing victim back toward the entrance as the other spacer raised his pulser, blocking his line of sight, forcing him to step to one side to aim at their erstwhile captive. By the time he'd done so, the captain had acquired a rock-steady two-handed firing grip on his own weapon. He fired first, three rapid rounds, two into the spacer's chest, the third at the center of his face as he yelled in pain and shock and began to fold forward over himself. The man dropped his pulser and slumped bone-lessly to the deck. Pernaska turned back to the wailing spacer inside his cell and fired one more round into his head, killing him instantly.

He shook his head in a vain attempt to clear his head of the sudden deafness caused by the hypersonic discharge of the pulser's electromagnetic mechanism. Faintly, through the ringing in his ears, he heard the sudden whooping of the ship's alarm, followed by the impact of airtight doors slamming shut,

reverberating through the vessel's structure. He grinned
savagely.

*Thank you, you fools! You think you've locked me safely away from
the bridge. Instead, you've locked me in the same section of the hull as
all your off-duty watchstanders. They're my meat now! You may kill
me in the end, but not before I make you pay for my life in the blood of
your spacers!*

He swiftly searched both bodies. Neither carried spare
ammunition for their pulsers, but that was of minor importance.
He'd used four of the twenty rounds in the first weapon, and
there were twenty more in the other – more than enough for
what he'd need. He tucked the second weapon into a pocket of
his jacket, then called up the vessel's schematic on the screen
again. There were eight four-person berthing units for the crew
in the forward section of the hull, plus three two-berth units for
supervisors and four single cabins for officers. Many of the crew
would be at their stations, but according to the duty roster he'd
carefully memorized earlier, about a third should be in their
berthing units. By now they'd have locked their doors, of course,
in the vain hope that would protect them from him. He spat
contemptuously. They would soon learn otherwise... the last
lesson of their lives.

He walked out of the brig, moving slowly and carefully,
peering around the corner to make sure that no braver-than-
usual spacer had decided to wait in ambush for him. The passage
was clear. Grinning almost cheerfully, he moved up to the first
sliding door on the port side. It was locked, as he expected. He
reached for the keypad set in the bulkhead next to it, and entered
the standard merchant vessel emergency access code. It was used
on all commercial ships, in accordance with United Planets regulations, so that search-and-rescue teams could enter locked
compartments if necessary. Sure enough, the keypad beeped, and
the door slid back.

Two spacers inside the compartment screamed in fear as they

stared at the black-uniformed figure in the open doorway. Their cries turned to gurgles of agony as he pumped one round into each of their chests. They crumpled to the deck. He walked over, aimed carefully, and put a second round through the head of each man. *That's four,* he thought with grim, bitter, vengeful satisfaction.

A voice began yelling over the ship's speakers, begging, pleading with him to stop. He ignored it as he turned to the door on the starboard side of the passage, and entered the emergency access code once more.

ABOUT THE AUTHOR

P eter Grant was born and raised in Cape Town, South Africa. Between military service, the IT industry and humanitarian involvement, he traveled throughout sub-Saharan Africa before being ordained as a pastor. He later immigrated to the USA, where he worked as a pastor and prison chaplain until an injury forced his retirement. He is now a full-time writer, and married to a pilot from Alaska. They currently live in Texas.

See all of Peter's books at his Amazon.com author page, or visit him at his blog, Bayou Renaissance Man. There, you can also sign up for his mailing list, to receive a monthly newsletter and be kept informed of upcoming books.

BOOKS BY PETER GRANT

MILITARY SCIENCE FICTION:

The Maxwell Saga:
Take the Star Road
Ride the Rising Tide
Adapt and Overcome
Stand Against the Storm
Stoke the Flames Higher
Venom Strike (coming soon)

Cochrane's Company:
The Stones of Silence
An Airless Storm
The Pride of the Damned

The Laredo War:
War to the Knife
Forge a New Blade
Knife to the Hilt (coming soon)

FANTASY:
King's Champion
Taghri's Prize

WESTERN:

The Ames Archives:
Brings The Lightning
Rocky Mountain Retribution
Gold on the Hoof
A River of Horns
Silver in the Stones (coming soon)

MEMOIR:
Walls, Wire, Bars and Souls

Made in the USA
Coppell, TX
28 August 2022

82204587R00194